Border Hell

Border Hell

Jackson Cole

WHEELER
CHIVERS

This Large Print edition is published by Wheeler Publishing, Waterville, Maine USA and by BBC Audiobooks Ltd, Bath, England.

Published in 2006 in the U.S. by arrangement with Golden West Literary Agency.

Published in 2006 in the U.K. by arrangement with Golden West Literary Agency.

U.S. Softcover 1-59722-168-6 (Western)
U.K. Hardcover 1-4056-3701-3 (Chivers Large Print)
U.K. Softcover 1-4056-3702-1 (Camden Large Print)

The text of this Large Print edition is unabridged.
Other aspects of the book may vary from the original edition.

Set in 16 pt. Plantin by Elena Picard.

Printed in the United States on permanent paper.

British Library Cataloguing-in-Publication Data available

Library of Congress Cataloging-in-Publication Data

Cole, Jackson.
    Border hell / by Jackson Cole.
        p. cm. — (Wheeler Publishing large print westerns)
    ISBN 1-59722-168-6 (lg. print : sc : alk. paper)
    1. Large type books. I. Title. II. Wheeler large print western series.
PS3505.O2685B67 2006
813′.52—dc22   2005030650

Border Hell

1

Sitting his tall golden horse atop the high bluff that overlooked the blue waters of Corpus Christi Bay and the far-flung glitter of the Gulf beyond Mustang Island, Jim Hatfield recalled Colonel E. A. Hitchcock's description of the town of Corpus Christi:

"The most murderous, thieving, God-forsaken hole in the Lone Star State . . . or out of it! A town of smugglers and lawless men with but few women and no ladies!"

Hatfield chuckled at his recollection of the retort of Colonel Hank Kinney, the town's founder and presiding genius:

"Ladies are all right, I reckon, but I've never seen one yet that was worth a damn as a cook!"

Both men had been sincere in their observations. Colonel Hitchcock had proved his conclusively by personal experience. Kinney's remark had come from a heart embittered and a mind twisted by a tragically blasted romance that had made him a cynical wanderer over the face of the earth. Here on the shores of the bay where the notorious Gulf pirate, Jean Lafitte, once held rendezvous, he found a doubtful haven and established a town and gathered about him men of his own way of thought and living. The inevitable result was all Hitchcock claimed for it.

"And the years haven't changed her much," Hatfield told his horse as he gazed down upon the sprawl of buildings between the bluff and the wide, crescent-shaped beach. "Lots of big new houses, some of 'em up here on the hilltop, a railroad, and so on. But with much the same sort of folks, I've a notion. Still a cow town on the water, and with sheep coming in to pepper up the hell broth. Well, maybe we'll be able to get a line on our men down there. They were headed in this direction and I figure they'd hardly have passed up Corpus Christi on their way to wherever they're bound, which is somewhere in this section, I've a hunch."

He scratched the two weeks' bristle of black beard that darkened his lean cheeks. His face was lined with fatigue and lack of sleep, but his long green eyes were clear and steady behind their thick black lashes. It took more than two days and a night of steady riding to knock out the man a stern old Lieutenant of Texas Rangers had named the Lone Wolf.

Now Hatfield shook his head as his eyes rested on the sea of chaparral rolling westward. That belt of thicket was indicative of the wild country extending for hundreds of miles. Although the land was old in terms of human occupancy, man had in reality only made a scrape here and there in the tangled maze. It was hole-in-the-wall country, ideal for outlaws and hunted men. In their concealed hideouts reached by trails known only to them, they could laugh at peace officers and defy capture. Hatfield's jaw set hard as he pondered this fact.

"We'll see," he told the horse, and dropped his eyes to the nearer terrain.

His eyes swept moodily over the far-flung vista seen from the hilltop. The waters were bright with the sunlight of later afternoon, but far to the east was a belt of haze that hung like purple mist over the Gulf. It was like a stealthily creeping shadow of evil moving with relentless purpose toward the town huddled under the bluff. To the immediate north were the salt marshes, rippling in the wind, the bending grasses forming alternate bands of light and shadow. Farther north was the onward roll of the rangeland, tipped with amber, washed with gold. To the southwest the bluffs stood boldly against the skyline, buttressed by the never-ending monotony of the chaparral, the thickets bristling upward like clumps of lances as they marched in endless review into the red glare of the low-lying sun.

Along the bluff crests ran a trail, dipping and rising, twisting and writhing, a snake tortured by the reaching thorns of mesquite, cat-claw and prickly pear. Here and there a mesquite plant shot its skyrocket burst of starry blossoms high into the air. The dead white graveyard-flowers of yuccas waved gently like swung censers. The purplish sage was like slow clouds of incense drifting to the bannered roof of some high choir.

And under the bluff, the buildings of the town huddled like poor lost sheep awaiting the fury of a coming storm.

One building held Hatfield's attention. It was a huge, sprawling structure that crouched on the sands of the beach like a waiting beast of prey. Smoke poured from its chimneys. Its windows glared like blank unseeing eyes. Over it a miasma of death seemed to hover. And it was a house of death. It was Samp Gulden's great packing house, a stench in the nostrils of every cattleman.

Packing houses were not new to Texas. Shanghai Pierce owned a vast one on Matagorda Bay. Captain Dick King and Miflin Kennedy also owned packing houses. Others were in operation along the Gulf Coast from Galveston to Point Isabel. Many of the big Texas ranches were near the coast and transportation by ship was easy. These packing houses specialized in skins, hides and tallow, with the better cuts of meat salted down.

But Samp Gulden did not process cattle. He processed sheep.

Hatfield raised his eyes from the grim building on the beach. Far to the southwest a slow dust cloud was boiling up through the clear air. The sunlight caught the individual particles and reflected them in golden points that tossed and scintillated until the moving mass was a constant shimmer in the wind. Hatfield watched its gradual approach, waiting for solid substance to take form beneath the shifting veil.

"Sheep," he mused. "Cows would he moving a mite faster than that. Should be here in half an hour or so. Think I'll stick

11

around for a look at those woolies. Wonder where they're coming from? King's place around Kingsville, the town he's building over there on part of his million acres, perhaps? But they might be coming from one of the smaller outfits that have been drifting in. No wonder cowmen are pawing sod. Looks like the beginning of the end of the open range in this section. They'll be fencing next."

The dust cloud rolled on, boiling up behind a tall, thick bristle of chaparral that lined the trail where it curved around the edge of the two-hundred-foot bluff. And as if jerked forward by invisible strings, the flock bulged around the bend, something over a mile distant, but plainly visible in the crystal-clear air.

It was a good sized flock, trudging along wearily through the thick dust. Hatfield spotted three horsemen urging the tired woolies along. Hooking one long leg comfortably over the saddle horn, he watched the flock's approach. Then abruptly he was tensely alert, staring toward the bend.

One of the herders had thrown up his hands and pitched from the saddle. He hit the ground to lie sprawled and motionless before Hatfield heard the crack of the distant rifle. While the sound was still ringing in his ears, a second herdsman went down.

The third managed to get his gun in action. Hatfield could see the mushrooming spurts of smoke. Then the remaining herder fell. His riderless horse went tearing back the way it had come.

Out of the brush surged a number of horsemen. Straight for the milling flock they charged, ropes lashing, guns blazing. The terrified sheep crowded away from the shots and the stinging ropes. Hatfield could not hear their piteous bleating, but he saw the wooly bodies go tumbling over the edge of the bluff to the rocks two hundred feet below.

Long before the last sheep, kicking and bleating, fell to its death, the great sorrel was speeding westward on the trail. Hatfield knotted the split reins and let them fall on the horse's neck. He slid his heavy Winchester from where it rested in the saddle boot beneath his left thigh and cocked it.

"Trail, Goldy, trail!" he urged the sorrel. "Just a little more and we'll be within gunshot of those blasted killers. Trail!"

The sorrel responded with an even greater burst of speed. His steely legs drove backward like pistons. He slugged his head above the bit, blew through flaring nostrils. Showers of sparks flew from the stones as his irons crashed against them. The dust cloud of his passing boiled up behind him, while in front the air was crystal clear.

"Just a little more, feller, just a little more!" Hatfield pleaded. "Okay! Steady!"

Instantly the sorrel levelled off to a smooth running walk. Hatfield clamped the rifle butt to his shoulder. His eyes glanced along the sights.

Smoke spurted from the muzzle. The rifle barrel kicked up with the recoil, lined rock-steady again. Hatfield's finger tightened on the trigger.

The report crashed back from the hills. One of the raiders reeled in his saddle. Another booming explosion and a second rose in his stirrups. Hatfield could almost hear his yell of pain and anger.

Whitish spurts of smoke gushed toward Hatfield. Lead whined past. Other slugs kicked up the dust nearby.

"They're using sixguns," the Ranger muttered. "They haven't got the range. Steady, feller!"

Another shot! A hat sailed through the air as the last of the sheep went over the bluff. The raiders whirled their horses and went streaming back into the brush, one still standing in his stirrups, another reeling and rocking and clutching the saddle horn for support.

Hatfield emptied his rifle magazine after them. He stuffed fresh cartridges into the Winchester and shouted to his horse for speed. A few minutes later he swung down from the saddle with Goldy's hoofs sliding in the dust. Crouching low, he ran to the edge of the chaparral, paused behind the cover afforded by a thick bush and peered and listened. To his ears came, faint with distance, the click of irons on the hard soil and a crackling of the brush.

"Kept going," he muttered, and turned back to the three bodies sprawled in the trail.

A single glance told him the men were beyond human help. It also told him that all three were Mexicans or of Mexican extraction. This was not strange, however, for most of the shepherds of the section were Mexicans. He was just stooping over one of the victims when with a clatter of irons a horse came charging around the bend from the west. Hatfield jumped erect and hurled himself sideways at the same instant. There was a crash of a shot and a bullet whipped his face with the hot breath of its passing.

Hatfield's hand flickered down and up. His long Colt boomed in reply. There was a clang of metal striking metal, a gasping cry and the rider of the horse slumped forward, swayed and toppled to the ground.

His face a mask of horror, Jim Hatfield stood rigid for a crawling moment. For as the rider fell, a wide-brimmed hat was whisked off to reveal tumbled yellow curls flying in wild disarray.

The rider of the lone horse was a girl.

2

White to the lips, Hatfield ran to the girl and knelt beside her, searching frantically for the wound. There was no sign of a bullet touching her, only a purplish bruise on her white forehead. Hatfield breathed heartfelt relief as he understood.

"Blazes! what a break!" he muttered. "The good Lord Himself must have been standing beside one or both of us a minute ago. My slug hit her gun, knocked it out of her hand and slammed her 'longside the head. She isn't hurt bad. Should be coming out of it in a minute."

Her long lashes were already fluttering against her creamily tanned cheeks. Another moment and they raised. As her wide blue eyes gazed up at the bearded face bending over her, they filmed with terror. She struggled violently in his arms.

"Easy, Ma'am, easy," he soothed. "Just take it easy. You'll be all right in a minute."

But her pupils were still dilated with

fright. "Aren't — aren't you going to kill me?" she panted.

"Not if I can help it," Hatfield replied, with the suspicion of a smile. "But I came nigh to it, I reckon."

The smile abruptly left his lips and his face grew stern. "What's the big notion?" he demanded. "Throwing down on a perfect stranger like you did? It was just poor shooting that kept you from drilling me and pure dumb luck that kept me from drilling you."

The fear left the girl's eyes and they blazed with anger.

"Why shouldn't I shoot at you?" she asked. "After you killed our sheep and murdered our herders? I wish I'd hit you!"

"Ma'am, I didn't kill anything or anybody," Hatfield replied quietly. "I was a mile off when the ruckus cut loose. If I'd been closer, I might have been able to prevent it."

Her eyes still flamed, but as she met his steady gaze her expression changed.

"I believe you," she said simply. "I'm sorry."

"That's all right," Hatfield replied, as he assisted her to rise. "But what's this all about?"

"I saw the sheep go over from where the

18

trail bends around the bulge to the west of here," she replied. "You can look across from there. I tried to get here in time, but couldn't. I was riding to catch up with the flock before it reached Corpus Christi. I was delayed at the ranch this morning or I would have been with the flock."

"Reckon being delayed was about the luckiest thing that ever happened to you," Hatfield said gravely. "Chances are that bunch would have downed you before they realized you were a woman."

"I don't guess realizing it would have made any difference to those killers," she replied bitterly. "They wouldn't have left any witnesses. They're that kind."

"You know them, then?" Hatfield asked curiously.

"Of course I know them," she replied. "They were some of Craig Benton's men. Who else could they have been?"

"You recognized them?"

"No," she said. "I was too far away for that, but it could have been no one else."

"Accusing somebody of murder without corroborative evidence is a serious matter, Ma'am," Hatfield said gravely. "Who is this Benton gent and why is he on the prod against you?"

"Because my brother and I raise sheep,"

she answered the last question first. "Craig Benton owns the Lazy Eight ranch, the biggest and best in this section next to the great King spread. Much of his holdings is open range. He hates sheep and has sworn to run them out of the country."

"I see," Hatfield replied thoughtfully. "But I understand that Captain Dick King himself is running in sheep."

"That's so," the girl admitted. "And Benton hates him for it. They've had words over it already. I guess Benton will kill King if he gets a chance."

Hatfield considered the prediction serious rather than fantastic, despite the great wealth and prestige of King. Chapters of the saga of "Mary's Little Lamb" had already been written in blood throughout the West.

The feud between cattlemen and sheepmen was nothing new. In days of antiquity when the first sheep came bleating across the hill slope there was immediately the making of a row. The difficulties between sheep and cattle owners are chronicled in the Old Testament. When Joseph's brothers came to him for help to escape the drought in Canaan, after Joseph became a power in Egypt, Joseph took them to King Pharoah but warned them not to mention that they dealt in sheep. "For," he said, "every shepherd is an abomination unto the Egyptians."

And the prophet Ezekiel had something to say about the matter, putting his finger on one of the great causes of feud between the sheepmen and others who wanted to use the land — "Woe be to the shepherds of Israel . . . seemeth it a small thing unto you to have eaten up the good pasture, but you must tread down with your feet the residue of your pastures?"

That, as Hatfield well knew, was what sheep do when not properly handled. They eat a country bare when grass is scant, cropping it down to the roots. And their sharp chisel feet, driven by a hundred-weight of solid bone and flesh, cut out even the roots of the grass. Vegetation may be killed for years to come.

This is particularly true in arid lands where every bit of green stuff serves to conserve moisture. Once the land is bare rain is not absorbed but runs off the ground, forming arroyos and ravines. Over-feeding destroys good range and sheep are far more destructive than cattle.

So the cowman considered sheep his arch enemy and acted accordingly. Where cowmen held the land by priority of occupation, they resented bitterly the coming of sheep and used every means at their command to combat the intrusion of the hated woolies, all too frequently taking the law in their own hands. The sheepmen fought back and the inevitable consequence was bloodshed.

It had been established in many localities that sheep and cattle, when properly handled, could graze on the same ranges without injury to either grass or stock, but as a rule the cattlemen could not see or would not admit the fact. And all too often the sheepmen were callous in their disregard of their neighbors' fights and refused to take the trouble to graze their woolies with heed to sensible conservation of the land.

Hatfield knew all this and realized well that trouble was building up in the section. He shook his head, and dismissed the matter for the moment.

"How you feeling?" he asked the girl.

"I'm all right," she said. "My head aches a little, but that's all. It will pass. What in the world happened to me? All I remember is a blaze of light as something hit my head just after I shot at you."

"You pistol-whipped yourself with your own gun," Hatfield replied, with a grin.

"Chances are it was shock and excitement that caused you to sort of faint, rather than being really knocked out by the blow. Otherwise you'd hardly be as chipper as you are right now. That bruise isn't puffing up much. Figure you weren't clipped very hard."

He briefly explained what had happened. The girl shuddered, one hand pressed to her red mouth. Her eyes were suddenly wide with horror.

"It wasn't as bad as all that," Hatfield reassured her. "Luck was sort of with you."

"I wasn't thinking of that," she said. "I was thinking how awful it would have been if my bullet had hit you."

"A minute ago you were wishing it had," Hatfield smiled.

She colored prettily at his words and Hatfield abruptly realized that she was really quite attractive with her wide blue eyes, sweetly turned red lips, and her curly hair the color of ripe corn silk. She was small and gracefully formed.

He picked up her gun from where it lay in the trail. There was an unpleasant feeling in the pit of his stomach as he noted the splashing of lead on the lock.

" 'Pears to be in working order," he commented as he handed it to her.

She shuddered a little and holstered it. "I'm beginning to wish I'd never started carrying one," she said.

"Sometimes it's a good notion not to," Hatfield agreed. "There are plenty of folks pushing up the daisies who would be alive today if they hadn't been heeled at the wrong time. A gun can be a liability as well as an asset. If you haven't got one you can't use it, and the chances are less that some other jigger will use his on you."

"I notice you have two," she remarked dryly.

Hatfield smiled slightly. "They come in handy sometimes," he replied.

She studied him a moment but refrained from asking questions.

Hatfield turned to the dead men. His face was bleak as he surveyed the still forms. At his side the girl was crying softly.

"They worked for us quite a while," she said. "They were good boys. I feel terrible about this, as if I were to blame. Perhaps it was a mistake to bring in sheep. But much of our land is not good for cattle, and you know what's happened to the cow business. We were losing out fast."

"Sheep are all right, if they're handled right," Hatfield said. "Do you allow them to stray onto other range?"

24

"No," the girl replied, "our land is fenced, and we move them from pasture to pasture so as not to hurt the grass. But that doesn't mean anything to the cattlemen," she added bitterly. "They just don't like sheep."

"Well, I've a notion they will have to learn to put up with them," Hatfield prophesied. "Funny thing about the woolies. They can lose every battle but still win the war. Well, I guess we had better be riding to town to report this. By the way, my name is Hatfield, front handle whittled down to Jim during the past twenty-eight years."

"I'm Gypsy Carvel," the girl introduced herself. "My brother is Tom Carvel. We own the Cross C ranch, fifteen miles to the west. But what about the — the bodies? Shouldn't we take them with us? The horses are just around the bend. They wouldn't stray far."

Hatfield shook his head. "We'll reach town in less than half an hour and it wants two hours till dark," he said. "Corpus Christi is the county seat of Neuces county and there'll be a sheriff's office. The sheriff and maybe the coroner will want to ride up here and view them just as they are. They'll pack the bodies in and their disposal can be arranged for later."

He stepped to the edge of the bluff and gazed over. His face grew even more stern as he noted that some of the wooly bodies on the rocks below were still moving feebly. He looked up and his eyes focused on the jut of cliff a mile to the west that could be seen across the gulf. Three men were riding northeastward on the trail.

Hatfield strode back from the bluff lip. "Company coming," he told the girl. "We'll hang around and see who it is. You keep behind me and let me do the talking."

"I'm not afraid of anybody," she flared.

"Chances are there's nothing to be afraid of," Hatfield replied. "But just the same you stay behind me and keep out of my way."

She hesitated, her eyes rebellious, but a sudden tightening of his bearded jaw decided her to obey.

3

Lounging easily in the trail, his hands hanging loosely by his sides, Hatfield awaited the coming horsemen. A little later they jogged around the bulge.

One riding a little to the rear was a nondescript looking cowhand. Foremost was a big, bulky elderly man with a blocky face and truculent eyes. Beside him rode a much younger man, lean and tall, with a bronzed, straight-featured face and a well-shaped mouth.

There was a resemblance between the two men, Hatfield noted. The resemblance of a ponderous broadsword to a finely tempered rapier, but a resemblance that denoted kinship.

The old man was riding on the outside close to the bluff edge. He leaned in his saddle and gazed down.

"Well, ain't that a purty sight!" he exclaimed heartily. "That's the way I like to see sheep look."

Behind Hatfield sounded a scream of rage. He whirled, and knocked up the girl's arm just in time. Her gun blazed. The bullet turned the old man's hat sideways on his head. He ducked, his face scarlet with anger.

"You hellcat!" he roared.

The girl was struggling with Hatfield. "Let me go, damn you!" she screamed.

Hatfield wrung the gun from her hand and slammed it back in its holster. "You keep it there or I'll spank you with the barrel of it," he told her. He turned to the startled group.

"As for you fellers, get going," he said. "You've caused enough trouble hereabouts."

The old man bristled. "Listen, you, I ain't takin' orders —" he began.

Hatfield's voice blared at him — "Get going!"

The old man gaped and started to speak, but the look in Hatfield's blazing green eyes closed his lips. The Lone Wolf was leaning slightly forward, his hands, the fingers crooked and claw-like, hovering over the black butts of the big Colts flaring out from his sinewy thighs. The position of those slim, terrible hands said plainer than words — "Coming!"

The younger horseman clutched the oldster's arm. "Hold it, Dad," he said in clear, ringing tones. "You wouldn't have a chance. He'd do for all of us. Don't you see what you're up against?"

Hatfield, who missed nothing, noted that he never took his eyes off Gypsy Carvel's face.

The anger left the oldster's eyes and was replaced by a look of intense calculation.

"Yes," he said, his voice quiet, "yes, reckon I do." His hard gaze met Hatfield's eyes steadily.

"Fast-draw, two-gun man, eh?" he remarked. "Brought in by the damned herders to do their shootin' for 'em, eh? Well, I've helped bury a few of your sort."

Hatfield ignored the implied threat. "Get going," he said.

They got going, sweeping past Hatfield and the girl with faces straight to the front. Hatfield distinctly heard the young man exclaim, "Good God!" as his eyes rested on the sprawled bodies of the herders. Hatfield watched the riders till they took the dip of the bluffs, following the trail that zig-zagged down the slope to the town.

"Reckon that old feller was the Craig Benton gent you were telling me about?" he remarked to the girl.

"Yes, that's Benton," she replied. "The

beast! Why didn't you let me shoot him?"

Hatfield was silent. He couldn't very well see his way to censure her after his own blaze of rage. He had been ready and willing to shoot it out with Benton and his bunch. He knew that it was Benton's callous indifference to the sufferings of the mangled animals on the rocks below that set the torch to his anger. But just the same it was hardly the thing for a peace officer to do and Hatfield secretly felt a little ashamed of his outburst.

It reminded him of the day just before he graduated from a famous college of engineering, the day his father was murdered. Young Jim vowed to take up the vengeance quest and either kill or bring his father's killers to justice. But Captain Bill McDowell, the "Grand Old Man" of the Rangers, had convinced him that taking the law in his own hands was a dangerous business and might end with him finding himself one of the very sort he pursued, a man outside the law.

As an alternative, Captain Bill had suggested that Hatfield join the Rangers and thus have the backing of law and order. Hatfield agreed, and became one of that most famous band of peace officers the West ever knew. The day came when he brought his father's killers to justice.

Canny old Captain McDowell had assured him that once his self-appointed task was finished he could leave the service and take up engineering for his life work as he had planned. But the quest was a long one and before it was finished Jim Hatfield realized that he was a Texas Ranger to stay. And now Captain McDowell's Lieutenant and ace-man bore a reputation for cold courage and uncanny ability that stretched far beyond the borders of Texas. Now the Lone Wolf was a symbol, spoken of with a respect that amounted to awe by honest men, with fear and bitter hatred by the outlaw brotherhood.

"Tell me," Jim resumed his questioning. "Who was the young feller with Craig?"

"His son," Gypsy replied shortly.

"Didn't look like a bad sort," Hatfield commented.

"He couldn't be any good with Benton blood in his veins," Gypsy said bitterly.

Hatfield did not answer the remark. "Let's head for town," he said, scratching his chin. "I want to get something to eat and a shave. These darn whiskers are getting long enough to bite."

"You don't usually wear a beard, then?" Gypsy commented.

"No," Hatfield replied, "but I've been too busy riding of late to bother with a razor."

"You must have been riding quite a ways," she remarked.

"I have," Hatfield replied.

Gypsy gazed at him curiously but refrained from further questioning.

"First, though," Hatfield said, "I'll round up the herders' horses and get the rigs off them so they can graze. I've a notion they won't stray far."

It took but a short time to accomplish the chore. Then they set out for town.

"Were those herders Mexicans?" Hatfield asked.

"No," Gypsy answered, "they had Mexican blood but they were born in Texas. They lived over to the west of here."

"Left folks, I reckon?"

"Yes," she nodded, "and they won't forget."

Hatfield's black brows drew together slightly. The remark was significant. He knew the people the dead herders represented to be long on blood feuds. More trouble in the making.

"When we get to town I'm going to ask the sheriff to arrest Benton," Gypsy said suddenly.

Hatfield turned to glance at her. Her lips were tight set, her eyes hard.

"Ma'am," he said, "I wouldn't do that. I don't know who was back of what happened, but I do know that Benton and his bunch did not shoot your herders and kill your sheep."

"How do you know?" she demanded.

"The men who did the shooting and ran the sheep over the bluff left here in one devil of a hurry," Hatfield explained. "I heard them going through the brush for a long ways. You can't send a horse tearing through the brush that way and not leave marks on his hide. And sweat stains in this kind of weather. The horses Benton and his bunch forked were perfectly fresh, and they didn't have a hair out of place. And it's hardly likely that they had fresh horses to change to. In fact, it doesn't make sense to believe they would come riding back this way at all. I'm pretty sure I winged a couple of the bunch that raided the herd. They wouldn't be likely to come riding back along the trail after that. Especially as they couldn't be sure how good a look I got at them."

The girl pondered a moment. "I guess you're right," she admitted grudgingly, "but you'll never convince me it wasn't some of Benton's men who did it."

"Believing isn't knowing," Hatfield said, "and you'd have to convince the sheriff you had proof against Benton before he'd act."

"Chances are he wouldn't act, anyway," she said. "The law is on the side of the cattlemen in this section."

"Not necessarily," Hatfield disagreed. "The law is against law breaking no matter who is responsible. If the sheriff is an honest peace officer, he'll hold no brief for anyone who violates the law. Have you any reason to believe he isn't honest?"

"No," she replied, "but he used to be a cattleman."

Hatfield smiled and said nothing more.

Half an hour later found them threading the streets of the town. Gypsy led the way to the sheriff's office.

A single glance convinced Hatfield that the sheriff, a hard-bitten old frontiersman, would enforce the law without fear or favor. In terse sentences he told the sheriff what he saw. Gypsy nodded corroboration.

The sheriff tugged his mustache and opened his mouth to swear, but refrained in deference to the presence of a lady.

"You didn't try to follow them fellers?" he asked of Hatfield.

"Hardly," the Ranger replied. "In the

first place, I was sort of busy for a spell. In the second, I don't figure it's good sense for one man to go barging through the brush after a bunch of killers."

The sheriff admitted it was so. "I'll ride up there right away," he said, adding querulously, "Darn sheep, anyhow. Wherever they show up there's trouble."

Gypsy's red lips tightened ominously, but Hatfield laid a restraining hand on her arm and averted the imminent explosion.

"I'll be in town if you want to talk to me," he told the sheriff. "Right now I hanker for a bite to eat, a shave and a mite of shut-eye."

"Reckon Miss Carvel can show you a place," said the sheriff. "I'll want you both here in the mornin'. Guess the coroner will hold an inquest and you'll be needed to testify."

Hatfield promised to show up and he and Gypsy left the office.

"I know a good restaurant over on Chaparral Street and they have rooms for rent upstairs," she said. "There's a bar, too, if you care for a drink."

"Reckon I can do without the drink for the present," Hatfield answered. "But I'll want a stable for my horse."

"I use one right around the corner from

the restaurant," she said. "But first I'd like to stop at the packing house and see Samp Gulden who owns it. He was expecting our sheep today."

They approached the gaunt packing house which looked even more sinister in the deepening shadows. A light burned in what was evidently the office.

A man looked up from a desk as Hatfield and Gypsy entered. He was a big man in the prime of life and more than passably good looking. Hatfield judged him to be a little over thirty years of age, although deep lines in his face made him appear older at first glance.

"Feller has had a tough fight getting to where he is," the Lone Wolf shrewdly deduced.

The man had crisp tawny hair, inclined to curl, that swept back in a leonine mane from his broad forehead. His nose was straight and he had a jutting chin. He had a hard-set but well-shaped mouth. His hands, Hatfield noted, were long and powerful with slender, tapering fingers. He favored Hatfield with a quick, keen glance and stood up.

"Howdy, Miss Carvel!" he said heartily. "Bring in the flock? Hope it's a big one. I've been held up on some other shipments and I've got orders to fill."

"You won't get any sheep from me today, Mr. Gulden," the girl replied. Briefly she recounted what had happened.

Gulden shook his big head and clucked sympathetically. "This goes beyond all reason," he declared. "Something has got to be done. Did you tell the sheriff?"

"Yes, I told him," Gypsy replied, "but it won't do any good. Sheriff Oswell and Craig Benton are friends."

"I don't think the implication is fair to either Benton or Sheriff Oswell," Gulden said gently. "Do you have any proof that Craig Benton was responsible for the attack on your herders?"

Gypsy's mouth set stubbornly. "Only in my own convictions," she admitted. "But he has made threats. He swears he'll run every head of sheep out of this section."

"Well," Gulden remarked dryly, "he'll find it a pretty hefty chore running out Dick King's forty thousand head."

"He told King he would do it," Gypsy replied. "And he threatened to kill King, if necessary. He'll do it, too. You've heard his history — how he murdered his own partner to get complete control of the Lazy Eight."

A peculiar expression shaded Gulden's

keen eyes for an instant, as if granite walls had suddenly reared up in the back of them. He slowly shook his head.

"The crime was never proved against Benton," he pointed out.

"But plenty of folks will tell you Benton did it," the girl retorted.

"There are always folks who are ready to think the worst of anyone," Gulden replied judiciously. "A man is supposed to be innocent until he is proven guilty but in practical application the principle does not always work."

Gypsy made no direct reply but she still looked unconvinced.

Gulden again glanced questioningly at Hatfield who had been an interested listener. Gypsy belatedly performed the introductions. Gulden shook hands with a firm grip.

"Cowhand, Mr. Hatfield?" he asked.

"Well, I have been," Hatfield replied, with truth. "Right now I'm sort of chuck line riding so far as cow work is concerned."

Gulden nodded. "A tophand rider should have no trouble getting work in this section," he said, "though I'll admit you've made a bad start — antagonizing Craig Benton. But Dick King uses plenty of riders. He hasn't yet converted all his million-odd acres of holdings to sheep. You might talk with him. Or with some of the smaller owners. They don't all follow Benton's lead. Benton used to about run this section, but of late men like King and Miflin Kennedy have been extending their influence and Benton doesn't like it. Yes, you should have little trouble tieing onto a job of riding, even with Benton on the prod against you."

"I've a notion Benton won't be particularly riled against me once he cools down a mite," Hatfield predicted.

Miss Carvel's reaction to Hatfield's optimistic assumption could be dignified by no other appellation than a sniff.

"You don't know Craig Benton," she said. "He never forgets nor forgives an affront. He'll get even with you for making him take water."

"He didn't take water," Hatfield differed. "His sort doesn't. He merely showed he had too much sense to butt his head into a stone wall for no good reason."

"I noticed you didn't turn your back on him when he rode off," Gypsy retorted.

Hatfield chuckled. "Don't miss much, do you?" he smiled, his teeth flashing startlingly white against his bearded lips.

Samp Gulden seemed to think the discussion had gone far enough. He deftly changed the subject.

"Do you think it possible to get together another flock for me by the first of next week?" he asked the girl. "I have commitments."

"Yes, I think we can," Gypsy replied. "We still have some stuff we don't intend to save for shearing. We'll get busy on it as soon as I get back to the ranch."

"That'll be fine," Gulden said. "I'll depend on you. Drop in any time you are of a mind to, Mr. Hatfield," he added, tacitly ending the interview. "Perhaps I'll be able to throw something your way."

Hatfield thanked him and he and Gypsy left the office. It was black outside, the wind was rising and as they walked along Water Street leading their horses they could hear the waves pounding on the nearby beach.

Gypsy shuddered and moved a little closer to her tall companion.

"The bar is moaning tonight," she said. "It always does when there is trouble in the wind. I wouldn't be surprised if somebody dies before morning."

"An old wives' tale," Hatfield derided.

"Perhaps," she admitted with a little

laugh, "but don't forget, we Scotch have the second sight."

"Carvel isn't a Scotch name," Hatfield demurred. "It's English."

"My grandmother was a MacDonald," Gypsy replied. "She used to make my hair stand on end with her stories of witches and warlocks and wailing women of the glens, and of the second sight that could foretell what was to happen and predict death and disaster. She always said that when the waves moaned on the bar death for someone who heard it wasn't far off."

Hatfield laughed. He paused to look back toward where beams from the riding lights of a nearby ship glowed on the rear of the great packing house.

"If it comes in a real hard blow, Gulden is liable to find himself hunting for new quarters," he remarked. "He's tight on the waterfront. The back end of that shack of his rests on piling that the waves wash."

"Yes, he built it that way purposely," the girl replied. "There is deep water just off the shore and he can load directly on the ships. But he's safer than you think. Mustang Island forms a natural breakwater that shunts the waves away from this section right here. During the hurricane last year, a number of buildings to the north and

41

south were destroyed, but the packing house was not damaged."

Hatfield nodded, understanding something of the vagaries of ocean current and how the island could deflect the force of the waves and the wind during a storm although it was nearly twenty miles distant.

"Here's where we turn," the girl announced a moment later. "The restaurant is right around the corner from William Street on Chaparral Street."

They walked the short distance on William Street and then turned north. Gypsy led the way down the next alley to a stable where they found satisfactory accommodations for their horses. They returned to Chaparral Street, Hatfield carrying their saddle pouches. A few doors down and they came to a big combination saloon and eating house which they entered and occupied a table.

"There's Craig Benton and his son, Sid, at that table over there," the girl said. "That's Jackson Hawley with him. Hawley owns the Rocking H to the north of Benton's holdings. He's Benton's closest friend and hates sheep as badly as Benton does. He used to be Benton's range boss, years ago, before he bought the Rocking H."

Hatfield had already noted both the

Bentons and the burly giant of a man who was their table companion. He had a lean swarthy face, dead black hair as lank as an Indian's and brilliant black eyes. Hatfield decided he was a hard customer, but rather stupid, and judged him to be something over forty years of age.

Although the table was apparently oblivious to their presence, Hatfield knew that their entrance had been noted. Craig Benton and Hawley continued to converse composedly, but Hatfield noticed the younger Benton's eyes glint in their direction.

"There are people who say Hawley was an outlaw before he went to work for Craig Benton," Gypsy remarked as they waited for their order to be brought. "I wouldn't be a mite surprised."

Hatfield chuckled. " 'Pears most everybody in this section is sort of off-color, one way or another," he said.

"Oh, I wouldn't say that," the girl protested quickly. "There are plenty of good people here. There's Dick King over at the corner table, for instance. He's as fine a man as you would want to meet."

Hatfield eyed with interest the famous cattle baron whose vast herds were burned with the "Little Snake" as the Mexicans

43

called the Running W brand. King bid fair to replace the fabulous Shanghai Pierce as the most noted of the Texas cowmen.

King was a very old man, but it was plain from the brightness of his eyes and the alertness of his expression that he had far from lost the vigor of his youth. Hatfield liked his looks.

"Jackson Hawley is a dangerous man," the girl went on. "He's a killer, always in self-defense. But they say he can draw a gun faster and shoot straighter than anyone else in Texas. He can even crack a horseshoe with his hands."

"Evidently quite a gent," Hatfield replied with a slight smile. "Well, here comes the chuck. Let's eat. My stomach is telling me my throat's been sewed up."

Hatfield enjoyed the meal with his pretty table companion. He noticed more than one curious glance cast in his direction. Several men who passed by spoke to the girl in a friendly fashion.

" 'Pears not everybody is down on you because you raise sheep," Hatfield observed.

"It's a mixed company in here," Gypsy replied. "Most of the cattlemen eat and drink here when they are in town, but sheepmen come here too. Not everybody is so set against sheep as the Bentons and Jackson Hawley, especially since Dick King began grazing them on his hill pastures. King and his judgment are respected. There is money to be made from sheep, but very little from cattle at present."

Hatfield nodded sober agreement. What she said was plain truth. The bubble of the cattle boom had burst. Ranchers all over the West were ruined. Draughts, blizzards and overstocking had all gotten in their deadly work. Cows that formerly sold for twenty-five dollars a head now went begging at six dollars. The days of open range, free grass and no winter feeding were drawing to a close.

Experienced cattlemen saw at last, many of them too late, that the happy-go-lucky conditions which had dominated the production end of the cow business could no longer endure. Reforms were in order and were already under way.

But such reforms took time and men were turning to other sources of income to bolster up their declining finances. There was money to be made from sheep meat as well as from sheep wool. Many men who had formerly raised cows were turning to sheep to tide them over the period of depression.

But there were many old-time cowmen, Hatfield knew, such as Benton and Hawley, whose instinctive hatred of sheep and all they stood for was not assuaged. They would defend what they believed to be their rights. And the result would be violence and bloodshed.

"I *would* land smack in the middle of a cow-sheep war, with plenty of other business on my hands," Hatfield muttered under his breath. "Well, maybe the bunch I've been trailing have their headquarters in this section. I began to think so when they passed up Galveston. It's either here or around Point Isabel, and I don't think that's likely. Anyhow, it's up to a Ranger to enforce the law wherever he finds it being violated. Reckon I'll stick around for a spell."

4

After they finished eating, Hatfield rolled a cigarette. "I think I'll go to bed," Gypsy announced. "I was up before daylight." She beckoned a waiter.

"Please ask Mr. Russell to come over here," she requested. "Russell owns the restaurant and the rooming house upstairs," she explained to Hatfield. "We can arrange for rooms with him."

An affable looking fat man came waddling across to the table. The matter of sleeping quarters was quickly arranged.

"I'll see you at the sheriff's office tomorrow morning," Gypsy said.

"Okay," Hatfield agreed. "I think I'll stick around for a while and have that drink."

Gypsy nodded goodnight and departed, the fat proprietor politely opening the door that led to the stairs. Hatfield settled back in his chair and smoked leisurely, eyeing the occupants of the room the while.

The place was filling up and the crowd was growing more boisterous. The necessary chore of eating had been attended to by most and the serious business of drinking was getting under way. A couple of poker games had started and a roulette wheel was whirring over to one side. A Mexican orchestra filed in and took up chairs on a little raised platform that fronted an open space reserved for dancing. Several "ladies" of the dance floor appeared, garbed in short silken skirts glittering with tinsel, low-cut bodices and high-heeled slippers. Corpus Christi's night life was getting in its licks.

At the table across the room, Craig Benton and Jackson Hawley were engaged in earnest conversation. Young Sid took no part in the talk but sat toying with his glass, a frown on his rather good looking face. Hatfield had a feeling that the younger Benton did not approve of something Hawley and his father discussed.

Hatfield pinched out his cigarette butt, rose and sauntered to the bar. He ordered a drink and stood sipping it, meanwhile watching Craig Benton and his companions in the back bar mirror. Benton seemed to be protesting something Hawley urged. Young Sid took no part in the conversation. Finally Benton threw out his hands resignedly and settled back in his chair. A moment later Jackson Hawley rose to the full of his towering height and headed for the bar. Hatfield watched the reflection of his approach in the mirror.

Hawley walked straight to where Hatfield stood. As he bellied the bar, he jostled Hatfield rudely, although there was plenty of room. Hatfield moved slightly and continued to sip his drink.

A bartender hurried to pour the cowman a drink. Hawley ignored it.

"Beginnin' to stink like hell of sheep in here," he remarked loudly with a significant sideways glance at Hatfield.

Hatfield placed his glass on the bar and turned to face Hawley. "It's also beginning to smell of skunk all of a sudden," he said in low but clear tones that carried throughout the suddenly hushed room.

Jackson Hawley glared. His face flushed darkly red as the implication went home.

"Why, you damned range tramp —" he began.

Hatfield hit him in the mouth, hard. Hawley reeled back, fell over a chair and measured his length on the floor. He bounded to his feet, spewing blood and curses. His face was working with anger, but Hatfield noted his eyes were cool and calculating. His hands swooped down in a menacing gesture. Hatfield stood perfectly still, facing Hawley, his hands hanging loosely by his sides.

As Hatfield expected, Hawley did not go for his gun. His hand paused above the butt, the fingers spread. He looked slightly bewildered by Hatfield's unexpected reaction.

Hatfield laughed, mockingly. "No self-defense this time, Hawley," he said. "You're called! Either fill your hand or crawl back to your table."

The room was tense and still. Then suddenly somebody laughed. The sound seemed to sting Hawley to madness. His eyes blazed. He jerked his gun from its sheath. The hanging lamps quivered to the crash of a report.

Hawley reeled back with a bellow of pain. He clutched his blood-spouting hand and doubled up, moaning and gasping. His gun, one butt plate knocked off, lay on the floor a dozen feet away.

The room was in an uproar. Men were ducking wildly to get out of line. The bartenders were yelling, the dance floor girls screaming. The orchestra had stopped playing at the first sign of trouble.

Smoke wisping from the muzzle of his Colt, Hatfield flickered a glance to Benton's table. Craig Benton's mouth was hanging open. On his face was a look of amazed disbelief. Young Sid's lips spread in a slow grin. His eyes twinkled.

Hatfield spoke, his voice like steel grinding on ice. "Had enough, Hawley?" he asked. "If you haven't, pick up your iron and have another try. But I might miss next time, *inside* your gun hand."

But Hawley was too sick and shaken to make further trouble. A forty-five slug through the hand is no light matter. He lurched and seemed about to fall.

Craig Benton sprang to his feet and hurried across the room. Young Sid followed at a leisurely pace. Old Craig seized the wounded man's arm and steadied him.

"Come on, get out of here," he said. "You need a doctor." He shot Hatfield a single black glare and led the reeling Hawley from the room. At the door, young Sid glanced back over his shoulder and grinned.

Hatfield holstered his gun and turned back to the bar. "Think I'll have another one," he told the bartender.

The bartender refilled his glass with a hand that shook till the liquor splashed out on the bar. Hatfield raised the brimming glass to his lips and drank. Not a drop spilled over the rim. Behind him he heard low-voiced conversation.

"Gentlemen, hush!" a man was saying. "Was that shootin'! Hawley had cleared leather before that feller reached. And did you get that about missin' *inside* Hawley's gun hand, next time? I'd hate to have him miss me that way. I got a funny feelin' in my middle just thinkin' about it."

Hatfield's lips twitched slightly as he sipped his drink. He felt a touch on his elbow and turned to face old Dick King who looked him up and down with his faded but still keen blue eyes.

"Son, you did a good piece of work," King said. "Jack Hawley had been asking for it for a long time. But look out for him. You hurt him mighty bad tonight and he won't forget it."

"Oh, he wasn't hurt much," Hatfield replied. "Just a hunk of meat knocked off his hand. He'll be okay in a couple of weeks."

"I'm not talking about his hand," King said. "What you hurt tonight, and hurt bad, is his pride. Hawley gets himself up to be considerable with a gun. You made him look plumb foolish. That hurt him worse than shooting out one of his eyes would have done. Look out for him. He'll figure to even up and he won't be particular as to the methods he uses. Hope to see you again soon. Like to have a talk with you."

With a pleasant nod, the cattle baron walked back to his table. Hatfield was suddenly conscious of added respect on the part of the bartender. Evidently Dick King's approval packed considerable weight in the section.

Hatfield finished his drink, turned away from the bar and retrieved his saddle pouch from where he left it under the table. Russell, the fat proprietor, hurried to open the door for him.

"Your room is the last down the corridor, on the left, suh," he said. "Two doors beyond Miss Carvel's. Good night, and if you should want anything, I'll be down here till mornin'."

Hatfield thanked him and ascended the stairs. As he walked down the corridor, a door opened a crack and Gypsy Carvel peered out, then stepped into the corridor.

She wore a silken robe that clung revealingly to her sweetly curved figure. Her eyes were great purple pools in her white face.

"I heard shooting," she said. "Was anything wrong?"

Hatfield hesitated a moment, then

frankly told her just what happened. She shuddered, and her eyes seemed to darken.

"I told you Jackson Hawley is a killer," she said. "He'll never forgive what you did to him. He'll kill you if he gets a chance. I feel terrible about it. I feel that I am to blame and have brought you trouble."

"Ma'am, I've a notion you bring trouble to any man who gets a good look at you," Hatfield chuckled.

She blushed rosily under his regard and her lashes fluttered down.

"Not that I don't figure to be able to handle all the trouble that comes my way," Hatfield added cheerfully.

She flashed him a look through the silken veil of her lashes. "You might find you had your hands full," she retorted. "Good night. I'll see you tomorrow. And — and please lock your door. I don't put anything past those men. Good night!"

She slipped back into her room and closed the door. Hatfield stared at it a moment, hesitated, reached and knocked.

The door opened instantly. In Gypsy's eyes was a trace of surprise and, perhaps, something else.

"Ma'am," Hatfield suggested, "you might try locking your own. No telling what's liable to happen in this helltown and I don't want you getting a scare."

"I was waiting for you to — to walk down the hall," she replied. The door closed again with something of a bang. The lock clicked. He stared, shook his head, and continued to his own room.

Hatfield cleaned and oiled his gun before going to bed. He had the habit, common to men who ride much alone, of talking to his horse or even to his guns at times. Now he addressed the big Colt aloud.

"Something darn funny about that business downstairs tonight," he declared. "The whole thing doesn't make sense. Hawley was out to down me, but why? Just because Benton suspects I was brought here by the sheepmen to help them against the cowmen? Could be, but it still doesn't make sense that Hawley should take such a chance for no better reason than that. No, there's more to it than that. But what? That's the big question, and one I've got to find the answer to if I expect to stay healthy. Old Benton didn't 'pear to be much sold on the notion. I figure he tried to talk Hawley out of doing what he did. And young Sid seemed sort of pleased that Hawley got his come-uppance. Oh, to hell with it! I'm going to bed!"

Which he proceeded to do without delay.

Just as he was drifting off, he chuckled drowsily to himself, "Darned if I don't believe she was waiting for me to knock on that door! She sure looked cute in that thin kimono or whatever it was."

5

Hatfield slept soundly, but he was up early. He shaved and enjoyed a good clean-up before descending to the restaurant for breakfast. Hardly anybody was about at such an ungodly hour and he took his time eating. Then, before repairing to the sheriff's office, he dropped in at the stable to clean his rifle and make sure Goldy was properly cared for.

"Say!" exclaimed the old stablekeeper, "I hardly knowed you with the brush off your face. You ain't a bad lookin' feller with your hay mowed. Last night you looked like a Mexican *bandido* straight from the Carmens. Goin' to work for Miss Carvel?"

"Well," Hatfield smiled, "I'm not exactly a sheep herder."

"The Carvels run cows, too" said the stableman. "They got quite a few, but they were hit by the beef market bustin' like everybody else. That's why they started runnin' sheep. They been havin' trouble hirin' hands of late, because of the woolies. Hear even Dick King has been sort of up against it for riders since *he* began stockin' sheep. King's been hirin' Mexican *vaqueros.* I heard he says he ain't goin' to hire nothin' else from now on."

"Mexican riders are good hands once they're cured of their show-off foolishness," Hatfield replied.

"You're right about that," agreed the stablekeeper, who was himself a former cowhand. "Heard about what you did in the Lipan last night. A good chore. Jack Hawley needs to be took down a peg. He's been swallerforkin' over this section for quite a few years now. I knowed him when he didn't have two pairs of pants and was trailin' with a mighty bad bunch, when he went to work for old Craig Benton. Then all of a sudden he blossomed out and bought his Rockin' H from the Weston brothers. That was about sixteen years back, after he'd been with Benton a couple of years. Reckon he started savin' up his dinero after he went to work for Benton. Must have been luckier at poker than anybody figured to tie onto that many pesos, though he seemed to lose most of the time."

Hatfield had let the garrulous old keeper

run on in the hope he might drop some crumb of information. His eyes grew thoughtful as he listened and the concentration furrow deepened between his black brows.

"Heard Dick King 'peared to take a likin' to you," the stablekeeper remarked as Hatfield turned to go. "Good feller to get in with — King. If you don't coil your twine with the Carvels, I've a notion King would sign you up."

It was still early when he left the stable and Hatfield strolled along Water Street, gazing at the blue waters of the bay and listening to the pounding of the waves on the beach. He noted that the ship standing off shore the night before was loading from the packing house by way of a long gangplank. Considerable freight was also being transferred from the ship, doubtless supplies needed in the operation of the plant. He watched the loading for a while, then turned east on Belden Street and headed for the sheriff's office which was located on Gavilan Street.

Gypsy Carvel was in the office when Hatfield arrived. He walked up behind her and touched her on the shoulder. She turned with a startled exclamation.

"Why — why, I hardly knew you!" she

exclaimed. "You look quite different than you did last night."

"And you also look sort of different than you did last night," Hatfield replied with a glance at her well-worn riding costume.

Her color rose at the implication. Apparently she decided he needed taking down a peg, for she added, "But I think I liked you better the way you were last night. The beard covered up more of you."

"And I liked you better the way you were last night, for just the opposite reason," Hatfield instantly countered.

This time she really did blush, but she did not appear particularly displeased, although she deftly changed the subject.

"The sheriff has been so kind as to arrange to have the bodies taken to the ranch with an escort right after the inquest," she told him. "I am going to ride with them, but I wish you'd drop in at our place soon if you aim to stay in the section. You can't miss it — the first ranchhouse seen from the trail to the west of here. I'm sure my brother would like to have a talk with you."

"I'll do that," Hatfield promised, "maybe tomorrow."

It did not take the coroner's jury long to bring in a typical cow country verdict. The verdict 'lowed that the herders met their deaths at the hands of parties unknown, adding that such a thing shouldn't even happen to herders and advising that the sheriff run down the varmints responsible as quickly as possible.

The sheriff contacted Hatfield as soon as the inquest was over.

"I want to have a talk with you," he said. "I've got to get those bodies started back to the Carvel place, though, and I got a couple more chores to attend to. Drop around right after noon."

Hatfield loafed around town a while, had a bite to eat in Fats Russell's Lipan restaurant and then returned to the sheriff's office. Sheriff Oswell waved him to a chair. Hatfield sat down and rolled a cigarette. The sheriff regarded him with his frosty eyes.

"Heard tell about the ruckus in the Lipan last night," he remarked at length. "You must be purty good with your irons to shade Jack Hawley. Reckon it ain't been done over often."

Hatfield smiled slightly but did not reply.

"Can't understand what got into Hawley," rumbled the sheriff. "He don't usually go off half-cocked like that. You didn't say somethin' to rile him up, did you?"

"Not until after he started making his

play," Hatfield answered. "I was sort of surprised myself."

"Reckon Hawley was a mite more surprised," grunted Oswell. "He sets up to be considerable with a gun." He regarded Hatfield suspiciously for moment.

"You seem to have been mixed up in considerable hell raisin' since you landed here," he resumed. "Craig Benton told me you saved him from gettin' an air hole in his hide yesterday. Gypsy Carvel is a nice gal, but she's got her share of her Old Man's temper. Comyn Carvel, her dad, was considerable of a heller himself in his day. Craig Benton was mighty lucky you happened to be there."

"Understand Benton isn't exactly a sky-pilot himself," Hatfield commented. "Understand from a remark I heard Miss Gypsy let fall when she was talking to Gulden over to the packing house, he killed his own partner."

Sheriff Oswell shook his grizzled head. "It was never proved that he did," he replied, rather heavily. "Personally, I never believed he did, but lots of folks thought otherwise."

"How did the yarn get started?" Hatfield asked, sensing that the sheriff was in a mood to talk about the matter.

62

"The whole business happened about eighteen years back and sheep was at the bottom of it," said the sheriff. "Sheep always make for trouble, even talkin' about 'em. Craig Benton and Walt Garner owned the Lazy Eight in partnership. They were both short-tempered gents and they'd had more than one arg'fyin', but always managed to patch things up till they had the big one over sheep."

The sheriff paused to fill his pipe. Hatfield maintained an interested silence.

"Walt Garner was a mighty smart stockman," the sheriff resumed. "He saw, long before most folks, what was sooner or later going to happen to the cow business. Craig Benton has him to thank for being a hell of a lot better off right now than most ranch owners. Garner began improving stock and raising winter feed more than twenty years back. Benton thought it was all darned foolishness and said so. But he went along with Garner till Walt suggested that they run sheep onto their hill pastures against the time when the bottom would drop out of the beef market. He 'lowed sheep would tide them over till things got better again as they eventually would."

"Far-seeing jigger, all right," Hatfield commented.

"Uh-huh, he was," agreed the sheriff. "But Benton hated sheep. He had a brother killed by sheepmen durin' one of the sheep-and-cattle wars in Arizona. There was a grand row between him and Garner and finally Garner put it up to Benton to either buy or sell, seein' as they couldn't get along together. Benton elected to buy and paid Garner off in gold. Garner rode off without even sayin' goodbye. A little later, Benton rode off too, fumin' and cussin'. Later he said he just rode into the hills for a while to cool off. Took him considerable time and it was way late at night when he got back to the ranchhouse. The next mornin' Walt Garner was picked up on the trail about a mile outside of the town. He had a bullet hole between his shoulder blades and he didn't have the gold he packed away from the Lazy Eight ranchhouse."

"And then there was hell to pay," Hatfield remarked.

"Uh-huh, and no pitch hot," said the sheriff. "Garner had lots of friends, and they accused Benton of doing for Garner. Of course there was no proof that Benton had anything to do with the killin'. Folks took sides and there came nigh to being a few more shootin's over it. I was sheriff

64

then, servin' my first term, and I managed to hold things down. Garner had a wife livin' over in Leesville, Louisiana, and a kid. She came here to claim his body after Garner's friends had written to her. She brought the kid along, a nice lookin' boy about twelve or fourteen, I'd say. I happen to know that Benton saw her and tried to give her a section of the spread to make up for what she'd lost. But Garner's friends had got to her first, and she turned down the offer and accused Benton to his face of murderin' her husband. That hit Benton hardest of all, but there was nothin' he could do about it. She took Garner's body back to Louisiana."

"What became of her?" Hatfield asked.

The sheriff's eyes grew somber. "I heard tell from some of Garner's friends that she went to work in a factory over there," he replied. "A couple of months later she got drowned in Atchafalaya Bay. Garner's friends here 'lowed she killed herself, but I can't say as to that."

"And the boy?"

"Was sent to an institution, sort of orphan asylum, I reckon. Dropped out of sight a few years later."

Hatfield's face was brooding. "Funny, how one man's act will set up a chain of

65

events that will affect the lives of others over a course of many years," he remarked.

The sheriff nodded soberly. "Most of Garner's friends are dead or left the section," he concluded, "but there are still a few around, so the story won't down."

"Was Comyn Carvel, Gypsy's father, a friend of Garner's?" Hatfield asked.

"That's right," replied the sheriff.

"And Jackson Hawley worked for Benton when Garner was with him?"

"Uh-huh," the sheriff nodded. "He was a young hellion in them days and I reckon he ain't changed much. Him and Garner didn't hit it off over well because of his hell raisin' in town. Garner was a mite straight-laced. But Hawley was as good a range boss as ever throwed a leg over a bronk and Garner put up with him. He stayed on with Benton after Garner was killed until a couple of years later when he branched out for himself."

Hatfield nodded thoughtfully, and rolled another cigarette. Sheriff Oswell stared at him, a slightly puzzled expression on his bad-tempered old face.

"Say," he exclaimed in injured tones, "I brought you here to ask you a few questions about yourself and I've been doin' all the talkin'. And I ain't usually much of a talker."

Hatfield regarded him with smiling eyes. Sheriff Oswell didn't know it, but shrewder men than he had found themselves unexpectedly in the same position in the Lone Wolf's presence.

"Well, I'm ready to answer anything you want to ask," Hatfield chuckled. "Shoot!"

The sheriff was about to speak when there sounded a clatter of hoofs outside, jerking to a halt in front of the office. The door banged open and a wild-eyed young cowboy charged into the room.

"Bill Withersbee! Bill Withersbee!" he panted.

The sheriff stared at him. "What in hell's the matter with you, Hastings?" he demanded. "What about Bill Withersbee?"

"He's dead!" gulped the cowhand. "I saw him! He's got a bullet hole between his eyes."

6

Sheriff Oswell came to his feet with a roar. "What in the hell *are* you talkin' about?" he stormed. "Where's Withersbee? Who shot him?"

The cowhand began mouthing incoherent speech. Hatfield abruptly stood up, towering over the old sheriff who was himself a lanky six-footer, and laid his hand on the young fellow's shoulder.

"Take it easy," he said quietly. "Get a hold on yourself and start at the beginning."

Something in the level green eyes that held his steadied the boy and quieted his shattered nerves.

"I was ridin' down the north trail from our place, headin' for town, and I saw him," he said. "He was layin' down at the foot of the slope below the trail against Tom Carvel's wire. His horse was standin' 'longside the trail."

"You didn't go to him?" Hatfield asked.

"No. I knew he was dead, and I was scairt. I headed for town as fast as my bronk could travel."

"One thing you did right, anyhow," growled the sheriff. "Bill Withersbee is Craig Benton's range boss," he enlightened Hatfield. "I'll ride over there right away. Damn it! both my deputies are out of town."

"I'll ride with you, if you don't mind," Hatfield offered.

"Glad to have you," said the sheriff. "I'll need someone to help me. This kid ain't good for nothin'. Get your horse. I'll have mine in a jiffy and meet you here."

Ten minutes later they rode out of town at a fast pace. Five miles to the west they turned off on a track that wound through the growth to the north.

"This is a short-cut to the Lazy Eight ranchhouse," the sheriff explained. "How far to where you saw him, Hastings?"

"About a mile up the trail," the boy replied. "Just past where the chaparral belt peters out."

Another ten minutes of riding and they passed out of the growth and saw the body. It lay at the foot of a slope of bare, soft ground that dropped rather steeply to a seven-strand barbed wire fence beyond which was rocky grassland dotted with grazing sheep.

"Wherever you see them damned bleatin' things there's trouble!" swore the sheriff. He was turning his horse toward the slope when Hatfield stopped him.

"Leave the horses here," he advised. "No sense in cutting up the ground. There should be tracks in that mud that may mean something. Son, you stay here and hold the horses," he told Hastings.

The sheriff nodded agreement. He and Hatfield dismounted and headed down the slope on foot.

Hatfield's keen eyes were searching the surrounding terrain. He noted that the chaparral belt curved away to the east and ran northward in a solid bristle of growth that paralleled the trail, a couple of hundred yards to the east. Grazing just east of the trail was a saddled and bridled horse.

They reached the body, that of a middle-aged man with grizzled hair. His face was streaked with blood. His eyes were glazed, and between them was a blue hole.

Hatfield suddenly halted, one foot outthrust. "Sheriff," he said loudly, "don't you figure it would be a good notion for Hastings to ride on to the ranchhouse and tell them what happened?"

"Why —" the sheriff began.

"Tell him to go," Hatfield directed in low tones.

The sheriff stared. The Lone Wolf's eyes were hard on his face, and in them the sheriff read something of importance. "Okay," he grunted. He raised his voice.

"Get goin', Hastings," he called. "Tell 'em to bring somethin' down here to pack the body."

The boy rode off along the trail. The sheriff turned to Hatfield.

"Why in blazes did you want to get rid of him?" he asked.

"Because," Hatfield replied, "there are some things here that the less folks see the better, I figure. Things that had better not be talked about."

He moved his outthrust foot as he spoke, and the sheriff saw what it had covered. With a growling oath he stooped and picked up the metal object.

"Wire nippers!" he exploded. "What in hell?"

"Looks like somebody aimed to cut the wire," Hatfield said.

The sheriff glared. "You tryin' to tell me that Withersbee was down here cuttin' Carvel's wire?" he demanded.

"No, I'm not," Hatfield replied. "But I

am telling you that Withersbee was not killed down here."

"Not killed down here!" snorted the sheriff. "Here he is, ain't he? And if he ain't dead, some gents with shovels are sure goin' to play a mighty mean joke on him in a couple of days."

Hatfield was in no mood for humor, but his lips twitched slightly in a smile.

"I mean," he explained, "that Withersbee was packed down here from where he was killed."

"How do you know that?" demanded the sheriff.

"Look at his boots," Hatfield said. "You'll notice there is no mud on the soles or on the heels. And he couldn't possibly have walked down here without getting mud on them."

"Maybe he was down here on his horse when he was shot and fell off," hazarded the sheriff.

"Maybe," Hatfield admitted, "but I don't think so. Wait here — don't walk around — and I'll make sure."

He climbed the slope, taking care to follow the route by which they descended and approached the grazing horse. The animal made no attempt to escape. Hatfield loosened the cinches and removed the bit from its mouth, so it could graze in comfort. Then he raised first one front foot and then the other, scrutinizing them carefully. Giving the horse a pat he returned to where the sheriff waited.

"The horse was not down here," he reported. "None of this red mud on its hoofs."

"But what the blazes does it mean?" asked the bewildered peace officer.

"It means, I would say," Hatfield returned quietly, "that somebody shot Withersbee up there on the trail and then packed his body down here to the wire and presumably laid the nippers beside his outstretched hand."

The sheriff started to speak, but Hatfield stopped him. "Look there," he said, "there's a line of boot marks coming down from the trail to where the body is lying. A double line, left by two men. And beside them is another line going up the slope. You'll notice the marks coming down are deeper than those going up, meaning that coming down the men packed a heavy load. And there were horses down here, too. A mess of tracks right over there by that post. And the hoofmarks go back up the slope, slanting to the north."

The sheriff swore explosively, but was

forced to admit it was all true.

"But what does it mean?" he wanted to know. "Why was Withersbee killed and packed down here?"

"I don't know the answer for sure yet," Hatfield admitted, "but I'm beginning to have a sort of notion. I sure wish I knew which way Withersbee was facing when he was shot."

He stood silent for several minutes, gazing up the slope toward where the bristle of growth fanged up against the sky, east of the trail.

A rabbit was hopping along the edge of the growth, pausing from time to time to nibble grass or weeds. Hatfield watched it idly, his thoughts elsewhere.

Abruptly the rabbit halted, close to the growth, and stood on its hind legs. Then it whirled around and streaked back the way it had come on twinkling white feet.

"Now what scared that feller?" Hatfield wondered aloud. "He —"

Suddenly his long arm shot out and swept the sheriff off his feet. He hurled himself to the ground at the same instant.

Something yelled through the air over their heads. The clang of a rifle shot ripped the silence.

The sheriff, volleying profanity, started

to scramble to his feet, but Hatfield slammed him down again.

"Stay where you are!" he rasped. "I don't think the devil can see us down here under the lip. We'll know in a minute."

They lay rigid with the expectancy of the tearing impact of a bullet at any instant. But no further sound broke the stillness.

"I was right, he can't see us down here," Hatfield muttered. "It was the rabbit that saved one of us. I was eyeing the brush, wondering what scared him, when I saw the sun glint on the hellion's rifle barrel as he shifted it to line sights. Stay right where you are. Don't stand up if you value your life. Keep your eyes on the lip of the slope and your gun ready. If anybody shows, shoot first and ask questions afterward. I'm going to try and see if I can make something of that drygulching gent, if he didn't hightail right after he pulled trigger."

He was sliding away from the sheriff as he spoke, worming along on his stomach. With Oswell muttering protests behind him he inched along, keeping his head down. Not until he was well beyond where the belt of chaparral began did he rise to his feet. He slid noiselessly into the growth and moved forward with the stealth and utter silence of an Indian. He continued north until the edge of the chaparral began veering eastward and a little beyond. Then he turned sharply north, moving with ever greater caution. Finally he reached a point that he judged was directly opposite where he spotted the drygulcher's shifting rifle barrel. He turned west, moving at a snail's pace, pausing every few steps to peer and listen.

"He ought to be straight ahead and mighty close," Hatfield breathed to himself as he searched the growth. Nothing moved. Nothing broke the silence save the twittering of birds in the nearby bushes and the faint rustle of the leaves in a gentle breeze.

Then suddenly he heard a tiny sound, a soft crunching of dead leaves such as would be made by a man shifting his weight from one foot to the other. He glided forward a few steps in the direction of the sound and paused, peering ahead. His eyes fixed on something bulky beside a mesquite trunk. Another moment and he made out the crouching form of a man who peered through the screen of twigs and branches. A flicker of sunlight glinted on the barrel of a rifle.

Hatfield debated his next move. Killing

the drygulcher would be a simple matter, but he earnestly desired to take the fellow alive. A live man might be induced to talk, a result which could hardly be expected of a dead one. Moving slowly an inch at a time he edged forward, careful not to make the slightest sound until he was but a couple of yards distant from the crouching form. His hands stretched out for a crushing grip on the fellow's throat. And then the unpredictable happened.

Under the deceptively smooth carpet of fallen leaves was a crooked stick resting in a shallow depression. Hatfield's forward-reaching foot came down on it. It broke with a sharp snap.

The drygulcher whirled around, swinging his rifle to the front. Hatfield's hand flashed down and up. The two shots boomed almost as one.

Almost, but not quite. Hatfield heard a slug screech over his head as the rifle barrel flung up and the drygulcher crashed backward through the growth, his boot heels beating a spasmodic tattoo on the dead leaves.

Hatfield bounded forward, gun ready for instant action. But the fellow was dead when he reached him, a bullet laced through his heart.

With a single quick glance at the corpse, Hatfield pushed his way through the fringe of growth. Sheriff Oswell was scrambling over the lip of the slope, gun in hand. Hatfield waved him to come on and a moment later he panted to a halt at the Ranger's side.

"Why didn't you stay put like I told you to?" Hatfield asked. "You didn't know which had come out on top."

"You think I'd stay holed up safe while you were shootin' it out with the sidewinder?" the sheriff gasped indignantly. "Did you get the varmint?"

"Looks that way," Hatfield replied, "and 'pears he was by himself. Let's look him over and see if you know him."

They pushed their way back through the growth and dragged the dead man into the open. The sheriff gazed at the swarthy, thin-lipped face and shook his head.

"Never saw him before," he said. "Ornery looking hellion."

"Typical border scum," Hatfield agreed. "Looks to have a mite of Indian blood and maybe some Spanish or Latin. I hoped to take him alive but maybe it's a good thing I didn't come to grips with him. Built like a brick smokehouse. Not very tall, but almost as wide as he is long. Let's go through his clothes and see what we can find."

They turned out the dead man's pockets, revealing among other things a number of twenty-dollar gold pieces.

"Devil's been doin' all right by himself," the sheriff grunted. "Hatfield, this ain't no brush-poppin owlhoot or stray calf wide looper. I figure he was tied up with a big outfit of some sort."

"Looks that way," Hatfield agreed. He fumbled another pocket and drew out a flat, round tin box. He removed the lid and stared at the contents.

The box was filled with an almost black, sticky substance that gave off a peculiar acrid smell. The Lone Wolf's eyes glowed as he examined it.

"This *is* interesting," he said. "Gum opium, sure as shooting."

"What in blazes was he doin' with that stuff?" wondered the sheriff.

"He may have used it," Hatfield replied. "More likely, though, he stole it, knowing he could get plenty for it. This stuff is costly."

The sheriff nodded and they resumed their search, revealing nothing more of interest.

Hatfield slipped the tin box into his

pocket. The sheriff regarded him curiously but offered no objection.

"What about the money?" he asked. "Several hundred dollars here."

"Take it and put it in your poor box," Hatfield suggested. "No telling where it came from and I reckon this gent doesn't need it any longer."

"Reckon not," the sheriff agreed, pocketing the gold. "Where he's gone all he'll have use for is a coal shovel and he'll get that free."

"But I'm more up in the air than ever now," he added querulously. "Why did this hellion try to do for us? Did he hang around here after killin' Withersbee on the chance of somebody comin' along? Don't seem to make sense."

"No," Hatfield said, "it wouldn't. From the looks of Withersbee's body, I would say he was killed but a short time before young Hastings found him. I've a notion the gents who did it heard Hastings coming down the trail and holed up in the brush till he was past. Then they trailed after him and slid into town right after he did. They watched us ride out. Then one of them or somebody they selected for the chore tailed us here. Would have been an easy enough chore. I don't think we looked back once after we left town. And even if we had, we wouldn't have thought anything of somebody riding the trail behind us. I gather it's a pretty well used trail from the looks of it."

"Yes, it is," said the sheriff. "Lots of spreads to the west of here and a branch runs up to Kingsville. Most always somebody ridin' it."

Hatfield nodded. "If this fellow had been here when we arrived, the chances are he would have downed us all before we had a chance to get down the slope," he pointed out. "If he was pretty close behind us, he would just have about had time to slide around through the brush and get into shooting position. We would find his horse somewhere close."

"But why did he do it?" demanded the bewildered sheriff. "Why should he want to down us in the first place."

"The answer to that might be worth considerable to me," Hatfield replied. "I have a notion, but I'm not quite sure."

The sheriff was regarding Hatfield with a queer expression on his lined face.

"Son," he said, "just what are you, anyhow?"

Hatfield smiled slightly. He fumbled with a cunningly concealed secret pocket

81

in his broad leather belt and held out something for the sheriff to see.

Sheriff Oswell's eyes widened as he gazed at the object, a gleaming silver star set on a silver circle, the feared and honored badge of the Texas Rangers.

"Well, I might have knowed it," he said at length. "You're just everything a Ranger should be and usually is." Suddenly his eyes glowed with excitement.

"And by God, I know you!" he exclaimed. "I've got you placed at last. Was wonderin' who you reminded me of, especially after you shaved. Somebody I'd heard a lot about. You're the Lone Wolf!"

"Been called that," Hatfield admitted as he stowed away the badge.

The sheriff stared, almost in awe, at the towering figure of the man whose exploits were legendary throughout the Southwest.

"The Lone Wolf!" he repeated. "Well, I'll be darned! And what are you doing here?"

Hatfield chuckled. "I've begun to wonder about that myself," he replied. "I *was* trailing a smuggling bunch that killed a Ranger and two deputy sheriffs up around Crockett in Houston county. They have been shoving in opium and marihuana and stuff on which no duty has been paid for quite a while. The Customs folks know it mostly comes in by ship, but they haven't been able to drop a loop on the bunch. They called on the Rangers to lend a hand. Enforcing the Customs laws isn't exactly a Ranger chore, but such stuff as opium and marihuana is contraband under Texas law. So a trap was laid for the bunch coming back south on the Trinity River trails from Dallas which had been decided was the distributing point for the stuff. They slid out of the trap and left three dead men behind them, one of them a Ranger. Captain Bill McDowell handed me the chore of trying to run them down. I trailed them south and past Galveston and on southwest and then completely lost track of them. I kept on down this way, figuring their headquarters was somewhere in this section or down in the Point Isabel country. Now I 'pear to have gotten myself tangled up in a few other things."

"And you figure they might work out of Corpus Christi?" the sheriff asked.

"Not necessarily, although I regard it as likely," Hatfield replied. "There are bays and coves all along the coast where a ship might put in to unload the stuff. Up until a few minutes ago I wasn't even sure they worked from this section, but now I'm pretty well convinced they do."

"Why?"

"Because of one of the little slips the owlhoot brand always makes," Hatfield replied slowly. "Just the can of opium gum this hellion was packing with him. I figure it was part of one of the smuggled shipments. And that ties up this gent with the outfit. And as he evidently rode out of Corpus Christi after us, I figure that their point of operations must be somewhere near."

"Uh-huh, and it looks like they've spotted you and figure you're better out of the way," the sheriff surmised shrewdly.

"Could be," Hatfield admitted. "But let's get back to Bill Withersbee."

"Why in blazes would a smugglin' bunch want to kill Withersbee?" wondered the sheriff.

"That's got me plumb puzzled," Hatfield admitted. "It doesn't seem to make sense. But I've a strong notion that Craig Benton is the key to the puzzle."

"For the love of Pete!" gasped the sheriff. "You don't figure Benton is mixed up in smugglin'?"

"No, I don't," Hatfield replied, with a smile. "But I do figure that somebody connected with the smuggling is mighty anxious to do in Benton. Sheriff, suppose for the sake of the argument that Withersbee aimed to cut Carvel's wire. Why would he do it?"

"Why, to let Carvel's sheep stray onto Benton's range over here so Benton would have an excuse to kill them," replied the sheriff.

"Exactly," Hatfield said. "And if that happened, all the sheepmen would immediately be convinced that Benton was back of the killing of Carvel's sheep and herders yesterday. And then Benton's life wouldn't be worth a busted cartridge. Those herders that were killed left friends and relatives. Once they are certain in their minds that Benton was responsible for the killings, they will be out to get Benton, and the chances are they'll get him. What I believe is that Withersbee stumbled on somebody getting ready to cut Carvel's wire, somebody he may have recognized, and was killed because of what he saw. Then his body was planted with the nippers alongside of it to make it look like he intended to cut the wire and was killed, presumably by some of Carvel's herders who caught him in the act. Which would also make things look mighty bad for Benton. He's on a tough spot as it is and it's going to take some fast work to get him off."

"Uh-huh, and here he comes right now," said the sheriff as a band of horsemen bulged around the bend of the trail to the north.

7

Craig Benton was evidently in a black rage. He pulled his foaming horse to a slithering stop, waved to the sheriff and glared at Hatfield.

"What's that feller doin' here with you, Oswell?" he demanded suspiciously.

"This feller," replied Sheriff Oswell with dangerous quiet, "just saved me from gettin' an air hole in my hide, just as he saved you from gettin' one in yours yesterday."

Benton stared. The sheriff suddenly exploded in bellowing wrath.

"But I'm a heap more grateful than you are, you terrapin-brained old horned toad!" he roared, shaking his fist in Benton's face. "What in hell did you mean by sendin' Jack Hawley after him last night? I've a damn good notion to throw Hawley into the calaboose for attempted murder and you too for eggin' it on. If I see one more thing off-color from either of you I'll lock you up and throw the key away."

It was plain to Hatfield that when Sheriff Oswell meant business, he was not a man safe to trifle with. Craig Benton cooled down in a hurry.

"I didn't sic Hawley on him," he protested. "I tried to talk Hawley out of it, but he 'lowed if the sheepmen brought this feller in to do their gunnin' for 'em, he might as well get it over with pronto. I figure he aimed to back this feller down and make him trail his twine out of the section. It didn't work out just that way."

"No, I reckon it didn't," growled the sheriff. "He'd have about as much chance backin' him down as he'd have backin' down a Gulf hurricane. If he had the brains of an addled hyderphobia skunk, one look would have told him so."

"This feller told him he smelled like a skunk, last night," Benton remarked reflectively.

"This feller's got a good nose," said the sheriff. "I've been thinkin' along them lines myself for quite a spell. But he'd better not let me catch him takin' the law in his own hands again, and that goes for the rest of you. If there's any runnin' out to be did in this section, I'll do it. Now I figure you'd better pack what's left of poor Withersbee back to the ranchhouse with you and hold him for the coroner's inquest."

"But why in blazes was he killed?" Benton asked.

"I don't know, but I aim to find out," said Oswell. And I don't want any loose-latigoed gabbin' about the sheepmen bein' responsible, either. I don't figure to have any cow-sheep war in this section if I can prevent it and I've a notion I can. You can all see this jigger here on the ground ain't no herder. He's a puncher, or has been. His hands show that."

"Wonder what the hellion had against poor Withersbee?" said Benton.

"You never can tell what goes on in a feller's private life," the sheriff remarked wisely. "Fellers will get on the prod against one another over lots of things. Cards, a woman, most anything. You never can tell. Now get goin', you fellers. I got work to do."

As the dismal procession got under way, the sheriff remarked to Hatfield,

"Reckon that'll hold 'em. I sold them the idea the killin' was over some private feud between the two fellers. That's all to the good."

Hatfield nodded agreement and they began giving the nearby thickets a once-over. After considerable searching they found the drygulcher's horse tied to a tree. It was an average-sized bay with no outstanding markings or characteristics. The rig was well worn and serviceable and of conventional cow country pattern. The brand interested Hatfield.

"Turkey Track," he remarked. "That's an upper Trinity River country burn or I'm a heap mistook. That sort of ties up. Stolen horse, the chances are. Yes, I'm beginning to feel pretty certain this gent belonged to the bunch I trailed down from the Trinity River country. We'll take the horse to town with us. Maybe some stablekeeper or somebody will recall seeing it and be able to tell us something about the man who owned it."

"And I'll put him on exhibition, too," said the sheriff. "I'll have all the barkeeps drop around and look him over. One of them may remember him and who he was with, if anybody."

It was well past dark and a thin drizzle was beginning to fall when they reached town, the dead drygulcher roped to his saddle.

"We'll corral this gent in the office and then head for the Lipan and somethin' to eat," said the sheriff. "Tanglin' with varmints always makes me hungry."

90

Hatfield and the sheriff had dinner together, after which they sat and smoked and talked a while. Several of the Lazy Eight cowhands put in an appearance later and the news of Bill Withersbee's killing was spread around. Men stopped to comment to the sheriff about the matter but the old peace officer was noncommittal in his replies, inferring that he figured it was just a grudge killing and that the killer himself had been taken care of and the matter closed.

A tall, finely formed man pushed his way through the swinging doors and stood looking around.

"It's Samp Gulden," exclaimed the sheriff. He waved his hand. "Howdy, Samp?" he called. "Come over and have a drink."

The packing house owner crossed the room. "Howdy, Sheriff?" he said, nodding in friendly fashion to Hatfield. He sat down and bared his tawny head. A waiter hurried off to bring him a drink.

"Understand you had a busy day," Gulden remarked to the sheriff.

"Oh, so-so," the peace officer replied. "Hatfield here did most of the work. I just kept my head down."

Gulden's finely formed lips moved in a

91

quick smile. "I have a notion Mr. Hatfield usually gets into action fast," he remarked rather cryptically. "Wonder why Withersbee was killed? I don't recall ever hearing of him having any enemies."

"Never can tell about a feller," the sheriff replied sagely. "Reckon there's things in most every man's life he doesn't talk about or even think about if he can help it."

Gulden's mouth tightened a little and it seemed to Hatfield that the granite walls were again suddenly up in the depth of his brilliant eyes as if to shut off the vision of a terrible memory.

"Yes, I guess that's right," he said slowly, "but it is only the very dull or the very fortunate who can refrain from thought."

The sheriff nodded vague agreement. "Think I'll go to bed," he said. "What about you, Jim?"

"Believe I'll take me a little walk before turning in," Hatfield replied. "I always like to walk in the rain, especially where I can look at the sea or a river."

"Everybody to their notion," grunted the sheriff. "I prefer to keep dry. Okay, see you in the morning."

"Believe I'll follow your example, Sheriff," said Gulden, rising to his feet. "Good night, Mr. Hatfield."

Hatfield sat on at the table for a while longer watching the crowd at the bar. He had a drink, then pinched out his cigarette and ascended the stairs to his room. He unstrapped his long slicker, donned it and buttoned it tight. The rain was coming down hard now but he still felt like a stroll. Leaving the Lipan, he walked down William. He turned into Water Street and strolled slowly north toward Samp Gulden's packing house. From time to time he dropped into one of the dingy waterfront bars, sipped a drink and studied the occupants who were principally seafaring men. They were of many races and nationalities, for although Corpus Christi had not yet developed a thoroughly adequate port, it was already visited by ships from all over the world.

Sometime after midnight Hatfield reached the relatively dark stretch of street adjacent to the packing house. The street was practically deserted but from a dimly lighted saloon there came a sound of revelry. He hesitated, then walked in. As he approached the bar he did not notice a face peer through the window, then fade from sight.

Hatfield ordered a drink and studied the place in the dingy back bar mirror. It was

93

fairly orderly but occupied by some hard looking customers. Hatfield catalogued them as chiefly waterfront workers rather than seafaring men. Some were quite drunk and talking loudly. Hatfield hoped a word might be dropped that would bear on the smuggling operations he was about convinced were centered in Corpus Christi or nearby. But as the minutes passed he heard nothing of significance. He grew weary of the din, placed his empty glass on the bar and headed for the door. He pushed it open and stepped into the street. The door closed behind him and the street was dark.

As he turned to walk away, something struck him a crashing blow on back of his head. Red flashes stormed before his eyes, he reeled, half off balance and partially dazed. Powerful arms encircled his body from behind and he was hurled violently to the ground. Other hands gripped him, holding him helpless.

Hatfield went limp and lay without sound or movement, his eyes closed. His quick mind realized that it was hopeless to attempt to put up a fight at the moment. It would only mean another blow on the head that would render him unconscious. It was wiser to "play 'possum" and hope for a better chance. His attackers were making no move to search him and he fervently hoped they would not notice his guns under his buttoned slicker. If they did discover them, he would have to take his chances on immediate resistance.

Low-voiced talk among his captors that began at once somewhat reassured him. The men were evidently sailors who were doubtless not familiar with belt guns.

"He's out," said a deep and growling voice. "Hope you didn't thump him too hard, Pete. A dead one ain't no good and killin's sometimes cause trouble."

"Ah, I just tapped him," said a whining voice. "He'll be comin' out of it in a minute. Don't see why the Captain wanted us to load this 'un anyhow. He ain't no sailor and you can lay to that."

"A trip around old Cape Stiff'll make a sailor out of any landlubber," replied the growling voice. "He'll learn. And the Captain knows his business. Chances are he's gettin' paid plenty to crimp this swab by somebody this blighter is afoul of. A flap around the Horn takes a wab off your course for quite a while. All right, there's nobody in sight. Carry him across and dump him in the dinghy. Shake a leg. The tide turns in twenty minutes and we put out with it."

Two men lifted Hatfield, head and heels, grunting under his weight, and carried him across the street to the wharf. He was bundled roughly into a small boat. His captors piled in after him. Oarlocks creaked and the dinghy forged through the water toward where the dark bulk and the riding lights of a ship could be dimly seen through the rain and mist. Hatfield understood that he had been shanghaied by a crimping gang, apparently at the behest of somebody ashore.

A few minutes later the oars were shipped and the dinghy bumped against the vessel's side. Hatfield groaned, and rolled his head from side to side to simulate returning to consciousness. He had decided it was about time to act.

"Blighter's comin' out of it," said the whining voice. "Told you I just tapped him."

Hatfield felt hands grip him. He struggled slightly, then relaxed and mumbled incoherently.

"Steady, me lad," said the growling voice. "Up with you, and don't make no funny moves if you don't want another whack with the persuader. Up you go!"

Hatfield was hauled to his feet in the rocking boat. His hands were shoved against the rounds of a rope ladder and he was given a significant prod from behind.

He began to climb, mumbling and groaning, making hard going of it. A hand reached down from above and gripped his collar. He was hauled onto the ship's deck where lanterns cast considerable light. He staggered and clutched at the rail for support, lurching sideways so that his captors could not see the fingers of his other hand deftly unfastening the buttons of his slicker.

The men in the dinghy climbed the ladder and came over side.

"All right," said the growling voice that belonged to a squat, powerfully built man with long, gorilla-like arms, "haul her in. Shove this swab into the foc's'l."

Hatfield whirled from the rail and leaped back. His hands flashed down and up. The astounded sailors stared into two yawning black muzzles. Hatfield's voice blared at them, hard as steel —

"UP! One move and it's your last! Up, I say!"

The sailors shot their hands high in the air. They shrank back from the grim figure back of the rock-steady guns.

"Hey, what the hell's going on down there?" shouted a voice from the raised poop deck. "Drop them guns, you!"

Hatfield saw a flash of metal. His gun muzzle tipped up and blazed the instant before a shot was fired from above. A bullet knocked splinters from the rail. On the poop sounded a yell of pain and the clatter of something falling.

The squat man leaped at Hatfield, clutching hands outstretched. Hatfield shot him before he covered half the distance. He went down with a scream of agony, thrashing about on the deck and clutching at his blood-spouting shoulder. Hatfield's voice thundered at the others —

"Back! Get going! Run, damn you!"

They ran, dashing across the deck, volleying curses. Hatfield slammed his guns into their sheaths and went down the rope ladder hand over hand. He shoved away from the vessel's side and grabbed the oars.

As the dinghy swirled out of the shadow, fire spurted from above. A bullet thudded against the boat's side. Another knocked spray into Hatfield's face. He shipped one oar, jerked his Colt and sent a stream of lead hissing over the heads lining the rail. The heads vanished amid a storm of yells and cursing. Hatfield bent to the oars again and sent the dinghy foaming through the water. As he drew away, he studied the receding vessel.

"It's the tub that was loading from Gulden's packing house yesterday morning," he muttered.

A moment later the dinghy bumped against the wharf. Hatfield swarmed up the piling and ducked into the shadow.

Across the water drifted a sound as of a great clock being wound. There was a creaking of yards swung around, a slatting of canvas.

"She's getting up anchor," Hatfield growled. "The tide's running out and she's going with it. No stopping her. Well, to hell with her! But I'd sure like to have had a gabfest with that captain jigger. Might have persuaded him to tell who paid him to shanghai me for a trip around Cape Horn. A smart try, all right. I'd have been out of the way for quite a spell and nothing to tie onto anybody. Just another drunk picked up by the crimps to fill out a crew. Some gent hereabouts who doesn't like me has plenty of savvy."

He buttoned his slicker and headed for Chaparral Street and the Lipan. He decided that he had had enough of the waterfront for one night.

8

Sheriff Oswell swore in wrath the following morning when Hatfield regaled him with an account of the happenings of the night before.

"I hope you drilled that varmint on the poop deck dead center," he declared vindictively.

"Don't think so, from the way he yelped," Hatfield replied. "But it made him drop his iron. Have a notion he was the captain who arranged to have me shanghaied. Hope so. It was a nice try all right, but I came out of it lucky with nothing worse than a knot on my head. Didn't even lose my hat. Picked it up in front of that rumhole where they grabbed me. Reckon it was the hat that saved me. The gent who swung that billy didn't realize how thick and stiff the crown of a good 'J.B.' rainshed is."

"I wish I knew where to start and clean out the whole nest of sidewinders," fumed the sheriff. "You learned anything so far, son?"

"Nothing for sure," Hatfield admitted. "But I'm getting a sort of a notion. It's not much more than a hunch so far, but I figure to play it. Won't tell you about it just yet. Chances are you'd laugh at me if I did. It's a plumb funny notion with very little to base it on so far. Just a story or two and a few little slips like the owlhoot brand always make. I want you to send a telegraph message for me. The answer will come to you. Hold it for me. And put a flea in the operator's ear. He's sworn to secrecy by the rules of his company, but a little extra prod from you to keep his mouth shut won't hurt."

The sheriff stared in bewilderment at the message Hatfield wrote out, but he refrained from asking questions that he decided wouldn't be answered.

"To Bill McDowell," he remarked as he stowed away the message.

"Yes," Hatfield said. "I want Captain Bill to do a mite of backtracking for me. He's good at that. We should have an answer in a few days. Captain Bill works fast. That answer may have an important bearing on the business we have at hand. In fact, my hunch just about stands or falls on it. I

101

have another one to play, but we'll let that go till we hear from Captain Bill. Now I figure to ride out to the Carvel *casa*."

"A good notion," approved the sheriff. "Miss Gypsy is a mighty fine gal and a mighty purty one, too."

"She's all of that," Hatfield agreed. "By the way, I've a notion young Sid Benton is sort of sweet on her. I noticed he couldn't keep his eyes off her in the Lipan the other night."

"Could be," admitted the sheriff, "but I've a notion Samp Gulden will give him a run for his money in that direction. I figure Samp has the inside track. He's always findin' some excuse to ride out to the Carvel place. Sometimes stays a couple of days."

"He's a fine looking man," Hatfield observed.

"Uh-huh, and a purty nice feller even if he does work with sheep," said Oswell. "He sure knows the packin' business."

"Been in this section long?" Hatfield asked.

"Somethin' less than two years," the sheriff replied. "He showed up here right after Dick King built his packing house. I've a notion that's why Gulden turned to sheep. King was already processin' beef and dealin' in hides and tallow. Gulden handles wool on the side. He's smart, all right. He 'lowed, after the big storms wiped out the old port of Indianola, that the trade and shippin' of Matagorda Bay would shift to Corpus Christi. He was right. I've a notion that's why he decided to build his plant here. He ships mostly by sea, and it's a heap sight cheaper than by rail. I rec'lect he said right after he come here that it was only a matter of time till folks would be growin' cotton and stuff on the black lands back of town and darned if they aren't beginnin' to do it. Uh-huh, Gulden's plumb smart. Well, be seein' you when you get back."

Hatfield rode southwest at a good pace. As he neared the track that led to the Lazy Eight ranchhouse a big freight wagon rolled into view. Behind the wagon rode four cowhands. On the seat was a big man with a bandaged hand. Hatfield recognized Jackson Hawley.

Hawley favored him with a black glare as the wagon rumbled past, but did not speak. The cowboys rode with stiff necks, eyes stonily to the front.

"Nice sociable bunch," Hatfield chuckled to Goldy. "That jigger must figure to pack back the whole town with him from the size of that contraption."

Five more miles of riding and Hatfield sighted a two-story white ranchhouse built in the Spanish style in a grove of scattered pinons. He turned into the track that led to the yard. A girl in a white dress was seated on the porch. He recognized Gypsy Carvel. She ran down the steps to greet him.

"So you really did come," she said. "I'm surprised."

"I'd have come if I had to walk all the way," Hatfield replied as he dismounted.

"I don't believe you," she said. "No cowboy would walk ten miles just to see a woman. Come on, I'll help you stable your horse. There's nobody around right now to do it. He's a beauty."

She reached out a fearless hand to Goldy who regarded her suspiciously.

"It's all right, feller," Hatfield told the sorrel. "She's a hell-cat, but she won't bite."

"Don't you be so sure," she retorted. "I might, under certain circumstances."

"I'll try and shy away from those circumstances," Hatfield smiled. "Might not be so bad at that, though. You've got mighty nice teeth."

"Yours are not so bad, either," she said. "But I've a notion some folks have learned, since you showed up there, that you *will* bite, under certain circumstances. One of the boys was in town and told us about Bill Withersbee and what happened afterward."

After Goldy's wants were taken care of they returned to the ranchhouse.

"Come on in and I'll fix us some coffee," Gypsy said. "Tom is out on the range but I expect him back in an hour or so. The cook is out somewhere too, fooling around. He's an old Mexican who was here when I was born. He's hundreds and hundreds of years old and does as he pleases, but he sure can cook."

She quickly and deftly prepared the coffee and they sat together in the living room to drink it.

"You're going to spend the night, aren't you?" she asked. "I won't take no for an answer. Come on and I'll show you your room in case you want to brush up."

She led the way up the stairs, opened a door and revealed a bright and airy chamber.

"Tom sleeps two doors farther down in the back of the house," she said. "Mine is right across the hall."

"Reckon I won't need to lock the door here," Hatfield bantered.

"Oh, you can," she said, "if you're afraid.

I never lock mine except when there is company in the house — some company."

On impulse, Hatfield tried a shot in the dark.

"Such as Samp Gulden," he said.

Her eyes widened. "How in the world did you guess it?" she asked. "Yes, I'll admit I'm afraid of Samp Gulden. And for no good reason at all. Nobody could be more courteous or considerate. I know it sounds silly, but somehow his eyes frighten me. There seems to always be a hint of madness in them. A look like that in the eyes of a cruelly mistreated wild beast. The look that says, 'I'm waiting!' "

Her voice dropped to almost a whisper as she pronounced the last words. Hatfield stared at her, wonderingly. A tinge of gray had touched her red lips and the color was gone from her cheeks. She laughed a little, embarrassedly, but Hatfield felt the laugh was rather forced.

"Remember, I told you we Scotch have the second sight," she added jokingly. "And, besides, I believe a woman's instinct always tells her who to fear and who not to fear."

Hatfield smiled down at her. Suddenly he reached out and cupped her round little white chin in his hand and tilted her head back. The wide blue eyes met his unflinchingly.

"I'm not one — bit — frightened!" she said, and was gone down the stairs.

Hatfield stared after her. "Now what am I letting myself in for?" he demanded of the closed door across the hall. "Women are pizen!"

But as he combed his thick black hair before the mirror a little later, he added.

"Just the same, she's sure a cute little tyke."

Gypsy was seated in the living room when Hatfield descended the stairs. She glanced up shyly at him and her color rose under his regard. He sat down and there was silence between them for the moment.

Hatfield was about to speak when the door opened and an old Mexican entered. His hair was snow white, his face crisscrossed with wrinkles, but his eyes were bright.

"This is Miguel, our cook," Gypsy said. "Miguel, Mr. Hatfield will be our guest for dinner."

Hatfield rose with quiet courtesy and took the old man's hand. The Mexican gazed up into the sternly handsome face so far above him.

"It is well," he said. "It is good to know

this one." He smiled and for an instant his wrinkled face seemed wonderfully youthful. With a bright nod he passed on to the kitchen.

"Miguel doesn't make mistakes," Gypsy said. "He doesn't like — everybody who comes here. I've learned to rely on his judgment."

Tom Carvel arrived a little later. He was a slender pleasant-faced young man of medium height. The resemblance to his sister was strong, but Hatfield instinctively sensed that he lacked the little yellow-head's fiery disposition. Hatfield couldn't see Carvel pulling a gun on Craig Benton or anybody else.

Carvel shook hands warmly. "You're all Gypsy's been talking about for the last couple of days," he said. "Hope you'll see fit to sign up with us. We could use a few more good hands."

"Chances are I will if I decide to stick around a while," Hatfield replied. "Right now I figure to take it easy for a few days."

When Hatfield awoke the following morning, it was to hear Gypsy singing somewhere outside the house in a clear sweet voice. He dressed leisurely and went down stairs and wandered into the kitchen where Miguel was busy cooking breakfast.

"The Senorita is happy," Miguel remarked, pausing to listen. "*Ai!* it is wonderful to be young and to love."

"What do you mean by that?" Hatfield asked.

"Ask of yourself, *Capitan,* or of her," Miguel replied and busied himself with his pots and pans.

After breakfast, Hatfield rode the range with Tom Carvel. He wanted to give the Cross C a once-over.

"You've got a good holding here," he told Carvel. "And when the market picks up, as it will, you should do all right. It was a good idea, taking on sheep to tide you over."

"More and more of the progressive cowmen are doing it," Carvel returned. "But there are some, like Craig Benton, who are dead set against the notion."

"Benton will have to be enlightened, perhaps somewhat as Pharoah was enlightened," Hatfield replied with a smile. "I've a notion he'll come around in time. He's just a stubborn old shorthorn and set in his ways."

"You know," Carvel observed thoughtfully, "I can't believe that Benton had anything to do with what happened on the bluff trail outside of town. That's not his way. His methods are direct. I can't see Craig Benton doing anything underhanded despite what has been said about him."

"I'm glad you feel that way," Hatfield replied gravely. "I have something of the same notion. But a mistaken man can often cause a deal of trouble through his mulishness. I'm afraid that's the case with Craig Benton."

Carvel nodded and they rode on. A little later they came to the east wire and gazed across to the rutted and hoof-scarred track winding in a northly direction through the brush. They were not far from where Bill Withersbee's body had lain against the wire.

"The trail leads to Craig Benton's ranchhouse and to Jackson Hawley's farther to the north," Carvel observed. "It's an old track. Was here long before Benton or Hawley were born. Oldtimers say it was used by smuggling outfits and raiders riding up from around the Point Isabel country and the Rio Grande. About twenty miles farther on it joins with the Old Spanish Trail that runs clear across Texas."

"Seems I rec'lect the Spanish Trail branches not far to the east, one fork running through the upper Trinity River country to the Red River and on into

Oklahoma," Hatfield commented.

"That's right," said Carvel. "The Tonkawa Trail it's called. From the Tonkawa Indians who used it to raid the Comanche villages up toward Dallas."

Hatfield nodded thoughtfully. "And you say Benton and Hawley have their ranch-houses alongside that track over there?"

"The trail is a short-cut to them," Carvel replied. "But you can't see their *casas* from it. They set more than a mile back."

Hatfield nodded again, his eyes even more thoughtful. "Carvel," he said suddenly, "I'm heading for town. Just remembered a little chore that needs attending to."

"Hoped you'd stay on with us a few days," Carvel answered, plainly disappointed. "Gypsy will feel bad about it. She expected to go riding with you this afternoon."

"Tell her goodbye for me and that I'll go riding with her in a day or two," Hatfield promised.

"There's a gate down to the south where you can get through the wire," Carvel said. "I'll show you."

Hatfield smiled a little and touched Goldy with his knee.

"Take it, feller," he ordered.

Goldy took it, soaring over the high wire

111

and landing easily on the slope beyond.

"Good Lord!" exclaimed Carvel. "He went across like he had wings. And that's a seven-strand fence."

Hatfield waved his hand and rode on down the track. On reaching the main trail he speeded up. Considerably less than an hour later he drew rein in front of the sheriff's office.

"Hello?" greeted Oswell as he entered. "Didn't expect you back so soon. You and the gal have a row?"

"Nope," Hatfield replied. "I just decided to play a hunch. String along with me?"

"Sure for certain," said the sheriff. "Anything you say."

"Your two deputies in town?"

"Yes."

"And can you tie onto a couple of specials you can depend on to keep their mouths shut?"

"Easy," said Oswell.

"Get 'em together," Hatfield directed. "Have them slip out of town after dark, one at a time. Tell them we'll meet them where that track that runs up past Benton's ranchhouse joins the main trail."

It was well past dark when Hatfield and Sheriff Oswell slipped out of town and rode southwest. They met no one until they reached the trail fork. They pulled up and a moment later the four deputies rode into view from the brush.

"Straight north," said Hatfield on whose broad breast gleamed a deputy sheriff's badge. "Now if we can only slide past the Lazy Eight *casa* and Jack Hawley's place without being spotted, everything should be okay."

Hatfield and the sheriff rode a little in front, the deputies jogging along behind. "As I said," Hatfield remarked in low tones, "I'm just playing a hunch. I believe a bunch of contraband was unloaded in Corpus Christi yesterday."

"From that damn ship that tried to shanghai you?"

"That's right," Hatfield agreed. "And I believe it will be run north over the Tonkawa Trail tonight, probably by mule train. If I'm right and we have luck we may drop a loop on the bunch packing the stuff. Chances are some of 'em will talk to save their own necks and we'll be set to smash the whole outfit. I got to thinking about it when Tom Carvel mentioned this track leads to the Old Spanish Trail and that it used to be used by smugglers coming up from Point Isabel and the Rio Grande. It would be just as handy for a bunch working out of Corpus Christi."

"I sure hope you're right," growled the sheriff. "Nothing would suit me better than to tangle those hellions' twine for 'em."

They rode in silence, their horses' irons thudding softly in the deep dust of the trail.

"We're passin' Craig Benton's ranch-house now," the sheriff said. "Don't 'pear to be nobody in sight." A half hour later he spoke again,

"Jack Hawley's place is just over that ridge to the right."

Hatfield studied the track winding up the slope. So far as he could see it was deserted.

"So far so good," he commented.

The eastern sky was brightening. The upper rim of a gibbous moon pushed its way over the horizon. Soon the prairie was flooded with wan and ghostly light. Groves and clumps of thicket stood out black and solid. A faint wind stirred the grass heads. They passed bunches of grazing cattle.

"Right ahead is the Old Spanish Trail," the sheriff announced about an hour later.

They came out upon the broad track that spanned the width of Texas and beyond. Hatfield called a halt and outlined his plans.

"We'll hole up at the first good spot to the east," he said. "We'll try and stay close enough to watch the forks. If the bunch is really riding tonight, they should come up from the south."

"There's sure to be no legitimate trains coming that way," observed one of the deputies. "From the west, yes, though not so often as they used to come, but not from the south."

Hatfield nodded. "Anything showing from the south will bear inspection," he said. "Let's go. There's a belt of thicket about three hundred yards farther on. I've a notion that will do."

Where the trail ran between the encroaching growth was a dark tunnel into which the moon beams did not pierce. It proved ideal for their purpose. They halted in the black shadow and faced their horses to the west.

"Reckon we can risk a smoke," Hatfield said. "But keep an eye on the forks and pinch out the butts if you spot anything moving. I want to take 'em alive if we can, but I'm scairt they won't be grabbed without a shooting. Don't take any chances. It's a salty bunch. They've already proved that."

9

A long and tedious wait followed. An hour passed and the better part of another. Hatfield began to wonder if his hunch was a cold one or if the smugglers had moved faster than he anticipated and had already passed the spot. The moon swung across the zenith and began moving down the long western slant of the sky.

A sound broke the silence. It quickly loudened to the muffled beat of hoofs. The posse tensed for action. Movement showed at the forks of the trail. Another moment and a string of pack mules swung up from the south. Bulky *aparejos* were roped to their backs. In front of the mules rode several men. Two more paced on either side of the train.

"All right," Hatfield whispered. "Take over, Sheriff."

The posse rode out of the shadow when the leading horsemen were less than a dozen yards distant. Sheriff Oswell's voice rang out — "In the name of the law! Halt!"

A startled oath sounded, and a popping of saddle leather as the horses were jerked to a stop.

"Look out!" shouted a voice. "It's a trap! Get them!"

Hands flashed to holsters. Both of Hatfield's Colts were blazing before the owlhoots could pull trigger. The posse's guns joined in. Red flashes spurted back and forth between the groups. Two of the outlaws whirled from their saddles. Another went down. A horseman streaked away from the tangle of braying mules, squealing horses and cursing men and rode back along the trail.

Hatfield sent Goldy charging straight forward into the storm of lead that hissed all around him. Instantly he was tangled in a mad scramble of plunging horses and terrified mules. Precious seconds were lost before he could win free. He saw the fleeing horsemen swerve south. The bristle of growth flanking the track swallowed him up.

"Trail, Goldy, trail!" Hatfield roared.

The sorrel won out of the mess by main strength and weight. Hatfield swerved him south and sent him racing down the winding track. He could neither see nor hear the fugitive. He covered a mile and another. The chaparral thinned and the trail stretched ahead for hundreds of yards and was utterly deserted.

Hatfield muttered an oath and pulled to a halt. "Gave us the slip," he told Goldy. "He couldn't possibly be this far ahead of us if he'd kept the trail. Slid into some hole somewhere. Chances are he knows this section like he does the palm of his hand. And I've a notion he was the hellion we want most. Well, we might as well head back and see how the sheriff made out. Okay, I should reckon. The shooting had stopped before we were out of hearing."

The sheriff was bandaging a posseman's bullet-drilled arm when Hatfield arrived at the scene of the fight. Another man had a gashed cheek. A third was bleeding from a flesh wound in his thigh.

"Nobody hurt bad, though," said Oswell. "And we got five of the varmints."

"All dead?" Hatfield asked.

"Yes, damn it," replied Oswell. "A plumb salty bunch. They wouldn't give up. Kept blazing away as long as they could pull trigger. It was them or us. How about the one you chased?"

"Got in the clear," Hatfield replied briefly. "Well, we thinned 'em out a bit, anyway. Let's see what's in those packs."

The *aparejos* were stuffed with contraband.

"Here's some more of them tin cans of opium," said the sheriff. "And sacks of dried and ground marihuana. It's a good haul."

"Not as good as I'd hoped for," Hatfield replied, "but it helps. Well, reckon we'd better be heading back to town. Be daylight when we get there as it is. Anybody know any of those jiggers on the ground?"

There was a general shaking of heads.

"We'll pack 'em to town and give them a careful once-over," Hatfield decided. "Too dark here."

The bodies were roped to the backs of the horses which were rounded up without much difficulty. The mules, tractable brutes, had quickly quieted down once the excitement was over. The cavalcade got slowly under way. Hatfield and the sheriff rode in front, alert and watchful. However, they reached the main trail to Corpus Christi without incident. Hatfield drew rein at the forks.

"I'm heading for the Carvel *casa*," he told the sheriff. "Rather not be seen riding in with this procession. I figure nobody in town knows I was with you tonight and

119

that's as it should be. Look those punctured gents over carefully and save everything you find in their pockets. Chances are you won't dig up anything worth while, but you never can tell. I'll see you tonight or tomorrow."

"Okay," agreed the sheriff. "Be careful a herder don't take a shot at you when you ride up to Carvel's place. I've a feelin' they're pretty jumpy over there."

"I'll risk it," Hatfield replied, and rode west.

However he cast a slightly apprehensive glance at the bunkhouse when he turned into the ranchhouse yard. The bunkhouse was some distance from the *casa,* and as it was the dead hour when folks usually slept the soundest he figured he didn't have much to worry about. He dismounted in the shade of a tree that grew close to the veranda and gazed at the dark and silent building, debating how to gain entrance without arousing everybody. His eyes focused on an open window that he knew belonged to Gypsy's room.

"Hope she isn't one of the yelpin' sort of females," he chuckled as he searched around for a small stone. He found one suitable for his purpose and deftly tossed it through the window. It hit the floor inside

120

the room with a considerable thud. He stepped back and removed his hat, so the moonlight fell on his face, and whistled softly.

There was a moment of suspense, then Gypsy's face appeared at the window.

"Jim!" she exclaimed in a low voice. "What in the world are you doing here at this time of night? Heavens! You nearly scared me to death."

"Got a bed for a tired man?" he called softly.

"Of course," she answered. "I'll be right down and let you in."

As he swiftly removed Goldy's rig and turned the sorrel loose to graze, not caring to risk stabling him, he heard Gypsy's bare feet pattering on the stairs. She opened the door and he mounted the steps and crossed the veranda.

"Come in and close the door," she urged. "If anybody sees us here, and me in nothing but a nightgown, I won't have a shred of reputation left. I was so excited I forgot to put on a robe."

He entered and closed the door. "Wait," she said. He heard her moving across the room. A match scratched. A lamp flared and Hatfield stared in admiration, as well he might. The thin silken gown which was her only garment was revealing, to say the least.

Gypsy met his eyes and blushed crimson. She crossed her arms over her breasts.

"I forgot again," she said. "You've got me all in a whirl." She turned and fled up the stairs, her bare feet twinkling.

Hatfield chuckled. He sat down by the table and rolled a cigarette.

She was back down in a few minutes, wearing a gaily colored robe and little golden slippers.

"Now," she said, "I feel a little less like something escaped from a dance hall."

"*I* sure wouldn't want to escape from a dance hall you were in," he smiled.

"You didn't act like it," she pouted. "Running off without even saying goodbye. What have you been up to? Is the sheriff after you?"

"Just left him," Hatfield replied. He studied her a moment, arrived at a decision.

"Trusting a woman has been the ruination of many a man, but I believe you can be trusted," he said as he laid the star of the Rangers on the table.

Gypsy stared at the gleaming badge, her eyes wide, something very much like terror in their blue depths.

"So that's it," she said, her voice low and trembling a little.

"Yes, that's it," Hatfield answered. Briefly he recounted the night's happenings. Gypsy shuddered as she listened.

"I suppose you're always getting mixed up in something like that," she said. "Is there something you want me to do for you?"

"Yes," Hatfield admitted. "I want to stay here today, but I don't know what your brother will think."

"I'll take care of that," she said. "I'll tell him I was sitting up reading — I often do. He sleeps in the back of the house and won't know how late it was when you came."

"That'll be fine," Hatfield said, "and it will help a lot. I don't want to show up in town today."

They ascended the stairs together, her golden head coming barely to his shoulders. He waited as she slowly closed the door, then entered the room across the hall.

10

Tom Carvel apparently saw nothing unusual in Hatfield's unexpected return. After breakfast he rode off to town to attend to some chores. Later, Hatfield and Gypsy also took a ride. It was a day of golden sunshine, so still and quiet that even the gossamers hung in motionless webs of pale argent. The touch of autumn was in the air and the bills were warrior monks in scarlet clad and gold, marching along the skyline to hopeless conflict with the legions of the frost. The grass heads were tipped with amethyst that glowed warmly against the emerald garment of blocks magically suspended in a sea of crystal arched over with cerulean blue.

"A mighty pretty country," Hatfield remarked as they sat their horses on the crest of a long ridge. "You'd think folks would be happy and content with all it has to offer and not be continually hell raisin' and making trouble for others."

"I imagine," the girl said slowly, "that is because most everybody wants something besides what they already have."

Hatfield nodded, his eyes somber.

"I don't believe you ever want anything much," she added, "or if you do, you take it."

"You may find out about that," he smiled.

"I hope so," she returned briefly and moved her horse, leaving the Lone Wolf to follow with something to think about.

Tom Carvel was excited by the news he had gathered in town when he got back to the ranchhouse.

"Reckon you missed it by not being in town last night," he told Hatfield. "Seems Sheriff Oswell got a tip a smuggler train was coming over the Old Spanish Trail. He laid a trap for the jiggers and bagged all but one of 'em. Grabbed off ten mule loads of stuff. He's got five bodies laid out in the undertaker's place and has been having folks look 'em over. A couple of barkeeps recognized three of 'em as fellers who had been hangin' around their places in town for the past few days. And a barkeep from a saloon on Water Street, up by Samp Gulden's packing house, remembered seein' that sidewinder who shot Bill

125

Withersbee. Said he came in his place frequent."

There was a pleased expression on Hatfield's face as he listened. Evidently the sheriff had done a good job of covering up for him. He only hoped the remaining members of the smuggling outfit were fooled by the scheme.

Hatfield rode to town the following morning and immediately got in touch with Sheriff Oswell.

"Got a little chore to do," he announced. "Want you to get me an interview with the president of the bank here in town or with somebody who's been with the institution for a long time."

"Cary, the president, has headed the shebang for the past twenty years and more," said the sheriff. "He's a good egg and an old friend of mine. We'll go see him right away."

Sheriff Oswell introduced Hatfield to the old bank president who regarded the Ranger with interest.

"And what can I do for you fellers?" he asked.

"First," said Hatfield, "does Jackson Hawley have an account with your bank?"

"Yes," the banker replied with a surprised look.

"And how long has he had it?"

"Well," said the banker, "I can't say off hand, but more than fifteen years. He opened it shortly after he set up in business for himself with the Rocking H ranch, of that I'm pretty sure. I can ascertain definitely from our records."

"And did he have one with you before he bought the Rocking H?"

The banker shook his head. "No, I'm pretty sure he did not," he stated. "However, I'll check on that also, if you desire."

"I wish you'd do that," Hatfield suggested.

The president called a clerk and instructed that certain records be brought to his office. A careful check of the old files corroborated his statements.

"Anything else?" he asked.

"No, that is all," Hatfield told him. "And thank you, suh. Of course you understand this conversation is strictly confidential."

"Naturally," the banker replied, with a smile. "We don't make a practice of discussing the affairs of our depositors with others."

"Now what?" asked the somewhat bewildered sheriff when they were outside the bank building.

"I was wondering," Hatfield said, "if you

happen to know whether the two brothers from whom Hawley bought the Rocking H are still alive and if it is possible to get in touch with them?"

"Billy Weston, the older one, is dead," the sheriff replied. "Ab Weston is still alive. He lives right here in Corpus Christi over on Tiger Street. Reckon there wouldn't be any trouble gettin' in touch with him. He's mighty old and stays at home most of the time. We'll walk over there if it's agreeable to you."

Hatfield nodded agreement and they proceeded to Tiger Street which paralleled Galivan Street to the east.

"You ask the questions," Hatfield said. "I'll line you up as we walk."

They found Ab Weston on his front porch, a wizened octogenarian with bright eyes.

"What the hell do you want, Oswell?" he asked politely as they mounted the steps. "I ain't stole nothin', 'least not since before you were born. Take a load off your feet, you don't look nacherel standin' up."

The sheriff introduced Hatfield, refraining from mentioning his Ranger connections, and took a chair.

"Want to ask you a few questions, Ab," he said.

"You're good at askin' questions," grunted Weston. "If you was as good at findin' the answers to a few we'd have a more peac'ble community hereabouts. Shoot!"

"Reckon you rec'lect sellin' your ranch to Jackson Hawley?" said the sheriff.

"Well, I rec'lect hearin' somethin' about it," Weston returned sarcastically. "Was right before I got out of the cow business, I've a notion."

Hatfield's lips twitched slightly in a smile. He decided the oldster was a character.

"Remember what Hawley paid you with?" asked the sheriff.

"What in hell do you suppose he paid me with, you ganglin' idjit?" snorted Weston. "He paid me with money. You figure he paid me with manzanity berries?"

"What kind of money?" persisted the sheriff.

"Hard money," said Weston. "Gold. There waren't much soft money floatin' around hereabouts in them days as you very well know."

"All in gold? No check?"

"Check!" jeered Weston. "That young hellion wouldn't have knowed a check in them days if he'd met one in the middle of the road. Reckon he never seed a bank

129

teller before then, 'less he looked at one over a gun sight durin' a holdup. I always felt a mite funny about that *dinero*. Couldn't but help wonderin' if it was stole somewhere. Anything else you want to know?"

"Reckon that's all," replied the sheriff.

"Then get goin' and stop clutterin' up the scenery," said Weston. "I don't see why you didn't drown yourself long ago in the interest of humanity. You're in bad company, Hatfield, but maybe it ain't catchin'."

He winked one of his bright eyes at the Ranger as they turned to go.

"Ab's a card," chuckled the sheriff as they walked up the street. "The time I had typhoid he stayed right beside me for fifty-six hours hand-runnin', keepin' the flies off me and spongin' me with cool water. Saved my life, I reckon. Wouldn't let nobody spell him 'cause he was the only one who could do anything with me when I was out of my head. Folks who thought they knew said he'd kill me, puttin' water on me that way and givin' me all I wanted to drink. But Ab had his old Smith & Wesson forty-four with him and swore he'd put six of the best through anybody what interfered. When it was all over and I'd passed the crisis and was asleep, they had to carry him from the room, he was so stiff and cramped and wore out. Yes, Ab's a card. Hatfield, do you believe Jack Hawley stole the money he used to buy his ranch?"

"Yes," Hatfield said, "I believe he did. I believe he paid Ab Weston with a dead man's gold!"

"A dead man's gold!"

"Yes, the gold Craig Benton paid Walt Garner for his share of the Lazy Eight."

The sheriff halted in mid-stride, and stared at his companion.

"And you mean Hawley killed Walt Garner."

"Yes," said Hatfield. "Jackson Hawley, the man who never had a cent and who spent all his spare time drinking and gambling and raising hell in general, but all of a sudden not long after Garner was killed and robbed, he was able to put out thousands of dollars in gold for a good spread. I can't understand why folks didn't wonder about that."

"Well," said the sheriff, "I reckon nobody thought to pay it much mind. Hawley had been workin' steady for several years, and the row over Craig Benton was still goin' strong and occupyin' folks' attention."

"Our talk with the bank president

showed that Hawley was not a man who didn't believe in banks and packed his dinero with him," Hatfield resumed. "As soon as his spread got under way he began banking money and has been doing so ever since. If he owned honest money before, why didn't he bank it instead of packing a small fortune around with him? Doesn't make sense. And he couldn't have possibly saved anything like that amount in a few years, working at forty-per. His reputation was bad, also, and it was known that he and Walt Garner did not get along. And of course he knew that Benton paid off Garner in cash money before he left the ranchhouse. I understand his signature is on the papers as a witness to the transaction."

The sheriff tugged his mustache. "You sure make out a case against him," he admitted.

"Though not one that would stand up in court," Hatfield said. "But I hope to soon have a case against him that will if things work out the way I expect them to."

"And you figure Hawley is head of the smugglin' outfit?" the sheriff deduced.

Hatfield shook his head. "No," he replied. "Hawley is only the tool of a much smarter man who took him in tow because he figured Hawley would be useful. The smart jigger made a mistake there when he thought he was being smooth. The owlhoot brand always makes such mistakes. Hawley is salty and utterly unscrupulous, but he's stupid. He does things that give him away. Like making that blundering try at going for me in the Lipan restaurant, assuming that folks would think it was because I had a run-in with Craig Benton, his friend. And like driving his freight wagon to town to pick up the smuggled goods and pack them to his ranchhouse where the mule train was made up."

"I never would have thought anything of that," protested the sheriff. "And I don't believe most folks would have."

"Perhaps not," Hatfield admitted, "but in Ranger work you learn to notice things like that, especially if you are suspicious of a man. All of a sudden apparently commonplace acts take on significance."

"Hawley also had to jog along with the mule train for a while the other night," Hatfield added. "Perhaps because he has the owlhoot's justified distrust for all other owlhoots and wanted to be sure they were on their way. No, I didn't recognize him the other night, but I did notice that he was the only one of the bunch who didn't pull a gun. That's because his gun hand is out of condition. And he immediately streaked it south instead of taking the logical escape route west on the Old Spanish Trail to the nearby hole-in-the-wall country over there. That's why I gave up chasing him the other night when I figured he'd turned off the track somewhere. I knew he would make it to his ranchhouse by ways with which he would be thoroughly familiar long before I could hope to catch up with him."

"And now what?" asked the sheriff.

"Wait," Hatfield said. "Wait until we get an answer to the wire I sent Captain Bill. A great deal depends on that. Meanwhile I want one of your men to keep tabs on the waterfront. When a ship puts in to load from Gulden's packing house, I want to know it at once."

"I'll take care of it," promised Oswell. "I know just the feller for the chore. I won't use one of my deputies. He'd be sort of conspicuous, loafin' around the waterfront. There's a feller who's done jobs for me before, a bright young Mexican. He peddles stuff to the sailors in the bars and restaurants and nobody will think anything of him being around. He's a plumb smart boy and will handle the chore proper."

"That will be fine," said Hatfield. "Tell him to keep his eyes skun and report anything unusual he may happen to notice."

The sheriff nodded. "And you really think Samp Gulden is mixed up with the smugglers?"

"I'm convinced of it," Hatfield said. "But proving it is something else again. Gulden tipped his hand a mite when he tried to have me shanghaied. Only you and Gulden knew I intended to walk the waterfront that night. I'm pretty sure I wasn't spotted when I left the Lipan rooming house. I left by way of the outside stairs and it was very dark. I rather absolved you from having anything to do with it, and that left Gulden as a logical suspect."

"Nice of you," commented the sheriff.

Hatfield smiled. "Gulden may know I'm connected with the Rangers," he said. "Or he may just be suspicious of me on general principles. What's puzzling me, though, is how did they move the stuff from the packing house to Hawley's freight wagon without attracting attention."

"I think I can explain that," said the sheriff. "Right across from the packing house on Belden Street, which still isn't much more than a poorly lit alley, is a stable. I happen to know Hawley puts up

135

his horses there when he is in town. It would be easy to slip the stuff across to the stable in the dark and stow it in Hawley's wagon along with the stuff he'd bought at the general store earlier in the evenin'."

"That's it," Hatfield agreed. "A perfect set-up. Just as the packing house is a perfect set-up for receiving the stuff smuggled in on shipboard."

"Funny that a jigger with a good business would go in for such monkeyshines," remarked the sheriff.

"Those mule loads we tied onto the other night were worth a small fortune in the illegitimate market," Hatfield pointed out. "Even if a train gets looped now and then, the profits are still tremendous."

11

Hatfield had become quite friendly with Arch Russell, the owner of the Lipan. Russell, fat and good-natured, was nevertheless shrewd and observant. And Hatfield had learned he could be a salty hombre if necessary. His fat was deceptive, being but a covering for great slabs of iron-hard muscle. And he was quick as a cat on his feet.

As Hatfield sat eating a late dinner, Russell came over and dropped in a vacant chair. For some minutes they chatted about various inconsequential subjects.

"Don't see much of Jackson Hawley's bunch around of late," Hatfield remarked.

"They never did come in here over much," Russell replied. "They mostly hang out in La Golondrina, down at the end of the street where the bridge crosses the crik. The crik ain't much, but the gulley it runs in is wide and deep. Bridge across it, by way of which you can curve around and get to the southwest trail."

"*La Golondrina* — The Swallow —"
Hatfield translated. "Not a bad name for a saloon."

"Reckon that's so," agreed Russell. "Place ain't thought overly well of by the better element here, including the sheriff, who's threatened to close it a couple of times. Stiff poker games there and plenty of gals and dancin.' Mostly cowhands and fellers sort of 'ridin' through' hang out there. Well, be seein' you. Got to look after business."

Hatfield nodded, his eyes thoughtful. He smoked a cigarette in leisurely comfort, then pinched out the butt and rose to his feet. He had a certain curiosity about La Golondrina and decided it might not be a bad notion to give the place a once-over. Following Russell's tip as to the location, he walked south on Chaparral Street, pausing now and then to glance in windows.

As he walked, the buildings grew fewer, the lighting less adequate. He realized he was drawing near the bridge by way of which the street crossed the creek and made connection with the southwest trail. The street was now practically deserted and a couple of hundred yards ahead loomed an open space that boasted no buildings.

To men who ride much alone with danger as a constant stirrup companion, there comes a subtle sixth sense that ofttimes warns of menace when none is obviously present. This sense was highly developed in the Lone Wolf. Abruptly, for no apparent good reason, Hatfield became acutely uneasy. Nothing stirred amid the shadows ahead. The rows of buildings flanking the street were silent and to all appearances deserted. He glanced right and left, peered ahead. Instinctively, however, he refrained from turning.

Across the street were warehouses, their dark windows like hollow eyes. And those windows, some of them set at an angle, provided good substitutes for mirrors. Hatfield's gaze fixed on them as he strolled slowly along.

At first he saw nothing. Then, outlined vaguely in the glass, he noted the forms of five men who were walking the street some distance behind. They walked in a close group and their attention appeared to be centered on something ahead.

Hatfield paused to gaze at the window display of a closed shop. From the tail of his eye he noted that the five men paused to gaze into another. When he moved on, they also moved. He quickened his pace.

The others quickened theirs. When he slowed down, they slowed down.

"Tailing me, all right," he muttered. "Now what's in the wind?"

He was almost to the dark open space. Ahead, at a distance of perhaps fifty yards, was a building with light gleaming from its windows. Doubtless it was La Golondrina, for directly beyond the structure Hatfield could just make out the shadowy loom of the bridge.

Suddenly he quickened his pace, his long legs covering the ground at an astonishing rate although he was not really running. His keen ears caught the sound of beating feet behind him.

"Thought so," he grunted, increasing his stride still more. "Figured to close in on me in the dark. Well, we'll just put a crimp in that little notion."

He realized that the men behind him were running now, swiftly closing the distance. But directly in front was La Golondrina. With the apparent pursuit still quite fifty yards in the rear, he swerved sideways and through the swinging doors of the saloon, instantly curbing his speed to a leisurely saunter.

Hatfield spotted a vacant table near an open window and sat down. He was rolling a cigarette when the five men entered, breathing hard and glancing keenly about. They moved to the bar and ordered drinks, their heads drawing together over their glasses. One, Hatfield noted, was tall and gangling with bony features and a wide, reptilian slit of a mouth. Another was short and broad with long, dangling arms. The other three were of medium height with no outstanding physical characteristics.

"Salty hombres, all right," was Hatfield's mental decision. " 'Pear to be cowhands, but I've a notion they haven't been for quite a spell."

While keeping an eye on the ominous quintette at the bar, he gave the room a careful once-over.

La Golondrina wasn't very large or crowded. It was apparently a one-room place. If it boasted a back room, the door leading to it was not conspicuously in evidence. There was a dance floor and a three-piece Mexican orchestra. The dance floor girls were good looking and had a bold look and calculating eyes about them. Their costumes were not readily described through masculine eyes. In fact, there wasn't enough to them to merit an expansive description. However, both girls and costumes seemed to suit the La Golondrina patrons for the girls did not lack partners.

The room was lighted by two hanging lamps, one near the bar and the other casting its beams over a couple of big poker tables near the center of the room. The building, Hatfield had noted from the outside, was built close to the creek bank. Its back, in fact, was supported by stout wooden piling.

A game was in progress at one of the poker tables and the tenseness of the players indicated that the stakes were high. Of the seven players, three had the appearance of well-to-do ranch owners. Three more were evidently mill or mine owners.

As he sat sipping the drink he ordered, it seemed to Hatfield that there was also a certain tenseness at the bar. The five men had edged along it until they were directly in line with where he sat, with the dance floor on one side and the poker tables on the other flanking an open lane from the bar to the table he occupied. The lone bartender, a swarthy, hard-eyed and alert looking individual, apparently knew the five men for he exchanged remarks with them, then moved to the end of the bar where he stood polishing glasses.

The other bar patrons appeared to have

conceived a notion for bunching together. They had crowded away from the five, leaving room on either side.

Hatfield knew that the five men were watching him in the back bar mirror. However, he sat unconcerned, his eyes apparently fixed on the poker games.

An argument started among the five. Their voices raised. They gesticulated angrily. Suddenly the short man bellowed a curse and leaped back toward the middle of the floor almost directly in line with where Hatfield sat. His hand dropped to his belt.

Instantly the tall man, who was facing him angrily, went into action. He jerked his gun and lined sights in the direction of his short companion.

And as instantly, Jim Hatfield went sideways from his chair to the floor even as the gangling man pulled the trigger and the bullet thudded into the back of the chair, he, Hatfield, had occupied the second before.

Prone on the floor, Hatfield drew and fired from the hip, two reports blending as one. With a clang of breaking glass the two hanging lamps went out. Black darkness blanketed the room.

Hatfield rolled over with a sideways,

slithering motion. Guns roared across the room and lead hissed through the air to thud solidly into the wall behind him. He blazed two shots in reply and heard a howl of pain and a sound as of a body thrashing about, a sound that was instantly drowned by the pandemonium that had burst loose. Men were yelling and cursing. The dance floor girls were screaming. The orchestra members screeched in frightened Spanish. A table crashed to the floor and the curses of the poker players added to the tumult.

Hatfield came to his feet like a released spring. His guns boomed again, the muzzles tipped up. The back bar mirror crashed to splintered ruin. Hatfield holstered one gun and side-stepped along the wall, groping in the darkness. His hand encountered a chair that he hurled at the dimly outlined opening above the swinging doors. The doors banged open under the impact.

"There he goes!" a voice bawled. "Out the door! After him!"

There was a pounding of boots, a crackle of shots, with no more bullets coming in Hatfield's direction.

Hatfield was going, all right, but not through the door. He was going through the open window, feet first. He hit the ground outside, staggered, regained his balance and raced toward the rear of the building. An instant later he was crouched under the overhang of the building, gripping a piling to keep his balance on the sloping creek bank.

The night air was quivering to angry voices tossing questions back and forth. Hatfield groped about on the ground until he found a loose stone. With all his strength he tossed it toward the bridge across the gulley which was only a few yards distant. The stone hit the floor and went bounding along, giving a very creditable imitation of boots pounding the boards.

"He's on the bridge!" somebody bellowed.

Hatfield saw dark figures flashing past in the starlight. Real boots pounded the floor boards. More shots were fired. The tumult outside died away in the direction of the grumbling stamp mills on the far bank.

But there was still plenty inside La Golondrina. All the girls seemed to be squawking at once like so many hawk-pounced chickens. Male voices cursed and boomed. There was a sound of breaking furniture, indicating that perhaps a private fight or two had started between irritated customers. A thrown bottle hurtled through the open window. Inside, more glass splintered. Hatfield chuckled, edged from under the overhang, and cautiously raised his head above the lip of the bank.

Standing within arm's reach was a man who peered downward. Hatfield caught a glint of metal. The man started a triumphant yelp.

The yelp rose to a howl of fright as Hatfield's iron grip closed on his ankles. Around and around the Lone Wolf whirled the screeching victim, then he let go. The howl thinned downward and ended in a tremendous splash.

Watery curses followed Hatfield from the black depths of the gulch as he scrambled over the bank and raced away from the still boiling La Golondrina. By way of a wide circle he reached the lighted street and headed for the Lipan at a leisurely pace, chuckling in remembrance of the shindig.

"A nice try, though, and smart," he told himself. "Start a phony fight, one jigger shooting at another misses and plugs me plumb by accident. Everybody sorry. Uh-huh, a nice try."

12

As a result of all the excitement and activity, Hatfield was hungry by the time he reached the Lipan. So he paused at the lunch counter for a sandwich and a cup of coffee. Then he mounted the stairs to his room, carefully bolted the door, and forgot all about the window — an inexcusable oversight, as he later told himself, in the light of subsequent events. The window opened onto a vacant lot reserved by Russell in the event that he ever needed more space for building.

Before going to bed, Hatfield carefully cleaned and oiled his guns. He laid them out close by and stretched out comfortably. For some time he lay drowsing comfortably and listening to the noises in the street that gradually subsided as the hour grew late. Finally he drifted off.

His awakening was decidedly more abrupt. He found himself sitting bolt upright in bed reaching for a gun. What had aroused him he did not know, but it had been a sudden and unwonted sound. He shot a glance at the closed door, shifted it to the rectangle of the open window dimly outlined against the glow of the street lights outside. There was nothing in sight.

Then he heard another sound from the direction of the window, a sibilant hissing.

"What in blazes?" he muttered.

He craned his neck toward the window. Then he hit the floor in a flash of movement.

Something was crawling along the floor beneath the window ledge. Not a snake, but a wavering flower of fire that spurted a shower of tiny sparks.

Hatfield dived for it, groping in the darkness. His hand encountered something rounded and greasy to the touch. It was a tightly tied bundle of dynamite sticks, three of them. And the fire of the burning fuse was almost lapping the cap.

Straightening up, Hatfield hurled the lethal bundle out the window with all the strength of his arm. He saw the sputtering fuse describe a parabola of flickering light and dodged back from the window.

Just before it hit the ground, the dynamite exploded with a roar and blaze of yellowish flame. Hatfield was hurled clear

148

across the room by the concussion. He hit the wall with a crash and sagged to the floor, half stunned. Dimly he heard the tinkle of the shattered window panes. The whole building rocked and quivered. There was an instant of paralyzed silence, then doors banged open in the corridor. Excited voices arose in a bewildered babble. Boots and bare feet thudded the floor boards.

Shaking his ringing head, Hatfield got to his feet and lurched across to the window, stepping carefully to avoid the broken glass that littered the floor. He peered out and saw a slowly dissipating cloud of yellowish smoke. The air was heavy with the tang of burned powder.

Men began appearing in the street, running up from every direction, shouting and gesticulating. Hatfield watched them crowd onto the vacant lot, and exclaiming. The drone of their babble loudened. There were curses, ejaculations, shaking of heads. Then gradually the crowd dispersed. Hatfield heard steps mounting the stairs. He opened the door and peered out as Arch Russell hove into view, half-dressed.

"What happened?" Hatfield asked innocently.

"Darned if I know," growled Russell. "Some loco coot must have figured it to be the Fourth of July and was chuckin' dynamite sticks around. Blew a hole in the ground out there you could hide a hogshead in. We didn't find anything of the feller what set it off. Maybe he ain't come down yet."

He cast a suspicious glance at Hatfield. "Say!" he exclaimed, "you don't know nothin' about it, do you?"

"Why you ask me that?" Hatfield evaded.

"I don't know," grunted Russell, "but ever since you showed up around here, things has been happenin'."

"Maybe they'll be quieter after I'm gone," Hatfield replied with a significance that was lost on the saloon-keeper.

"I'm beginnin' to figure it might be so," said Russell. "Well, good night, I'm goin' to try and sleep once more. Be busy tomorrow repairin' busted windows. Lucky the buildin's still standin'."

"Yes," Hatfield replied, again significantly, "I've a notion you are at that."

Something about the tone of his voice caused Russell to shoot him another keen glance, but he did not put his suspicions in words. With a grunt and a growl he stalked off down the corridor to his room. Hatfield closed his own door with a chuckle.

"Don't have to lack for fresh air, anyhow," he remarked, glancing at the smashed window. "Reckon the jigger will hardly come back for another try. Nice section, this."

With which he crawled back into bed and was soon asleep.

Despite the hectic events of the preceding day, Hatfield was up early, but before sitting down to breakfast he sauntered around the corner of the building to view the scene of the explosion.

Russell had not exaggerated in his estimate of the crater hollowed out by the dynamite. Hatfield, however, gave it but a passing glance. What interested him much more was something he found beneath the shattered window of his room.

It was a long and slender pole, evidently a trimmed sapling. One end was forked by means of lopping off two widespread branches.

"So that's the way he did it," mused the Lone Wolf. "Wedged the dynamite in the fork, shoved it over the window sill and jiggled it loose. It was the scraping of the pole on the ledge and the thump of the bundle dropping on the floor that roused me. Sidewinder sure had plenty of nerve. If the sticks had come loose and dropped back to the ground, there wouldn't have been enough of him left to take up with a blotter. A salty outfit, all right, and plumb snake-blooded."

He sat down to breakfast in a very thoughtful mood. The two deliberate attempts on his life were a trifle hard on the nerves.

Although he was pretty well convinced that Corpus Christi was headquarters for the smuggling band, Hatfield was missing no bets. He decided to ride he southwest trail in the direction of Port Isabel. He knew that hidden coves, bays and inlets were frequent, each of them providing a likely spot for unloading contraband cargo. He got the rig on Goldy and set out. He expected to reach the river town of Camina some time in the afternoon.

For some distance the trail crossed the mesquite and cactus flats which were a riot of color ranging from flaming red to delicate tints of mauve, pink and cream. Spanish dagger, sotol, century plant, catclaw, rattail cactus, barrel cactus, devil's pincushion, devil's fingers, ocotillo, and various forms of yuccas added their grotesque shapes and varied colorings to the landscape.

The ocotillos, their tall, curving, graceful wands springing from a central root were like green jets from a fairy fountain.

A mile after passing the Cross C ranch-house, the trail wound through a tall and dense stand of chaparral. The bends were numerous and Hatfield could seldom see ahead for more than a hundred yards. He was approaching the bulge of one of the curves when from not far ahead there came a thudding crash, a chorus of curses and a woman's scream of fright. Followed a booming report and a crackle of shots.

"What in blazes?" the Lone Wolf wondered. "Hit the dust, feller, let's see what's going on around that bend!"

13

The Camina-Corpus Christi stage pulled out of Camina, a couple of hours after daybreak. Old Lafe Woodard, the driver, made sure that his lone passenger, a slender girl whose dark eyes were startling in contrast with her curly golden hair and fair complexion, was comfortable.

"Here's a footstool for you, Miss Benton," he said, shoving a heavy iron box into the body of the coat. "Not a bit too good for such puffy feet, either," he added gallantly, "even though there's twenty thousand dollars gold in it."

"Twenty thousand dollars!" exclaimed the girl, looking somewhat askance at the strongbox.

"Uh-huh," said Lafe. "Twenty thousand dollars in gold coin headed for the Corpus Christi bank. Came in by boat."

"Aren't you afraid of robbers?" asked the girl, still regarding the box.

"Nope," Woodard replied cheerfully.

154

"Nobody but me and Ralph, the guard, and the band folks know the stage's packin' it. Besides, Ralph has his shotgun and I got my old hogleg. We'd make it sort of hot for anybody what tried to stop us."

"I hope you won't need to," said the girl.

"Don't worry none about it," said the garrulous old driver, suddenly feeling that perhaps he might have talked a mite out of turn. "Nothin's goin' to happen. We'll get you to Corpus Christi okay. Reckon your dad will meet you there."

"I'm not sure," the girl replied. "I'm getting home a few days earlier than I expected, but I won't have any trouble getting somebody to drive me out to the ranch."

"Sartain, sartain," agreed the driver as he closed the door. He climbed to the high seat, gathered up his reins.

"All set?" he asked the guard who sat beside him, double-barreled shotgun across his knees, rifle ready to hand. "Okay! Here we go!"

He whooped to his four mettlesome horses and the stage roared out of Camina in a cloud of dust.

The sun was climbing to the zenith when the stage boomed through Camina Canyon and past busy mine buildings, the shafts and the huddle of shacks that served as makeshift quarters for those of the miners who preferred not to take the ride to and from town each day. Old Lafe shouted cheery greetings to acquaintances and whooped to his speeding horses.

Nearly three miles northeast of the canyon, a second trail flowed from the northwest to join the Corpus Christi trail. It was a little-traveled trail that led straight to the Rio Grande and Mexico. Old timers who knew its history called it the Raiders' Trail.

Just below where the Raiders' Trail joined the southwest trail, the brash was thick and high and sprinkled with large trees whose overhanging branches cast their shadows across the track. At one spot the branches interlaced so thickly that no ray of sunshine pierced their entwined foliage. The gloom beneath was cavernous.

At top speed the coach hurtled toward the junction of the two trails. It swooped into the shadow beneath the arch of the trees. The shadow was so dark that neither guard nor driver saw the rope stretched tightly across the trail from tree trunk to tree trunk.

The lead horses hit the rope. Down they went in a wild tangle of splaying hoofs, squeals and snorts. The unwieldy coach slewed around on cramped front sheels. One rear wheel struck a projecting fang of stone with a crash. The spokes splintered to matchwood, the tire rolled free and the denuded hub thudded to the ground. The coach reeled and rocked and only a tree trunk against which it slammed saved it from a complete overturn.

Guard and driver volleyed curses and clutched the seat railing for support. The thing had happened so suddenly neither realized what had taken place. From the body of the coach came a frightened scream, cut off short.

Out of the brush bulged four mounted men. Black masks covered their faces. They held levelled guns in their hands.

"Elevate!" boomed a voice.

The guard was game. He flung his shotgun to his shoulder and pulled both triggers.

The double charge ripped the mask and most of the face from one of the owlhoots. Then guard and driver toppled from the seat to lie beside the dead outlaw, their bodies riddled with bullets.

"Haul the box out and hightail," shouted a voice from the brush. "Never mind Hank. He's done for. Move, before an ore wagon comes along."

The three masked men started to dismount, holstering their smoking guns.

"Look out!" the voice suddenly yelled a warning.

Around the bend raced a great golden horse, like a flicker of flame amid the shadows. And very real was the flame that gushed from the roaring muzzles of the guns held by his tall rider.

Down went a second raider, to lie crumpled and motionless in the dust. Another howled with pain, reeling in the saddle and gripping his blood-spurting shoulder. But he recovered himself and jerked his gun. His companion was already blazing away at the horseman.

Shot for shot, Jim Hatfield answered the outlaws, ducking, weaving and slewing from side to side. Goldy did a wild dance that made a most elusive target of his rider.

The wounded outlaw reeled and fell. An instant later the remaining raider rose upright in his stirrups, stood rigid for a moment and then slowly toppled sideways to lie beside his dead companions.

With Goldy still dancing and weaving, Hatfield threw one leg over the saddle and dropped to the ground. A gun boomed from the brush and a bullet turned his hat sideways on his head. He slewed his Colts around and raked the growth with his remaining bullets. He caught a glimpse of brown flickering between the branches. There was a crashing of brush and a drumming of hoofs dimming away from the trail.

Hatfield started to remount, then abruptly changed his mind. He recalled that terrified scream that had ceased so suddenly an instant after the crash of the wrecked coach. He staffed fresh cartridges into his guns, his eyes never leaving the bodies sprawled on the trail. Then satisfied that there was nothing more to fear from the owlhoots, he strode to the stage and jerked open the door.

Huddled on a seat was a girl with tumbled golden curls clustering about her white face. Her eyes were closed and she lay limp and unconscious.

Muttering under his breath, Hatfield reached in and lifted her from the seat.

"Breathing, anyhow," he exclaimed in relief. "Did one of those hellions plug her?"

Then, again with intense relief, he sighted a purpling bruise on her white forehead just below the hairline.

"Hit her head when the coach went over," he understood. "Knocked her cold. Blazes! now I have got my hands full."

For a moment he stood wracking his

brains, the unconscious girl still in his arms. Then he recalled the ranchhouse he passed but little more than a mile back along the trail.

"I'll take her there," he decided quickly. "Wonder what those devils were after?"

He peered into the coach, saw the iron strongbox.

"So that's it," he muttered. "Well, can't leave it here. Don't think the one that got away will come back for it, but anything is liable to happen in this darn section. Besides, he might have some sidekicks holed up somewhere near waiting for him."

He gently placed the unconscious girl on the grass at the edge of the brush. Then, working at top speed, he got the fallen horses to their feet. Neither seemed much worse for the experience, save for some bruises and skinned places. He unharnessed one and haltered it with one of the trailing reins. He lifted the heavy box from the coach and with the other rein deftly diamond-hitched it to the horse's back. Just as he was tightening the last knot, he heard a gasping cry behind him. He whirled, hand streaking to his gun.

The girl was sitting up, a dazed look on her face, her eyes wide with terror.

"Take it easy, Ma'am," Hatfield cautioned, crossing the trail to her side. "How you feel?"

The girl shrank back as he drew near, her face ashen. "Wha-what are you going to do to me?" she gasped.

Although he was in no mood for mirth, Hatfield chuckled. Then he smiled down at her, his even teeth flashing white against his bronzed cheeks, his green eyes sunny.

The girl stared up at him. Some of the fear left her eyes.

"You're — you're not one of the robbers?" she asked.

"Reckon not," Hatfield reassured her. "How you feeling?"

"I feel rather dizzy," she replied, passing her hand across her bruised forehead. "And my head feels queer."

"You got a bad knock," Hatfield said. "Must have hit your head on a door handle or something. You need to be in bed and have it looked after. I'm taking you to a place I passed on the way down here."

Before she could protest, he gently raised her in his arms, strode to where Goldy stood waiting and deftly mounted. He scooped up the halter of the stage horse with the strongbox on its back and secured it to the saddle horn.

"Get going, feller," he told the sorrel.

Goldy moved forward at a good pace, the led horse trotting behind him.

The girl appeared to be recovering somewhat. "Can't you tell me what happened?" she pleaded. "The last I remember was the stage going over."

" 'Peared to be a try at a holdup," Hatfield replied. "I heard the crash and heard you scream just before the shooting started. I'd say they were after that box back there."

"There's twenty thousand dollars in it — the driver told me so," said the girl.

Hatfield nodded. "Figured something like that," he replied.

"But those men back there," questioned the girl. "Did the guard kill them?"

"Reckon he got one with his shotgun from the looks of him," Hatfield replied.

"And the others? Oh, you must have killed them!"

"Reckon so," Hatfield replied briefly.

The golden-haired girl stared up at him her dark eyes widening. What manner of man was this who could shoot down three of his fellowmen and apparently not be in the least affected?

But something about the sternly handsome face and the steady eyes so far above her was infinitely reassuring. She hadn't the least notion where he was taking her, but to her own astonishment she realized that she didn't particularly care. Her head ached and her nerves were strung to the breaking point, but the feel of his arms about her was very comforting. It seemed that there was no longer anything to worry about. Everything was bound to be all right with this tall stranger in charge.

Hatfield glanced down at her. "How come you were on the stage, Ma'am?" he asked. "Where were you heading for?"

"Corpus Christi," the girl replied. "Then on to my home, the XT ranch, to the north of the town. I'm Mary Benton."

Hatfield's interest in her suddenly increased. "Craig Benton happen to be your father?" he asked.

"Why, yes," she answered. "Do you know him?"

"I met him," Hatfield said. "Had a talk with him. Well, here we are. Let's see if there's anybody home."

He let out a shout. A moment later Tom Carvel appeared in the doorway, garbed in a ragged and very dirty shirt. A four days' stubble of reddish beard did not add to the attractiveness of his face which was liberally smeared with axle grease, Carvel having been working on a buckboard.

Hatfield heard the girl gasp. He chuckled.

"Don't worry, honey, he's just a human like the rest of us," he said as he slipped to the ground, deftly cradling her in his arms.

"What in thunder?" exclaimed Carvel in astonishment.

"Lady's been hurt," Hatfield told him briefly. "Needs attention."

"Bring her in! Bring her in!" Carvel interrupted. "Gypsy isn't here, but I'll get Miguel. He's a better doctor than half the sawbones in Texas. Bring her in!"

Hatfield carried the girl into the ranch-house. Miguel came pattering from the kitchen.

"Put on bed," he directed. With deft fingers he probed the bruise.

Tom Carvel was staring at the girl in a dazed sort of way. He absently raised a muscular hand, scratched at his bristle of whiskers, continued to stare.

Miguel straightened up. "Be all right," he said. "Need rest. Hombres get out!"

"Come on, feller," Carvel instantly said. "I learned better'n to arg'fy with him, years ago."

Hatfield chuckled, smiled down at the girl and followed Carvel out the door.

"Who is she?" Carvel demanded.

"Said her name was Mary Benton," Hatfield replied.

Carvel stared, his eyes widening. "Old Craig Benton's daughter!" he exclaimed.

"So I gather," Hatfield admitted.

Carvel's lips pursed in a soundless whistle. "Haven't seen her for two or three years," he said. "She's been away to school. Was just a leggy kid the last time I saw her. Feller, won't you please tell me what this is all about?"

Hatfield told him, tersely. "You take care of that money box," he directed. "And send a man to Corpus Christi to notify the sheriff."

Several of the Cross C hands were in the yard now, listening with avid interest. Carvel snapped orders.

"A couple of you fellers better ride down and look after the stage and the horses," he concluded.

"Where you going, Jim?" he asked as Hatfield swung into the saddle.

"I'm going to see if I can trail that jigger who got away," Hatfield replied.

"Think you can do it?" Carvel asked curiously.

"Figure it's worth trying," Hatfield said. "I got a sort of personal interest in that gent. He came nigh to drygulching me from the brush. I 'low he's the he-wolf of the pack. Hung back and gave the orders. I'd like to get a look at him."

"Want me to come along?" Carvel offered.

Hatfield shook his head. "You stay here and look after Miss Benton," he said. "Reckon you'll have to drive her up to her dad's place. Don't let her ride a horse till a doctor looks at that bruise and pronounces her okay. An injury like that will sometimes produce a concussion that can't be detected except by a trained physician. I think she's all right, but she's too pretty a girl to take chances on. That sort don't happen along every day."

"You can say that again!" Carvel declared with emphasis.

Hatfield shot him a quick glance, an amused and pleased light in his green eyes.

Accompanied by two of Carvel's cowhands, Hatfield rode back to the stage. He dismounted and ripped the masks from the faces of the dead owlhoots.

"Recognize any of them?" he asked.

At first the cowboys shook their heads. Then one peered closer.

"I *have* seen this ganglin' jigger hangin' around the bars in town," he said. "That short, square one over there looks sort of familiar, too."

Hatfield nodded. The unsavory pair "looked familiar" to him also. He instantly recognised them as two of the group that had staged the fake gunfight in La Golondrina the night before.

"Well, I sort of evened up that score in a hurry," he told himself with satisfaction. "Now if one of the others just happens to be the dynamite chucker!"

With the cowhands watching him curiously, he emptied out the dead man's pockets, revealing a rather surprising sum in gold and silver coin.

"Hellions been doin' all right by themselves," one of the punchers observed. "Feller, I believe you got a few of the bunch that's been raisin' all the hell hereabouts of late. A prime chore. Hope you get the other one."

Nothing further of significance was discovered. Hatfield replaced the coin and the other objects.

"Maybe the sheriff can make something of that stuff," he told the punchers. "And maybe he'll know some of these horned toads. Might help him to run down the rest of the outfit."

"I'm scairt Oswell ain't much good at runnin' down things," volunteered one of the cowboys. "He's a nice feller and plenty salty, but I'm scairt he's a mite light in the upper story for such a chore. It's a bad bunch operatin' in this section, feller, and one with plenty of savvy. A pet fox is plumb foolish 'longside that bunch."

Hatfield was inclined to agree with the puncher on both scores, but refrained from saying so.

At that moment a ponderous ore wagon lurched around the turn from the south. The driver pulled up his mules with a yelp of astonishment.

Leaving the cowboys to explain matters to the driver, Hatfield twisted Goldy's reins over his arm and walked into the brush to the south of the trail.

As he anticipated, he had little trouble picking up the trail of the fleeing stage robber. Nor was he surprised when it circled to enter the little used Raiders' Trail that led to Mexico.

He was somewhat surprised, however, when a couple of miles farther on it turned off to follow a faint track that threaded brush grown ravines and trended steadily east through a spur of the hills. Gradually the direction changed to northeast with a continued veering to the north.

"Hellion didn't head for *manana* land as I figured he would," Hatfield mused.

"Darned if it doesn't look like he's following a way back to town."

The owlhoot had taken no pains to conceal his tracks and they were absurdly easy to follow. Hatfield decided that the fleeing man had doubtless felt that he could not afford to take time to be careful.

"Chances are he figured I'd be tied up with the girl and the strongbox and couldn't hightail after him right off," the ranger concluded. "Figured right, too. All he needs to do is cover distance and perhaps swing back to the Camina where there'll be no picking out his tracks. Well, here goes for a look-see, anyhow."

The trail, little more than a game track, continued to worm its way into deeper canyons choked with brush and littered with boulders. The trail, Hatfield soon determined, had been used more than once in recent times, a fact that interested him and caused him to advance with greater caution.

"Darn snake track could well lead to a hole-up somewhere in this mess of gullies," he told himself.

The sun was behind the western peaks and the canyons were growing shadowy, but still the tracks of the quarry showed plainly on the soft ground. For the present, at least, it would be impossible for him to turn off anywhere because of the steep walls that hemmed the canyon in.

Hatfield slowed his pace, however, and redoubled his caution. The darkening gorge was sinister in its silence. As the gloom deepened, the walls seemed to draw closer together like stealthy monsters crouching for a spring.

Hatfield sensed a disquieting feeling of uneasiness, though why he did not know.

Suddenly he sniffed sharply and jerked Goldy to a halt. To his nostrils had come the indubitable tang of burning wood. For some minutes he sat tensely in his saddle, listening and peering.

No sound dulled the sharp edge of the silence. Nothing moved amid the encroaching growth. But the woody whiff of smoke persisted.

Hatfield resolved a plan of action. It was certain that somebody had kindled a fire no great distance ahead. Although the thing did not seem reasonable, it could possibly have been done by the man he was pursuing. And if so, it was logical to believe that others were with him. Perhaps this was a hideout frequented by the band that had been terrorizing the section for some time.

Glancing about, the Lone Wolf located a dense thicket whose deeper green hinted at water near at hand. He turned Goldy from the trail and forced him through the bushes. He was not surprised to see, close to the canyon wall, a small spring from which seeped a trickle of water.

"You can just hole up here for a spell, feller," he told the sorrel. "There's a nip or two of grass around and a drink. If I go gallivanting along with you kicking over rocks at every step, somebody is mighty liable to hear us coming and perhaps cook up a hot reception for us. I'll sneak along on my bootheels till we see which way the pickle is going to squirt."

Leaving the thicket, Hatfield proceeded with caution. He really doubted that his quarry was holed up somewhere ahead, but he acted on the assumption that he might be. He knew that the hills and canyons of the section were dotted with old cabins, shacks and even former Indian lodges, occupied at one time or another by prospectors or trappers. Likely as not the builder of the fire ahead was some harmless old desert rat who spent his days chipping the ledges and washing the creek beds for color. But the Ranger preferred to take no chances. With the greatest care he eased along the faint trail, keeping to the shadows, refraining from breaking any twig or dislodging any stone. Even in the thickening gloom he could still make out the hoof prints he had been following during the afternoon.

Stronger and stronger grew the smell of wood smoke. And abruptly he saw its source.

Near the canyon wall was a dilapidated old cabin strongly built of logs with a split-pole roof and a mud and stick chimney. From the chimney rose a streamer of blue smoke. Light gleamed through the dirty panes of a single window. The door was closed. Behind the cabin and slightly to one side was what appeared to be a lean-to stable, but whether horses were tethered under the sloping roof Hatfield could not make out in the deepening dusk.

Standing at the edge of a thicket, he surveyed the cabin. Aside from the drifting coil of smoke and the faint gleam of light, there were no signs of occupancy. The canyon remained silent and devoid of motion. Hatfield peered and listened, debating the advisability of crawling to the building and risking a glance through the window. Between where he stood and the old shack was open space. Should someone open the door he could hardly hope to avoid detection. He resolved to wait until full dark closed down before making a move. He relaxed comfortably, wished for a smoke but decided he could not take the chance of striking a match.

A split second too late his straining ears caught a sound of stealthy movement directly behind him. Even as his hands streaked to his belt, the hard, cold circle of a gun muzzle jammed against his back.

"Hold it!" warned a harsh voice. "Make a move and I'll blow your insides around your breast bone. Elevate, slow!"

14

Hatfield obeyed the command. There was nothing else to do. He was caught settin'. Slowly he raised his hands shoulder high, seething with anger at himself. He cursed his own stupidity for blundering into a trap.

"Keep 'em there," warned the voice. A hand plucked his guns from their sheaths.

"All right, Val, I got him," said the voice.

There was a rustle in the growth and a man stepped into view, wearing an evil grin. He held a cocked six in his hand. He kept carefully to one side of Hatfield, the gun ready for instant action.

The circle of steel prodded Hatfield's back. "Get goin'," said his captor. "Head for the shack. Right through the door, and keep your hands where they are. I got an itchy trigger finger."

Again the Ranger obeyed. With the gun muzzle against his back he moved forward. The second man kept pace with him, still considerably to one side. He reached the door.

"Kick it open," said the man behind. Hatfield did so. A significant prod sent him into the room. He glanced quickly about, noted a small iron stove with hot coals glowing through the grate bars. In the middle of the room was a table and a couple of chairs. There were bunks built against the walls. Several rifles stood in a corridor. Cooking utensils hung on pegs back of the stove. The room was lighted by a single bracket lamp with a smoky chimney. A doorway was cut in the far wall, evidently leading into a second room. No door closed the opening.

"Put your hands down, behind you, wrists together," ordered his captor. "Hold your iron on him, Val. Plug him if he makes a move. Don't see any sense in not doin' it anyhow, but orders are orders."

Working with speed and efficiency, the man behind him lashed Hatfield's wrists together with a length of hair rope that cut viciously into his flesh.

"Right through the door over there," came the order. "Lay down on the bunk."

Hatfield moved forward. A bar of light from the bracket lamp revealed a bunk built against the far wall of the inner room, which was much smaller than the other. Without a word he lay down on it. Another moment and his ankles were securely bound. His captor stepped back and Hatfield got a look at him. He instantly recognized him as another member of the group that had staged the row in La Golondrina. The second man, a scrawny specimen with a cadaverous face and muddy colored eyes, he did not recall having seen before.

"And that's that," said the first man. "Now we'll throw together a surroundin' and eat. Then we'll go get the Boss."

"I don't see the sense in all this loco foolin' around," whined the man called Val in a thin, querulous voice. "Why not plug him and get it over with?"

"Shut up," rumbled the other as he busied himself over the stove. "The Boss said to hold him, didn't he? The Boss knows what he's doin'. He wants to talk to this gent, ask him a few questions. He wants to find out what he's doin' here and where he comes from."

"What difference does it make?" whined Val.

"It may make considerable difference," grunted the other. He lowered his voice to a mutter, but Hatfield's unusually keen ears caught broken sentences — "that business over west — maybe — them fellers stick to trail — may be more of 'em around — got to find out."

"Don't see why the Boss didn't stick around and help grab this hellion," creaked Val, " 'stead of ridin' off to town."

His companion's voice rose in irritated tones. "And not be there meetin' somebody he'd promised to see," he growled. "That sort of thing starts talk. Old Benton 'spects folks to be around when he wants 'em. And he's always suspicious of everybody. Let him start wonderin' about somethin' and he's liable to put things together. Things ain't been goin' right hereabouts of late. You let the Boss do the thinkin'. He figgers things out, that's why he's the Boss. Just like he figured that feller tied up in there would come snoopin' along the trail he left for him to follow. You let him do the thinkin' and foller orders. You'd better. You talk too darn much, Val. I've seed him sort of lookin' at you of late, and you know what that means. Want him to do a chore of man breakin' on you?"

Craning his neck, Hatfield could see the scrawny man's face twist as if in fright.

"I don't mean nothin'," he whined. "It's just that I figger a feller like this one ain't the sort to take chances with. When you get him hogtied, finish him, that's what I say. You don't get more 'n one chance with that sort."

"One chance is all we need," the other declared grimly. "Now shut up and eat. We got a ride ahead of us."

Silence followed, save for the rattle of knives, forks and tin plates. Hatfield's anger against himself increased.

"See now why that trail was so easy to follow," he muttered under his breath. "Hellion was just luring me on and I fell for it like a dumb sheepherder. Well, I'm liable to pay for being so terrapin-brained."

Finally the two finished their meal. The bigger man stood up, wiping his mouth.

"All right," he said, "let's go. Never mind the dishes. We'll take care of 'em when we get back. If the Boss got held up in town we'll have to go there to tell him, and it's better'n an hour's ride."

"He said he'd come back here as soon as he finished in town," observed the other. "Maybe we'll meet him on the way."

"Maybe," agreed the first speaker, "but we got to get goin'."

"Figure it's safe to leave that feller here by himself?" asked the scrawny man. "Maybe I'd better stay and keep a eye on him."

"Don't you worry about that," grunted the other. "When I tie 'em they stay tied. He'll be right here when we get back. Better for us to stick together. No tellin' what we might run into. That damn sheriff will be gallivantin' around somewhere, chances are. He's dumb, but he's salty, don't forget that. We can't afford to take chances. Blow the lamp out and come along."

An instant later the cabin was dark save for the faint glow of the stove grates. Hatfield heard the two stump out, banging the door shut behind them. He heard the muffled thud of horses' hoofs dying away up the canyon.

Lying alone in the darkness, the Lone Wolf set himself to some very hard and serious thinking. He knew he was on a tough spot with little chance, so far as he could see, of getting off it. The Boss, evidently the man who had directed the stage holdup, apparently desired to ask him some questions before doing him in. And undoubtedly he had highly unpleasant ways of getting answers from his victims. Answer or not, Hatfield knew he would have but a short time to live after the Boss arrived at the cabin. He figured that at the very most, he had a little over two hours to work out a means of escape. He tried to recall the layout of the cabin, but could remember no projection or bits of metal against which he might chafe the cords that held his wrists. He strained at them with all his strength but only increased the pain of the hair rope cutting into his flesh. Sweat dewed his face and soon he was trembling in every limb. The man who did the tieing made no idle boast when he said when he tied 'em they stayed tied. The knots refused to loosen.

The glow of the stove grates, the only gleam of light in the black darkness, drew Hatfield's gaze. His eyes focused on the reddish glow. And suddenly there came to him a thrill of hope. Hair rope burns very easily.

This was all very well, but he knew that it would be impossible to get the cords against the fire in the stove. He knew he could flop from the bunk and roll and hunch his way to the other room, but to rear up on his tightly bound legs and reach the grates was out of the question.

"I've got one chance," he muttered. "Might as well take it. If I slip it up, it won't be a nice way to pass out, but even that will be better than what that devil is liable to hand me when he gets here."

With a convulsive writhe he flopped off the bunk and hit the floor with a bone-creaking jar. Then he began rolling over and over until he reached the door. Inching through the narrow opening was a tedious and exhausting struggle, but finally he made it. Then he rolled again until he was close to the rickety stove. His plan was to kick it over and scatter the glowing coals from the grate.

It was practically certain that the greasy, worm-eaten and tinder-dry floor boards would almost immediately catch fire. But he hoped to be able to get his bound wrists over a coal and char the rope enough to break it before he was roasted alive. It was a desperate gamble, but the Lone Wolf was resolved to take it. He drew up his bound legs and kicked out with all his strength. Both boot soles caught the stove amidships with all the drive of the Ranger's sinewy legs behind them.

Over went the stove with a crash. The upper and lower halves rolled apart. Hot coals scattered over the floor boards. Instantly smoulders began that quickly increased to flickering flames as the fire ate into the wood.

With desperate haste, Hatfield writhed and twisted until he got his bound wrists

181

over one of the coals. He winced as the heat seared his flesh, but pressed the rope hard against the coal. An odor of burned hair mingled with the whiff of wood smoke.

Enduring the agony of his scorched wrists, Hatfield continued to press down on the ember. When he felt that it was cooling, he flopped and twisted his way to another that still glowed brightly red. Again he repeated the painful process, tugging and straining at the charring rope. For what seemed untold ages he struggled with the stubborn cords. The floor boards were well afire now and the air was thick with smoke. Hatfield coughed and choked and fought madly to free himself. His wrists were a searing agony and still the ropes held.

But the increasing odor of scorched hair told him he was making progress. He pressed down hard on the coal and tugged with all his strength. A moment of despairing resistance and suddenly the rope snapped. Hatfield tore his wrists free from the loosened cord and levered himself to a sitting position. With numbed fingers he drew a knife from his pocket and slashed the ropes that bound his ankles. He struggled to his feet and instantly pitched headlong. His legs were wooden and refused to support him. Frantically he massaged them until the agonizing "pins-and-needles" of returning circulation began. He struggled erect again and stood lurching and weaving. He started for the door, then realized that to open it would send in a draft that would fan the creeping flicker out of control. Choking and gasping, he stamped out the strengthening flames one by one.

The smoke thickened, but soon the last flicker had been reduced to a smoulder. He staggered to the door and flung it open, gulping in great drafts of life-giving air. He gave a little attention to the smoulders and the still glowing coals, then leaned against the wall for a moment till his strength returned somewhat. He found a match and lit the bracket lamp. Its smoky radiance revealed his guns lying on the table. With an exultant exclamation, he seized them, made sure that they were loaded and in perfect working order and then thrust them into their sheaths.

There was a pot half full of still warm coffee on the table which had escaped overturning in the course of his struggle with the stove. He poured a cup and swallowed, following it with another. Then he dipped grease from a pan and smeared his smarting wrists. The burns he decided, though painful, were not serious. He drank more coffee and felt decidedly better, though he was still half dazed from smoke poisoning.

Without the slightest warning the door crashed open and his two captors bulged into the room, bellowing curses, guns out. Hatfield had a fleeting glimpse of a third man looming in the darkness.

Hatfield hurled himself sideways, his arms lashed out and slammed the lamp from its bracket. Darkness swooped down, darkness split by red flashes and quivering to a thunder of reports as Ranger and owlhoots blasted death at each other through the murk.

Ducking, weaving, Hatfield shot with both hands. He felt the lethal breath of passing lead and the hot burn of a bullet grazing his ribs. Another whispered through his hair. He reeled and nearly fell as a third knocked half the heel from his left boot.

Then abruptly he realized that no more spurts of flame were coming from the direction of the open door. Thumbs hooked over the hammers of his guns, he held his own fire and listened intently. A gurgling and gasping swelled somewhere in the dark, then ceased. Then a quick beat of hoofs broke the silence.

Hatfield bounded forward, tripped over a sprawled body and fell through the door. Instinctively he rolled over and to one side before attempting to rise. No shots came in his direction. He scrambled to his feet.

Far up the canyon a speeding horseman was but a flicker in the starlight. Hatfield fired twice but knew the range was too great for anything but a lucky hit. A moment later the rider vanished from his sight, still firm in the saddle.

Leaning against the side of the cabin, Hatfield started to eject the spent shells from his empty gun. Without warning a figure bounded from the cabin and crashed into him. The gun was dashed from his hand. Fingers like steel rods closed on his throat. He had no chance to draw his other gun. Barely in time he gripped the fellow's other wrist and forced his hand up and back. There was the crash of a shot but the bullet whistled wide. A sharp click rewarded a second pull on the trigger. His opponent's gun was also empty.

The owlhoot was a big man, heavier even than the tall Ranger, and he seemed to be made of steel wires. Back and forward they

185

wrestled in grim silence save for their gasping breath. Hatfield tore at the hand gripping his throat but could not break the other's hold. His senses were whirling, there was a thin, ruddy mist before his eyes. In his ears was a great roaring. Another moment of that throttling grip and his senses would leave him.

With a final desperate effort, he hurled himself backward and down. He struck the ground with a thud. The other catapaulted over him, grip torn from Hatfield's throat.

Panting, gasping, the Ranger rolled over on his face. His clutching hands closed on a large boulder. He surged to his feet, gripping the rock, as the other also scrambled to his feet and rushed, empty gun clubbed for a lethal blow.

Hatfield raised the stone above his head and hurled it with all his strength. His aim was true. It struck the outlaw's skull with a dull crunching sound. The man dropped, twitched for a moment and lay still. He was satisfactorily dead, dripping blood and brains, when Hatfield bent over him.

For a moment he stood listening for sounds of life in the cabin against the chance that another of the hellions had only been creased. All was silent. Recovering his gun, he loaded it, fished a match from his pocket and struck a light.

He stepped into the cabin, groped about and found the remains of the shattered lamp. The wick was still in the battered brass burner. He twisted it up and touched a match to it. He surveyed the wrecked cabin, wedged the burner in a crack and by its uncertain light gave the dead men as careful a once-over as the circumstances would permit. Their pockets held nothing of significance.

Hatfield retrieved the burner and carried it outside. Nearby stood two saddled and bridled horses. They bore Mexican brands that told the Ranger nothing. Saddles and bridles were ordinary gear and of no significance. Hatfield got the rigs off the animals and turned them loose to graze.

"And now I'd better see about my own cayuse," he decided. "He'll be thinking I got myself lost for sure. Well, I pretty nearly did at that."

As an afterthought he re-entered the cabin and examined its contents by the last flicker of the dried-out lamp wick. The building showed signs of considerable recent occupancy, but revealed nothing else of note.

Leaving the cabin and its grisly occupants, Hatfield made his way down the canyon to where he left Goldy.

"A close call," he told the sorrel as he fitted the bit into his mouth. "A couple of 'em, in fact. I've a notion, feller, that I'm growing feather-brained. I should have remembered that if those gents came back and saw a light burning in the cabin they'd know something wasn't just right. If they'd used a mite better judgment, they could have potted me through the window, but the owlhoot brand always make slips like they did by bulging into the room. Lucky for me that they do, considering the ones I've been making of late. Well, we got the breaks, that's all. But I don't 'low to rely on getting any more of 'em. Can't afford to play my luck too strong. From here on, horse, we're moving slow and easy and on the lookout for anything. It's a bad bunch we're up against. But, anyhow, we're thinning them out a mite. Okay, feller, let's go. I gather this crack leads back to town somehow. We'll chance riding the trail of that sidewinder who got away."

15

As Hatfield surmised, a few miles farther on the canyon opened onto the rangeland. Plotting his course by the stars, he rode north. Another half hour and he sighted the lights of Corpus Christi winking like fallen stars in the distance.

In a fairly equable frame of mind, he rode on to town. Aside from blistered wrists, bullet-skinned ribs and numerous bruises, he was in good physical condition and his injuries were none of them serious enough to warrant concern. One sleeve hung in tatters, mute proof of the shooting ability of the dead outlaws, just as his scorched overalls were reminders of his tussle with the stove and its contents.

Reaching town, Hatfield stabled his horse, washed up a bit and went in quest of something to eat. A spare shirt from his saddle pouch improved his appearance somewhat, but just the same Arch Russell stared in astonishment when he entered the Lipan.

"Well, been havin' yourself a time, eh?" remarked the saloonkeeper. "What happened? Oswell rode in about dark, cussin'. They still ain't got the stage fixed up and brought in. Hauser had the strongbox full of the bank's money with him. A little later Tom Carvel drove by in a buckboard with Craig Benton's gal. He stopped and asked for you and the gal asked, too. Seemed plumb interested. She's a purty little thing. Takes after her mother, I been told. Sure didn't get her good looks from Craig. They stopped at Doc Cooper's office. Doc looked her over and told her she had nothing to worry about. Then they drove on to the ranch."

Hatfield enjoyed a good meal. With the elasticity of youth he had already thrown off his fatigue. He joined Russell in a drink and rolled and smoked a cigarette.

"Think I'll amble over to the doctor's office and let him put something on these wrists," he announced. "It's nothing serious, but I figure they should be looked after a mite. I'll drop in again before I go to bed."

When Hatfield returned from the doctor's office, a slender young cowhand of medium height, attired in nearly new, neatly fitting rangeland garb was talking

190

with Arch Russell at the end of the bar. His lean cheeks were clean shaven and he was immaculate in every respect.

Hatfield chuckled, his green eyes sunny as summer seas. The man was Tom Carvel!

Hatfield joined the pair at the bar. Carvel greeted him warmly.

"Arch was just telling me about the shindig you had," he said. "I told you I should go along with you. Might not have happened to both of us together."

"Might not have," Hatfield agreed, "but it worked out all right and I've a notion you did better by staying back. Get the little lady home all right?"

"Uh-huh, I got her home all right," Carvel replied. "Her dad was sure surprised to see her. Didn't expect her for another week. He started to swell up like a pizened pup. But the little gal soon cooled him off. He ended by shaking hands with me. Maybe he didn't overly hanker to, but he did shake hands."

Carvel paused a moment. "You know," he added, "I've got the notion that maybe he isn't such a bad old jigger, after all. Say, what's so funny?" He stared at Hatfield in puzzled surprise.

For the Ranger was shaking with silent laughter.

"The Arabs," said Hatfield with apparent irrelevance, "the Arabs have a word — *kismet.*"

"Uh-huh," said Carvel. "It means fate or something like that, I believe."

"That's right," Hatfield nodded. "When something unexplainable or utterly unexpected occurs, they call it kismet — fate. Funny, isn't it, how fate steps in every now and then to lend a hand at straightening things out? Well, so long, gents, I'm going to bed."

"Now what the blazes did he mean by that?" Carvel demanded of Russell as Hatfield took his leave.

But fat Arch, a twinkle in his faded blue eyes, refused to hazard an opinion.

16

The sheriff received Captain McDowell's answer the following day and sent for Hatfield at once.

Sanford Garner, son of Walter and Mary Garner, (wired Captain Bill) spent three years in Louisiana institution for orphaned children. Upon leaving institution he went to work for the La Salle Packing and Provisions Company of New Orleans. Was industrious. Did well. Became a floor foreman in packing department. Discharged on suspicion of being connected with gang accused of stealing meat. No court action. Dropped out of sight. Nothing learned of subsequent movements.

Hatfield's eyes glowed as he read the message. "This ties up some of the loose threads," he told Oswell. "I'm beginning to see where Craig Benton comes into the picture. My hunch was a straight one. Now we can only keep our eyes skun and await developments."

Two days later the young Mexican slid furtively into the sheriff's office with news.

"A ship loads from the *Senor* Gulden's packing house," he announced.

"And is she unloading anything?" Hatfield instantly asked.

"*Si, Capitan,* she unloads barrels of rock salt and other packages."

"Could be legitimate," Hatfield said. "Used in curing hides and in meat processing, but a salt barrel would make a fine hiding place for something else. Go back on the job, Pedro, and keep your eyes skun. You might spot something else of interest."

The Mexican youth nodded and slid out again by way of the back door which opened on a little-used alley.

"Still nothing to do but wait and watch that packing house," Hatfield told the sheriff.

"You think Hawley will run his wagon in again?"

"Depends on what they deduced from the raid we made on their mule train the other night," Hatfield said. "If they really fell for the yarn you put out, that you acted on a tip that a train was coming east over the Old Spanish Trail, he may. If they are suspicious of your story, they may try another method."

"Funny they'd risk another shipment so soon," commented Oswell.

"Chances are they have no choice in the matter," Hatfield explained. "The ships bringing the stuff in are hot to get rid of it. They know the Customs people are liable to swoop down on them at anytime. No matter what the government folks may think, if no contraband is found on a vessel they have no case. So the captain is anxious to unload as quickly as possible. Once it's off his ship it's somebody else's headache."

The following day the sheriff came hurrying in, his face mirroring consternation.

"A freight wagon just came in," he announced. "But it ain't Hawley's wagon. Craig Benton and a cowhand brought it in. Benton is buyin' stuff at Harper's general store right now. What's the meanin' of that?"

"I don't know," Hatfield replied, the concentration furrow deepening between his black brows. "May mean that Benton really is in town just to buy supplies. Just a coincidence that he happened in at just this time. But it may mean something else. Reckon it's up to you to find out. Mosey around and 'accidentally' bump into Benton. You should be able to learn something from him. We've got to do something in a hurry, I figure. The way I've been in your company of late is bound to make somebody wonder."

The sheriff was gone for more than an hour. When he finally returned, he was exultant.

"It is Hawley's wagon!" he exclaimed. "Benton and one of Hawley's punchers brought it in. Benton told me Hawley is having trouble with the hand you drilled for him and is laid up. Asked Benton to do his buyin' for him today. The cowhand will take the wagon back tomorrow."

"Beginning to shape up," Hatfield said. "They'll load the wagon some time tonight."

"Shall we keep a watch on 'em and grab 'em off?" the sheriff asked.

Hatfield shook his head. "No," he said. "We'd only grab off some hired hands. There wouldn't be a thing against Gulden or Hawley. They could deny any knowledge of what was going on and make it stick. And unless we round up the whole bunch, especially Gulden who I figure is the brains of the outfit, we've just been wasting our time. Sit tight and await developments. Don't go near that stable tonight."

"What about the ship?" Oswell asked.

"It's up to the Customs folks to worry about her," Hatfield replied. "If things work right for us, you can notify them and they can take such steps as they see fit. There'll be nothing against the ship unless we can induce somebody to talk."

"Somebody will talk if I get my paws on him," the sheriff promised significantly.

Early the following afternoon the wagon rolled out of town, tarpaulins tightly lashed over its bulging load, Hawley's cowhand on the driver's seat. A couple of hours later, nearly the whole of the Rocking H cowhands rode into town and hitched their horses at the racks. Hatfield observed this incident with satisfaction.

"A good sign," he told Oswell. "They're in for a bust. Hawley wants them out of the way for the night. Those are his legitimate riders and have nothing to do with the business."

Shortly afterward the sheriff had more news.

"Samp Gulden just left," he told Hatfield. "Said he was ridin' out to the Carvel place. Nothing unusual in that, though. He visits out there frequent. But do you think I'd better have Pedro trail him? Pedro's good at that."

Hatfield shook his head. "Don't think it's necessary," he replied. "I've a good notion where he will eventually end up. Oswell, it's working out, I hope."

"What you mean by that 'I hope'?" asked the sheriff.

"I mean," Hatfield replied slowly, "that if things go as I figure they will, we should be able to drop our loop on the whole bunch. That is if they don't outsmart us. If they do, there's a good chance that neither one of us will be talking about it tomorrow," he added grimly.

The sheriff looked startled. "You mean they may set a trap for us?"

"They might," Hatfield admitted. "Depends on how suspicious they are and how desperate. I think I have it figured how they will try to outsmart us, but I could be wrong. If I am, my mistake will be something in the nature of a doctor's mistake."

"A doctor ain't allowed but one mistake," observed the sheriff. "One is usually plenty." He essayed a laugh, but it was not a very hearty one.

"Yes," Hatfield agreed, with a smile, "in this case, one will be plenty. Well, we'll have to risk it. Get your men ready for business. We ride tonight."

"Goin' to hole up for 'em in the same place as last time?" Oswell asked.

Hatfield shook his head. "If we did, we'd never see them," he predicted. "My notion is that they'll cut across Hawley's north range and hit the Old Spanish Trail far to the east. They will start from his ranchhouse, of course. Do you think you can make it to the ranchhouse from that thicket where we holed up on the Trail the other night?"

"Plumb sure I can," the sheriff said. "I've lived fifty years in this section and I know every foot of it."

"Then things should work out nicely if I've analyzed the situation rightly," Hatfield said. "If we only had Hawley to deal with everything would be comparatively simple. I think I could figure just how his mind would work. Hawley's methods are direct. But it is different with Gulden. He has plenty of savvy. A cold, calculating brain that plans every move in advance and counts possible consequences. I'm basing everything on the assumption that he will be subtle in his moves. He's already

199

showed that, at least to a certain extent. If my estimate of him is wrong, well, it'll be just too bad for us."

"Stop it, will you?" exploded the sheriff. "You've got me jumpy as a rabbit in a houndawg's mouth!"

17

The sheriff was jumpier still as they rode the north trail hours later. It was nerve wracking work riding the dark and silent track, listening and peering, ready for instant action. The openings in the chaparral were like coal-black caves from which might come at any moment a thunder of gunfire. Jim Hatfield was not especially afflicted by nerves but his palms were moist as they passed the forks that led to Jackson Hawley's ranchhouse. He breathed deep relief when the broad belt of the Old Spanish Trail lay before them.

"Now if we don't run into a corpse and cartridge occasion when we reach that thicket everything should be okay," he observed.

"Uh-huh, 'if'!" grumbled the sheriff. "No moon tonight. The hellions have got everything in their favor."

They approached the thicket with caution. In the dark tunnel formed by the encroaching growth all was silent. A couple of hundred yards and Hatfield pulled up.

"Take over, Sheriff," he said. "And make as good time as you can. We'll be lucky now if they don't pull out before we get there."

Followed an hour of hard riding over broken country. But Oswell was thoroughly familiar with the terrain and they made good speed.

"Just beyond that next grove is the ranchhouse," he finally said. "Less than a quarter of a mile from here."

They left their horses at the outer edge of the grove and stole forward under the trees. The growth thinned and the solid bulk of the ranchhouse lay before them and not more than a hundred yards distant. There was no moon but the sky was brilliant with stars and objects were dimly visible. Through chinks in the closed shutters seeped beams of light.

"Looks like they're in there, all right," Hatfield breathed. "There are the mules, loaded, and standing by the corner of the house."

"Yes, and there's a jigger with a rifle standin' guard down where the trail comes up the sag," whispered the sheriff.

Hatfield nodded. He had already spotted

the guard. "I'll see what I can make of the jigger," he said. "Think I can get within reach of him by sliding along at the edge of the brush down there. Have to chance it. He must be gotten rid of before we make a move."

He started forward in the shadow cast by the trees, then abruptly halted. The guard had suddenly alerted and was gazing down the trail. A moment more and Hatfield heard a thud of hoofs swiftly drawing nearer.

A horseman loomed. He drew rein beside the guard and engaged him in low-voiced conversation.

"It's Samp Gulden, sure as blazes!" muttered the sheriff.

"Yes," Hatfield breathed in reply. "He rode to the Carvel's place to provide himself a nice alibi if he happened to need one. This is working out fine."

Gulden rode on, dismounted in front of the veranda and mounted the steps. The door showed a glowing rectangle as it opened. Gulden passed in and it closed behind him.

Hatfield waited a moment, then began stalking the guard who had relaxed and was leaning on his rifle. In utter silence the Lone Wolf glided along the edge of the growth, keeping in the shadow and taking advantage of every bit of cover. The sweating watchers were barely able to follow his progress. Breaths caught as the guard suddenly straightened up as if he had heard something. However, after staring toward the growth a moment, he began pacing up and down, drawing close to the bristle of thicket each time before he turned.

The posse had lost sight of Hatfield. Their eyes fixed on the moving guard. They could see the white blur of his face as he strolled toward them. He reached the end of his beat and turned. Behind him a tall shadow developed form and movement. The watchers saw Hatfield glide forward on the unconscious sentry's back, saw him leap, his hands outstretched.

The two bodies merged into one, twisting and writhing. Through the tense stillness a sharp crack sounded as if a rotten stick had been snapped in two. The guard's boot heels beat a weird tattoo on the grass. Hatfield gently lowered his limbs to the ground and stole back to the shadow of the growth.

"Busted the hellion's neck with his hands," muttered the sheriff, wiping his streaming face. "That big jigger don't know his own strength!"

A moment later Hatfield came gliding back to the waiting posse. "All ready to go," he said. "We've got to work fast. Straight for the door and through it. Don't take any chances. It's a salty bunch and I don't think they'll be taken without a shooting. No telling how many are in there and there are only six of us. But the advantage of surprise should be on our side."

With quick, light steps he led the posse across the ranchhouse yard. They reached the steps and bounded up them, Hatfield in the lead. His face was set in lines bleak as the granite of the hills. On his broad breast gleamed the star of the Rangers.

Hatfield hit the door with his shoulder, his two hundred pounds of bone and muscle behind it. The door crashed open and the posse poured into the room.

Seated around the table were Samp Gulden, Jackson Hawley and five more men. Gulden was apparently outlining something. They leaped to their feet at the crash of the opening door.

Hatfield's voice rolled through the room —

"In the name of the State of Texas! I arrest Sanford Garner, otherwise known as Samp Gulden, Jackson Hawley, and others for murder. Anything you say —"

Jackson Hawley screamed with rage and terror. He went for his gun. Gulden's hand flashed down at the same instant.

Hatfield shot Hawley with his left hand, Gulden with his right. The room rocked and roared to the thunder of sixshooters.

In a moment it was all over. Gulden, Hawley and two more men were on the floor. The remaining three owlhoots were backed against the wall, hands in the air, howling for mercy.

While his men covered them with their guns, Sheriff Oswell hurried forward to secure the prisoners.

Hatfield knelt beside Samp Gulden who lay with his life draining out through his shattered lungs. He gazed up into Hatfield's face.

"Should have pulled out when you first showed up," Gulden panted through the blood that frothed his lips. "Wanted to get Benton first."

"Gulden," Hatfield said, "you can rest easy on one score. The man who killed your father died tonight."

"What!" Gulden gasped. "Benton — where — how —"

"Benton did not kill your father," Hatfield told him. "Benton is an innocent man who has lived for years under a cloud because of another man's crime. Jackson Hawley killed your father."

Gulden stared with glazing eyes. "Funny — how — things — work out!" he breathed. An expression of peace and contentment crossed his pain-wracked features. His eyes closed wearily and he was dead.

"He's gone," said Sheriff Oswell, who had joined Hatfield. "And the world hasn't lost much."

"Well, it didn't give him much, did it, the poor devil?" Hatfield replied. "So let's not think too badly of him."

He repeated Gulden's last words: "Funny how things work out. Gulden, unintentionally and indirectly, brought his father's killer to justice. If he hadn't taken Jackson Hawley in tow, figuring to use Hawley against Benton and because Hawley and his isolated ranchhouse came in handy to further his smuggling operations, Hawley would doubtless have never paid the penalty for his crime. I want to ask the prisoners a few questions. I've a notion they'll be ready to talk."

The prisoners, their souls numbed by fear of the rope, talked volubly.

"Just as I figured," Hatfield told the sheriff. "After he was discharged by the packing company, Gulden stayed on with the robbing and smuggling outfit he'd gotten in with, finally getting control of the band. He was a smart man but his mind was warped and twisted by the bitter tragedies of his youth. His whole life was an obsession to take vengeance on the man he believed killed his father and drove his mother to suicide. That's why he worked back this way. He conceived the idea of using his packing house as a receiving station for the smuggled goods. He learned about Jackson Hawley's early outlaw connections and induced Hawley to throw in with him. He planned to use Hawley against Benton, playing on Benton's insane hatred for anything that had to do with sheep. Of course it was Gulden's men, directed by Hawley, who killed Tom Carvel's herders. Gulden figured the relatives of the herders and the other sheep men would get Benton sooner or later if he could keep fanning the fires. The cattle and sheep trouble here played right into his hands."

"Wonder why he didn't just shoot Benton and have it done with," remarked the sheriff.

"Gulden wasn't the killer type," Hatfield replied. "That would have been Hawley's way. The subtle, indirect method appealed to Gulden's nature. Also, he wanted to keep in the clear himself. He had no desire to stretch rope just to gratify his hate. But when his men killed a Ranger and the deputy sheriffs up in the Trinity country, his neck was in a noose and he knew it. You know that under Texas law, if a murder is perpetrated in the course of the commission of a crime, all involved in said crime are adjudged equally guilty of the murder. Well, it's finished, and I've a notion it will mean the end of the cattle and sheep trouble, too. When he learns the truth of things, Craig Benton will come down off his perch and eat crow."

"Uh-huh, I've a notion the stubborn old shorthorn will," Oswell agreed. "He's not a bad jigger at heart."

Hatfield nodded. "Well, reckon we might as well head for town," he said. "I'll be riding in the morning. Captain Bill will have another little chore lined up for me by the time I get back to the post. I want to stop off at the Carvel place before I leave."

Hatfield spent part of the following day at the Carvel ranch. Gypsy walked to the trail with him when he departed.

"Will you be coming back to me some day?" she asked.

Hatfield smiled down at her. "A Ranger

rides a lone trail and a long one," he said. "But there never was a trail so long that it doesn't have a turning. Yes, I'll come back some day."

She watched him ride away to where duty called and danger and new adventure waited, tall and graceful atop his great golden horse, the sunlight etching his stern profile in flame.

"A woman's destiny," she murmured as the distances swallowed him up. "A woman's destiny — to wait!"

We hope you have enjoyed this Large Print book. Other Thorndike, Wheeler or Chivers Press Large Print books are available at your library or directly from the publishers.

For more information about current and upcoming titles, please call or write, without obligation, to:

Publisher
Thorndike Press
295 Kennedy Memorial Drive
Waterville, ME   04901
Tel. (800) 223-1244

Or visit our Web site at:
www.gale.com/thorndike
www.gale.com/wheeler

OR

Chivers Large Print
published by BBC Audiobooks Ltd
St James House, The Square
Lower Bristol Road
Bath BA2 3BH
England
Tel. +44(0) 800 136919
email: bbcaudiobooks@bbc.co.uk
www.bbcaudiobooks.co.uk

All our Large Print titles are designed for easy reading, and all our books are made to last.

PRAISE FOR

'A ROLLERCOASTER OF SUSPENSE AND SURPRISE ...'
Guardian

'FUNNY, THOUGHTFUL ... WISE AND LIVELY...
ANOTHER COUP FROM COWELL'
The Sunday Times

'HIGHLY RECOMMENDED ... A GREAT NEW WORLD'
The New York Times

'THE DETAIL OF COWELL'S WORLD IS A DELIGHT ...
THIS ONE WILL RUN AND RUN'
Observer

'COWELL IS MOVING TOWARDS NATIONAL TREASURE'
Big Issue

'A FUNNY, CLEVER ADVENTURE'
Sunday Express

'THIS IS A TRIUMPHANT RETURN FOR COWELL'
The Telegraph

this book is dedicated to dearest
CLEMENTINE
with so much love

HODDER CHILDREN'S BOOKS

First published in Great Britain in 2018 by Hodder and Stoughton

1 3 5 7 9 10 8 6 4 2

A CIP catalogue record for this book
is available from the British Library.

ISBN 978 1 444 94140 1

Printed and bound in Great Britain by CPI Group (UK) Ltd, Croydon, CR0 4YY

The paper and board used in this book are made from wood from responsible sources.

MIX
Paper from
responsible sources
FSC® C104740
FSC
www.fsc.org

Hodder Children's Books
An imprint of
Hachette Children's Group
Part of Hodder and Stoughton
Carmelite House
50 Victoria Embankment
London EC4Y 0DZ

An Hachette UK Company
www.hachette.co.uk

www.hachettechildrens.co.uk

The Wizards of ONCE

Twice Magic

written and illustrated by

CRESSIDA COWELL

Hodder
Children's
Books

This is a story with two heroes.

The girl, Wish, is a Warrior, BUT she has a Strange and powerful Magic-that-Works-on-Iron.

The boy, Xar, is a Wizard, but he has a Witchstain on his hand that may be impossible to remove..

QUERED

TERRITORIES

Warrior Capital

THIS WAY

The Sweet Track

Iron Warrior Fort

THE

QUEENDOM
of
SYCHORAX

WARRIOR

EMPIRE

Queen Sychorax's New Wall (built on the

WILDWOODS

remains of the LAST Wall...)

Ragged River

Prologue

Imagine an age of giants.

It was a long, long time ago, in a British Isles so old it did not know it was the British Isles yet, when the country was all wildwood, and there were two types of humans fighting in the woodlands.

The WIZARDS, who had lived in this forest for as long as memory, and were as Magic as the wood itself, and rode on the back of the Giant Snowcats. And the WARRIORS, who hunted the Magic down with bright swords and fire, so they could build their forts and their fields and their new modern world.

The Warriors were winning, for their weapons were made of IRON. . .

. . . *and IRON was the only thing that Magic would not work on.*

This is the story of a young boy Wizard and a young girl Warrior, who were both cheerful and hopeful and full of good ideas, but they had been taught since birth to hate each other like poison. It is the tale of how they met, and learnt to be friends and to see things from each other's point of view, and it really wants to be a HAPPY story . . . but unfortunately in the course of their last joyful adventure . . .

They accidentally let the KINGWITCH out
of the Stone where he had been imprisoned so safely
for century upon century . . .

And WITCHES had returned to the wonder of the
wildwoods.

Now, I do not want to scare you, dear Reader. But Witches had feathered wings, and acid blood, and every clawed hand ended in five talons as long and as slice-sharp as a freshly sharpened sword.

Which would be *fine* if they were well-intentioned.

But Witches were the kind of evil that hates all things good and eats the hearts of robins and wants to destroy the world and everything in it.

And the Kingwitch commanded them all . . .

Nobody knows where the Kingwitch was now hidden. But *I* do.

I want the boy, thought the Kingwitch, in cramped, wicked thoughts. *I want the Boy-who-is-Very-Nearly-Mine, for HE can help bring me the Girl-who-has-Magic-that-Works-on-Iron . . . for if I GET that Magic, I shall at last be invincible . . .*

But fear not, dear Reader! This must be impossible. Xar had been locked up in the great prison of Gormincrag. And nobody gets *out* of Gormincrag, which may not be very nice for Xar, but it also follows, as night follows day, that the Kingwitch and his Witches cannot get *in*.

And as for Wish, why Wish's scary mother, the great Warrior queen Sychorax, has built a gigantic Wall across the entire western edge of her kingdom, a Wall so high that even a Longstepper High-Walker Giant couldn't see over it on tiptoes, to protect her people from the attacks of the Witches.

So our heroes can't possibly meet each other, or the Kingwitch, in a story as short as this one.

It was extremely unlikely that they would ever have met in the first place.

It happened ONCE.

Surely it couldn't happen TWICE?

I am a character
in this story...
who sees everything,
knows everything.
I will not tell you
who I am.
Have You GUESSED yet?

Follow the ink path of the
story
(don't get lost,
These woods are DANGEROUS.)

GORMINCRAG PRISON

Gormincrag prison is surrounded by a smoken forest in a sea filled with Bladder bones, Bloody Bones and Daggerfins — things are oozing skulls of the battlements

NOBODY gets out of the terrible prison of

GORMINCRAG →

Sea of
↙ Skulls

1. Escape from Gormincrag is Impossible

It was a quarter past midnight, four weeks before Midwinter's End Eve, and a thirteen-year-old boy was dangling precariously from a disintegrating home-made rope hanging from outside the darkest tower of Gormincrag, the Rehabilitation Centre for the Re-Education of Dark Magic and Wicked Wizards.

(That, by the way, is a long and fancy name for a jail, and not just any old jail, the most secure and impregnable jail in the wildwoods.)

The boy's name was Xar – (which is pronounced 'Zar' – I don't know why, spelling is weird) and he really, really, *really* should not have been there.

He was supposed to be INSIDE the prison, not OUTSIDE it, dangling fifty feet above sea level from one of the windows. That's one of the most important rules about prisons, and Xar really should have known that.

But Xar was not the kind of boy who followed the rules.

Xar *acted* first, and *thought* later, and this was exactly what had led him to be put in the Gormincrag Rehabilitation Centre in the first place, and given him

the reputation of being the
naughtiest, wildest boy born into
the Wizard kingdom in about
four generations.

See if you think that reputation
is justified . . .

In the past week, for example, Xar
had:

*. . . put what was supposed to be Sleeping
Potion into the Rogrebreath guards' wine, but it
turned out to be Cursing Potion instead . . . glued the
bottoms of the entire Drood High Command to their chairs in
the hope that it would give him time for a quick getaway - but
forgot to glue the chairs to the floor, so the Droods just ran
after him with chairs stuck to their bottoms . . . treated*

himself to some stolen Invisibility Potion, but unfortunately
it had only made his HEAD disappear, giving the Drood in
charge of Reprogramming a terrible shock because he imagined
on visiting Xar's cell that the prison had been invaded by
headless GHOSTS . . .

None of these disobedient things had been
intentional, exactly. They had all just happened by
accident, in the course of him trying to escape, for
even though Xar was a happy-go-lucky cheerful sort of
person, two months of imprisonment had given even *his*
high spirits a bit of a battering, and his quiff of hair had
drooped a little under the pressure, and he had
been feeling, at times, a little desperate.

Gormincrag was well known to be
impossible to escape from, but Xar never
let a little thing like impossibility put him
off. So although to an outsider his present
predicament might have looked pretty bad,
Xar was remarkably pleased with himself for
a person who was hanging on to a crumbling rope
swaying violently above seas known to be infested with
such dreadful monsters as Blunderbouths, Daggerfins,
and Bloody Barbeards.

His wide-awake eyes were bright with excitement
and hope.

'You see!' Xar whispered triumphantly to his

Squeezjoos

companions. 'What did I tell you? We're doing brilliantly! We've *nearly* escaped already!'

And Xar was right, they had really done a very good job to get this far.

The Gormincrag Detention Centre for the Re-education of Dark Magic and Wicked Wizards had been designed to imprison some of the most terrifying monsters in the entire Magical world. Bogeymen. Ogres of all sizes and savageries. Jack o' Kents, Bugbears, Kelpies, Grim Annises, you name it, and even, once upon a time, dare I say it, WITCHES, that were once extinct, and had recently re-emerged in that part of the wildwoods.

NO ONE, no Dark-sprite, no Rogrebreath however large and terrifying, no Wicked Wizard of spells the most fiendish, had EVER escaped from Gormincrag before. People had tried of course, and the legends of brave but failed escape attempts from Gormincrag were told from sprite to sprite across the years. But no one had

Bumbleboozle

ever successfully made it out of there alive.

Even if, by some extraordinary chance, you made it beyond the prison perimeter without the skulls screaming, the grim towers of Gormincrag were built on seven islands set in a sea called prettily '*the Sea of Skulls*', and the treacherous waves would get you, or those vicious merfolk, the Bloody Barbeards, would swim out of their holes in the Drowned Forest on the seafloor and get you, and bring you back.

As the son of a King Enchanter, and a boy with a great deal of personal charisma, Xar had quite a few followers.

At the moment he was accompanied by five sprites (Tiffinstorm, Timeloss, Hinkypunk, Ariel, and Mustardthought) – and these were beautiful, fierce-looking creatures, resembling a cross between a very small human and an angry insect, and three hairy fairies, (Squeezjoos, Bumbleboozle, and The Baby), smaller, more bee-like animals, who were too young to have climbed into their cocoons and metamorphosed into proper adult sprites yet.

Sprites can light up like stars in the night-time, but these ones did not want to be detected at the moment, so they had subdued the light of their little bodies to the very dimmest of glows.

The
Baby

15

These sprites all belonged to Xar, and loyally, quietly, invisibly, they had smuggled themselves in to Gormincrag to try and help him escape.

'Yous right, Master!' Squeezjoos, one of the hairy fairies, whispered back. Squeezjoos was a tiny little six-legged creature, larger than a bumblebee but still so small he could fit into your hand, and he was buzzing excitedly around Xar's head. 'Yous ALWAYS right! That'ss why youss the Leader and you never leads uss into any trouble! Oo! What's this fasscintressting cave?'

This 'fasscintressting cave' was in fact a large skull with its mouth open. Squeezjoos buzzed in to investigate and the mouth snapped shut with an ominous clang, and the eyeholes squeezed tight closed as if they still had lids on them. 'Helloooo?' buzzed Squeezjoos in anxious echoes from within. 'Helloooo? I think I iss stuck!' The sprites nearly fell out of the air they were laughing so much, but Xar intervened in quick alarm, hissing, 'Don't go over the boundary of the battlements anybody! There's a Magical forcefield around this castle, and it's fine getting IN, but you can't get across it to get OUT !'

At some considerable danger to himself, because the skull was just out of reach, and he had to tie the end of the rope to his ankle and dangle upside down to get his

17

I can't look...

hands on it, Xar then very, very carefully and delicately released the mouth bone of the skull so that Squeezjoos could buzz out triumphantly squeaking, 'I is fine! Don't worry everyone! I is FINE!'

And then Xar swung himself back onto a safer ledge again, and explained to his interested companions that those skulls were the screaming kind, and they were one of the final defences of Gormincrag.

I is FINE!

If you put one finger tip beyond the perimeter of the prison, the skulls would open up their mouths and scream blood-curdling yells, which would wake the guards of Gormincrag and bring them down upon you.

This was typical of Xar. Although he had spent his entire young life leading his followers into considerable trouble, to do him justice, he always tried his hardest to get them OUT of it, even if it put him personally in great peril.

Xar was also accompanied by a talking raven – who had his wings over his eyes, such was his horror at the whole dangling-upside-down-and-rescuing-hairy-fairies-from-screaming-skulls episode – and a seven-and-a-half-foot Loner Raving Fangmouth werewolf called Lonesome, who made anxious grunting noises when Xar mentioned the Gormincrag guards.

Xar had met Lonesome in the prison, and while it is not really advisable to make friends with Loner Raving Fangmouth werewolves, neither Xar nor the werewolf had a lot of choice in the matter. They both wanted to escape.

The werewolf gave a smothered howl of discontent.

'What is the werewolf saying?' asked the raven.

The talking raven was called Caliburn, and he would have been a handsome bird, but unfortunately it was his job to keep Xar out of trouble, and the worry and general impossibility of this hopeless mission meant his feathers kept falling out.

'I think he's saying, why are we heading in *this* direction?' said Xar.

Xar was the only one of them who had been taught werewolf language, but Xar wasn't great at concentrating in class, and the problem with werewolves is they did mumble their words, so sometimes you could mistake a grunt for a gurgle, or an oooarrghh for an eerrggagh, and completely misunderstand what they were talking about.

'We're going *this* way,' explained Xar, 'because we're just going to drop into the Drood Commander's Room . . . it's an important step in our escape . . .'

The werewolf gave a smothered howl of horror and waved his shaggy paws around with such alarm that he nearly fell off the rope.

'You shouldn't be escaping! And we shouldn't be helping you!' said Caliburn in a flurry of anxiety, 'but surely if we *are* helping you to escape, the idea would be to do it *quietly*? Crusher and the animals are waiting for us down at the bottom of the Western battlements . . .'

(Crusher was a Longstepper High Walker Giant, and he and the wolves, the snowcats and the bear were also Xar's companions.)

'We should be joining Crusher and the others!'

Caliburn pointed out. 'Hopping over the back of the wall, without telling anyone, not presenting ourselves to the head of the prison for a jolly little chat and a cup of herbal tea!'

'Yes, well, that's why no one has ever got out of this armpit of a jail before,' said Xar. 'How many times have YOU tried to escape from here, Lonesome?'

The werewolf mumbled something that might have been 'twenty-three' . . .

'You see?' said Xar. 'Trust me, everyone! I have a plan that could just be the cunning-est, most brilliant and daring escape plan in the entire *history* of the wildwoods . . .'

Xar had a lot of good qualities, but modesty wasn't one of them.

Inch by inch, the little party crept down the ropes, landed on the windowsill outside the Drood Commander's Room, and peered inside.

The room might have been the shape of a star, or a circle, or a pentagon, who knew? For the walls had a habit of moving around while you were looking at them, and the floor looked like the sea, and the ceiling might have been the sky. It was enough to make you feel a little bit sick just to look at it.

The only still point in the room was a gigantic desk.

Three Wizards were sitting around the desk, talking.

One of the Wizards was the Drood Commander of Gormincrag, and Xar pointed to the spelling staff the Drood Commander was holding.

'That's the reason we're here . . .' whispered Xar. *'Because the Drood Commander's spelling staff controls everything in this Castle.'*

'Ohhh no . . . oh noo . . .' whispered Caliburn the raven, in a frenzy of alarm. 'Don't tell me that your plan is to steal the Staff-That-Commands-the-Castle?'

Xar nodded. That was indeed his plan.

'Itsss brilliant! Is brilliant!' squeaked Squeezjoos, buzzing around in such an over-excited fashion that he was very nearly sick.

'Sssshhhhhhhh . . .' everyone else whispered back.

The werewolf gave a small grunt that might have been approval. It was quite a good plan actually. At least, it was something the werewolf had never tried before.

But as Xar peered into the room, the shaggy weight of the werewolf's fur on his shoulder, he started so violently he nearly fell off the windowsill.

For he suddenly recognised the other Wizards who were talking to the Drood Commander of Gormincrag.

'*My father* . . . and my *brother* . . .' whispered Xar.

It was indeed Xar's father, the Great Wizard Enchanter, Encanzo the Magnificent, King of Wizards, and Xar's older brother, Looter.

Xar could feel a mixture of fear and shame rising within him, starting with a queasy flip of his stomach, and then bubbling up into a hot flush of shame.

When Xar had been arrested by the Drood Guards, Encanzo and Looter had been travelling, on a mission to the Witch mountains, to find out how bad the threat from the Witches was.

So they did not yet know why Xar was in here . . . and Xar really, really didn't want them to find that out . . .

Xar could just about hear what the Wizards were saying, if he leaned in through the window.

'Your Droods have crept into my kingdom while I was away and stolen my son from me!' raged Encanzo. 'I demand that you release him this instant!'

Xar's father, Encanzo, was a tall, immensely powerful Wizard, of such Magic strength that it was curiously difficult to look at him. His outline was blurred by Magic, shifting, moving, and great steaming clouds of enchantment drifted off his head as he spoke. He was looking a little weary, for he was at his wits' end, trying to lead his people in the fight against the Witches.

The Drood Commander was taller still, a rake of a man, spitefully thin, and with eyebrows so long he had braided them. He had grown so old in the forest that there was something of the tree about him. His fingers

had bent and twisted into twigs, and his face was as
green and wrinkled as ancient bark.

The Drood Commander was well
intentioned, but he was convinced that he
was right about absolutely everything,
and everyone else was absolutely wrong.
Over time that can make you bitter
rather than gentle, for whatever
we are tends to concentrate as
we get older, and it had distilled
him into a pungent, poisonous
drink indeed. Cross, judgmental
little eyes glittered
in his tree-bark
wrinkled face, and
his claw-like hands
closed jealously over
his spelling staff.

'I am not keeping
Xar here for my
own amusement!'
snapped the Drood
Commander. 'Your
wretched son has
completely disrupted
my prison!

The Drood Commander

IS SO FUNNY!

He has;

> . . . *for no reason whatsoever, cut off some tail hair of the Great Howling Hairy Hindogre while it was sleeping in its cell, and the Great Howling Hairy Hindogre is still howling in fury five days later, keeping everyone in the western tower of the prison awake all night . . .*

'Ah,' said Encanzo thoughtfully, 'is that the distant moaning sound I can hear?'

'That *wasn't* for no reason!' objected Xar in a whisper to his companions, 'I needed that hair so I could escape in an absolutely foolproof Bigfoot-soldier-with-a-beard disguise . . .'

'*Nobodysss* going to think you're old enough to have a beard, Xar!' objected Caliburn. 'And Bigfoot soldiers are at least six feet tall!'

'That *was* a slight flaw in the foolproof plan,' admitted Xar.

It wasn't the only flaw.

When their winter coats

tee hee he hee.

come in, Howling Hairy Hindogres are an attractive shade of midnight blue, and Xar had been caught within about five minutes because the Drood Guards agreed with Caliburn that there was no such thing as a five-foot tall Bigfoot with a bright-blue beard.

The Drood Commander was really getting going now, with a long list of Xar's offences:

. . . Put itching powder in the knickers of my Guards on patrol . . . stolen a prison Guard's cape and hood and dropped it in the vampire-dog pit . . . dropped the stinky socks of a Rogrebreath Guard into the breakfast porridge so that it tasted disgustingly of rotten eggs . . .

'Accidents . . . all accidents and misunderstandings . . .' whispered Xar from the window.

'And then, out of sheer wanton mischief,' the Drood Commander ended, 'he glued the behinds of Drood High Command to their chairs while they sat quietly and peacefully eating their dinner! Indefensible, inexplicable, *inexcusable* behaviour!'

This last incident had particularly upset the Drood Commander, for he was a man of great dignity, and he had not liked having to visit the Sanitorium with a chair stuck firmly to his bottom. He had draped a cloak over it, but it was quite a large chair and the Rogrebreaths, still stuffed to the tips of their hairy ears with Cursing Potion, had made quite a few personal remarks that still stung when the Drood Commander remembered them.

'That was quite funny,' admitted Xar, smiling at the memory of it, 'but that, too, was an accident! They shouldn't have locked me up if they didn't want me to try and escape!'

'All of these things you are describing are just disobediences,' said Xar's father Encanzo, with relief. 'Annoying, I grant you, and Xar ought to have grown out of such stuff, but there's nothing *wicked* in those things . . . he'll just be getting fed up with being in here, and I don't blame him, quite frankly . . .'

'I do have a prison to run,' said the Drood, his lips pursing. 'I cannot let your son completely disrupt it. He is here because he represents a severe threat to the entire Magic community,' continued the Drood Commander, getting to his feet. 'But I can show you he is safe. Come with me . . .'

All around the Drood Commander's room were gigantic mirrors, and they were not normal mirrors. If you looked into those mirrors you could see into every single room in the castle. So at any point the Drood Commander of Gormincrag could know exactly what was going on, all around the prison.

The Drood Commander pointed at one of the mirrors, and the mirror clouded up, before gradually showing the view inside a small cell in the high security block.

'It's empty,' said Encanzo the King Enchanter.

The cell was indeed, as Encanzo said, empty.

The Drood Commander stared at the empty cell in astonishment. 'I don't understand it!' said the Drood Commander. 'That is most definitely Xar's cell . . . Where on earth is he?'

'I thought you were supposed to be the most secure, maximum high-security prison in the wildwoods?' snapped Encanzo. 'And you are telling me, that you have somehow *mislaid* my thirteen-year-old son?'

'This is most unusual . . .' blustered the Drood Commander, blinking at all the mirrors so that they rapidly clouded up to reveal cell after cell, each one containing a captured Rogre, or Grim Annis, or Venge-sprite . . . but absolutely no sign of Xar. 'Of course there must be some perfectly reasonable explanation for all this . . . the Guards must have moved him without telling me . . .'

'Dear, oh dear . . .' purred Encanzo, 'that's not very organised is it? Rather poor communication with your guards, I'd say . . . I repeat, Commander, *where is my son?*'

'Here I am,' said a voice behind them.

Unfortunately, when the three Wizards stepped away from the Drood Commander's desk and stood in

front of the mirrors,
they had forgetfully left
their Spelling Staffs lying on
the desk behind them, in full
view of Xar who had an empty
pouch, just the right size for a
couple more staffs.

So now when they both slo-o-owly
turned round . . .

. . . *there was Xar.*

He was accompanied by a seven-foot werewolf,
standing by the desk. Above Xar's head buzzed his
sprites, and a very guilty looking Caliburn.

There was a sprite word for the way that the Drood
Commander and Encanzo and Looter were looking at
Xar in that moment.

And the sprite word for it is: 'goggle-smarked'.
Absolutely 'flabberwastedly, jiggerdroppingly goggle-
smarked', to be precise.

Ariel

Squeezjoos

The Baby

Bumbleboozle

Xar's Sprites

Tiffinstorm

Mustardthought

Timeloss

Hinkypunk

2. Did I Mention that Escape from Gormincrag is Impossible?

'Hello, father,' said Xar defiantly, annoyed to find himself trembling. 'Hello, Xar,' said the Enchanter calmly. 'We were just looking for you, and here you are ... What are you doing?'

'I'm escaping,' said Xar.

'Escape is impossible from Gormincrag!' blustered the Drood Commander.

Both Xar and the Enchanter ignored him.

'If you're escaping,' said the Enchanter thoughtfully, 'then what are you doing *here*? I would have thought that the Drood Commander's office is not the perfect place to come to if you want to make an escape.'

'That's what *I* said!' said Caliburn in agreement.

'I suggest you put the staffs down,' said the Enchanter, 'and then we can talk reasonably. How are you? Are you all right?'

For Xar was looking shaken, and somewhat worn. His quiff of hair had drooped, and there was something a little desperate about his usual cheeky swagger. He looked like a thirteen-year-old boy who had got himself into a LOT of trouble.

'What have you Droods been doing to him?'

snapped Encanzo, turning to the Drood Commander. 'How DARE you treat the son of a king in this way?'

'Ask the boy what he's done to be put in here,' sneered the Drood Commander. 'And then perhaps you will see why we acted as we did. Go on! Ask him!'

'Why did they put you in here, Xar?' said Encanzo calmly.

Xar would not answer his father's question.

He could not look his father in the eye. He could feel himself burning red with embarrassment.

'Aren't you going to tell your father the truth?' jeered the Drood Commander. 'Are you . . . ashamed?'

Xar gripped the spelling staff tighter. 'Don't tell him!' pleaded Xar.

'He is here,' shouted the Drood Commander, 'because he has been using the Magic of a Witch!'

There was an uncomfortable silence.

'Is this true?' said the Enchanter, and it was every bit as bad as Xar had dreaded. He sounded so very, very disappointed.

Unfortunately, it was, indeed, completely true.

Wizards are not born with Magic, the Magic comes in when they are about twelve years old. Xar was thirteen, and his Magic still hadn't come in, and that was deeply embarrassing, particularly for a boy like Xar who had a lot of pride. The son of a King Enchanter to be a boy without Magic? Inconceivable!

So six months earlier, Xar had taken desperate steps to get hold of some Magic of his own.

Desperate, stupid, *dangerous* steps.

He had deliberately pricked his hand with Witchblood, so that the blood mixed with his own, and he was able to use the Magic of the Witch.

On his right hand there was a tell-tale green cross that marked where the Witchblood had gone in. He had managed to conceal this for a while, but the Droods had a way of knowing when people were using dark Magic, and they had taken Xar from his father's fort while Encanzo was away.

'That arm the boy is holding behind his back has a Witch-stain he has been using to perform banned Magic,' said the Drood Commander. 'I'm surprised,' he continued, 'that an all-powerful Enchanter like yourself did not notice your own son using dark Magic, right under your nose . . .'

How indeed had Xar's father not noticed?

Well, the truth is, sometimes parents do not want to believe the worst about their children, even if that worst is staring them right in the face.

'Show me your hand,' said Encanzo, although one look at Xar's guilty face let him know that the Drood Commander was telling the truth.

Quickly, to get it over with, Xar brought his arm out from behind his back, and took off the glove that he wore to conceal the Witch-stain.

'It's not as bad as it looks,' said Xar, hopefully.

Encanzo stiffened with shock, his outline pulsing with furious energy.

It was a gruesome sight.

The sprites hissed with horror when they saw it, and little Squeezjoos stuck his tail between his legs, crouching down and trembling in the air.

'Poor Xar ...' whispered Squeezjoos.

The green of the Witch-stain had moved beyond Xar's hand, up his wrist, and looked as if it was spreading further, like a creeping bruise, or ivy slowly growing around and strangling a tender young tree.

Poor Xar indeed.

He had been well punished for his one moment of madness in a midnight wood.

'Of all the stupid things you have ever done, Xar,' said Encanzo, bitingly, 'this is undoubtedly the stupidest.'

'I told you, Father!' jeered Looter. 'A Wizard with *no Magic*, who is using the Magic of a Witch! He's a disgrace to our family! No wonder they locked him up!'

Xar could feel himself going red with shame, and tears pricking away at the back of his eyelids.

'It was because my Magic should have come in!' explained Xar. 'You don't know what it's like, Father, growing up without Magic when everyone else has it!'

'Oh, Xar . . .' said the Enchanter, shaking his head. He could feel himself getting angry. Why did Xar always put him in these situations? He had come to demand Xar's release, only to find his son had been put in jail for perfectly understandable reasons.

'Why didn't you tell me you had this Magic, and then I could have helped you try and get rid of it?' asked Encanzo, his brow descending like a thunder cloud. 'And you, Caliburn? Ariel? Why did *no one* tell me about this?'

Caliburn looked even guiltier. 'The boy trusts us,' said Caliburn. 'We cannot betray him.'

'You made us Xar's advisorsss, not his jailersss . . .'

"It's hot as bad as it looks," said Xar

hissed Ariel, moving protectively towards Xar's shoulder, and showing his fangs in a snarl at the Enchanter.

It was Encanzo's turn to redden. '*I* did not jail him!'

'Well, thank goodness *we* jailed him!' said the Drood Commander. 'The boy represents a severe threat to the entire Magic community, and until we can get rid of the dark Magic he has stolen, he cannot possibly be released.'

'But why can't you help me *control* the Witchblood magic?' said Xar. 'I can command it, if you teach me . . . it's fine . . .'

'Witchblood Magic is almost impossible to control,' said the Drood Commander. 'Particularly for a boy like you, selfish and impulsive—'

'He's *thirteen*!' protested Encanzo. 'Were *you* never young and a bit foolish, Commander? Did *you* never make

"I promise I'll make everything right again"

40

a mistake, and regret it?'

'I was once young, but never foolish,' said the Drood Commander, lips pursing.

Xar turned to his father.

'I'm sorry, Father, I didn't mean for this to happen. I'm sorry I got this dark Magic . . . I'm sorry I didn't tell you about it . . . I'm sorry for everything, I really, really am . . . ' he said, hanging his head sadly, and he did mean that.

But Xar could never stay sad for long.

His face brightened, and he carried on eagerly, 'But I promise you, I'll make everything right again! I'm going to make you SO PROUD of me!'

"I'm going to make you So PROUD of me, father!"

'I'm *already* proud of you!' said Encanzo, now seriously alarmed. 'Exasperated sometimes . . . Infuriated . . . but what are you planning to do now?'

'I'm going to make amends,' said Xar. 'I'm going to break out of here and destroy the Witches on my own, and *that* will get rid of the Witch-stain!'

There was a stunned silence. Encanzo tried not to laugh.

But Looter didn't try.

Looter was a lot bigger than Xar, and he was handsome and clever and smug and good at everything, including Magic.

'Oh, come ON, little brother!' Looter laughed. 'You can't possibly do that!'

'Why not?' Xar asked belligerently.

YOU?
THE BOY
of DESTINY?

HA! HA! HA!
scoffed Looter

42

'Because you're just one small, stupid little kid!' scoffed Looter. 'This is all part of Xar's silly idea that he is some kind of boy of destiny.'

'I AM the boy of destiny!' cried Xar, punching the air.

Looter and the Drood Commander laughed even harder at that, and now even Encanzo joined in.

'Oh, *don't laugh* . . .' begged Caliburn, putting his wings over his eyes. 'Think of Xar's dignity . . . Don't laugh, Encanzo!'

'It is a worthy ambition, Xar,' said Encanzo, hastily recollecting himself, 'and I'm impressed that you are truly sorry, and you want to make amends. It is a sign that at last you are growing up. But trust me, I will make amends *for* you, and try and get rid of the Witches on your behalf. Just give me the staff.'

Calmly, Encanzo the Enchanter held out his hand.
Xar paused.

'So you will get rid of the Witches?' he asked warily.

'It could be impossible to do that entirely,' admitted Encanzo. 'But there may be other ways of removing that Witch-stain . . .'

'And you'll let me help?' Xar asked. 'You'll get these Droods to set me free?'

'I'm sorry, Xar, but the Drood is right. Until we have got rid of that Witch-stain, you mustn't leave the safety of Gormincrag,' said Encanzo. 'The Droods are the greatest Wizards in the wildwoods, and if anyone can find a way of removing that Witch-stain, *they* can.'

'I can *control* the Witch-stain, even if they can't remove it!' said Xar, backing away from his father. 'Why are you so gloomy about everything? Why do you listen to this Drood here rather than me? *Caliburn* thinks I can get better. *Caliburn* believes in me.'

'Caliburn and Ariel have shown themselves to be completely unworthy advisors!' snapped the Enchanter.

'They're better advisors than YOU!' roared Xar. '*You'll* NEVER get rid of the Witches, for you are too COWARDLY to fight Warriors or Witches with the strength of our ancestors!'

The Enchanter lost his temper.

'You will stop this nonsense, Xar!' yelled the Enchanter. 'You will stay here until the Witch-stain can be removed, and you learn self-control and your place in this world. I am your father and I ORDER you to hand over that spelling staff this instant!'

Xar backed away, his brows descending thunderously. 'You don't trust me! You think I should be in jail! You think I am selfish! Well, I can be good! I can make amends! *I'LL* SHOW *YOU!*'

Encanzo realised his mistake. 'No! I'm sorry, Xar, I do trust you, it's just that I think you need help. You can't do this on your own!'

But it was too late. The moment when Xar might have changed path was lost.

The Drood Commander blinked, two swift blinks that brought out a bolt of Magic from his eyes, speeding towards his staff that Xar was holding.

There was instant pandemonium.

Don't perform Magic
when you're angry, Xar!

Xar pointed
the staff at the
Drood Commander, and a great blast of
Magic came out of it, a blast so wild that it
stopped the Commander's Magic in its tracks.

Looter leapt forward to try to wrest the staff out of
Xar's hands, but Xar pointed the staff, keeping as calm
as possible and whispering the words of a freezing spell
that he vaguely remembered from one of his spelling
lessons.

After so many years of trying to perform Magic
with no results, Xar could not help his heart lifting in

joyous triumph as he felt the extraordinary tingling
feeling, like pins and needles, in his right arm, that built
and built, until the Magic came blasting out in a great
satisfactory electric burst, hitting Looter in the stomach.
Looter stopped, frozen, mid-action, mouth open, arms
stretched forward.

'You see!' said Xar, glowing with happy pride. '*I
can do it!*'

But hardly had the confident words left his
mouth, before the frozen Looter's nose melted
and swelled, grew to twice its original size
and dripped violet-coloured snot on
the floor. Then Looter's

entire body shrunk into something small and furry
that is hard to describe except to say no one had ever
seen anything like it before.

WHOOPS. Um...,
I am
So sorry
Looter.

'Oh!' said Xar, in surprise. 'I'm not sure what happened there ...'

'*What have you done? Is this your idea of being good?*' raged Encanzo.

'It was an accident,' said Xar, panting and shaking the staff, as if it was a bottle of potion that wasn't working, and as if it were all the staff's fault, and not his.

Shaking the Staff-That-Commands-the-Castle wasn't a very good idea. Magic ricocheted madly around the room with such curving, bending ferocity that the Drood Commander's desk burst into flames.

The castle responded instantly to the flaming desk, for the building was equipped with the very latest in Magical defences. Rain poured out of the Magical ceiling above with such intensity that, not only did it put out the fire, but the Wizards were drenched within seconds, stumbling about trying to see through the downpour and the clouds of smoke.

'Oh dear!' said Xar.

'Escape!' roared the werewolf, picking up Xar. (Actually he said, 'Gruntsnar-ugh-rowarr,' but that

is what he meant.) The werewolf leapt up and out
the window, followed by Xar's sprites and Caliburn,
dropping feathers like dark rain.

'*I'll be good, Father, I promise!*' shouted Xar from the
windowsill.

And then, 'Shut!' cried Xar, waving the Staff-That-
Commands-the-Castle.

The - Creature - that
Once - was - Looter

← 3 ears

hairy
bottom

long
dribbly
nose →

And the window turned into wall behind them like the closing of an eye.

The Enchanter and the Drood Commander were too late with their next bolts of Magic. They rebounded harmlessly off the window-that-was-now-wall.

The two Wizards staggered towards the mirrors. The Drood Commander winked again, and the mirrors flicked through views of the outside of the castle, until they could see in one of them Xar and the werewolf, hanging by a couple of home-made ropes from the exterior.

'They can't get away . . . Watch!' said the Drood Commander.

As Xar and the werewolf edged towards the outskirts of the castle, the skulls begin to open their eyes. And as the tip of the Staff-That-Commands-the-Castle got nearer to the barrier Xar had been so careful to avoid touching earlier, the skulls opened their mouths, and an unbearable screaming noise – like five hundred foxes cornered by dogs – came out of the toothy skinless grins. It was a noise so loud that they could see the sprites shaking in the air, their lights going on and off with the soundwaves.

'There!' said the Drood Commander, pointing with satisfaction at the mirrors. 'The Drood Guards are out.'

Sure enough, you could see the winged forms of cockatrices flying up from the guardhouses situated within the castle walls. On the back of every cockatrice was a Drood Guard, each armed with an array of ominous-looking spelling staffs.

'We have a reaction time of under two minutes,' said the Drood Commander with smug satisfaction.

'Do you?' said the Enchanter thoughtfully.

The little party of would-be escapees was panicking like mad, as they peered over the battlements to where, far down below, Xar's loyal companions were waiting for him, his giant Crusher, and his snowcats, wolves and bear. These had clung to Crusher's back as he swam across, braving the terrors of the Sea of Skulls in order to help Xar escape, for Xar may have had his faults, but he inspired great loyalty in his companions.

A sprite called the Once-sprite was sitting on a peregrine falcon, peering up at Xar, with his hand shielding his eyes. Behind him, one of the Witch feathers Xar had collected on his previous adventure was glowing with a weird, ominous light.

'Why'sss aren't they jumping?' asked the Once-sprite nervously, for he could smell a horribly familiar scent in the air, carried to his sensitive sprite nostrils on the wind and the mists of the seas they were standing in.

A deadly nightshade reek of rotten rat and choked-up corpse with a little bright stinging note of viper venom, as strong and as poisonous as the arsenic of an apothecary . . .

The smell of *Witches* . . .

Witches must be watching, and they were somewhere out there in that mist.

'*Mmmfff?*' replied Crusher absent-mindedly in answer to the Once-sprite's question. Giants are big, and they tend to have BIG thoughts. Xar's giant was a Longstepper High-Walker giant, and they are the biggest thinkers of all.

Behind the
Once-sprite, a
Witch-feather
was glowing,
with a
strange,
unnatural
light...

'I wonder,' said Crusher slowly, 'if the fate of human beings is predetermined by the stars, or do they forge their own destiny? Is there really such a thing as "luck"? And what *exactly* do we mean by the concept of "free will"?'

Which were all interesting questions, but perhaps not *entirely* helpful right at that particular moment.

'They hassss to get a move on . . .' whispered the Once-sprite, peering nervously upwards, then out into the mist, where he thought he might have seen wings, or talons, or the beak of a Witch. 'We need to get out of here RIGHT NOW!'

'What are we going to dooooo?' moaned Caliburn, up on the battlements.

'Wings!' whispered Squeezjoos. 'Whys doesn't humans beings have wings?'

'It's a design fault,' admitted Xar, 'and a nice idea, but I haven't really got time to evolve them, Squeezjoos. Don't worry . . . I have a plan!'

'I really, really hope it's a good one . . .' muttered Caliburn.

Xar shook the Staff-That-Commands-the-Castle, shouting the words of a spell.

And then he threw the spelling staff as hard as he could, so that it fell down, down in a great arc into

CRUSHER (Xar's Giant)

the sea below, before jumping down after it. The werewolf followed, and the sprites, and Caliburn the talking bird.

And Xar fell, down, down, like a falling star, towards the sea, where his faithful companions were waiting.

'What did he say before he jumped?' said the Drood Commander, watching Xar in the mirror.

'He said: "Everything Open,"' said Encanzo.

The smug smile was instantly wiped off the Drood Commander's face, as C-R-E-E-EAAAKKKKKK! The door of the Commander's Room unlocked itself and swung wide open. S-L-AAMMMMM! The windows shot open, letting in the moonlight, and the Wizards winced as the cold outside wind hit them.

Through every mirror they could hear the commotion of doors opening, portcullises rising, bars melting, invisible Magical barriers dropping with electric hisses.

And then there was the sound of many, many pairs of running feet and opening wings.

'Oh by the steaming droppings of the Big-bottomed Bogburper!' swore the Drood Commander, his eyes popping with disbelief. 'He's used the Staff-That-Commands-the-Castle to open all the doors so EVERYBODY can escape!!!!!!'

'Your guards are going to have their hands full *now*, Commander,' said Encanzo drily. 'We'll get to see how they deal with those Grim Annises, Rogrebreaths, and all those other terrible things you mentioned, *now*. I suspect they might be so busy fighting with those particular villains that they may not have time to catch my son.'

The Drood Commander shot him a filthy look. With a swirl of wet cloak he swooped out of the open door, shouting: 'Jailbreak! CODE RED! WE HAVE MULTIPLE ESCAPE ATTEMPTS! SOMEONE FETCH ME MY COCKATRICE AND GET ME IT *NOW*!!!'

And Encanzo stood, watching in the mirror, as his son disappeared from view.

Then he sat down at the Drood Commander's desk.

'Mff!' said a small, insistent voice at Encanzo's

elbow. Sitting on the desk was the rather odd unknown creature that Xar had turned Looter into, a very unattractive little thing, slightly smaller than a rabbit, with a long dribbly nose and a high-pitched squeak.

'Yes, I'm sorry, Looter,' said Encanzo. 'I can't turn you back into human form until I find out exactly what Xar has turned you into . . . I'll look you up in my Spelling Book. In the meantime, you'll have to be patient I'm afraid. There are more important things at stake here. Xar is in real trouble . . .'

The Creature-That-was-Once-Looter was not used to being anything other than the most important thing in his father's life. He looked panic-stricken, letting out a rather revolting jet-black liquid from his nostrils and then sitting down dejectedly in his own puddle.

'Maybe it serves us both right,' said Encanzo with a sigh, desperately flicking his way through his Spelling Book, searching, searching, searching for a spell that could cure a Witch-stain. 'Could you be a Winklefutt? No, too many ears . . . We were rather hard on the boy. We jeered at him, offended his dignity . . .'

There was a curious mixture of expressions on Encanzo's face. Now that his anger was retreating, he felt a reluctant pride in the sheer breathtaking cheek and ingenuity of his younger son. There are not many people who would have the brazen nerve to turn up in the Drood Commander's room and nick his staff from him.

He was also feeling guilty, for Encanzo had not been able to prevent all this from happening.

But his dominant emotion was *fear*. For, despite everything, Encanzo loved his son, and he knew that Xar would now be in the most terrible danger.

Two ancient sprites settled gravely on Encanzo's shoulders.

He drummed his fingers with furious fright on the table in front of him. 'That Witch-stain is not getting better . . . it is only a matter of time before we lose Xar entirely to the dark side. We HAVE to find a cure . . .' He sighed. 'But firstly we have to find Xar himself, before his time runs out.'

'Could I have prevented this?' said Encanzo to himself. 'Caliburn was right . . . I should have listened to Xar. I should have reasoned with the boy, not hurt his pride.'

But then Encanzo's face hardened. 'But just because I am sorry for him does not mean that he isn't extremely dangerous. I fear the boy's faults are greater than his strengths, and we will all suffer for his mistakes.'

Ah, being a parent is so much harder than it looks.

And just because you are old, does not mean that you do not make mistakes.

59

So that is the story of the Great Jailbreak of Gormincrag. For the first time in a thousand years, not only was there a successful escape attempt, but, indeed, the ENTIRE PRISON POPULATION broke out in one single night.

The sprites would tell that story for many, many centuries afterwards. It was too good a tale not to tell. All of the escapees were recaptured, of course. Apart from two.

A werewolf.

And Xar, son of Encanzo.

The first human being EVER to escape from the detention centre of Gormincrag did it by merely travelling across the Sea of Skulls through the Drowned Forest on the back of his Snowcat, his animals and the werewolf swimming by his side.

'I am the boy of destiny!' said Xar as he struggled out of the sea on the far shore. 'And fate is on my side!' And he vanished, glorious, wild and jubilant, into the freedom of the wildwoods.

But was Xar REALLY the master of his own destiny, and did he really just escape through his cleverness and his luck?

I have to tell you that the Bloody Barbeards, the Daggerfins, the Blunderbouths that would have dragged Xar and his companions to the bottom of the ocean, were eliminated by a talon between the ribs, an acid breath to the lungs, a whiff of dark Magic in their ears, before they could attack.

The Witches got rid of them.

Xar and his companions escaping underwater through the Drowned Forest →

WANTED

Xar, son of Encanzo

Recently escaped from
the prison of Gormincrag.
GENEROUS REWARD
offered to those who help
recapture him.

Signed:
the
Drood Commander

I am the Boy of Destiny !!

BUT WHY WOULD THE WITCHES WANT
XAR TO ESCAPE?

I told you that stories take you in unexpected directions.

I cannot apologise more, but we are only at the end
of Chapter TWO, and I have to take you back to the
Kingwitch. He is still suspended there, in that chamber that I
told you about, miles away, in the Witch Mountains.

Deep below those mountains, there were secret caverns where the Witches had been hanging in great dark cocoons, sleeping out the centuries. The cocoons had been cracking for some time. A limb poked out here, a feather there. A beak, a nose. And the Witches spread their dreadful wings, and flew up and out of the caverns in numbers so huge they were impossible to count, and across the landscape to work their destruction.

The Kingwitch alone was frozen and unmoving. He sent out his troops to wage his War, but he had not moved, for he was waiting, and I fear he may have been conserving his energy for a greater battle that was to come. His great head, with those jaws that could unhinge to swallow a deer in one gulp, was drooping on his breast. He was hanging so high that, despite his immense size, if you walked into that chamber once built for giants you would not even know he was up there.

I would not be doing my duty as a storyteller if I did not warn you that the Kingwitch was up there, poised like a sword about to drop, hiding in the shadows.

But he was still a long, long way away from our heroes, dear Reader. And although Xar may have escaped from the prison of Gormincrag, our other hero Wish was still hidden behind her mother's Great Wall, way, way to the east in the Warrior territories. And as long as she stayed there, she was absolutely safe . . .

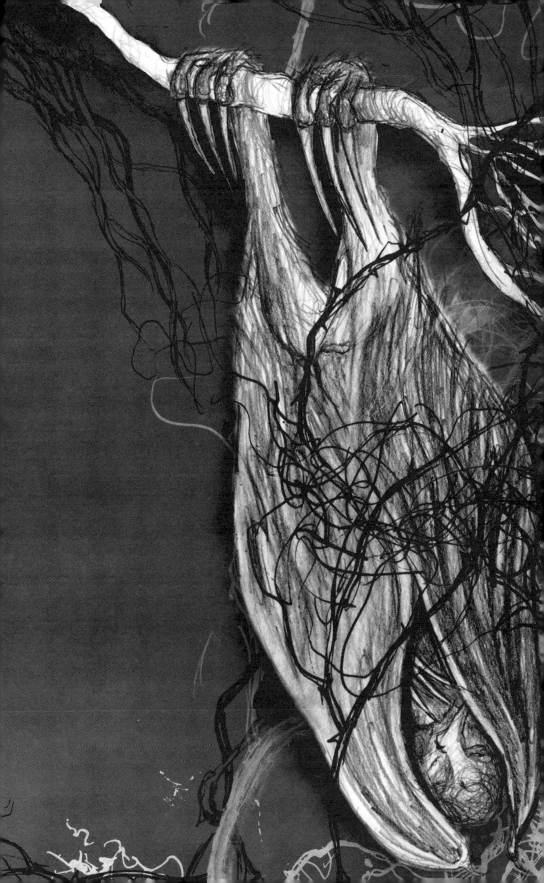

Queen Sychorax's
IRON
WARRIOR
FORT

The feathers fly on, and we have
to follow. I told you these woods were
DANGEROUS...

3. Inside the Punishment Cupboard

Two weeks after Xar made his spectacular escape from Gormincrag, a young Warrior princess called Wish was sitting inside a locked cupboard in the Tower of Education in Queen Sychorax's iron Warrior fort, when she made an important, and perhaps unfortunate, discovery.

Iron Warrior fort was the largest hill-fort you could possibly imagine, protected by seven great ditches cut into the hill, and the Great Wall Sychorax had recently rebuilt. It was constantly patrolled by Warriors looking out for Witches, who would shoot anything Magic that they saw on sight.

Like Xar, Wish was having imprisonment problems.

That's right.

I *did* say she was sitting inside a locked cupboard.

Queen Sychorax, Wish's terrifying mother, was expecting visitors, and whenever Queen Sychorax had visitors she got Madam Dreadlock, Wish's tutor, to lock Wish and her bodyguard in the Punishment Cupboard of the schoolroom until after the visitors had left.

So Wish and her bodyguard had already been sitting in this locked, cramped cupboard for hours and hours and hours, and Wish had been whiling away the time by reading and writing stories.

Wish didn't really like small spaces, so she was keeping her spirits up by singing softly to herself as she read and wrote.

'*NO FEAR!* That's the Warrior's marching song! *NO FEAR!* We sing it as we march along! *NO FEAR!* Cos the Warriors' hearts are strong! Is a Warrior heart a-wailing, is a Warrior heart a-failing, is a Warrior heart a-railing? *NO FEAR!*'

Now, Wish wasn't entirely what you might expect from a Warrior princess. Warrior princesses were supposed to be like Wish's six older stepsisters, tall and tough and good at things like archery, and shooting ogres with their arrows from a distance of thirty paces.

But Wish was small, and sweet-natured and determined, with an eyepatch over one eye, and hair so disobediently flyaway that it looked as if it was being blown about by some personal independent wind.

But worse than that, she was MAGIC.

Wish had always been a little clumsy and forgetful, but when she turned thirteen her Magic had come in, and the problem had got worse. Objects she touched slipped through her hands like water, or tingled with electricity when she put her fingers on them, clothes ripping, shoes coming loose, keys missing, needles wriggling to life in her hands, rugs inexplicably moving beneath her feet, or curled up at the edges when she stepped on them . . .

Goodness knows HOW she was Magic, as she was a Warrior, but the fact remained that her eyepatch was hiding a Magic eye, and it wasn't any ordinary kind of Magic, it was Magic-that-works-on-iron.

And up until now, iron had been the only thing that Magic could not work on.

There was a spoon standing upright on one of Wish's shoulders.

It was a perfectly ordinary iron dinner spoon . . .

Except that it was *alive.*

Alive, and bending this way and

that, and dancing to the sound of Wish's singing, along with about thirty or so little iron pins, which were also swaying and jumping and regrouping to the rhythm. The spoon had a gentle glow coming from the bowl of its head that lit up the cupboard and the iron pins, and the book Wish was reading.

This was a Wizard's Spelling Book, and it was yet another enchanted object that Wish really, really should not have owned. It had once belonged to Xar, but Caliburn had given it to Wish in case Witches came after her in the future.

The spelling book is a complete guide to the entire Magical world, so it is filled with recipes, potions, fairy stories, everything you might need to cope in a world of Magic.

It was in this book that Wish made her important, and perhaps unfortunate, discovery.

'Bodkin!' Wish exclaimed excitedly. '*Look!* I've found a SPELL TO GET RID OF WITCHES*!*'

Bodkin was an anxious skinny boy about the

About thirty little Enchanted Pins...

same age as Wish. He was finding being the Assistant
Bodyguard to the princess really rather testing, because
he didn't like fighting very much, he had an unfortunate
tendency to fall asleep in situations of physical danger,
and trying to control the uncontrollable little princess
was an impossible task, because she seemed to have
absolutely no idea what rules were at all.

He too was reading – a book called *The Rules of
Warrior Bodyguarding: THE NEXT LEVEL* – but he put
the book aside, excited but a little wary, to look over
Wish's shoulder.

And there it was, in a section of the book entitled
'Write Your Own Story'.

On the left hand side of the page,
Wish had written down her
New Year's Resolutions:
'Noo Year's
Ressolushuns:

Noo Year's Ressolushuns

1. I will work hard at my
reading and riteing and arithmatick
so I can be topp of the Klass.

2. I will make a gud impreshun
on the teacher.

will impres my Muther
lots not thre

A Spell to G

Gather all ingrede
a living spoon.

Ingredients

one: Giant's Last Bre
Castle Death.

1. I wull work hard at my reeding and riteing and arithmatick so I can be topp of the klass. 2. I wull mak a gud impresshun on the teecher. 3. I wull impress my muther so she dus not think I am a Dissapointment.'

And on the right hand side of the page Wish had written down in completely different beautiful curly writing, the words of a spell.

A Spell to Get Rid of WITCHES

Gather all ingredients and STIR with a living spoon

Ingredients
One: Giant's Last Breath from Castle Death
Two: Feathers from a Witch
Three: Tears from a Frozen Queen

But after 'Three' the writing got a bit smudgy, as if the writer had suddenly been surprised in the middle of doing something.

'And do you want to know something *truly* extraordinary?' said Wish, eyes shining like stars.

Not really, thought Bodkin, who was beginning to get a very, very bad feeling about this.

'*I wasn't even looking for it!* I was just starting to write a story in this section of the book, because Caliburn gave me one of his feathers to do that with, and *suddenly the feather started writing all by itself!!!*'

'Oh dear . . .' said Bodkin, whose bad feeling was getting worse. 'Are you sure it wasn't just *you* writing it? That's a bit spooky . . .'

'I'm certain!' said Wish. 'It's not my writing, and it *definitely* isn't my spelling.'

It was true.

Wish was very clever, but she had certain difficulties in the 'reeding, riteing and arithmatick' departments. It may have been something to do with being Magic, but somehow all the letters and the numbers wandered about doing complicated alphabet dance exercises in her head, and they wouldn't stay still however hard she concentrated. It was very wearing.

Only that morning, her teacher, Madam Dreadlock, had been so exasperated with Wish's spelling that she

Madam Dreadlock was not, perhaps, the most sympathetic of teachers...

had made Wish write 'I am a Fule' on a piece of paper and hang it around her neck as a punishment.

But every single word on the page Wish was showing Bodkin was spelled absolutely correctly.

'You're right,' Bodkin confirmed. 'That doesn't look anything like your spelling . . .'

'Don't you see what this *means*?' said Wish, excitedly waving her arms around. 'The Witches have come back, but now we have a spell to get rid of them! We HAVE to get this spell to Xar, so he can give it to his father, and then the Wizards can fight back against the Witches . . .'

Bodkin looked at her in horror. There were so

many things wrong with this plan that he didn't know where to start.

'Princess,' said Bodkin, carefully, as if talking to a dangerous lunatic. 'I hate to mention this, but we are sitting inside a locked cupboard, in a Warrior fort encircled by seven ditches, each one protected by your mother's guards, and Xar is somewhere out there, we have no idea where, on the *other* side of your mother's Great Wall. How are we going to get out of the cupboard? How will we get over the Wall? How would we find Xar?'

Wish frowned, thinking for a second. 'We will go to my mother,' said Wish, 'and explain everything, and ask for her help.'

'Everything?' squeaked Bodkin. 'We can't explain everything! What about your Magic, and the spoon and the pins and the Spelling Book? Look!'

There was a large notice attached to the inside of the cupboard door.

The notice read:

THE PUNISHMENT CUPBOARD WOULD
LIKE TO REMIND YOU THAT

ALL MAGIC IS BANNED IN THIS CASTLE

NO SPRITES, NO SPELLING,
NO CURSING, NO CHARMING
AND ABSOLUTELY
NO ENCHANTED OBJECTS

By order of the queen who will
most unfortunately remove your head
if you disobey.

Queen Sycorax

'Right there! It says, quite clearly, **NO ENCHANTED OBJECTS**! It's against the rules!' Bodkin was a boy who really *believed* in the rules.

'The spoon isn't really an enchanted object,' argued Wish. 'Admittedly he's a little ... *lively* ... overexcitable perhaps ... but he's only young, you have to make allowances. He can be quiet if he needs to be, can't you, spoon?'

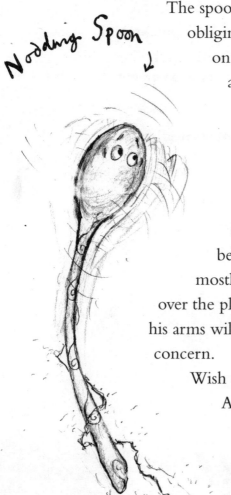

Nodding Spoon

The spoon nodded and very obligingly went rigid, falling flat on its face on Wish's shoulder and playing dead.

'Look!' said Wish proudly. 'Just like a normal dinner spoon!'

'Normal dinner spoons don't nod! Normal dinner spoons don't pretend to be dead! It's quiet *now*, but mostly it's moving around all over the place!' said Bodkin, moving his arms wildly up in the air in his concern.

Wish thought for a moment. And then eventually she said in a very small voice:

Spoon pretending to be dead ...

'Do you think if I told my mother I was Magic, she would be terribly disappointed?'

'Of COURSE she's going to be disappointed!' said Bodkin, so alarmed he spoke without thinking. 'She's already so ashamed of you that she's locking you in Punishment Cupboards so that visitors can't meet you, and she doesn't even *know* about the Magic yet!'

Too late, Bodkin realised he had said the wrong thing.

Wish swallowed hard.

And then three large tears fell down her cheeks.

In her heart of hearts, Wish knew that she was a disappointment to her mother – she could see it in her mother's eyes when she looked at her. *She wishes I was more like my stepsisters . . .* But to hear it confirmed by another person made it even worse. 'WHY doesn't my mother want me to meet visitors? WHY doesn't Madam Dreadlock like me, however hard I try? It's because I'm a bit weird, isn't it?' said Wish desolately.

My mother thinks I'm WEIRD, doesn't she?

Bodkin patted her on the back sympathetically. 'Your mother doesn't know you like I do, princess. You're going to be a brilliant Warrior one day, you have loads of wonderful Warrior qualities, it's just going to take a little time ...'

Wish wiped away the tears with the end of her sleeve, leaving big teary smudges on her cheeks.

'My mother is a magnificent person,' said Wish fiercely, 'but she shouldn't be ashamed of me, and I'm going to tell her that we need to get out there, and help the Wizards!'

'But the Wizards are our enemies!' said Bodkin, a little hysterically.

'They're fellow human beings!' said Wish. 'And Xar is our *friend*! My mother's built this Great Wall, to keep all us Warriors safe, but what about all those poor Wizards who she's left to fight the Witches all on their own?

'Sometimes, when I lie awake at night,' said Wish, with big eyes, 'I think I can hear, beyond the Wall, the sound of giants howling, as if they're being attacked by Witches . . . Don't you hear that, Bodkin? Are we supposed to just stay here, safe behind our Wall, and let that carry on?'

Oh dear, Bodkin *did* sometimes think he heard that. You see, this is the problem with meeting your enemies. Once you have met them, it's really quite difficult to carry on hating them in the way you absolutely ought to.

'*Xar* wouldn't let his father lock him up in cupboards when visitors came,' said Wish mutinously. '*Xar*

stands up to his father when he thinks he is wrong. That
is what *I* should be doing, not sitting around in dark
horrible cupboards, too scared of my mother to stand up
to her . . .'

'You're quite right to be scared of your mother!'
said Bodkin, now thoroughly confused and beginning
to panic. 'Queen Sychorax is super scary! Scarier than
Ghostshrieks! Scarier than Hellhounds! Scarier than
an Ice Warlock in a really really bad mood! Oh by the
green gods . . . *what are you going to do*???'

'I'm going to break out of this stupid Punishment
Cupboard, and go down there, and tell my mother that
we need to find Xar and his father and get this spell to
them,' said Wish. 'There is good in my mother, she is
firm but fair, and she will see my point and help us.'

This was one of the most annoying things about
Wish. She persisted in thinking the best of people even
when they quite clearly did not deserve it.

'Your mother is not firm but fair!' objected Bodkin.
'Your mother is a terrifying tyrant who locks people up
in Punishment Cupboards for a really long time when
they've done absolutely nothing at all!'

'Well that's exactly my point,' argued Wish, 'she
needs to understand that what she is doing is *wrong*.'

'You don't tell terrifying tyrants they're wrong!'
gibbered Bodkin. 'You just do what they say! And I take

it back – there's probably some excellent reason for her keeping us in this cupboard . . . it's quite comfortable in here, wouldn't you say? They've given us some food, so we won't starve . . .' There were indeed a couple of bowls of soup in there with them, and some bread. 'And a bit of legroom . . . I can wriggle my toes! Quite cosy, don't you think? Nice and warm for midwinter and *SAFE*! It's very safe in here . . . not many cobwebs . . . There's plenty of oxygen for two people . . .'

'It's a cupboard,' said Wish. 'We can't stay in a cupboard forever. And she's leaving us in here for longer and longer amounts of time . . . No, we're getting out.'

'WE NEED TO STAY IN THE CUPBOARD, WISH!' said Bodkin in a strangled whisper.

We need to stay in the cupboard, Wish!

But Wish knelt down and looked at the keyhole.

The Spelling Book had a handy alphabet at the beginning, and when Wish tapped her fingers on the letters to spell out 'U-n-l-o-k-k-i-n-g L-o-k-k-s' the pages Magically turned themselves to the 'Spells for Unlocking' section in the book*.

Wish pushed up her eyepatch just a smidgeon (not too far – the Magic eye was horribly powerful), then muttered the words of the spell under her breath and the key on the other side of the door wriggled out of the lock, and shot underneath the bottom of the door to their side of the cupboard, picking itself up off the floor, and making them both a small bow.

The handle of the key formed the shape of a mouth, and the key said in a tiny, creaky, excitable little voice: 'How can I help you?'

may I help?

'It's speaking!' whispered Wish, delighted, for she had never made an enchanted object speak before.

'*Will . . . you . . . stop . . . BRINGING THINGS TO*

---

* The Spelling Book didn't seem to mind a little creativity in spelling out words as long as you made a reasonable guess at them.

LIFE?????' whispered Bodkin through gritted teeth.

'You can help us unlock the door, key,' said Wish, and the key bowed again, absolutely delighted, for there is nothing that enchanted objects enjoy more than doing the things they were created for. The key hopped up the door and unlocked their side of it with such overenthusiasm that there was a small explosion, and the wood of the door split in half.

'Whoops,' said Wish, as the half-broken door swung open.

'It's not too late to stay in the cupboard!' cried Bodkin, as Wish scrambled out.

'Oh, brother . . . she's not staying in the cupboard! I'm going to have to follow her . . .' groaned Bodkin, grabbing his weapons.

'She's exploded Madam Dreadlock's cupboard! She's left the schoolroom without permission!' moaned Bodkin, eyes wide open with horror as he stumbled out of the cupboard, through the schoolroom, and onto the battlements. 'We're going to be in SUCH TROUBLE . . .'

Clank! Clank! Clank! Bodkin staggered after Wish, as fast as he could, given that he was wearing two sets of body armour.

'Wait . . . for . . . me . . .' puffed Bodkin.

Wish slowed down a little. 'Oh! I'm so sorry, Bodkin. Am I going too fast for you? Wow, you're wearing a lot of armour . . .'

CLANK! CLANK! CLANK!

It's important not to

Bodkin paused for breath a second. 'You see, Wish, *this* is why Madam Dreadlock doesn't like you . . .' groaned Bodkin. 'What about your New Year's Resolutions?'

It was true, Wish's New Year's Resolution number 2, 'mak a gud impresshun on the teecher', wasn't going so well, what with one thing and another.

'Bodkin,' said Wish, 'I'm sad that Madam Dreadlock doesn't like me, but there are some things that are more important than teachers and exploding cupboards. Look! Somewhere out there, over that Wall, Xar and the Wizards are in trouble, *and we can help them!*'

Bodkin swallowed hard.

'Oh dear, you're right, you're right, we have to help them . . . It's just that Witches are SO SCARY . . . And they're invisible until they attack so they could be anywhere!' whispered Bodkin with boggling eyes. He tried to look over his shoulder, but the weight of his helmet and body armour meant he had to shuffle his entire body around a hundred and eighty degrees. 'I keep thinking they're here already . . . that we're being *followed*! That's why I'm wearing so much body armour!'

'Yes, it's probably better not to wear so much armour that you can't actually *move*, Bodkin,' advised Wish.

'And your mother's busy . . . It won't be a good

Wear so much armour
that you can't MOVE

moment . . . She's expecting visitors . . . I can see her already, up on the Royal Stage!' Bodkin pointed down, into the courtyard.

'My mother's ALWAYS busy! There's never a good moment. Don't worry, I've been practising my Visitor Manners, Bodkin . . .' said Wish.

And she dashed off down the stairs.

Bodkin hopped unhappily from foot to foot, in an agony of anxiety. There was no stopping the little princess when she was in this kind of mood. He left the shield and the backpack behind because they were too heavy and slowing him down, and Clank! Clank! Clank! he staggered after Wish down the stairs.

'At the very least,' begged Bodkin, catching up with Wish as she reached the bottom of the tower, because she'd lost one of her shoes and had to go back for it, 'give me all the enchanted objects. You can't go on the Royal Stage with your pockets full of banned Magical things . . . I'll look after them while you're up there.'

Wish did see Bodkin's point.

Wait... for... me...

She gave him the spoon, the Spelling Book, and all of the enchanted pins, who neatly pinned themselves all over Bodkin's shirt. And then she hurried off, pushing her way through the crowd towards the stage, practising saying very firmly, 'You are wrong, Mother, wrong. We have to help the Wizards!' and her Visitor Manners, just in case: 'How do you do? What do *you* do?'

The Executioner, who was a kind man when he wasn't doing his job, helped her up onto the stage beside her sisters.

Wish's six older stepsisters were tidy, handsome Warrior girls, as muscled and hairy and unwelcoming as six well-groomed blonde gorillas. When she scrambled up beside them, the sister nearest to her in age, Drama, gave her such a big shove in the stomach with her elbow, that Wish nearly fell off the stage.

'What are *you* doing here, you weird little rat?' growled Drama. 'Mother is ashamed of you. You're not fit to be seen by company.'

CLANK!

Clank!

Clank!

Puff

puff

puff

Queen
Sycorax

And the next oldest sister but one, Unforgiving, gave a great stamp on Wish's toe, and added, with satisfaction, 'Mother is going to be SO ANGRY . . .'

It seemed they could be right.

The great queen Sychorax was sitting in a magnificent throne, right in the centre of the courtyard. She was dressed in elaborately regal armour, with one black earring, and one white.

Wish, already gasping for breath and hopping on one foot from her stepsisters' rather violent greeting, felt her stomach plunge with anxiety.

What had seemed such a good idea in the cupboard suddenly didn't seem such a good idea *now*.

Even to Wish's hopeful eyes, her mother didn't look firm but fair.

She looked absolutely hopping mad.

'What are *you* doing here, Wish?' hissed Queen Sychorax in the voice of a sweetly striking cobra. 'How dare you disobey my orders?'

And then she gave Wish *That Look*.

In most people's eyes, Wish's mother Queen Sychorax was the most petrifying Warrior leader in the entire western wildwoods, known for her stern punishments, her short temper, and her dungeons of interminable depth.

In *Wish's* eyes, her mother was the most wonderful,

beautiful, splendid person in the entire world, and more than anything else in the world Wish longed to please her mother, get her golden approval.

Wish had meant to tell her mother she was wrong.

She meant to explain about the spell to get rid of Witches, and how they needed to get it to Xar and his father, and how they shouldn't be building Walls that left the Wizards and the poor Magic things to be attacked.

But when her mother gave her *That Look*, a Look of Deepest and most Furious Disappointment, all the brave words Wish had been *intending* to say went completely out of her head.

She opened her mouth . . . and shut it again.

'I will deal with *you* later,' snapped Queen Sychorax through gritted teeth.

It was too late for Wish to leave the stage.

For Queen Sychorax's visitors had already arrived, one of them stepping towards the throne, in a curiously crab-wise, menacing fashion.

'Be quiet, and don't draw attention to yourself!' Queen Sychorax ordered Wish. 'Don't droop! Don't fidget! Don't move! Don't blink!'

'Oh! Yes, mother, I won't cause any trouble I promise . . .' said Wish miserably.

Queen Sychorax's visitor was a tall, alien figure, of such alarming aspect that Wish felt a little sick and her hair began to move and stand up on the back of her neck, softly wriggling itself into a bird's nest of tangles as if each little individual hair had a life of its own.

'Who, or *what* is *that*?' exclaimed Wish, in a kind of fascinated horror, desperately trying to flatten down her hair in the hope that no one would notice.

'Don't you know anything, you ignorant little ant?' demanded her stepsister, Drama, trying to sound careless, even though she was extremely frightened herself. '*That* is the Witchsmeller.'

We should have stayed in the cupboard! thought Bodkin, who had reached the royal stage and was peering up at the Witchsmeller. *We should have stayed in the cupboard!*

I should have
stayed in the cupboard!

4. The Pointing Finger of the Witchsmeller

The Witchsmeller had a face that seemed to be entirely composed of nose. A nose that quivered and trembled sensitively at the tip, as if at any moment it might wander around to left and right like a pointing finger.

The Witchsmeller had bony fingers, that quivered like the legs of a praying mantis, as if he could smell with his very fingers themselves.

Beards of dwarves hung from his cloak. Little skulls of poor sprites hung from his neck.

From his belt hung goblin hearts, and the beards of elves, and toenail clippings of famous giants he had killed (AFTER they gave themselves up, for the Witchsmeller did not think you needed to keep promises you made to giants).

He was a little annoyed at having to come so far out west to this godforsaken uncivilised jungle. He supposed the food would be terrible out here, but the emperor had insisted. He gave Queen Sychorax a very perfunctory bow.

'Ah, the pest controller,' said Queen Sychorax, inclining her head.

'My name,' said the Witchsmeller, stiffening somewhat, 'is the Witchsmeller.'

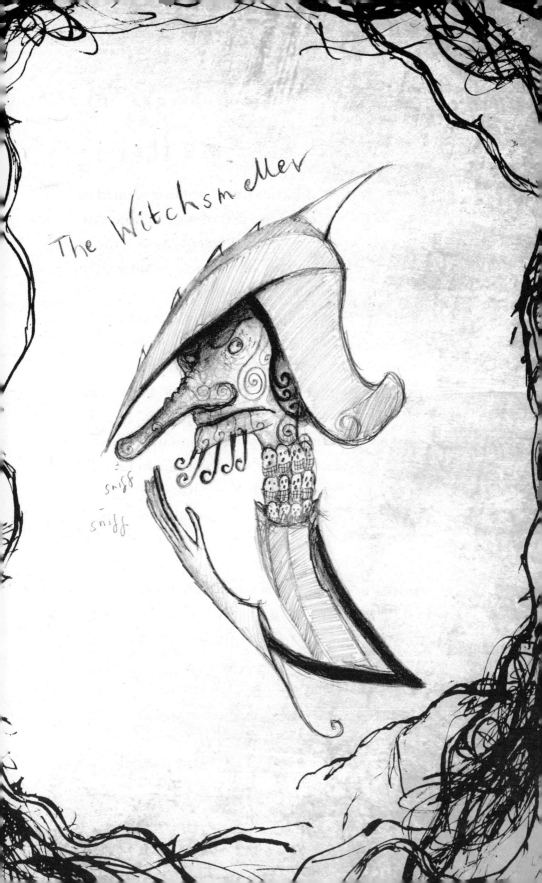

'Excellent,' said Queen Sychorax. 'Welcome to iron Warrior fort. I have summoned you here to my queendom because we have made the unwelcome discovery that Witches are not extinct after all, and I need you to hunt some down for me.'

Oh! thought Wish, cheering up a little. So my mother ISN'T leaving the Wizards to fight the Witches on their own! But I'm not sure she's chosen the right person to help her . . .

'You have come to the right person,' said the Witchsmeller with a smile. He didn't quite like the word 'summoned'. Who did this backwater queen think she was?

'Let me explain my problem. This stone here used to be my Stone-That-Takes-Away-Magic,' said Queen Sychorax.

She gestured to the back of the stage, where Wish realised for the first time, the stone had been carried up from the dungeon where it was normally kept. 'And for many years I have successfully removed the Magic from many a giant and sprite. But about six months ago, the stone was found to contain a Kingwitch, who then escaped from the stone and as a result we have something of a Witch infestation in the western territories.'

The Witchsmeller took a good look at the stone. There was a sword sticking out of the great jagged

split that cracked the stone from side to side. The
Witchsmeller tried to remove the sword from the
cracked stone. It would not budge. The Witchsmeller
made tut-tutting noises.

'I have built a Wall along the entire western edge of
my kingdom to protect Warrior territories, but I need
you and your troops to go out there and hunt down the
Witches,' said Queen Sychorax.

The Witchsmeller shook his head condescendingly.
'Ah, your Majesty, I am quite surprised that you used a
Magical object like this stone in the first place. And you
should have been KILLING the Magic, not removing it
... The emperor would not be pleased. Such softness is
not the Warrior way.'

There was an uncomfortable murmur from Queen
Sychorax's subjects, and they all took a step backwards,
as if moving away from the edge of a volcano that was
about to blow.

Nobody spoke like that to Queen Sychorax.

Queen Sychorax's eyes sharpened to flinty arrows.

'Softness? *Softness???? Not the Warrior way?* How
dare you question my methods?' she said in a voice
that could have frozen the very bone marrow of a
lesser man. 'I merely use Magic to destroy Magic, in a
modern civilised manner. The ends justify the means. *I*
am a great monarch and YOU are a mere common-or-

garden *rodent-operative*. I have commanded you to go out and hunt Witches. So go out and do it!'

The Witchsmeller jumped as if he had been bitten.

He had never before met someone with quite the force of Queen Sychorax's personality. Mostly people cowered before him. He, the Witchsmeller, was the Terror of the Empire. He looked behind him at his soldiers, the emperor's crack Magic-hunting troops.

The sunlight glistened off their iron helmets, their bristling weaponry, their Magic-catching equipment.

'I believe *I* am the expert on Witches, your Majesty,' snapped the Witchsmeller. 'Your problem is not the Witches out *there*, but the Witches here in this courtyard!'

Oh dear, oh dear, oh dear, oh dear! thought Wish. This is DEFINITELY not the right person to help . . .

'What on earth are you talking about?' snapped Queen Sychorax, out-snapping him by double. 'I've told you, no Witches can get over my Wall!'

'YOU HAVE INVITED ME HERE LOOKING FOR WITCHES AND I INTEND TO FIND THEM!' shouted the Witchsmeller, pointing one quivering finger in the air.

He sidled forward, and began to sniff at the nearest person, as if he were a dog.

'I smell *Witches* . . .' hissed the Witchsmeller, in a high, squeaky voice.

A murmer of horror went around the courtyard.

'Oh for goodness sake,' said Queen Sychorax with a sigh, thinking, *Oh no, just my luck, he's a nutcase,* and thoroughly regretting inviting this lunatic into her queendom in the first place.

Sniff

Sniff

Sniff

Sniff

Shiff

She generally had perfect control of her subjects, but they were a superstitious lot, and she could see this might get out of hand.

'I smell WITCHES!' cried the Witchsmeller again, holding his shaking finger to the heavens in a voice of DOOM.

Mad as a box-load of frogs. Nuttier than a tree-full of squirrels . . . thought the queen.

'I can sniff out Magic, wherever it may be hiding,' snarled the Witchsmeller. 'I will move through the crowd, and point at any person who is concealing Magic . . .'

Oh for goodness sake...

Now there was a dreadful silence in the courtyard, and you did not need the nose of a Witchsmeller to detect the smell of fear.

Nerves and sweat.

Wish could feel herself getting very hot, and her clothes itching her neck and back.

'Murmuring mistletoe, you've never actually met a real *Witch*, have you, pest controller?'

said Queen Sychorax drumming her fingers on the arms of her throne in great irritation. 'You'd know it if you saw one . . . a big feathered thing with green blood and talons . . .'

'Those kind of Witches are extinct!' screamed the Witchsmeller. 'I'm talking about the *modern* Witches!

sniff

The Witches in our midst!'

'You won't find any Magic here, pest controller,' said Queen Sychorax, yawning, 'I keep a very clean castle.'

Wish tried to half-hide behind her stepsister Drama, to make herself even smaller, so she would not be noticed. Her hair was so alarmingly frizzy and alive that she was having to hold it down forcibly with both arms. Maybe no one would notice.

Please don't let the finger land on me . . .

Please.

If that finger lands on me, I'm never going to be allowed out of that Punishment Cupboard EVER AGAIN . . .

My mother is going to be SO disappointed . . .

But that will be the least of my worries because I also may be DEAD . . .

And here the quivering nose was right behind her. Sniff, sniff, sniff.

The fingers paused, she could almost feel them, the bony digit about to press itself into her back, like the spooky white bone of a chicken. It would happen in one second, two . . .

Wish could not bear it, the agony of suspense. She closed her one eye.

Please don't let the finger land on me.

Please.

The finger paused behind her – it was about to land on her, she knew it . . .

5. The Finger Lands on Wish... and Everything Gets a Bit Chaotic

The spooky chicken finger of the Witchsmeller landed right in the middle of Wish's back.

'Aha!' crowed the Witchsmeller triumphantly, swinging her round to face him. 'A Witch!'

The crowd gave a moan of astonishment.

'How do you do?' gabbled Wish, rather desperately falling back on her Visitor Manners. 'Welcome to Warrior Castle. Did you have a good trip? Very-pleasant-weather-for-the-time-of-year, I-do-hope-you-are-well and ... er ... what-do-YOU-do-?'

The Witchsmeller blinked at her in amazement.

'I ... *hunt* ... *WITCHES* ...' he snarled.

You have to hand it to Queen Sychorax. She was absolutely cool as a cucumber in a crisis. She glided out of her throne in a graceful golden flash, and she laid a restraining hand on the Witchsmeller's arm. She even managed to sound a little bored.

'That is not a Witch, pest controller,' said Queen Sychorax. 'That is my daughter, Wish. She may be a bit

of an incompetent disgrace to her tribe, but she most
certainly is not a Witch.'

'She couldn't possibly be the daughter of a Warrior
queen!' hissed the Witchsmeller. 'She's very odd-
looking . . .'

'I think I know my own daughter,' said the queen
witheringly. 'Hair disgraceful, height poor, general
Warrior turnout utterly substandard – where are your
weapons, Wish?'

'I left them in the cupboard . . .' said Wish,
miserably looking down at her feet to avoid her
mother's scathing gaze.

107

'Spelling appalling, disobedience unspeakable, deportment tragic,' continued Sychorax, brutal even by her own standards, for Sychorax was CROSS. 'Yes, it's definitely her.'

'But this notice on her chest here says she's a *Fule* . . . what is a Fule?' spluttered the Witchsmeller suspiciously. 'Is that some kind of weird western Magical being?'

'*You* are the fool, pest controller,' said Queen Sychorax in her cold, reasoned voice. 'Witches cannot hide themselves in people. I keep telling you, Witches are a very different thing altogether. Witches have green blood, and feathered wings. They are not extinct, which is the reason I summoned you here in the first place.'

The Witchsmeller had regained his composure. He held up his finger.

'THE FINGER IS NEVER WRONG!' shouted the Witchsmeller. 'SEARCH THE FULE!'

Sychorax drew herself up to her full royal height.

'My daughter, however hopelessly unworthy, is of royal blood and a direct descendant of Grimshanks the Ogre-wrangler!' said Queen Sychorax. 'You most certainly will not search her or I shall be complaining to the emperor personally! Wish will turn out her pockets on her own, won't you, Wish?'

Thank GOODNESS Bodkin had taken all those

enchanted objects off her, thought Wish. He was the best bodyguard in the world. And she really, really should start taking his advice.

Wish felt in her pockets, confident at least of finding nothing there, and turned a little white. She slowly drew out her hand, opened it, and there sitting in the palm was . . .

The Once-sprite.

And out of the other pocket, in terrified alarm there buzzed . . .

Squeezjoos . . . who just had time to squeak at Wish: 'I's ssorry, Wisssh!'

Wish blinked at him in astonishment. *What was he doing here anyway?????*

Out of nowhere a peregrine falcon dived down in a blurr of wings and hovered for a split second above Wish's hand. With impeccable timing (if Wish had been in the mood to admire it), the little Once-sprite hopped on the bird's back and Squeezjoos hung onto one of the falcon's claws, and they soared up, up and away, Wish looking after them with her mouth open.

There was a nasty silence.

And then there was absolute chaos.

'She has sprites in her pockets!' screeched the Witchsmeller. 'SHE'S A WITCH!'

'Is this your idea, Wish,' said Queen Sychorax,

The Enchanted Spoon

through teeth so gritted they were practically grinding, 'of *not causing any trouble?*'

'I didn't know they were in there, honestly, Mother . . .' pleaded Wish with a very white face.

'SEIZE THE FULE!' screamed the lunatic Witchsmeller, drawing his sword.

'The princess may have a few sprites in her pockets,' cried Queen Sychorax, incandescent with annoyance, and drawing her own sword. 'But that doesn't make the

to the Rescue!

disobedient little excuse for a princess a *Witch*. Warriors!
DEFEND THE PRINCESS!'

And then she gave a start as . . .

CLANG! CLANG! CLANG! CLANG! CLANG!
Across the Royal Stage came the Enchanted Spoon,
rushing to Wish's rescue. He had a curious way of
propelling himself, like he was doing headstands, and
then jumping back onto his feet again, cartwheeling
from bowl to handle, and then back to bowl again.

CLANG!
CLANG!
CLANG!

'What is *that???*'
hissed Queen
Sychorax in disbelief,
as quick as a whip, the
Enchanted Spoon danced
right up the baffled
Witchsmeller's long
black body.
CLANG!
CLUNK! CLANG!
CLANG! The
Enchanted Spoon
was clanging the
Witchsmeller's
helmet from left
to right so loudly
that the Witchsmeller
dropped his sword and
staggered, his ears ringing
with the noise.

And, just as if things weren't
confusing enough already . . .

'*WITCH ATTACK!*' screamed Bodkin as, with a
strength born of fear, the Assistant Bodyguard managed,
despite his two sets of armour, to clamber onto the
Royal Stage.

For Bodkin, his mind full of Witches, had seen something that nobody else had noticed. The problem with invisible attackers is that you start seeing them everywhere. But this time Bodkin *knew* he was right.

There was a Witch's talon levitating in the air, heading in the direction of Wish and the Witchsmeller . . .

So Bodkin stormed the Royal Stage, screaming 'WITCH! WITCH!' which, as you can imagine, didn't exactly calm the situation.

'WITCH, Wish! There's a Witch right behind you!' yelled Bodkin.

'SEIZE THE FULE!' screamed a whole crowd of Magic-hunters, storming the stage right behind Bodkin.

'DEFEND THE PRINCESS!' yelled the Warriors loyal to Queen Sychorax, storming the stage after them.

I told you it was chaos.

'AHA!' crowed the Witchsmeller in triumph, as eventually he managed to grab the thing that was attacking him and pull it off his head.

The spoon immediately stopped struggling and pretended to be dead.

The Witchsmeller blinked at it in astonishment. 'I'm being attacked . . . by a *spoon*?'

He leant down and sniffed the spoon all over, the revolting tip of his nose snuffling up and down like it was a bloodhound's.

The spoon tried as hard as it could to be rigid. But eventually he couldn't quite bear it, the sniffing was so ticklish. Little ripples shook his sides like giggles, for one second, before he turned hard again.

The Witchsmeller blinked. Surely he hadn't seen that. A spoon couldn't move.

Tentatively he put the spoon in his mouth, because that was what you *did* with a spoon, after all. The minute it touched his lips, the spoon struggled wildly, thrashing around from side to side, desperate to escape.

The Witchsmeller spat the spoon out in horror, and screamed like he had been stung by a hornet: '*It's alive!!!!*'

It was hard to know who was the more revolted, the Witchsmeller or the spoon.

Yucky.

The spoon leapt up,
rapped him sharply on
the sensitive end of his
nose, and hopped down
the Witchsmeller as fast
as he could hop, before
disappearing through the
nearest person's legs.

'*Catch that spoon!!!!!!!*'
yelled the Witchsmeller,
holding onto his nose.

I wish I had a sword . . . thought
Wish, looking desperately around her.

She was standing right next to the Enchanted
Sword, which was stuck fast in the Stone-That-No-
Longer-Took-Away-Magic.

So Wish reached out and took it.

Queen Sychorax watched Wish do this with her
royal mouth slightly ajar. Sychorax had spent the last
six months trying every trick in the book that she knew
to get that beastly Witch-killing sword out of the stone
– for with the return of the Witches to the forest, she
really, really needed it – and it would not budge.

Six months!

She'd had giants, Rogrebreaths, strong men and
women from all over her queendom try to pull it out.

115

She'd even secretly tried *spelling* it out (for Queen Sychorax was a very tricky and unusual person, and she was not above using Magic to destroy Magic, as we have seen).

To no avail. Nothing had worked. And here was her odd, unsatisfactory little daughter just *reaching out and taking it*!

Queen Sychorax was reluctantly not only impressed but perhaps also a little confused. There were things going on here that Queen Sychorax did not perfectly understand, and Queen Sychorax absolutely hated that.

Wish wasn't normally all that good at swordfighting.

But the Enchanted Sword had the rather satisfactory effect of turning whoever was wielding it into the Best Swordfighter in the World, so Wish disarmed, one, two, three, Magic-hunters in a row ('Nice work,' said Queen Sychorax to herself, watching this).

Wish then ran to help Bodkin, for he did now seem to be fighting what looked very like a Witch's talon that was floating in the air – clumsily, poor Bodkin because, as Wish said earlier, it's very important not to wear so much armour that you find it difficult to *move*.

He couldn't turn his head to face the invisible opponent that he thought he was fighting, he had to turn his ENTIRE BODY three hundred and sixty degrees and shuffle around, very, very slowly.

116

To make matters worse, Bodkin's impressive but completely blind-making visor then came down, and he couldn't see a thing. The sword was so heavy that when he eventually managed to lift it and make a wild swipe at where he guessed his opponent might be, the weight of it carried him with it, and he lost his balance, and . . .

CLANG!

That was the sound of Bodkin's helmeted head hitting the floor.

Being a bodyguard is so much harder than it looks...

He immediately passed out, for Bodkin had a slight problem. He had a medical condition that caused him to fall asleep in situations of extreme danger.

'Bodkin! Wake up!' yelled Wish.

'Who? Where? What? How?' Bodkin sat up, holding his head.

'Iron Warrior fort! Possible Witch attack! Watch out! I think it's going to dive!' shouted Wish.

She was about to lunge with the Enchanted Sword towards where she thought the invisible assailant might be . . .

And then she checked herself just in time.

Could this be . . .?

6. And a Little More Chaotic Still

Indeed it could be.

The invisible assailant sl-o-o-owly became visible in front of Wish's eyes, as the iron of the soldiers surrounding him made whatever invisibility spell he was using wear off. It was the Wizard boy, Xar-son-of-Encanzo.

'XAR!' exclaimed Wish, completely forgetting where they both were in her delight at seeing her old friend again. 'But . . . but . . . what are you doing here?'

'I'm saving you, even though you've completely sabotaged my mission!' shouted Xar.

'That tricky wretch of a Wizard boy!' gasped Queen Sychorax

Xar, you see, had gone to considerable trouble to get into iron Warrior fort. He needed his Spelling Book.

Caliburn had begged him not to involve Wish in all this trouble, but Xar had said he would just sneak in and take back the Spelling Book without her realising. Everything had initially gone to plan. He had got through the Wall by the simple trick of approaching the gate wearing Queen Sychorax's hooded cloak, which he had stolen from her six months ago. Queen Sychorax made a habit of wearing these spectacular cloaks that didn't show her face, so she could come and go through her own Wall without people recognising her. Xar passed through the gate unchallenged by the sentries, the sprites hidden underneath the folds of fabric.

It took a while for them to find Wish, creeping through the corridors of the fort, using invisibility spells and lurking in quiet corners.

When Wish and Bodkin had run out of the schoolroom, they had been followed by an invisible Xar and his sprites. Xar had tripped Wish up at the bottom of the stairs, so that the Once-sprite and Squeezjoos could search her pockets for the Spelling Book, but once they were in the courtyard, all the surrounding iron had turned them both visible, and by the time Wish had reached the Royal Stage it didn't seem a very good moment for the sprites to escape.

Tiffinstorm and Hinkypunk were all for leaving Wish to fend for herself when the Witchsmeller accused her of being a Witch.

But Xar was determined to stick to his resolution to be good. He couldn't abandon Wish . . . particularly when it was his sprites in her pockets that had got her into trouble.

So he made his invisible charge at the Witchsmeller . . . only to be tackled round the legs by Bodkin the bodyguard, who mistook Xar's drawn sword for the talon of a Witch.

But this was all news to Wish, who hadn't realised any of this was going on.

Saving me? Sabotaged his mission? What IS Xar talking about?

Blink! Blink! Blink! Blink! Blink! Blink! Out of nowhere, six sprites came blinking into visibility, and then Blink! Blink! Blink! three smaller lights of the hairy fairies.

Wish had been missing these sprites so badly, and at any other time she'd have been thrilled to see them, but right now . . .

'I have to say, I don't want to be unwelcoming, but this is a really, really bad moment for you to drop by,' said Wish.

This was the understatement of the Iron Age.

The effect of a Wizard boy, a talking raven, six sprites and three hairy fairies rapidly appearing in an iron Warrior fort full of blood-crazy Magic-hunters who have already been whipped into a Witch-finding frenzy by a barking mad Witchsmeller, is a rather similar one to that of a large plump juicy chicken with ten dear little yellow fluffy baby chicks suddenly appearing in the middle of a pack of ravenous wolves who've had a bit of a lean streak lately.

'A WIZARD and its WITCH COMPANIONS!' shrieked the Witchsmeller.

(He really couldn't ever have seen a real Witch if he thought a Witch looked like Squeezjoos, but the other Magic-hunters weren't in a mood to be picky about their species identification so they all joined in joyfully.)

'GET THEM!' they cried.

Now, *this* was a crisis.

Queen Sychorax's Warriors might rush to stop the Magic-hunters from seizing their unsatisfactory little princess, but they weren't going to do the same for Xar. Indeed they might even join in. After meeting him six months ago, Xar wasn't exactly top of Queen Sychorax's Midwinter's-End Eve present list.

Yes, it was most definitely a crisis.

But Wish, though she didn't look much like her mother, did in fact have a few things in common with Queen Sychorax.

She was rather good in a crisis. Cool. Collected. *Tricky*, if by tricky you mean clever.

In that split second when it became apparent that Xar might be killed if she didn't come up with a pretty nifty solution *right now*, Wish reviewed her options.

She was a bit hampered by the fact that no one had taught her how to use her Magic properly, so these choices were a little limited.

She could take her eyepatch off entirely.

That would make the castle fall down, which would create a diversion, but would also be dangerous, and a little messy.

She could use the Spelling Book to do a Spell of Invisibility, or Transformation.

But Bodkin had the Spelling Book, and it would

take way too much time for him to retrieve it, carefully hidden as it was beneath many layers of body armour.

Or . . . She could cast a spell that she had seen someone do before, so she could copy it.

Wish thought back to six months ago, when Tiffinstorm had cast the spell that made Xar's bedroom door shrug out of its frame like an old man shrugging out of his jacket, and turned it into a flying door so that they could escape from Wizard fort.

She wriggled up her eyepatch, just a tiny, tiny smidgeon, and looked up towards the Tower of Education. She imagined the door of the Punishment Cupboard (she knew that door well) gently shrugging out of its door frame in the same way as Xar's bedroom door had done. She spelled out the word that Tiffinstorm had said as she cast the spell: M–O–U–V–E . . .

Luckily, Magic did not seem to care about the exact positioning of the letters. Indeed, it seemed to positively LIKE creativity in the spelling department. It invigorated the Magic, like adding oxygen in some kind of chemical experiment.

As the Magic–hunters thundered towards them, swords drawn, shouting, 'KILL THE WITCHES —'

BOOOOOOOM!!!!!!!!!!!!!

Above their heads, the broken door of the Punishment Cupboard EXPLODED out of the top window of the Tower of Education and rocketed at breathtaking speed, neck-height across the courtyard. Everybody had to stop charging towards Xar and the sprites-misidentified-as-Witches and throw themselves on the ground for fear of being decapitated.

The Witchsmeller rubbed his eyes and stared upward at the door sailing up into the air and turning round back again for another dive.

'What's that?' whispered the Witchsmeller in a hollow voice of disbelief.

'It seems to be a door, sir,' said his sergeant smartly.

'I know it's a door, *idiot!*' spat the Witchsmeller, 'but what is it doing flying through the air like a bird?'

The door came to a screeching, manic, hovering halt in front of Xar and Wish.

'The Wizard boy's kidnapping me!' shouted Wish, grabbing Xar by the arm and dragging him on to the door. The sprites, already finding it difficult to fly because of all the iron around, threw themselves down on the door beside them.

Xar grinned. 'Quick thinking, princess.'

Neither he nor the sprites could make this door fly themselves, because the door had iron hinges, and an iron lock.

'How do I make it work?' panicked Wish. She'd never driven a flying door before.

'Use the key!' advised Caliburn.

Without thinking, Wish put her hand on the key, and then moved her arm back sharply, as if she had been stung, as the head of the key moved like a mouth, asking: 'Where would you like to go?' in its cosy, creaky, upbeat little voice.

'Up . . .' said Wish, 'we want to go UP!'

She put her hand on the key again a little more cautiously this time and moved it gently upwards, and the door went shrieking up into the air so wildly that all of them nearly fell off.

'We have to go back for Bodkin!' yelled Wish. 'We can't leave him there – my mother is hopping mad, and she'll say it's all his fault for not looking after me!'

'HA!' said Xar. 'Do we have to? He does kind of get in the way. If it wasn't for Bodkin interfering, I'd have SMOOSHED that horrible guy with the sniffing nose . . .'

'Er . . . I's thinks that Bodkin might have the Spelling Book, Boss,' wheezed Squeezjoos. 'It wasn't in Wisssh's pockets . . .'

'We go back for Bodkin!' said Xar, punching the air.

Wish slammed the Enchanted Key to the right and the door of the Punishment Cupboard veered violently round in a circle, and made a great swooping dive back down again, sending everyone who was beginning to get up BACK onto their stomachs for the second time.

Xar and Wish both had to lean over and drag Bodkin

onto the door, such was the heaviness of his armour.

'Nobody shoot, or the princess will die!' shouted Wish over the side of the door, as it sailed up into the air, a little shakily because of Bodkin's weight, and swooped backwards and forwards over the crowd.

The only person still standing on the Royal Stage was Queen Sychorax. She would have DIED rather than throw herself on her stomach.

Nonetheless, she was rattled, really rattled.

The situation had got thoroughly out of hand.

She waved her sword up at the door shouting, not with her usual cool, for Queen Sychorax had lost her temper. 'COME DOWN *IMMEDIATELY*, WISH! A Warrior princess does not fly about on the back of doors! A Warrior princess does not allow herself to get kidnapped!'

'Oh dear, she really *is* cross,' said Wish, peering over the edge of the door. 'I'm so glad we didn't leave you down there with her, Bodkin ...

'You're right, you don't ALLOW yourself to be kidnapped, Mother!' Wish shouted back down, 'A kidnapping just happens ...'

But Queen Sychorax was not fooled. She knew perfectly well who was kidnapping who.

'DO NOT, ON ANY ACCOUNT, LEAVE THE SAFETY OF THIS FORT!' commanded Queen Sychorax. 'DO NOT, ON PAIN OF MY *MOST*

SEVERE DISPLEASURE, GO OVER THAT WALL!'

Take the usual look of disappointment on Queen Sychorax's face when she looked at her daughter, and then times that by about TEN, and you'll have an idea of what Queen Sychorax looked like as she gazed up at Wish and her disreputable companions lying on their stomachs on the back of the flying door.

'I'm so sorry, Mother!' said Wish guiltily. 'Don't worry! I'll be right back, I promise I will!'

And then the door of the Punishment Cupboard sailed UP, UP and away . . .

Over the battlements . . .

And on towards Queen Sychorax's Wall.

Queen Sychorax gave a sigh of fury and resignation. Maddening though her daughter might be, she really did not want her shot down.

She called up to the sentry on the Tower of Education. 'Nobody shoot down the door! The princess is going over the Wall!'

And the astonished cry went up from sentry to sentry, and tower to tower, all along the fortifications and the battlements of Queen Sychorax's Great Wall.

'Orders of the queen! Nobody shoot down the door!'

The Wall of Queen Sychorax was supposed

to be impregnable, unclimbable, unbreachable by Witches and everything Magic. The arrow-hands of those sentries were absolutely *itching* to shoot that door down as it sailed majestically and a little erratically over their heads, particularly when Xar leaned over the side of it and gave them all a cheeky wave.

But they were all far too scared to disobey orders.

Queen Sychorax watched it go. She closed her eyes for a second as the door lurched wildly this way and that, went into nosedives several times, before flying, on, on, over the forest.

With her clumsy little daughter in charge, it really was going to be a miracle if they made it for more than five minutes through that forest without crashing.

But in among all the anger in Sychorax's face there was the blink of an emotion much more unusual for her.

Fear.

For she knew now that her daughter was in real and terrible danger.

Tap tap tap . . . went Queen Sychorax's furious little foot on the Royal Stage as the Witchsmeller and his Magic-hunters got cautiously to their feet, looking as though they felt a little at a disadvantage, for the queen was the only one who had stayed standing throughout.

Queen Sychorax's Warriors remained where they were, curled up like hedgehogs, their arms over their heads, for they knew that their queen was about to speak her mind and it was better to lie low until she had.

Queen Sychorax narrowed her eyes.

And then she *struck*, every single word a snake-bite, dripping with poisonous sarcasm and contempt.

'I hold *you* entirely responsible for this mess, you miserable little pest controller!' flashed Queen Sychorax. 'Thanks to *your* pathetic inability to follow orders and do your job, MY DAUGHTER has left the protection of MY castle and has been carried off into terrible danger! Because OUT THERE, beyond MY Wall, are REAL LIVE Witches, not that *you* would know one if it bit you on the nose, and those *real live Witches* are going to be chasing my daughter and trying to kill her! And this is *ALL . . . YOUR . . . FAULT!*'

The Witchsmeller's mouth opened and shut.

And then he drew himself up and put his finger in the air for full scariness. He trembled with indignation. He had never met a woman so dreadful in all of his life. 'None of this is *my* fault. It is *you* who is in big trouble, Queen Sychorax! You tried to cover up the fact that your daughter is an extremely dangerous "FULE" and is fraternising with evil Magic elements!'

'She was *kidnapped*!' said Queen Sychorax. 'And there's no such thing as a "FULE", you unbalanced ignoramus!'

Shaking with fury, the Witchsmeller whirled round

to face his Magic-hunters in a swoop of cloak, the sprite-heads around his neck rattling against the giants' toenails.

'AFTER THEM!' yelled the Witchsmeller. 'MAGIC-HUNTERS, ONTO YOUR HORSES! FAIRY-CATCHERS, HAVE YOUR NETS READY! GIANT-KILLERS, SHARPEN YOUR AXES! WE WILL *HUNT ... THEM ... DOWN!*'

The Witchsmeller vaulted onto the back of his horse, and with terrible cries the hunt poured out of the castle gates.

The Enchanted Door was so small in the distance now that it was beginning to disappear into that great dark greenness. After it raced the Magic-hunt, the raving Dogwolves barking, as mad and out of control as if they had seen a fox, the insane scream of the Witchsmeller at the front, his cloak flying behind him as they charged after the door and into the forest.

I don't know if *you* have ever seen a hunt in full cry, but it is a truly terrifying sight.

'That hunt is going to tear Wish to pieces when it catches up with her,' said Drama with satisfaction.

'It most certainly will not,' said Queen Sychorax, grimly. 'For *I* will reach the Witchsmeller first. Warriors!' She stamped on the Royal Stage, once, twice. 'Up and on your feet! Saddle up my hunting horse! There's no time to lose! *We have a princess to catch*!'

7. On the Other Side of the Wall

s they approached Queen Sychorax's unbreachable, impregnable, invincible Wall, Xar let out a long crow of triumph.

'I did it!' cried Xar, punching the air.

'You mean, *we* did it!' Wish corrected him.

'Which way now?' asked the Enchanted Key chattily.

'I've never seen an enchanted object that talked before,' said Xar.

'I don't know what I'm doing!' replied Wish, slightly hysterically. 'I don't mean to bring things to life at all!'

Wish was struggling to keep control of the flying door. It had looked so easy when Xar did it six months ago. But somehow the door, when *she* was enchanting it, seemed to be going way too fast, and zig-zagging out of control all over the place . . .

A bit like Wish's emotions.

Wish knew she should be feeling horrified, and anxious. She knew that Warrior princesses really oughtn't to fly on the back of doors in the company of Wizards. She had tried so *hard* to be a Warrior princess, to concentrate on all the maths-work, and the sword-work, and the letter-work.

But the truth was, in her heart of hearts, she was absolutely fed up to the back teeth with trying to work out whether 'i' went before 'e' or what happened when you took 'x' from 'y', and whether she should be getting Madam Dreadlock's homework to the schoolroom or the stables because it was every second Thursday.

Of course she was scared and sad that her mother was going to be so disappointed, and so angry.

But part of her was just absolutely thrilled to be back in the adventure of it, soaring high, high, over the battlements . . . high, higher still to get over Queen Sychorax's Wall, the wind blowing her hair back. Oh my goodness, they were really going to get over it! Peering over the edge of the door she could see the little figures of the Warrior sentries, shouting but not shooting up at them, way, way down below . . .

Her heart beat fast . . . they were over the Wall! The great forest stretched out for miles and miles like an enormous green carpet in every direction, full of excitement and possibilities of danger.

The peril was instant, for the out-of-control door

was sinking fast, and Bodkin pointed to the tiny
distant figures of the Magic-hunters, pouring
out of the gates of the fort. They had to get as
far away as possible if they were not going to be
caught very quickly.

'Bodkin!' ordered Wish. 'Take off your armour!
It's weighing us down!'

And as Bodkin threw away breastplate after
breastplate, spears, swords, leg-protectors, arm-
protectors, and they fell down into the forest below,
the nose of the door lifted, and though it became
no slower, in fact it even speeded up, it
became easier to control. Wish's heart
lifted too.

The Enchanted Door shot over the forest canopy as fast as a speeding arrow, and Wish thought joyfully, *They'll never catch us now! Or . . . not tonight, at least . . .*

They zoomed over the Ragged River, and on, on and beyond, out of Queen Sychorax's territory, out of the boringness of real life and Punishment Cupboards and horrible stepsisters, and into the drama and excitement of the Wizard wildwoods.

However, once they were away from Queen Sychorax's territory, and flying above the forest, Wish's elation died. For there was something odd about the land she was looking down on, something different from the last time she had flown over it. Normally there was the friendly smoke of wandering giants moving slowly across the countryside, or the bonfires from the Wizard camps, or great swarms of chattering sprites migrating south, or north, depending on the season. Now there was not a breath of smoke, not a sound.

The forest was weirdly quiet, and worst of all were the sinister blackened circles cut into the woods, like a child had torn into them with a wicked pair of scissors.

'Oh my goodness . . .' whispered Wish. 'This has all been done by . . .'

'Witches,' said Xar, grimly finishing the sentence for her.

'I had no idea all this was going on!' said Wish.

It was a horrid thought, that while life was going on just exactly as normal in the Warrior territories, and they'd been doing their training, and their maths-work just like they always did, terrible battles had been carried out on this side of the Wall.

'Yes, well, that's your mother all over,' said Xar. 'As long as you are safe, she doesn't care about us. She's left us to be exterminated.'

'That's not entirely true,' said Wish. 'She hired the Witchsmeller and his Magic-hunters, didn't she?'

'If "the Witchsmeller" is that guy with the sniffing nose and the weird pointing finger, do you really think he is going to improve the situation?' said Xar.

Wish had to agree, the Witchsmeller's arrival in the wildwoods could not be described as an improvement.

'No, it's all down to ME,' said Xar moodily. 'I AM the boy of destiny, after all.'

Bodkin had shut his eyes at the word 'Witches'. Witches were all he needed to make him feel thoroughly sick, particularly because he'd now got rid of most of his armour. He was a reluctant flyer at the best of times, but as a first-time pilot, Wish was sending the door swooping up and down and swaying side to side in such a wild and uncontrolled manner that his stomach seemed to have been left behind somewhere back in the castle.

'Which way should I take it?' said Wish.

Xar pointed down to the right. 'The snowcats and Crusher are waiting for us somewhere over in that direction,' he said.

It was a bit of a bumpy landing.

When they got below the tree canopy, Wish had quite a lot of difficulty getting the door to slow down, and because she always got a tad confused between left and right, the door slalomed rather manically through the tree trunks until eventually she found a small clearing, and they slammed down into the ground with such energy that all three of them were catapulted off the door.

'Woah,' said Xar with reluctant respect, picking himself up and brushing himself off, 'you are one crazy door-driver, Wish!'

And then he punched the air and shouted, 'I DID it! Quest accomplished! Look at ME, O gods of the trees and water, and bow down in respect!'

'Oh yesssss, well done Xar, well done!' squealed Squeezjoos excitedly. 'You're brilliant, you really are!'

'I most certainly am,' said Xar with a grin. '*One thirteen-year-old boy, flying very low, has achieved the impossible double! Breaking out of Gormincrag Prison AND getting over Queen Sychorax's supposedly unbreachable Wall . . . not ONCE but TWICE!* I AM THE BOY OF DESTINY! FEEL MY POWER!!!!'

And then he threw back his head, and howled too.

'Urrr urr URRRR! Urr urr URRRRR!!!!!'

Wish and Bodkin, picking themselves up, and realising the enormity of what had just happened, looked at the so-called boy of destiny very, very balefully indeed.

'Aren't you going to thank me for saving you?' said Xar, just to add insult to injury. 'Or don't Warriors do thank yous?'

The cheek of it!

'Ha! *HA!* You saved US??' exclaimed Wish in outrage, her hands on her hips. 'WE saved *YOU*! If I hadn't enchanted that door those Magic-hunters would have killed you! And now Bodkin and I are in big, big trouble!

'Helping me out of there was the least you could do when all your relatives were attacking me!' said Xar. 'You Warriors are not very friendly to your guests!'

'*Guests???* Guests are *invited*! Guests are *polite*! *Guests* don't sneak in invisibly and try to *steal* things off you!' said Wish. 'I think the word you may be looking for is "burglar", not "guest" . . .'

'That Spelling Book is mine!' howled Xar. 'I need it for a very important Quest! And talking of burglary, you Warriors know all about that, don't you, because you're the biggest burglars in the world, and you've been stealing this forest off us

SIGH... these human beings
never seemed to change...

for as long as anyone can remember!'

'You can't steal a forest!' yelled Wish. 'The forest belongs to everyone!'

'Try telling your mother that.' Xar glowered.

'*Your father is just as bad as my mother, I've seen him!*' said Wish.

Wizard and Warrior stood nose to nose in the forest, bellowing insults and curses at each other, as their ancestors had done throughout history, ever since Warriors first invaded from across the seas, and the two sets of humans met in battle in the wildwoods centuries before.

Caliburn sighed.

However many lifetimes he lived, these humans never seemed to change. He'd hoped for better from these two, but maybe they were going to be just like the others . . .

But Xar wasn't feeling too pleased with his father, so he had to agree with Wish's last remark. And Wish was feeling rather the same about her mother.

They both paused.

'We shouldn't be fighting, Xar,' said Wish at last, sticking out her hand for him to shake. 'I've been really worried about what happened to you, and I'm so glad you're safe. I thought we were friends . . .'

Xar didn't have all that many friends at the moment, what with one thing and another. And he rather liked Wish. Even if she *was* an enemy. He was even rather fond of the odd bodyguard who kept falling asleep. So after a while, he said, 'Thank you for helping me out by enchanting that door.' Xar shook her hand and grinned back. 'And I like your style of door-driving.'

Maybe there *was* hope for the humans after all.

'And it WASSSS really funny, wassssn't it?' hissed Tiffinstorm, blinking into life beside them. 'The Witchsmeller, screeching like a ssscreech owl . . . "This spoon is alive! This spoon is alive!"'

Now the danger was over, it really was quite funny. Wish and Xar, the sprites, and even Bodkin were laughing at the memory of the Witchsmeller. The spoon did a brilliant impression of bonking him on the nose.

Even Caliburn's shoulders were shaking, before he remembered himself, and gave a little cough. 'I'd just like to gently remind you that you're supposed to be meeting everyone else here, Xar . . .'

Xar stopped laughing.

'Oh yes! You're right, Caliburn.' He whistled a
couple of times. 'Now where ARE those snowcats?
And Crusher? I TOLD them not to wander off.

'Oh, there you are!' exclaimed Xar as, out of
the gloom of the forest, there burst three stunningly
beautiful lynxes, who padded over to Xar and greeted
him as enthusiastically as if they had been three
little kittens, knocking him over onto his back, and
slathering his face with licks.

'Nighteye! Kingcat! Forestheart! Crusher!' sang
Wish delightedly, as with great crashing noises the
giant lumbered into the clearing, pushing the trees
aside, his head on a level with the topmost branches.

She hugged the snowcats, burying her face into the

Snowcats

deep softness of their fur, and then ran to embrace the
giant around the ankle. 'Oh, I've MISSED you all . . .'

'And weezus missed you!!!' trilled Squeezjoos happily,
flying into her hair and making a joyful little nest in it.
'Ridunculous humungular being!'

'Ssssome of us have . . .' said Hinkypunk, and just to
show that not ALL sprites were as soppy as Squeezjoos,
he blew a little sprite-breath, which froze Wish's fringe
and stuck it to her forehead. 'Nots *me* though . . . I
hatesss Warriors . . .'

'And this is the Once-sprite,' said Xar, pointing to
the little sprite sitting on the back of a peregrine falcon
that had landed on his shoulder. 'He's a new member
of my sprite team. Your wicked mother took his Magic
away, but he's learning to live life without it, aren't you,
Once-sprite? His wings don't work any more but he's
learnt to fly on the back of this peregrine falcon.'

The Once-sprite was sprite-sized, and sprite-shaped,
but no bright light shone from his chest. His colour had
faded till you could hardly tell what it might have been
. . . *once*. His wings had withered on his shoulders, and
the sharp little points of his ears had turned and drooped.

'It's very nice to meet you,' said Wish, giving the
Once-sprite a shy wave. The Once-sprite did not look as
if he had forgiven Wish for her mother's actions. He stared
stiffly into the distance, as though Wish were not there.

But Wish was too happy in that moment to mind.

The truth is, if you spend most of your life with your only real friends being an Assistant Bodyguard and a spoon, it's very nice to meet up with some other people who are on the same wavelength, even if some of them *are* a little annoying sometimes, and supposed to be your deadly enemies.

Bodkin drew his sword and screamed, 'Werewolf! Get behind me, Wish! There's a werewolf!' as he saw Lonesome for the first time, prowling in the shadows behind the other wolves, his tail swaying ominously from side to side.

'Oh, no, that's fine, he's a friend,' explained Xar with a careless wave of his hand. 'I met him in Gormincrag.'

'A *friend*? You're friends with a *werewolf*?' said Bodkin. This really was too much, even for Xar. 'But werewolves used to be known as companions for Witches . . . and what were you doing in Gormincrag? Isn't that some kind of prison?'

'Lonesome was innocent. He should never have been in prison in the first place,' said Xar. 'And for a Loner Raving Fangmouth werewolf he's really quite friendly. He just needs a bit of help with his manners.'

'Doesn't EVERYONE in prison say they're innocent?' said Bodkin, looking very dubiously indeed at the werewolf, who was pawing at the ground in a manic sort of way, as if he was barely repressing the urge to rip them all to pieces.

The werewolf bared its teeth menacingly at Bodkin.

'Oh, Bodkin, don't be so prejudiced,' scolded Wish. 'This werewolf may be a very *nice* werewolf for all we know . . .'

The werewolf paused for a moment, stiffening a little in surprise. He had never met Warriors before, having spent his whole life locked up in Gormincrag, and this was the first time that anyone had ever described him as 'very nice'. Mostly people just ran away screaming.

'Why were you in prison, Xar?' asked Wish. 'And why do you want the Spelling Book? I'd have just *given* it back to you, you didn't have to sneak in and steal it.'

'Caliburn didn't want me to get you involved,' said Xar. 'And I need a Spelling Book so I can make my father's staff work properly. I'm going to need all the Magic I can get in the quest I'm going on . . . A quest to get rid of . . . *this*.'

Xar took off his glove.

Wish and Bodkin let out horrified gasps.

'I *wish* you'd stop doing that,' moaned Caliburn, putting one wing over his eyes as the sprites burned with green fire, hissing and cursing in alarm, and the snowcats and the wolves crouched down, growling. A trembling Squeezjoos flew into Wish's hair and made a little nest there.

'Oh . . . my . . . goodness!' whispered Wish in horror. 'What happened to your hand? It's the *Witch-stain*, isn't it? But I thought the Stone-That-Takes-Away-Magic had taken the Witch-stain away? We all saw it happen, in my mother's dungeon!'

'Yes, well, it didn't take all of it,' said Xar. 'The great thing about it is that I can do Magic now, and that was wonderful, at first. But the bad thing about it is . . .'

'It's *Bad* Magic,' finished Caliburn. 'Very, Very *Bad* Magic. And, as you can see, it's getting worse.'

Bodkin and Wish shivered as they looked at Xar's hand.

'It looks so *awful*. You don't think . . . you're not worried that . . . it might turn YOU to the bad, Xar?' suggested Wish tentatively. She laid a gentle hand on Xar's arm.

She could feel a slight coldness as she touched him, like ghost-breath on the back of the neck. Xar wasn't looking well. His hair was damp, as if he had a temperature. The green of the Witch-stain had crept all the way beyond his wrist, there was a feverish look in his eye, and he shivered now and then, as if he was about to catch a nasty bout of the flu. Sometimes his hand stiffened, and his fingers curled and turned into claws . . .

147

And even Xar found that a little scary.

'The Droods found out about the Witch-stain and shut me up in Gormincrag. They said they were trying to find a cure, but they were *lying*, and my father believed them,' said Xar moodily. 'They all just want me to stay in Gormincrag forever. My father doesn't care ... Well, I'll show *them*!'

'But what are you going to do, Xar?' said Bodkin. 'The Stone-That-Takes-Away-Magic is broken, you can't use that any more!'

'The only way to get rid of a Witch-stain is to get rid of the Witches *themselves*,' said Xar. 'So that's what I'm going to do. I'm going to go out there and destroy them.'

Bodkin looked at him with an open mouth. He had met Witches before, and knew exactly how scary they were. 'You're going to go out there and face a whole horde of acid-blooded nightmares *all on your own*? On *purpose*? But you're just one small boy!'

Caliburn coughed. 'And it's all very well saying you're going to destroy them, Xar, but HOW, exactly? That's been my point along ...'

'Well, that's why I need my Spelling Book,' said Xar. 'I'm sure there will be something in there that can

The Spelling Book FLEW up into the air and into Wish's hands...

help me . . .'

'This is the most extraordinary coincidence!' cried Wish excitedly.

'What coincidence?' moaned Caliburn, feeling the beginnings of a serious worry coming on. 'I hate coincidences . . .'

'*I've JUST TODAY found a spell in the Spelling Book to get rid of Witches!*' said Wish triumphantly. 'In fact, that's exactly why I broke out of the Punishment Cupboard – I wanted to get the spell to you and your father . . . Bodkin, show Xar!'

As soon as she said these words, the Spelling Book flew out of Bodkin's pocket, and up into the air and into Wish's hands, growing larger as it flew.

Wish tapped the letters on the 'Contents' page to take them to the right part of the book.

'It was quite strange really. I didn't *find* it so much as *write* it,' admitted Wish. 'I was using the feather that Caliburn gave me to write with, and it was almost as if Caliburn's feather was writing *on its own* . . .'

They all crowded around the Spelling Book to see the page.

THE SPELLING BOOK
Bloody Barbeards

Bloody Barbeards are dangerous mer-people who live in the Drowned Forest. They have a grudge against all Wizards, the reasons for which have got lost over the centuries, but any Wizard found swimming in the Sea of Skulls will be dragged down to the bottom of the ocean by a Bloody Barbeard.

page 3,284,956

Three-headed Bugbear

Bugbears are large, annoying creatures with great tracking abilities. Once they are on your trail, they will very rarely give up.

The third head on this Bugbear is invisible

page 3,284,957

THE SPELLING BOOK

Telekenesis

Moving things with your mind...

?
?
?
?

The power of moving things with your mind. Most Wizards have to use a staff to move things through the power of mind control, but a few can use their hands, and in this case, a Magic eye.

It takes years of practice to perfect this art.

The Magic Eye

Wizards with a Magic eye are extraordinarily rare, and will have more than one life. The Magic eye allows the Wizard to perform Magic without a staff (normally a skill that takes decades to learn). However the Magic is so powerful it is extremely difficult to train and control.

A Magic eye only appears once in every couple of generations.

page 58½,130

Transformation

Transformation is one of the most difficult Magic spells, and extremely dangerous. For it is one thing to transform into another form – it is quite another to come back. If you stay too long, there is a risk that you might remain as the creature you transformed into forever.

The stronger the Wizard's Magical powers, the longer they can stay transformed and still come back.

House Sprites

Most forts, either Wizard or Warrior, are infested with house sprites. These mischievous little creatures hide like mice, in the walls or under the floorboards, and they come out at night to steal food, or play tricks on the inhabitants of the forts.

PAGE 60,486

The SPELLING BOOK
Write Your Own Story
Noo Year's Ressolushuns

1. I wull work hard at my
reeding and arithmatick so
I can be topp of the klass.

2. I wull mak a gud impreshun
on the teacher.

3. I wull impress my muther
so she dus not think I am a
Dissapointment.

sined:

Wish

page 2,304,587

The Spelling Book
Write Your Own Story

A Spell to Get Rid of Witches

Gather all ingredients and STIR with a living Spoon.

Ingredeents:
One: Giant's Last Breath from Castle Death
Two: Feathers from a Witch
Three: Tears from a frozen Queen

page 2,304,588

The Spelling Book Thanks You For Reading,

and Would Gently Remind You That Things

Generally Turn Out All Right

IN THE END.

(Hopefully)

DIE!

SnOcats FoREVER

Niteye eating Looter

When my MAGIC
comes in I will bee
the MOST MAGIC ~~pursonn~~
purson
in the
UNIVERSE

I ♥ Spoons

This bOOK has ben lent
to mee. Wish

'Look! It's a recipe! Maybe the Ssspelling Book wants us to EAT the Witches?' said Squeezjoos, excitedly, for Squeezjoos was always hungry.

'That's not a recipe!' said Xar. 'Oh my goodness! *You're right!* It's a Spell to Get Rid of Witches!!! I knew it!'

They all gazed hopefully at the spell.

'You wrote this with MY feather, did you, Wish?' said Caliburn, so worried now that the feathers were dropping from his back like leaves in autumn. 'Oh dear, oh dear, oh dear ... Sometimes I forget what happened in my former lives, but the memory lives on in my feathers.'

'You've lost me there, Caliburn,' said Bodkin, shaking his head. 'I have no idea what you're talking about. Former lives?'

'Yes, I have lived many lives as a human but this is the first time I have been reincarnated as a bird,' explained Caliburn, as if this was the most normal thing in the world. 'So perhaps the feather is writing a message TO me, FROM me in one of my former lives?'

Bodkin's head was going round and round. These Wizards and Magical things were so complicated. Having just the one life as a Warrior Assistant Bodyguard was so much simpler than all this reincarnating, turning-into-birds business.

'But I've never heard of a spell so strong that it could actually get rid of Witches ENTIRELY,' said Caliburn.

161

'Did I really know that in a former life? *What does this mean?*'

'It means,' said Xar animatedly, '*that we're going spell-raiding, guys!* Oh, this is so exciting!'

Spell-raiding was a rather disreputable part of the Magic world. Spells needed ingredients, and some of those ingredients were hard to get hold of. So wild wingless young sprites called 'spell-raiders' specialised in collecting and stealing spell ingredients. They flew at night, on the back of specially trained peregrine falcons, in order to make a quick getaway.

The Once-sprite cheered up no end. He had been drooping sadly on the back of the peregrine falcon, but now he sat up, so excited that he might have an important role to play in the world once more that he accidentally fell off his bird, scrambled up on its back again, and saluted Xar, saying, 'I won't let you down, Xar! Youssss can rely on me!'

'Me too! Me too!' squeaked Squeezjoos. '*I's* wants to be a spell-raider too!'

'Youss too young to be a ssspell-raider . . .' said the Once-sprite. 'It'sss very dangerousssss . . . you can guard some of the collecting bottles that we're going to put the ingredients in . . .'

The Once-sprite rustled in his spell-bags and gave a few collecting bottles to Squeezjoos, who said, 'Is'll guard them with my life!'

'All right, let's see, what's the first ingredient?' said Xar excitedly. '*The Giant's Last Breath from Castle Death* . . .'

The werewolf started to growl and gesticulate urgently. What he said was: '*REOOWR, grunt, GROOWGGRGLE, grunt, weoorrrrr!*' And then a loud spitting noise, and a stamp of the hairy foot, followed by, '*Creargle Urgh.*'

'Look! Lonesome is agreeing with us! He's saying we have to go IMMEDIATELY to Castle Death,' said Xar.

'You speak werewolf?' asked Wish, deeply impressed.

'Oh yes, fluently,' said Xar, carelessly.

'Would you say *fluently*?' said Caliburn, to no one in particular.

'Fluently,' repeated Xar firmly. 'We Wizards all get lessons in werewolf language.'

'Xar's *brilliant*, issn't he?' said Squeezjoos proudly. 'Speakss werewolf like he'ss a werewolf himself.'

'Your lessons sound so much more interesting than *our* lessons,' said Wish longingly.

'What's he saying now?'

'*Grunt, weoorrrr!*' Stamp! Spit! repeated the werewolf rather more urgently.

'Don't worry, Lonesome, I understand,' said Xar. 'We need to go to Castle Death. Immediately.'

Unfortunately that *wasn't* what the werewolf was

saying. Xar really should have concentrated harder
in the werewolf language classes. *'Creagle Urgh'* does
indeed mean Castle Death, so Xar had got that bit right.
But 'go to' in werewolf language is *'grunt, weeiiiroh,'*
whereas *'grunt, weoorrr*!*'* means 'stay away from'.

The spit and the stamp was just for emphasis.

So what the werewolf was *actually* saying was: 'For
goodness sake STAY AWAY from Castle Death!'

The werewolf got more urgent still.

'Reaaghhh cccroooglle sfocccan Burgan!' Stamp! Spit!
*'Purgan GRUNT WEOORRR, nurgan GRUNT
WEEIIROH! GRUNT WEOORRR Creagle Urgh! Pi
urglly discottle agly rewooooow perooooooow.'*

And what *that* meant was, 'That's not what I *said,*
you stupid human! "Stay away", not "go to"! STAY
AWAY from Castle Death if you want to hang on to
your pathetic little human lives!'

And then Lonesome threw his head back and started
howling.

'Lonesome's just becoming a little frustrated because
he thinks we should be getting a move on,' said Xar.
Xar patted the werewolf kindly on the paw. 'Don't
worry, Lonesome, we're going there, we're going there
as fast as we can . . .'

'I think *we* should go too,' said Wish decidedly.

'Whaaaaaaaat????' said Bodkin.

THE SPELLING BOOK

Two-Headed Sabre Tooth
werewolves

Werewolves do not only come out at night, as the
legends suggest, and some are more friendly than others.
This Two-Headed Sabre-Tooth
werewolf is remarkably speedy
and very savage, so best
avoided (unless you are a
very fast runner).

Best avoided, unless
you are a
very fast
runner.

8 · Following the Sweet Track

'But you promised your mother!' said Bodkin in an agonised sort of way. 'You said you'd go back home straight away! This isn't our problem!'

'It IS our problem,' said Wish. 'We ALL let the Kingwitch out of the stone, and Xar is our friend, so we have to help him. We can't just sit behind the Wall twiddling our thumbs while Xar goes through all this on his own.'

'I have to agree with Bodkin the bodyguard,' said Caliburn. 'That's a REALLY, REALLY bad idea! Your type of Magic is very dangerous, Wish . . . and the Witches WANT that Magic. On the other side of the Wall, the Witches can't get at you, but over *here* . . .'

'You need our help!' argued Wish. 'The spell talks about how you should "stir the ingredients with a Living Spoon", and *I'm* the one who has the living spoon!'

The Enchanted Spoon, delighted to be playing such an important role, gave a small, proud bow to the rest of the company.

'You should both go back to your parents!' moaned Caliburn to Xar and Wish. 'I know they're a little unreasonable, but if you explain everything to them, maybe they could help you. This is a bigger problem than the two of you can deal with ... MUCH bigger ... MUCH more dangerous. This is a Longstepper High-Walker GIANT of a problem!'

'All right, Crusher, what do YOU think?' Wish shouted up to Xar's giant.

Crusher was picking leaves from the topmost branches of the trees and eating them.

He put his face down a little closer, and you could see that it was covered with wrinkles and laughter lines like the wandering paths on an old map, and his eyes were kind and wise.

'I was thinking,' said Crusher dreamily (speaking v-e-r-y slowly, for giants operate in a different timescale from everyone else), 'about LANGUAGE and how in *English* two negatives make a positive, but in *spriteish*, a double negative is still a negative. However there is NO language in which two positives make a negative ...'

'Yeah, right, like THAT'S the problem,' said Xar, sarcastically.

'I hadn't thought of that!' said Crusher in gentle surprise, but delighted that Xar was engaging with his mental processes. 'You're correct, Xar. "Yeah, right" IS a statement in English where two positives make a negative ...'

Crusher was a wonderful giant companion, but he could sometimes be on a different planet from everyone else.

'That wasn't what I meant!' said Xar, in exasperation. '*Stop thinking Big Thoughts, Crusher!* The *real* problem is, should Wish come with us or go back to her scary mother?'

'Oh!' said Crusher, even more thoughtfully.

He paused for an impressively long time, and then said, 'Well, Wish should come with us, because I like her.'

Strangely enough, it was this simple statement that changed Caliburn's mind.

'All right!' he said with a sigh. 'I suppose this is all such a disaster that it doesn't really matter WHAT we do, as long as we're with our friends and we do it TOGETHER.

'And as long as everyone promises that we will take breaks for lessons along the way,' he went on. 'I don't want any of you getting behind in your studies! You three need all the education you can get.'

They looked up the way to Castle Death in the 'maps' section of the Spelling Book, which very helpfully lit up the various routes across the wildwoods with different colours of sprite dust. Purple dust was a warning to the traveller to be careful, red dust meant

exceptional danger, and yellow dust marked the safer
passages.

Castle Death, on the edge of the Witch Mountains,
was across a land to the west called the Slodger
territories, a vast, bog-like desert that stretched for miles
in every direction.

And the Slodger territories were dangerous, for
Grindylows and Greenteeth lived in those marshes,
strange, part see-through creatures, with huge sad eyes,
who reached out skinny arms, and dragged you down
under the muddy water, with little satisfying belches of
the bog.

The only safe way, marked in yellow, across the
Slodger territories was the Sweet Track, an ancient
road like a long, winding bridge, built and blessed by
Wizards long ago. You can't be attacked on the Sweet
Track, for it was guarded by a very ancient power, and
Spells too old to unravel.

They didn't want to use Magic to get there, for
Magic was tiring, and Wish was already so exhausted by
the effort of making the door fly and keeping it in the
air by her sheer will, that she could feel every muscle in
her body aching. Also, the use of Magic would make it
easier for Witches or other bad things to trace them.

The broken door had smashed to pieces on landing,
but they might need it later, so it was the sprites who

put it back together again with their wands.

A fairy making a spell is a little like someone taking a golf shot, or a baseball swing in another time, another place. It's not just a matter of pointing the wand in a careless fashion. The spell is thrown up in the air, the wand goes right behind the head and then smashes the spell towards the thing that it is wanting to enchant, preferably, for full power, with a great deal of follow through.

ZING!!!! The spells spun through the air, singing the word 'reconstruct', and scoring a direct hit on the smashed door, and the pieces instantly sorted themselves out, organising themselves swiftly on the floor like a puzzle rearranging itself, at first forming a ridiculous pattern that didn't look like a door at all, before whizzing back together again magically in the right place, as if magnetically attracted to one another.

Crusher put the Enchanted Door in his pocket, and Xar, Wish and Bodkin climbed aboard the snowcats' backs, and the giant slowly walked his way through the holloways to the beginning of the Slodger territories, the wolves and the snowcats running by his side, the sprites and Caliburn flying overhead.

After six hours of walking, they
reached the famous bridge, beginning in
the woods itself, and then stretching way,
way into the distance across the marshes,
like the coils of an enormous snake.

They decided to camp on the bridge of
the Sweet Track for the night.

'And we should lay the campfire on
the bridge itself,' said Caliburn. 'For once
it gets dark, that is the only place where we
will be truly safe. What is the best wood for
a campfire that might put off Greenteeth?
Bodkin? Wish?'

Bodkin and Wish had absolutely not
the foggiest of an idea. A Warrior education
tended to focus on maths-work, and letter-
work, and sword-work, and
farming skills.

The start
of the Sweet Track
(ancient Way across the marsh)

Wood-work was not really part of anything they knew.

'Goodness gracious!' said Caliburn, very shocked. 'Don't they teach you anything over there in iron Warrior fort? This is elementary stuff. How do they expect you to survive in the forest if you don't know *that*?'

'I's know! I's know!' said Squeezjoos. 'Alder or rowan is for protection . . . and hawthorn makes a nice hot fire . . .'

So Xar and Wish and Bodkin gathered alder wood from the forest, and then they arranged a little ring of stones to put the wood on to make their campfire.

'Let *me*
practise lighting it
with staff-Magic!' said
Xar.

'I'm not sure that's a
good idea,' said Caliburn
hastily.

'I have to practise controlling
the Magic! And you were the one
who said we should be doing lessons!'
said Xar. He looked up the spell in the
Spelling Book and then held out his arm with the
Witch-stain on it, his father's yew spelling staff grasped
firmly in that hand.

'Let the Magic come out slowly,' advised Caliburn,
'in a controlled and focussed manner . . . Think gentle,

calm, happy thoughts . . . Be patient . . .'

But nothing happened. And Xar was not a patient person.

He went red in the face with exasperation. He shook the staff crossly. 'Why isn't it working?'

'Oh, I've been looking up about spelling staffs. I think you might be holding the staff at the wrong end – you hold it like *this*,' said Wish, helpfully putting her hand on the staff to show him the grip she had read about in the Spelling Book.

And the moment that Wish put her hand on it as well . . .

BOOOOOOOM!!!!!!!! The Magic came screaming out of the staff with such force that the little campfire of alder and hawthorn twigs EXPLODED, and Wish and Xar and Bodkin and the wolves and the snowcats and the werewolf were all blown off their feet by the force of the explosion, and into the bog.

'Don't get discouraged, everyone!' announced Caliburn, as they all staggered muddily to their feet, amidst a strong smell of burning feathers, and singed-fur-of-werewolf. 'It can take quite some TIME to learn

how to control Magic.'

The explosion had blasted a great big
hole in the bridge of the Sweet Track,
where the ancient timbers, which had
lain there quietly and peacefully for so
many centuries, had been smashed
in two, and now smouldered
ominously with little flickering
green flames at the blackened
edges.

'Oh dear, was that me?' said Wish apologetically.
'I'm so sorry, I've always been a bit clumsy . . .'

'No, no . . . it could happen to anyone!' said
Caliburn, with a nervous glance at Wish, for the power
that protected the Sweet Track was a very ancient
power indeed, and the bridge really ought to have
remained intact whatever spells were thrown at it. He
had never heard of any Magic, past, present or future,
that could have an effect on the Sweet Track.

It didn't seem the best of omens for the start of their
expedition.

They regathered wood, and relaid the fire a bit
further down the bridge, and Bodkin lit it by the
Warrior method of using a little iron fire striker
against flint, which deeply impressed the sprites. Less
spectacular than Xar's way, but more effective.

The sprites then blew *out*
the fire, in order to show off to
Bodkin that they could relight
it with their sprite-breath, in
all sorts of beautiful colours –
yellow, red, green, blue.

Look what I've
done to my father's
Spelling Staff !!

Wish tore up the note she wore around her neck saying 'I am A Fule' and put it on the fire, and the note burned happily, with rainbow brightness.

And then they made a delicious nettle stew. Crusher gathered the nettles, stuffing his pockets with handfuls and handfuls of them, for they would need food for the journey ahead, and not much food was to be found in the Slodger territories. Wish and the sprites found water and Bodkin did the cooking. The werewolf, *thoroughly* overexcited by his new-found freedom in the wildwoods, returned from his own hunting expedition with an entire mouthful of worms, which he deposited triumphantly in Wish's lap as a helpful addition to the stew (the werewolf seemed to have taken a bit of a shine to Wish).

'That's a LOVELY idea, Lonesome!' said Wish tactfully, not wanting to hurt his feelings. 'But maybe you could have those on the side or as a starter? I think Bodkin may be allergic to worms, aren't you, Bodkin?'

'Definitely allergic to worms,' said Bodkin firmly.

Xar wanted to try one, but Caliburn wouldn't let him.

The Enchanted Spoon stirred the stew with such enthusiasm that he turned it into a positive *whirlpool*, and on a couple of occasions he very nearly fell in and had to be rescued by Xar or Bodkin or Wish.

Bodkin announced that the stew was ready and the werewolf leapt up and thrust his entire head into the saucepan and began noisily slurping. Xar pulled him out, and Caliburn explained to the rather crestfallen werewolf about manners, while the sprites cartwheeled through the air in fits of giggles.

Xar had managed to steal a saucepan while he was on the run, but he hadn't got any plates, which was fine, because they just ate off large leaves.

And I don't know whether it was the cold night air, and the adventure of the day, or the way that the Enchanted Spoon stirred that stew, but it was the most delicious stew that anyone had ever tasted.

That was a happy, happy evening. Even Bodkin was happy. He couldn't quite think why. He had lost most of his armour, which should have left him more anxious, but somehow he felt lighter and braver. At least he could bend over.

He joined in with the songs around the campfire.

The moon came up over the marshes, a big round full one, and the werewolf howled at it, and Xar joined in. *'URR URR URRRRR!'*

'Is is just me,' whispered Bodkin to Wish, 'or is that werewolf not a very good influence on Xar?'

'Give the werewolf a chance,' said Wish. 'He just hasn't been around people very much . . .'

Eventually they fell asleep on the boards of the Sweet Track, and even though the air was bitterly cold, they were all snuggled round with the wolves and the snowcats and the bear, and their shaggy coats kept them warm. The smoke from the fire curled gently upward, constantly changing colour – blue, red, orange, white.

Crusher stayed awake, watching out for Witches and other bad things. He sat cross-legged in the bog, humming and singing very softly to himself.

Much later, Wish woke up.

'Having trouble sleeping, little one?' said the giant, stopping singing for a moment and bending down to look at her.

'I'm worrying about

going to Castle Death . . . and the Witches . . .' shivered Wish. 'How can you *not* worry, Crusher?'

The giant laughed. 'What *I* generally find is that if there is some GIANT problem in the world some GIANT answer turns up just in time to solve it.'

The raven, who was also awake, harrumphed a little, but he did admit, 'That IS the lesson of history.'

'Worrying won't help it turn up any sooner. And look!' continued the giant, 'If you waste your time *worrying*, how will you have a moment to see how beautiful the world is?'

His giant fingers closed around Wish, and gently he carried her up, up, up into the air. Wish had a heart-stopping moment of excitement to find herself looking DOWN on the world rather than UP at it. Crusher put her into his pocket and she peered over its rim, the wind blowing her hair back. From here in the moonlight she could see for miles and miles across the wasteland, and way, way in the distance the misty outlines of the Witch Mountains. Somewhere out there was Castle Death . . . but from the safety of the giant's pocket, all she could think of was how calm it was, how still, with the moon above the marshes and the wind blowing steadily.

The giant began to sing.

'A GIANT heart
Needs a GIANT life!
GIANT arms
Can hold a world!'

Every time he sang the word 'GIANT!' he threw
out his arms wide and Wish bounced around unsteadily
in his pocket, giggling.

'Let me lead a GIANT'S life!
No LITTLE steps, no holding back!
A GIANT way, a GIANT'S track!

Let my mistakes
Be GIANT ones!

For I can't live in LITTLE worlds!

I need the space to run my fill
I need to jump from hill to hill

And if you take my woods from me
I'll wander out into the sea
And try to find another world

So I can live a GIANT life!'

And down on the Sweet Track, the sound of the
giant's singing woke Xar and Bodkin, and the sprites,
and it was so joyful it really put heart into the
little party. The werewolf even joined
in with his OWN song, which I
have translated here, because
otherwise it sounds mostly
like howling.

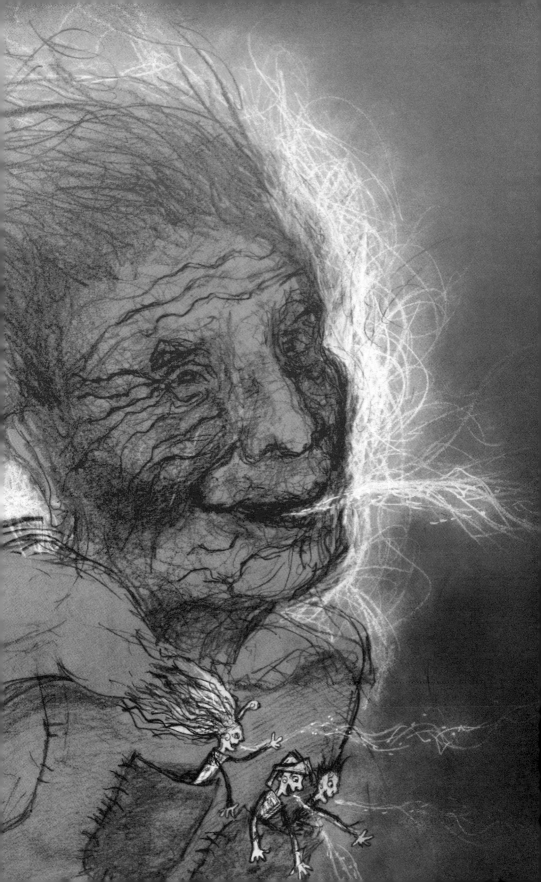

The moon and I
(The Werewolf's Song)

Me and the moon
The moon and me
When all the world gives up on me
When everyone thinks bad about me
I still have the moon
It's me and the moon
It's always the moon and me

My bad wolf heart wants what it wants
So I have to keep running ... Keep running ...
Can't stop in case I bite someone
Keep running ... Keep running ...
I thought I was good, and then I looked down
My shaggy coat, my wolfy paws,
I'm bad as a snake, and meaner than grit,
Don't try and stop me, cos you will get bit
Let me keep running ...

I'm running for the moon
Up to the moon where I can be good
When all the world gives up on me
When everyone thinks bad about me
I still have the moon
It's me and the moon
Mostly its me and the moon

Every now and then the werewolf would break off
to howl: *'Ooooww ooow OOOOOOOOWW!'*

And Wish and Bodkin joined in with the Warrior
War Song: 'NO FEAR! That's the Warrior's marching
song! *NO FEAR!'* While Xar and the sprites sang the
Magic Lament: 'Once we were Wizards, wandering
free, in roads of sky and paths of sea ...'

'Let me lead a GIANT'S life!' sang
Crusher.

'Mostly it's me and the moon!' sang
Lonesome. *'Ooww ooow OOOOOW! Ooooow ooow*
OOOOOOOOOWWWW!'

And as the songs blended on the midnight air, they seemed to be defying and taunting the many, many people and creatures who were now chasing Wish and Xar.

Xar's father was looking for him, searching the countryside in the form of a great golden eagle. And Queen Sychorax and the Witchsmeller.

And something WORSE was following them . . .

For as I said earlier, when Xar escaped from Gormincrag, there might have been some things that helped, things that had soft black wings, and feathers for arms, and talons like swords on the ends of their claw-like hands. Things that might have been Witches . . .

Well, they weren't helping him NOW.

They were AFTER him.

For Xar, all unknowing, had done what the Kingwitch wanted. He had brought Wish from behind the Wall, and now she was out in the open, unprotected, and if the Witches could get their claws on her and bring her to the Kingwitch sooner than expected, why, then, so much the better . . .

Xar and Wish are on
this Quest together now...

but they are being
CHASED by dark forces.
Can they get away?

Part One: Escape

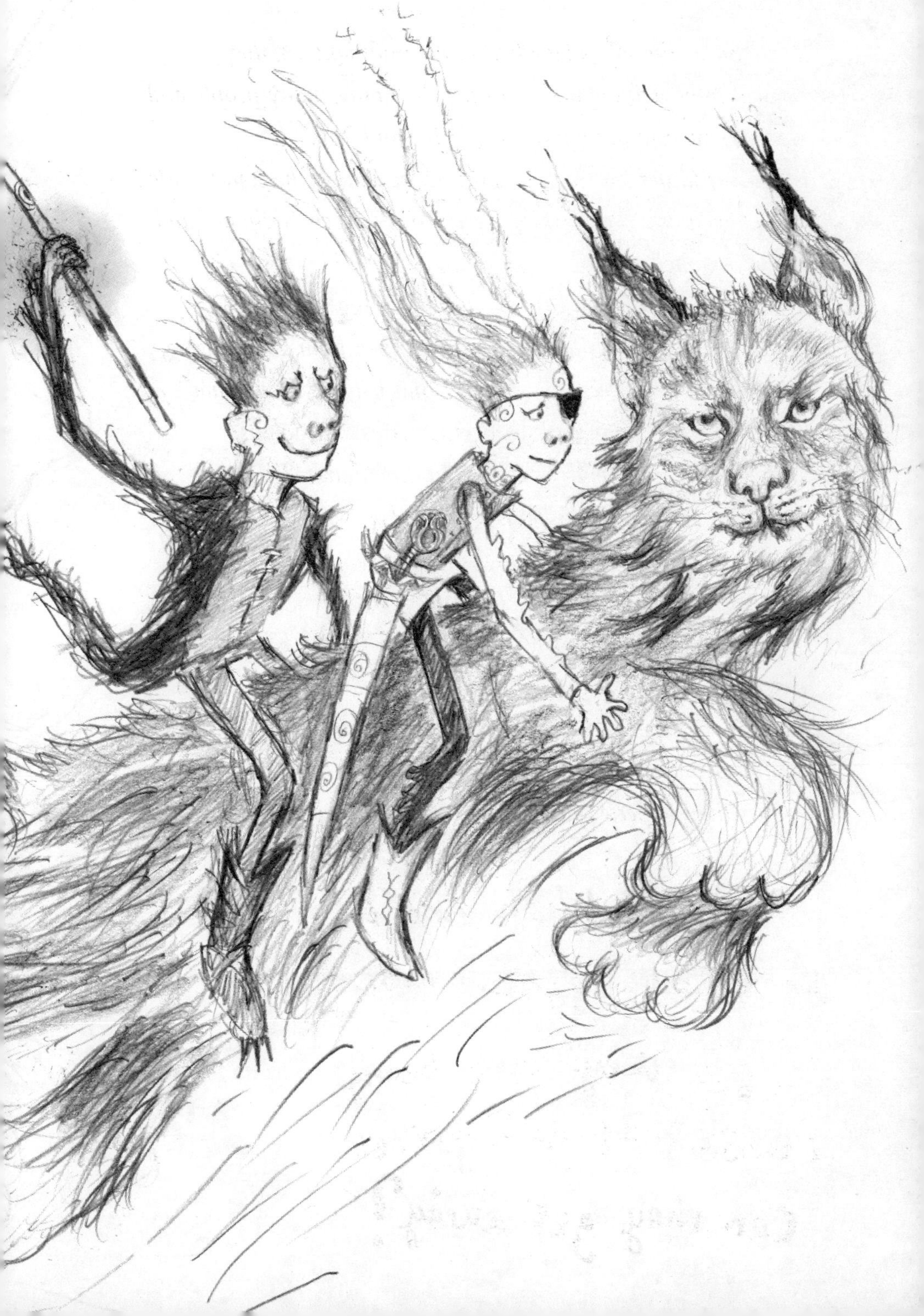

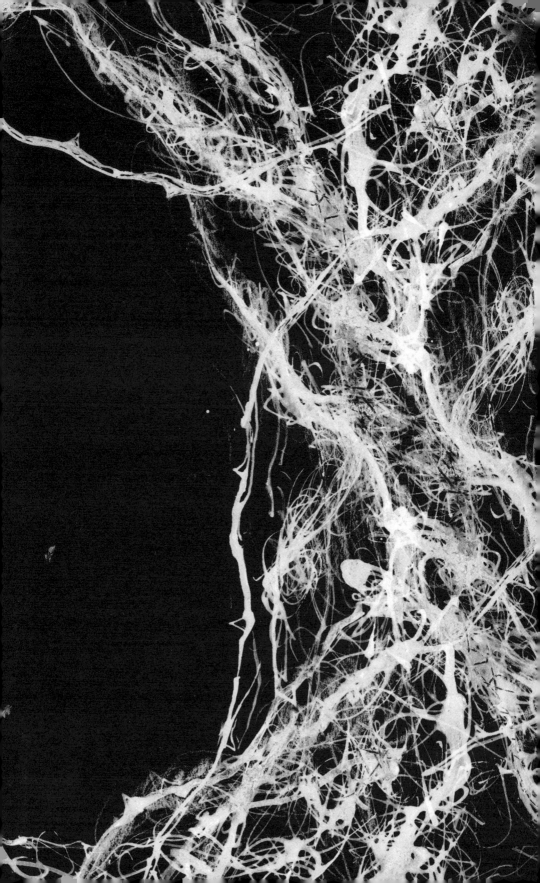

part Two
the
Witch
-Trap

9 · A Couple of Nasty Surprises on the way to Castle Death

Xar woke very early the next morning, his right arm aching and burning. He shook Wish awake, and within seconds of opening her eyes, her heart was beating as quick and panicked as that of a small forest creature who knows it is about to be attacked. There was a coldness in the air that they both remembered from before, a chill that sank into the bones and froze the blood and smudged the thoughts, and the hair on Wish's head rose up with electric, fizzing energy.

For the smell was familiar too: a stinking reek of decaying cat and corpses' breath and burning hair, with a sulphurous kick of rotten eggs . . . A smell that brought Xar out in a frightened sweat, for it was the smell of WITCHES.

All around them the animals were waking into instant, terrified alarm, their fur bristling around their necks in ruffs, and the sprites flew shaking up into the air, burning bright with fear, drawing their wands, sharp as thorns, reaching into their spell bags . . .

Wish felt for the Enchanted Sword, but to her horror she found that for some reason she couldn't take it out of the scabbard. It was stuck fast.

194

She could hear her own breath.

There was something under the bridge . . .

She had a glimpse from between the boards
of something dark and feathery, moving slowly,
nauseously, greasily beneath them.

'Ruuuuuuuunnnnnnnnnn!!!!' yelled
Wish at the top of her voice, as
with a high unearthly wail . . .

UH-OH...

There's
something
under the
bridge!

SLLLLLICCCCCCCCCE!

Three great talons came up from below, piercing right through the planks of the bridge a couple of yards back from where they were standing.

Wish and Bodkin and Xar ran for their lives alongside the snowcats, with the wolves and the werewolf, along the length of the Sweet Track, with the sprites and Caliburn flying terrified above, and Crusher

stumbling to his feet and splashing noisily through the
bog, following them all.

Wish looked over her shoulder as the snowcats ran
further, further along the bridge across the marshes.
There were the woods, dark in the distance. There was
the broken bridge. There was the place where they
had camped. There was the spot where Wish had seen
the Witch's talons, but there was nothing to be seen of
those talons now ... Where had the Witch gone?

They ran on, on, on, along the Sweet Track, until
the woods were just a distant smudge on the horizon,
and the snowcats were so tired that their weary
paws moved slower, slower, and ...
slower ... still, until they limped
and lumbered into a
panting walk.

'I think,' puffed Caliburn, 'that we're safe now. That Witch would only have been able to attack us because the explosion yesterday may have broken the Magic that protects the bridge at that particular point.'

'Why couldn't I draw the Enchanted Sword?' said Wish, puzzled and shaken. 'It wouldn't come out, however hard I pulled it, but it's coming out really easily now . . .'

Sure enough, now they were out of danger, she had taken the sword out of the scabbard with one light touch.

'I always said that sword was a bit wayward,' said Caliburn nervously. 'It has too much of a mind of its own.'

They all stopped to examine the sword.

'That's odd . . .' said Bodkin, noticing something for the first time. 'The writing on the blade looks different.'

'It must have got scratched or worn away at some point,' said Wish.

It was an unfortunate scratch. For somewhere since their last adventure a deep scrape on the blade had changed the inscription from: *'Once there were Witches . . . but I killed them,'* to: *'Once there were Wishes . . . but I killed them.'*

It was a much gloomier message somehow, the idea of 'wishes' being buried, and particularly gloomy when one of your party is actually *called* 'Wish'.

'It's just a scratch,' said Wish, firmly putting the sword back in the scabbard. 'It was an accident. It doesn't mean anything.'

They kept on walking, trying not to see this as a bad omen, and to put as much distance as possible between themselves and that Witch attack.

But it was only much, much later in the day that Wish's heart began to beat a little slower again.

That little incident made the spell-raiding band somewhat uneasy, as you can imagine.

But you can't stay frightened forever.

And over the next few days, there was absolutely not a hint of a Witch, or even a Grindylow or a Greenteeth, only curlews and kingfishers, lapwings and snipe, wheeling and calling and singing over the bog.

They got back into a happier rhythm, walking across the Sweet Track, across the endless marshes, and when they stopped for a rest, Caliburn would give them Magic lessons sitting on the bridge, their legs swinging.

For Xar, the lessons were based around patience, calmness, not losing his temper when he practised the spells. This was particularly important because Xar was working with his father's staff rather than his own one, which had been left behind in the Wizard fort when Xar was taken to Gormincrag. Encanzo's staff was not supposed to be used by beginners, particularly those who have a Witch-stain, so things often went wrong.

For instance, Xar helpfully tried to make Caliburn's feathers grow back, because the old bird had lost so many from the sheer worry of being Xar's advisor. He pointed his father's staff, as calmly as possible . . . and the feathers went on growing and growing and growing, until Caliburn had a tail as long as a peacock's, that trailed over the edge of the bridge and into the bog below. Squeezjoos and the hairy fairies were in fits of giggles. It took a couple of hours of concentrated spellwork for Ariel and the sprites to get the feathers to grow small again, and two days later, Caliburn still had an amusingly fluffy bottom.

Caliburn was a dignified bird, so he got very cross if he caught the hairy fairies pointing and laughing at it.

With Wish, Caliburn concentrated on things that were easiest for her first, to build up her confidence. Wish found things made out of iron the simplest to move, so Caliburn had her pushing up her eyepatch a little, and practising with her pins, making them dance,

BOING!

and moving them like little armies, and even getting
them to have pin fights with each other.

'I understand things so much better
when YOU'RE teaching me, Caliburn,
rather than Madam Dreadlock!'
said Wish triumphantly. 'Madam
Dreadlock is just a little too . . .
shouty . . . and it's difficult to focus
when someone is yelling at you.'

The key from the
Punishment Cupboard had
decided it was in love with the
Enchanted Spoon.

BOING

BOING

BOING

The head of the key formed a mouth, and every now and then it would shout in its enthusiastic, creaky little voice: 'Sppooooon!!! Where are yoooooouuuu?' The Enchanted Spoon was a bit frightened of the key, and had taken to hiding, because the key kept on wanting to kiss the spoon.

Wish was so delighted with her success in bringing the spoon and the key and the pins to life, that she

accidentally did the same with Bodkin's fork, and
regrettably that created a love triangle. The fork decided
that *it* was in love with the key, and that the unfortunate
spoon was its main rival. So Bodkin would be trying to
eat his supper, and the fork would leap heroically out
of Bodkin's hand to pin the Enchanted Spoon to the
ground.

Or the spoon would find itself being stalked . . . and
the fork would challenge it to a fight . . . and the spoon
would stick out its chest like a proud swordsman, and
the two of them would conduct a complicated spoon-
and-fork-fight, lunging and parrying and duelling and
ambushing each other across the Sweet Track.

Oh be careful, my love!

Caliburn progressed from lessons on 'moving things' into lessons on 'magnetism'. The Enchanted Spoon was very patient when Wish gave him many variations of hairstyles made out of pins that she made magnetically attach to his head.

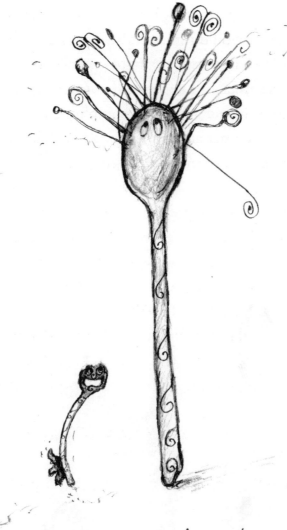

Nice hairstyle, handsome!

One day, Wish's hand slipped on her eyepatch and the spell from her Magic eye was a little too strong. It sent the Enchanted Spoon cartwheeling through the air like a spinning spelling staff, pins scattering in all directions, before he landed upside down, stuck fast to the top of Bodkin's forehead.

And there the spoon stayed, doing a headstand, his handle moving up and down like a kicking leg, as the key cuddled up to it, cooing, 'Poooor sppoo000n . . . poooor spoooooon . . .'

This all passed the time very merrily, until after a week or so, they reached the edge of the Witch Mountains, which rose eerily out of the edge of the marshes.

Castle Death was somewhere on the edge of those mountains, but all the paths on the map had petered out, so there was absolutely no sign of how to get to it.

'Whoever lived in Castle Death long ago didn't want to be found,' explained Caliburn.

'How are *we* going to find it then?' asked Bodkin, very reasonably. 'This mountain range is huge! We could be searching for this castle for the next twelve months!'

They had to leave the Sweet Track to get to the Witch Mountains.

This led to the SECOND bad thing that happened

on the way to Castle Death. And it was far worse than the first, even though in a way it solved their problem of how to find the castle.

Camping on the edge of the marshes, Wish was woken early one morning by a cold presence.

She tried to draw the Enchanted Sword . . . and for some wayward reason of its own, once again it would not budge, however hard she pulled it.

Crusher reached out his giant hand to protect Wish, the snowcats pounced . . . *too late.*

'*My spoon!*' cried Wish in horror. 'He's GONE!!!!'

No spoon,

Something's taken my spoon!'

'What do you think it was?' asked Bodkin. 'Was it a Witch? Was it a ghost? Was it a Grindylow?'

But neither Wish nor Crusher had seen what it was, and there were all sorts of nasty creatures that lived in the Witch Mountains.

'It can't have been anything Magical,' argued Xar. 'Magic things are afraid of iron . . . maybe it was a bear or something?'

They searched and searched, but they could not find the spoon anywhere.

Poor Wish was inconsolable. 'I should never have led my spoon into all this danger!' she wept. 'He's going to be so frightened . . .'

And then, a while later, and a hundred feet or so away from the edge of the campsite, the Enchanted Key gave an excited squeak, and it and the fork and the pins came hopping back to Wish, the key crying in its little creaky voice, 'We've picked up his trail!'

Wish's heart leapt, and the little party followed the enchanted things, who hopped purposefully ahead, pausing every now and then to smell some scent that only other enchanted things could detect, that was telling them which way the spoon had gone.

Sad Key

At first, Wish was hopeful that they might find him quite quickly, but minutes turned into hours, and darkness fell, and they still had not found the spoon, and eventually they had to decide to camp for the night, and carry on looking for him the next day.

And a broken-hearted Wish had to go to sleep without her spoon.

They didn't find him the next day either.

Or the next.

'Don't worry, Wish!' said Xar on the fourth day. 'We WILL find him, I promise! Don't give up hope . . . I know what it can be like, losing a great companion . . . We're constantly losing *you*, aren't we Squeezjoos? But we always find you again in the end!'

But each night they had to camp without finding him, it got harder and harder, and Bodkin lay awake by the campfire, looking up at the stars, realising bleakly that adventures were wonderful and exciting, but the stakes were high and the peril was real.

Even Xar understood that they had to find the spoon before they could start looking for Castle Death.

And though the snowcats' paws were weary, and Wish cried herself to sleep every night for love of the Enchanted Spoon, they followed the Enchanted Key and Fork deeper and deeper into the Witch Mountains.

When, long ago, the iron Warriors were on the

warpath, the Witches retreated further and further west, driving the giants out of their homeland of peaceful Gigantica, forcing many of them to wade out to sea along the way of the Giants' Footsteps, never to be seen again. It was the Droods who struck the final blow against the Witches, ambushing them in their stronghold between the woods and the sea, and getting rid of them entirely. That was when the Kingwitch was defeated, and put inside the stone . . .

After that, the country was ruled by a great Wizard called Pentaglion, but something terrible happened to him, no one quite knew what. It was rumoured that if anyone dared enter the ruins of Pentaglion's castle, Castle Death, a giant of unsurpassable size would take revenge with his very last breath. The Witch Mountains were built on a scale that was unimaginably huge. Up there, the clouds formed and reformed and fogs descended with such suddenness that it was hard to tell what was land

Oh, spooon!

and what was sky. Wish had a horrible feeling they were being followed, but every time she whirled around there was nothing there. Higher and higher they climbed, and the deer paths teetered over impossible crevasses, and at times turned into rope bridges half smashed out, so that they had to clamber across them on the backs of the snowcats in driving rain.

And then they climbed a peak that looked like it might be any other peak, exhausted, having almost given up hope that they would ever see the spoon again.

And it was there.

Not the spoon.

But *Castle Death*.

The Enchanted Key and the fork jumped in excitement, the fork pointing all of its prongs at the castle, and the key squeaking, *'The spoon's in there! The spoon's in there!'*

'We weren't looking for the castle but we found it anyway!' said Wish in delight. 'Oh, Xar, this is marvellous! We can get back my spoon AND the Giant's Last Breath all at the same time!'

'Oh dear, oh dear, oh dear,' moaned Caliburn. 'That's

quite a coincidence. I HATE coincidences . . . because, are they really coincidences, or did someone or *something*, really intend them all along?'

But Wish was too thrilled thinking that she might find her spoon again, and Xar was too pleased thinking that they were going to get the first ingredient in his spell, to be anxious that this coincidence was a little suspicious.

They pressed forward, even though the castle was not exactly inviting.

Castle Death was half buried in vegetation, a sad corpse of a building, surrounded by a mass of thorns and briars and treacherous fogs, and with such an ominous feeling of decay about it, that hopeful and determined as they were, it was still hard to resist the urge to run away as fast as possible in the opposite direction.

Crusher's eyes filled with tears. 'The halls of my ancestors . . .' he whispered. 'Ah . . . I never thought to see such a place . . .'

This had been the ground of many a battle.

In front of the castle was an extraordinary clatter of rock formations, covered in vegetation. But these weren't exactly what they at first seemed. As Nighteye slipped on a slimy boulder, Xar looked down, and realised it wasn't a stone at all, but the hilt of an enormous sword, a sword so huge that it could only have been wielded by a giant, wound round and round with layers of brambles and thick with a cushion of a century of moss.

And none of the rocks they were scrambling over were stones after all, but a carpet of these impossibly huge weapons – broken spears, the tip of a smashed, enormous shield, half-buried arrows – that the trees had grown through and up and around.

The sign of Pentaglion was a raven. So there were carved ravens on the shields of the giants, ravens scratched into the cracked stones, ravens decorating the broken ramparts of the castle.

'We shouldn't go in there,' groaned Caliburn. 'This is a really bad idea. I just know it's a really, really bad idea . . . it's CURSED! I mean, who thinks this is a good idea? Because *I* don't . . .'

The werewolf enthusiastically agreed with him, making loud gargling noises and pointing down the mountain to indicate the direction he thought they should be going. DOWN.

'The werewolf wants us to go in anyway!' said Xar. 'He says, "Look at how far we've come . . . we can't turn back now!"'

Xar was going in even if the castle WAS cursed.

CASTLE DEATH ↗

This could be his chance not only to get rid of his aching, worrying, burning Witch-stain, but also to get rid of the Witches themselves.

'We HAVE to go in,' said Wish excitedly. 'For the sake of Xar's spell, and to find the spoon. He's here, somewhere, I know he is! Spoo-oon! Where are you???'

And the Enchanted Key repeated after her, 'Spoo-oon? Yoooo-hooo!! Where are you?' and their two voices bounced together and mingled as their echoes came back spookily from the gigantic ruined rooms.

'Shhhhhh!' whispered Bodkin, who had drawn his sword. 'We don't know what's in here. And if there IS something, we don't want to wake it up!'

They tiptoed forward. Everything was built on such an enormous scale that it created the extraordinary impression that someone had waved their staff, and had turned the spell-raiding party into mice. And yet people their own size had obviously lived here too – giants and humans together.

When sprites are concerned, their hearts glow green, and they give off a sulphurous smell to warn the other sprites not to go further, and all around, those sprites were burning a hot chartreuse, green as emerald, smoky with fear, queasily circling and buzzing and hissing out protection spells with so many consonants in them that the words whistled and spat like hot fat in a pan. 'Bklftttllkprt! Kkllfrkkkfllff! Rkrbptt!!'

For the dead castle seemed to be coming alive again as they entered it, and the ears of the sprites could hear the music it was singing, and it was a terrible song indeed. 'A song without music, a sword in the senses, a storm in the heart, and a fire in the brain . . .'

The pointed ears of Ariel swivelled to catch the sound. He opened his little forked-teeth mouth and cautiously drank a bit of the air, and his face crinkled in disgust and alarm at the searingly bitter taste of it.

215

'Lissten . . .' whispered Ariel. 'Taste . . .'

'I can't hear anything,' said Bodkin, swallowing hard and holding very tight to his sword.

'Ssstupid humansss . . .' hissed Tiffinstorm in exasperation, holding equally firmly to her wand, sharp as any thorn. 'Your dull earsss can never catch the important sstuff . . . I don't know how you have ever sssurvived . . .'

'Let's leave now, Xar!' said Ariel. 'We must go no further! Trusst us, trust us, trussst us!'

'This castle wants revenge,' explained Tiffinstorm softly, blinking into visibility beside them. 'Every stone is singing of it . . . every creeper . . . every broken glass . . . the hum of revenge is all around us. Can you not taste the bitterness of it? Can you not hear the anger of it?'

Wish peered around. She could hear

nothing, but even *her* dull human senses could feel the
savage melancholy of the atmosphere. And then, was
it her imagination, or were the creepers, the ivy, the
bracken that had with infinite and minute slowness
pushed their green vegetative tentacles up through
the broken flagstones, were they now ... *moving?*
At a rate that was visible to the human eye?
Yes ... there it was, the ivy was moving like
snakes, rustling like serpents, reaching out either
pleadingly or menacingly towards them ...'
'Are any of US doing that?' cried Wish
in alarm, already knowing the answer,
but the werewolf and Xar and all of
the sprites had got out their staffs and
were performing encircling spells of
protection, to stop the encroaching
plants reaching out
towards them.
'Somebody
knows we're here!'
whispered Wish.
'We should go
back!' cried Bodkin.
And even as he
said the words the great
broken door slammed

behind them, and the vegetation choked up behind, closing the way, great roots and thorns spearing upwards like crossing swords.

Xar swallowed hard. 'Of course it's going to be frightening,' said Xar stoutly. 'We're looking for the ingredients of a spell to get rid of Witches, and Witches are not going to be vanquished by a smell of roses. Revenge is going to be a wonderful ingredient for our spell.'

'But we don't know who the castle wants revenge *on*,' Caliburn pointed out nervously.

He had a horrible, horrible feeling that he was returning to a forgotten past. It's a dreadful problem for a raven who has lived many lifetimes. He had some dim memory of the familiarity of the place, but he couldn't for the life of him recall any of the important details.

'Well, it stands to reason that this castle will want revenge on the WITCHES, won't it?' said Xar. 'The Witches took this territory from the giants, so of course the giants' castle is going to be cross with the Witches . . .'

'But Xar, you don't know that . . .' groaned Caliburn. 'Stories and histories are often more complicated than they look.'

And then they came across the shoe.

It was lying in front of them, on the steps, on one side, as if someone had been in a hurry and lost it. At first they thought it must be some sort of leather tent or house, before they realised it was in fact a gigantic BOOT, a shoe so large it dwarfed even Crusher, the top of the rim of it coming up to the Longstepper High-Walker's waist. Crusher peered over into the cave-like depths, an expression of mild worry on his face, which was a cause for concern in itself because Crusher did not normally worry about much.

'Impossible,' marvelled Xar. 'This can't be true! Giants don't grow that big . . . Something that huge just could not exist!'

'The ancient giants were supposed to be much larger than our present giants and ogres,' said Caliburn. 'Gog and Magog and their descendants . . . We are trespassing in lands we do not understand . . . with mysteries and forces much bigger than we know . . .'

But Xar was now thoroughly overexcited. 'There IS a giant in this castle after all!' he said, drawing both his father's staff and his sword at once. 'So that means we can get the Giant's Last Breath! And that breath will be the breath of REVENGE!'

'But the giant is HUMUNGOUS!' exclaimed Bodkin. 'If he's alive, we'd have to kill him if we want his last breath, and we couldn't possibly do that because I like giants and so does Wish and so do you! And if he's dead we can't get his last breath anyway!'

Xar wasn't listening.

'We'll just sneak up on him, and check the whole situation out,' said Xar.

'But whatever–it–is already knows we're *here!*' wailed Bodkin.

Now Wish knew what it must feel like to be the size of a sprite, for that is how small they were in comparison to this boot.

With shaking steps they inched forward, and the Enchanted Pins, Key and Fork led them to an enormous door, hidden in cobwebs and darkness. Behind the door was a staircase that led down, down, down underground. Crusher had to lift them all down the steps, and when they got to the bottom of this staircase they came to a hall that was way, way bigger than the last. It was impossible that a room could be that huge. A table so high that each one of its legs was as tall as one of those tree trunks from the High Forests outside. A chair so enormous its existence was beyond imagining. And underneath the table was a boot to match the boot outside, and a gigantic foot, with huge toes that were turning a rather unnatural green colour. And above the foot, way, way above, stretched the leg, and out of their sight, must be the body of the giant.

A giant larger than anyone had ever seen before, or dreamed of.

10. The Giant's Last Breath

It took every single ounce of nerve in their bodies to make them move forward. Bodkin could feel his heart beating so fast it felt like it might leap out of his chest and make a run for it. *He* wanted to do that anyway . . .

But then he thought of poor Xar, shivering in the night as the Witch-stain crept up his arm. Xar would have to stay forever locked up in Gormincrag if they could not find the ingredients for this spell. The Witches were not going to go away if they closed their eyes and hoped for it . . . So Bodkin walked on.

Each one of the toes of the giant came up to Wish's waist. The toes were absolutely still, unmoving. They appeared to be green, now they got closer, not because of gangrene, but because they had been there so long that moss was growing over them, so they must not have moved for a very long time.

'Is he alive, this giant?' whispered Wish. 'Or is he dead?'

'Find out, sprites!' ordered Xar fiercely.

Bravely, Tiffinstorm and Ariel and the Once-sprite flew up to the head of the giant.

Tiffinstorm flew back down first. 'Dead,' said Tiffinstorm.

'But it can't have been dead for very long,' argued Wish. 'Because after a while, don't dead bodies . . . sort of *decay*?'

'Yucky!' said Squeezjoos, inspecting the giant for signs of decay with delight. 'They's do! Letsss me look . . . letsss me look!' The hairy fairy buzzed around excitedly, but returned extremely disappointed. 'He'ss just the sssame assss when he wasss alive . . . No yucky bits . . . no squidgy bits . . . The green is just moss . . .'

'It's some kind of enchantment,' said Caliburn, shivering. 'An enchantment so strong I'm not sure I want to know what it is . . .'

'Which may mean,' said Xar triumphantly, 'that we CAN get his last breath! The spell to get rid of a Witch-stain must be true! And this giant here must have been waiting for us to come so that it can die . . .'

'You're making a whole load of assumptions there,' said Bodkin, terrified. 'Maybe it's waiting so that it can eat us.'

'We keep telling you! Giants are vegetarian!' said Xar.

'Yes but, Xar, we don't know much about the really, really big ones . . .' said Bodkin. 'Most of them waded out to sea hundreds and hundreds of years ago.'

But Xar wasn't listening. 'Follow me!' he ordered.

The snowcats and the werewolf climbed each table leg as if they were tree trunks, claws gripping either

side, with Wish and Xar and Bodkin on their backs.
Xar had never been on a giant's table before. The
plates were larger than any he had ever seen, more like
enormous silver lakes. The three young heroes steered
their way round the massive cups and
knives. The Enchanted Fork perched
on the rim of one of the spoons,
gazing down with admiration
at its unfeasibly enormous

cousin, a monster in spoon form. The fork shook its head, as if to say, 'Will I ever grow that big? Could I?'

Squeezjoos and Bumbleboozle and The Baby, always easily distracted, had a great time slipping down the centre of the giant's spoon as if it were some sort of gargantuan slide, until Xar snapped his fingers, to get them to concentrate.

'We're on a mission here,' whispered Xar. 'There's no time to mess about! Once-sprite, you're the Chief Spell-Raider. How do we get the last breath out of the giant, if there's still one in there?'

Up above them was the giant's head, tipped to one side. He certainly LOOKED dead. His eyes were closed. His great wrinkled map of a face was covered in bracken and ivy, and if they had not known that he was a giant, and seen that foot down below, they might have thought he was a rock face, or some other broken landscape, covered in a rich tangled mess of briars and thorns as if he wore a mask.

A sad face.

A broken face.

A lost face.

The Once-sprite flew the falcon upwards, and leapt from the bird's back. He swung for a second from one of the giant's nose hairs, peering up into the dark depths above as if it were some sort of enormous snot-filled cave.

He poked his spear into one edge of giant nostril.

The giant did not move.

'He's dead,' announced the Once-sprite, dropping back onto the falcon.

'Yes, I know he's probably *dead*!' said Xar impatiently. 'The point is, how do we get a last breath out of him?'

And then, as if in response to Xar's question, and making them all jump, there was a reverberating sound like the noise of a muffled distant drum, and a slight wheezing wind poured faintly out of the nostrils above like the breeze in coral caves.

Oh, by green things and white things and mistletoe and ivy . . .

The giant wasn't dead after all!

'The beassst isss alive . . .' whispered Ariel, burning so bright green with alarm that he shone like a torch.

The giant twitched.

'Ohhhhhhhhhh my! Ohhhhhhhh my! He's moving!' said Squeezjoos.

Slowly, slowly the great eye above cracked open the mess of thorns above it, and one enormous eye focussed grimly on the children – an eye you could lose yourself in, a mighty desolation like the desert of the ocean. And then the great mountain above them jerked upwards with such startling suddenness that the plates bowled over, and the young heroes lost their balance on the table, set a-shaking by his sudden coming-to-life. They all forgot that giants are not ogres, and that they're supposed to be vegetarian, even the really, really big ones, and they scattered like scurrying ants across the table, for safety under the plate rims, and to hide under the forks.

Their hearts beating like rabbits', they cowered, Bodkin under a plate rim, Xar flattened behind a salt cellar, Wish under the spoon.

'Don't move . . .' whispered Xar.

Was the giant friendly? Or was he *unfriendly*? Did he know they were there? Had he seen them?

They could hear the giant breathing now, the wheeze in and out of its lungs like some great wind, and suddenly it seemed that their quest might have been a little, well, *foolish*.

Bodkin held his breath.

Maybe the giant *didn't* know they were there . . .

Minutes passed.

There was silence again.

Bodkin began to breathe a little easier.

And then a very beautiful voice, one that definitely could not have belonged to a giant, said sweetly and out of nowhere: 'There's one hiding under the plate . . .'

And . . .

BLAM! The sheltering plate above Bodkin went spinning from above his head and sailing across the room, where it smashed with ear-shattering violence.

That was a little too, well, ROUGH for the giant to be entirely friendly, and when Bodkin looked up at the face looming above him like a great green god, the glowering fury of its expression was unmistakeable.

It's all very well, people telling you not to *move* when you're being charged by a forest animal, or if a great desolation of a giant is poised over you, but in those sorts of situations instinct tends to kick in, and Bodkin ran across the table with some considerable speed.

SLAM!!!! A fleeing Bodkin was caught by a mighty force from above that sent him sprawling – OOF! – onto his stomach, and when he scrambled, petrified, back to his feet, an immense hand imprisoned him like a great green cave.

Peering out from behind the spoon, Wish shouted, 'Bodkin's been trapped!' Forgetting all about how much she liked giants, she ran forward and jabbed one of the massive fingers with her sword, and it couldn't have been much more than a pin-prick, but the fingers startled upward, and then all three humans were scurrying and running, and weaving and dodging across the table with the giant and frankly not-very-friendly hand slamming down around them, trying to catch them.

Which it did, eventually . . .

Xar and Bodkin hid in the salt cellar, but the giant shook them out, and pinned them to the table between the prongs of a fork.

And then the giant took a cup and slammed it over Wish. For one horrible moment she thought she would be trapped there forever, but the giant flipped the cup over, picked her up and dropped her in it. And there she hung, peering with one terrified eye over the rim, into the grim eyes of the enormous and, let's face it, extremely annoyed giant.

An unintelligible noise came out of the giant's mouth. It was opening and shutting as if it were making words, but the wheeze of his voice meant it was impossible to hear what he was saying. He paused.

The three children looked at one another, terrified. None of them could make head nor tail of what he was talking about.

The giant spoke again, equally unintelligibly, soft anger in the wheezing.

Caliburn bravely flew up to the giant's mouth, so that he could hear more clearly.

The giant seemed to be choking,

fighting for breath, until from out of nowhere an ethereal little *something* appeared in a trail of light, something so bright it made you blink to look at it, and the something poured a little potion into the choking giant's mouth, and the dusty desolation drank it down greedily.

'What is *that*?' asked Wish, with an open mouth, trying to look at the brilliant little something as it dashed past. It didn't look quite like any other sprite, or elf, she had ever seen before.

'I am a Frost-sprite who once belonged to the great Wizard Pentaglion,' said the little *something*, moving so quickly they still couldn't see what it was, 'but you can call me Eleanor Rose ... That is not my name, but it's a very pretty one, don't you think?'

Eleanor Rose, for that was *not* her name, had a very beautiful voice that reminded you of running water, or bells. It must have been she who had told the giant where they were. 'And this big decaying chap here is Proponderus,' said Eleanor Rose, as if they'd all dropped in for a cosy chat, rather than broken into a ruined castle whose name was Death. 'So, since we're all here, perhaps you might introduce *your*selves? Proponderus and I have not had company for many a long year. And even when we do, uninvited guests tend not to stay very long ... particularly if they are burglars ...'

Eleanor Rose

There was something a little sinister in the last

statement, even though she said it perfectly good-naturedly, even somewhat sadly. They didn't need Caliburn to whisper, 'Don't trust her . . .'

Eleanor Rose didn't appear offended. She even agreed, and might have been nodding her head if she had been still enough for them to see her. 'Yes, it's probably wiser for human beings not to trust me . . . Frost-sprites have no hearts, you see . . .'

The giant spoke in a wheezy whisper, which was nonetheless very loud to human ears, for he was so very large a giant.

'Who,' said the giant, 'are YOU, little ants, little nothingnesses, and how dare you disturb the peace of a giant of the ancient lines who is on the verge of dying? Is nothing sacred?'

'Oh, you're on the verge of dying are you?' said Xar, without thinking, and heartily pleased to hear it. 'Excellent!'

The giant blinked down at them.

Bodkin prodded Xar frantically.

Xar started, suddenly realising that it wasn't very polite to be seeming to welcome the imminent death of your host.

'I mean, we're *very* sad to hear that,' said Xar hurriedly.

Eleanor Rose laughed again. 'Oh, don't worry!' she said kindly. '*You're* on the verge of dying too!'

'A-are we?' stammered Bodkin anxiously.

'Of course you are!' said Eleanor Rose with great humour. 'What did you expect? You are entering, uninvited, a castle whose name is Death, with the burglarous intention to steal something infinitely precious from one of the inhabitants within who also happens to be your unwilling host . . . Don't bother to deny it!'

For Xar had opened up his mouth in instinctive denial.

'Unless . . .' said Eleanor Rose.

'Unless?' prompted Wish, ever-hopeful.

'Unless . . . you are the people we have been waiting for, which is terribly unlikely, considering the amount of people there are in the wildwoods, and how surprising it would be if they were to accidentally make their way here,' said Eleanor Rose. 'Which is the reason we have been waiting such a very, very long time. So, who are you?'

Oh dear, oh dear, oh dear.

They had to hope the Spelling Book had not tricked them. They had to hope that their names would be good enough.

'Tell the truth,' Eleanor Rose advised them.

'I am Xar, son of Encanzo, boy of destiny,' said Xar. 'And this is Wish, daughter of Sychorax . . . and this is Bodkin, Assistant Bodyguard.'

There was a long, long silence, and Eleanor Rose was still enough for Squeezjoos to see her clearly for one, tantalising second, and for Squeezjoos to say with a sigh, 'Oh! How pretty you are!'

'Beauty is not everything,' said Eleanor Rose, on the move again, 'but the universe has found that, sometimes, it helps. And impossibility isn't everything either, but it is surprising, particularly considering the nature of impossibility, how often the universe is depending on *one* . . .

unlikely . . .

chance . . .'

Bodkin and Xar and Wish had been holding their breaths, but now they let them out again with relief.

'Of all the numberless names of people in these wildwoods, you ARE the right ones,' said Eleanor Rose.

'Thank goodness for that,' breathed Bodkin.

'At last!' said the giant. 'Are they worthy?'

Eleanor Rose hovered in front of all of them, and touched them one by one – Xar, Bodkin, Wish and finally Caliburn – testing them for worthiness. Each of them cried out at the moment of contact, as if they had been hit by a sharp electric shock.

Eleanor Rose circled the room twice before she gave her pronouncement.

'There is room for improvement,' said Eleanor Rose. 'Particularly in the one who calls himself the boy of destiny . . . but what can you expect from the humans? However, when it comes to the worthiness of the bird, why the bird . . .'

Caliburn ruffled his feathers, preparing to make modest protestations. This was his moment.

'The talking bird is the *least* worthy of all,' said Eleanor Rose.

'Oh!' cried Caliburn, very offended. 'I think you must have mistook me! I am Caliburn, the raven-who-has-lived-many-lifetimes, and I have been put in charge of Xar, precisely *because* of my wisdom and my worthiness!'

'Yes,' said Eleanor Rose, with an audible, dismissive sniff, that still managed to sound affectionate, 'and perhaps you might like to think, *why*, after all those lifetimes, you have ended up as a bird? I know perfectly well who you are, raven, and age is no proof of worthiness, or indeed of wisdom. We'll just have to make do, Proponderus, and hope for the best, as is often the case with the humans. We can't wait any longer. I am finding it harder and harder to slow down the dying process, and those are, after all, the right names.'

The giant snorted with relief.

'So,' said Eleanor Rose, 'you have come here to steal something? Don't bother lying, just tell me what it is.'

'We have come to take the giant's last breath,' said Xar defiantly. 'We need it as part of our spell to get rid of the Witches.'

'Ahhhh . . .' breathed the giant with desperate satisfaction in a great wind above them. 'They *are* the right ones.'

'That is precious, very precious,' said Eleanor Rose solemnly. 'It is not something the likes of you could *steal* from a giant of the ancient lines, but luckily for you he will give it to you willingly. I presume you have come prepared?'

'We have,' said Xar promptly. 'The Once-sprite here is a great spell-raider. He will catch the breath, and Tiffinstorm will shrink it, and between them they will put the breath in this collecting-bottle here . . .'

Eleanor Rose laughed again. 'Oh, you humans! You're so funny! Your plans are so inadequate and yet you keep making them! You hadn't a hope of doing that on your own, but I will help you.

'You shall have your wish,' said Eleanor Rose, 'and maybe, as is the way of things . . . a little *more* than you wished for, as well. Settle down, everyone, make yourselves comfortable.'

Eleanor Rose did not bring out a wand, or a staff, or make any sort of movement that could be interpreted as spelling, but the fork lifted itself off Xar and Bodkin, and the cup tipped over gently, depositing Wish on the table.

'The giant is going to tell you a story, and I am going to help . . .'

Way above them, the not-quite-dead giant's words came booming out with such loudness, they had to put their hands over their ears.

'LET ME TELL YOU A STORY!' said the giant.

'A story???' said Xar, between clenched teeth, for the words really were very, very loud.

'You don't like stories?' said Eleanor Rose in surprise.

'I love stories!' said Xar. 'But what is the giant doing, telling us a story? This is supposed to be his last breath! Surely you can't tell a whole story with one last breath? And we're in a bit of a hurry here . . . it's complicated, but the Droods and the Wizards and the Warriors and the Witchsmeller and the Witches themselves are all chasing after us and they could be here any moment . . . And my companion, Wish here, has lost her Enchanted Spoon, and we have to find it . . .'

'Have you seen him?' said Wish anxiously. 'My fork and key are convinced he's in here somewhere. He's about so high, made of iron, and—'

'What did I say?' interrupted Eleanor Rose. 'Plenty of room for improvement. You need to learn patience, boy and girl. There is *always* time for a story. The giant will give you his last breath and in return you will listen to his story, patiently, quietly, and humbly, for those are all things you need to learn. That is your payment, if you will.'

So in the heart of Castle Death, Wish and Caliburn and Xar and Bodkin and the snowcats and the sprites and Crusher the giant sat down cross-legged or put their shaggy heads on their paws, or folded their wings, or lay on their backs with their eight legs in the air depending on what or who they were. All of them listened quietly, obediently, and even *Xar* tried to be as patient and respectful as he could as they listened to the story.

Now, the last words of *anyone* who is dying have a Magical power.

But the last words of a giant of such extraordinary immenseness . . . why, those have more power than most.

In real life this story was being told by a great giant the size of a small hillside, in the last stages of dying, crumbling at the edges and a trifle fly-infested, in a voice that was sometimes louder than the loudest thunder and at other times breaking and wheezing and barely there, and when his voice broke at the edges, like the crumbling of his fingers, and became so faint that you could hardly hear it, the story was taken up by the Frost-sprite, who was the absolute opposite, tiny and ever-moving, with a voice like the never-heard music of the universe and turning stars and the tiny bell-like chime of time . . .

But if I tell it like *that* it will make it hard to concentrate on the story, and the story is important. So I will speak it in my own voice, the voice of the unknown narrator.

This was the story the giant told.

It was The Story of The Giant's Last Breath.

The story was dying to be told...

Once upon a time, there was a ferocious young Warrior
princess, as wild as any werewolf. She was afraid of nothing,
this Warrior princess, and her hunting skills were the talk of
the Empire. All alone, she fought the Frost giants of the frozen
north, all alone she captured the dreadful Grim Annis of the
west, all alone she scared off the Rogrebreaths that were raiding
the Warrior villages in the south.

The Warrior princess did not believe in love.

'Love is weakness,' said the princess.

'I'm really, really hoping this isn't
going to be a LOVE story!' said Xar
in disgust, before remembering
he was supposed to be quiet and
respectful and hurriedly shutting his
mouth again.

I'm really
hoping this isn't
a LOVE story...

One day, the princess was riding alone
and free through the wildwoods, in the
depths of midwinter, when she realised that
she was being chased by a couple of snowcats.
She shot arrows at the snowcats, and two of
them hit their targets, but still they pursued her.
Eventually she realised they wanted her to follow
them, and she was so impressed by their bravery,
that this she did.

The snowcats led her to a clearing where there was a circle of gigantic wolves waiting patiently at the bottom of a tree. There was a young man up in the tree, and the wolves were waiting for him to grow so tired he would fall out, like a large ripe apple. Two days he had been up there, and he was dropping with hunger and thirst and fear.

At the bottom of the tree lay the young man's Wizard staffs, for he had climbed the tree to rescue one of his sprites.

The young man (whose name was Algorquprqin, but that sounds like someone choking on a walnut, so everyone called him Tor), was singing, a very stupid song in the princess's opinion, which went something like this:

I am young, I am poor, I can offer you nothing
All that I have is this bright pair of wings . . .
This air that I eat, these winds that I sleep on
This star path I dance in, where the moon sings . . .

Now, the princess knew that she should have ridden on at that point. This young man was clearly a Wizard, and Wizards were the Warriors' deadly enemies.

And he was also clearly a very silly young man.

But there was something so human about the silliness of this song that it made her pause.

The princess loaded her bow, and shot an arrow towards the Wizard, not to hit him, exactly, but just to see if he would flinch.

He didn't . . . Even though it passed so bitingly close that it grazed his left arm. The princess was impressed, for she admired bravery, even in Wizards.

The wolves got to their feet, and snarled warningly at her, padding restlessly round the tree. The princess loaded her bow again, pointed it at the wolves, and called out sneeringly: 'What are you doing, talking to trees, you stupid Wizard?'

'I'm not talking to trees,' said the Wizard. 'I'm talking to YOU.'

He carried on with the song:

See the swifts soar, they live well on nothing,
You are young, you are strong, if you'll give me your hand
We'll leave earth entirely and never go back there,
We'll sleep on the breezes and never touch land

I promise you gales and a merry adventure
We'll fly on forever and never will part
I am young, I am poor, I can offer you nothing,
Nothing but love and the beat of my heart . . .

And then he just said 'Help me . . .'

'What will you give me if I rescue you, Wizard?' called the princess.

There was silence from the treetops, and then the Wizard replied, 'What do you want, most in the world?'

The princess replied, swift as one of her own arrows: 'I want to be the Warrior queen of this whole forest.'

The princess, you see, was always MEANT to be the queen of the whole forest, but her throne had been stolen when she was a baby by one of her evil cousins, so she was wishing for something she had wanted her very whole life.

The Wizard called Tor looked down at her.

'All right, I can't make you a Warrior queen,' admitted Tor, 'but I CAN give you a horse. A queen needs a good horse.'

'I already HAVE a horse, stupid!' said the princess, laughing. 'I'm riding it!'

'Back at home in my Wizard camp, I have a horse far better than that horse you are riding, a horse as black as night and as swift as spell-raiders . . . I will give it to you if you rescue me,' said Tor. 'It isn't Magic,' he added hastily. 'It's

just an ordinary horse. You'll like it . . .'

So the princess, who was really just looking for an excuse
to save this silly young man, shot her arrows at the wolves,
and the wolves began to chase her.

They hunted her through the forest, the princess shooting
back at them over her shoulder. And Tor climbed down from
the tree, picked up his Wizard staffs, and followed after her on
his injured snowcat. He caught up with her at just the moment
when the wolf pack took down her horse.

The princess drew her sword and he used his spelling staffs,
and together they fought the wolves, but there were so very
many of them that they had to climb aboard the snowcat to run
away, and leave the wolves with the horse.

'You've made me lose my horse!' protested the princess, as
they rode together through the forest on the back of the snowcat.

'It was the horse, or us . . .' said Tor, 'that's why I
offered you one of my own horses if you rescued me.'

And that was the moment that the princess realised that
Wizards were tricky.

The princess didn't mind that.

LOVE...
Y.Y.UCKY

She was tricky herself.

The Wizard, now that she could see his face up close in the moonlight, was a very silly, tricky young man, but undeniably a little bit handsome . . . and he hadn't flinched when she shot him . . .

And that was how the princess lost her heart in the forest.

'It IS about love!' said Xar in disgust.

'Shhh!' hissed everyone else, because they wanted to hear the end of the story.

The Warrior princess agreed to meet the Wizard, in the same clearing, a week later, so he could bring her the horse.

'This will be the last time I meet him,' said the princess to herself.

Tor gave her a horse called Thunderbird, which certainly wasn't swifter than spell-raiders, or darker than midnight. It was a perfectly normal horse . . . Except in one respect.

Every second Thursday, if she happened to be riding it, it would carry her off, and however hard she pulled on the reins it would take her through the forest, back to the clearing where she first met Tor.

"It IS = about love!," said Xar in disgust.

247

Tor would be waiting for her, and they would spend the afternoon being silly together.

The young Warrior princess swore that she would marry Tor. She promised on her heart that they would run away together, and find themselves a world where it did not matter where they came from, where Wizards and Warriors could love and live in peace.'

And then . . . And then . . . And then . . .

TRAGEDY.

The princess's wicked cousin died, and that meant that SHE was now queen of the Warriors.

She had all that she had ever been wanting, for her very whole life . . .

And now that she had it, she found that she did not want it after all.

O, you must be careful what you wish for, guys . . .

IT MAY COME TRUE.

For here is the thing about becoming a queen. It brought with it responsibilities, duties. The new queen's people needed her, for if she were NOT the queen, it would be one or other of the wicked cousins, with their taxes, and their wars-of-vengeance, and their endless thirst for such delicacies as blood-of-werecats as an aperitif, which may have been delicious, but was costly in human lives.

So the young princess felt she HAD to be the queen, and a queen of Warriors cannot marry a Wizard.

But how should she get rid of her love?

A true love's kiss is the strongest thing in the world. It cannot be got rid of by sneezing.

So the young princess did a terrible thing.

She had heard of an extremely powerful Wizard called Pentaglion, who was living all alone, and was doing experiments into looking into the future . . . dabbling in that dangerous practice. She travelled to see him. They looked into the future together, and what they saw there was that if she were to marry the young boy called Tor, the Witches would return to the forest . . .

SO THE PRINCESS HAD TO GET RID OF HER LOVE FOREVER.

And there was only one way.

PENTAGLION GAVE HER THE SPELL OF LOVE DENIED, WHICH IS A VERY, VERY DANGEROUS SPELL INDEED.

The sprites all gasped at the sound of the Spell of Love Denied. Squeezjoos curled himself up so tightly in Wish's hair that she let out a small squeal. Only Squeezjoos's eyes were peeping out, wide with alarm.

The Warrior princess drank the Spell and the love died in her heart.

She wrote a letter to the Wizard boy called Tor,

written in poison ink and bitterage, saying she did not love him, and never had.

Meanwhile, Tor waited many long weeks in the appointed waiting place and the Warrior princess never came. He got the letter. He read it, refused to believe it. Two years he waited. A hut grew around him, and the sprites in the forest felt so sorry for him, they brought him food and water. They called him 'the Wizard-who-waits'.

Tor knew in his heart of hearts that the princess had betrayed him, and eventually he came to believe the letter. He got word that the Warrior princess had married someone else, and was now calling herself the queen of the Warriors. The Wizard went so mad with unhappiness, he went to fight in the hinterlands and became a Shadow Man . . .'

'Oh, how cool . . .' breathed Xar, for the Shadow Men were legendary.

'And now we reach MY part of the story . . .' said the giant. 'You see, the castle you are standing in was once the castle of Pentaglion . . .'

Xar and Wish and Bodkin held their breaths. They had got so caught up in the story they had forgotten that it might be true. They looked at the smashed remains of the castle all around them. What had happened here?

'And the giant you are listening to is Pentaglion's giant, and this is where I come into the story.' The giant's voice was drenched in bitterness at this point. 'Unfortunately one of the essential ingredients of the Spell of Love Denied was the tears of a Drood, and Droods don't like having their tears taken. The Droods set about tracking the man who had taken their tears, and when they found him, they killed not only the extremely powerful Wizard Pentaglion, but they tried to kill his giant, and took his little baby werewolf into captivity . . .

'And that giant,' finished the giant, 'was ME. So many years, I have been angry, so angry at the injustice of it, that I have not been able to die.

'I have BURNED with anger!' roared the giant. 'The boiling impossible heat of my fury has kept me here . . .

'SO ANGRY!' thundered the giant, and the sound of the giant's anger, even though he was dying, rumbled out of his great giant chest like a thousand bears a-roaring, echoing its way around the room, sending the table shaking.

'I am not afraid to die, but I have had unfinished business . . .' said the giant. 'And with my last breath I urge you . . .'

Oh..h..h...

REVENGE!

The Giant Wants revenge!

There was a great pause.

For the last breath of giants is a terrible thing.

'Revenge!' whispered Xar, highly excited. 'He wants REVENGE! Don't worry, giant, I'm pretty cross with those Droods myself . . . You can pass that quest right on to me, Xar's your man!'

Xar was delighted because the last breath of a giant was one thing. But the dying VENGEANCE wish of a giant . . . that was a very powerful ingredient indeed. THAT would be extremely helpful if you wanted to get rid of the Witches.

'Get ready, everyone!' shouted Xar. 'The giant's about to go!'

'Oh poor giant!' said Wish. 'Have a little respect, Xar! These are his dying moments!'

'He's been dying for YEARS!' said Xar. 'We're doing him a favour! You're CROSS aren't you, giant? So angry you haven't been able to die . . . Give us your fury! We need all of it!'

'With my last breath I urge you . . .' said the giant. He clutched his throat . . . he was about to go, fighting for breath.

'I urge you . . .

'I urge you . . .

'FORGIVE THEM.'

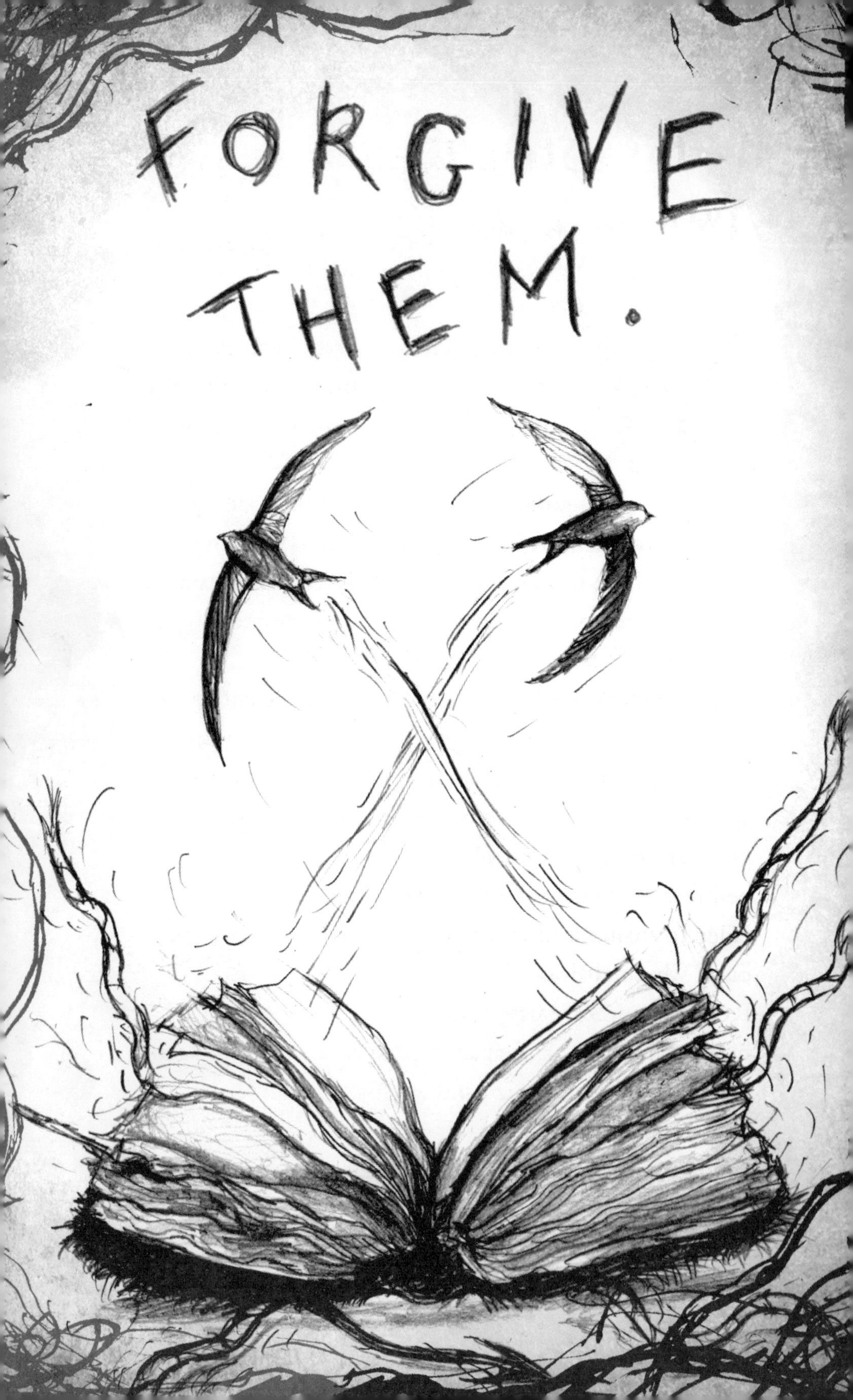
FORGIVE
THEM.

11. The Story Takes a Surprising Turn, as is the Way of Stories

'Whaaaaaat?????' said Xar, so absolutely flabbergasted, he momentarily forgot the quest.

'*GET THE BREATH!!!!!!!!*' yelled Bodkin.

It was a beautifully synchronised operation.

You'd have thought they'd done it a thousand times before.

The giant fell backwards, with a CRASSSHHHHHHHHHH! that shook the hall to its remaining foundations, and the last breath was up and out of his mouth in a great cloud. Tiffinstorm zapped an appearance spell to make it visible, and there it was, in a great shaggy cloud, for one tantalising moment before, *reoow!* Hinkypunk's shrinking spell failed to shrink it more than an inch or so – but that was where Eleanor Rose came in. She flew right over it, holding her little arms apart, and the breath shrank to pea-size and, with a glorious flurry of wings, the peregrine falcon swooped, and the Once-sprite caught the now-tiny little ball

Whaaaaat???..?

of breath in his collecting bottle, putting in the stopper as the falcon dived down and then up, up again, out of the way of the rising dust.

And then he dropped the little bottle into the waiting hands of Squeezjoos, the official sprite assistant to the spell-raiding team.

Wish ran over to the prone body of the giant. Eleanor Rose held up both her arms again, and in front of their eyes the great body of the giant simply melted away, into the ground beneath them.

'Where has he gone?' whispered Wish with round eyes.

'Where he should have gone a long, long time ago,' said Eleanor Rose. 'Do not be sad, he is free at last, the poor giant.'

'Oh, but we *are* sad!' said Wish, and all of them

were, for the giant had been so noble, and had been treated so badly.

'As am I,' Eleanor Rose said briskly. 'Not sad, of course, but free. And what a last breath it was . . . after all these years of anger, he forgives them!' she said in amazement. 'How wonderful!'

'Mission accomplished!' the Once-sprite said proudly, as the peregrine falcon came to rest on Xar's shoulder.

Squeezjoos held up the bottle. There, right in the middle, was a small, odd-looking round thing, curled up in on itself like a flower.

The sprites let out a great hissing cheer, the wolves and the snowcats howled their appreciation. '*We issss spell-raiderssssssssss!*'

The wolves capered up and down, the snowcats chased each other round the dinner plates, Lonesome sat down and howled.

The only one who wasn't dancing gloatingly around the giant dinner table in glee was Xar.

Which was unlike Xar, who was normally Gloater-in-Chief.

It was as if having to sit quietly for five minutes without fidgeting had been such an effort that he had to burst out now with his real feelings.

'It should be a *Revenge* Breath!' said Xar crossly.

'What use is a *Forgiveness* Breath, even a *giant* one, if you're fighting Witches, the greatest peril the world has ever known?'

It was only Xar who had failed to understand the true meaning of the story.

For most of the others in the room, the story had thrown all the pieces of what they knew up in the air, and when they came down again, everything had changed.

Stories can change lives . . .

And this was one of those stories.

Secrets had been told that had been kept buried and hidden away in human hearts for a very, very long time.

'Don't you understand, Xar?' said Wish. 'The princess in the story was my mother! And the young Wizard was your father Encanzo . . .'

'What?????' Xar's jaw fell open. 'Nonsense! The young Wizard was called Tor!'

'Maybe that was your father's name before he became an Enchanter,' suggested Caliburn, which was possible – Wizards did tend to take a new name when they rose to that status.

'But it's impossible,' said Xar. 'My father would never be so soppy as to fall in love with the human iceberg that is Queen Sychorax . . .'

'Is this why I am Magic, Eleanor Rose?' said Wish through white lips.

'Yes. A Warrior queen could have a daughter who was Magic, if she once loved a Wizard,' said Eleanor Rose. 'The kiss of a Wizard, if it was a true love's kiss . . . that could stay in the blood. The Magic could still be in there, even after the love had died.'

So there was the truth of it.

Once, long ago, Sychorax and Encanzo had been in love.

And Sychorax had taken the terrible Spell of Love Denied . . .

And the love had died.

She had married a Warrior, like she was supposed to . . .

But somewhere, somewhere behind Sychorax's iron breastplate . . . the lingering true love's kiss of a Wizard had made her daughter Magic, even though she was the daughter of two Warriors.

'Oh dear, oh dear, oh dear,' moaned Caliburn. '*They broke the rules*! And rules are there for a reason! Wizards and Warriors aren't supposed to fall in love . . . And now we see why! A child has been born – Wish – who has Magic-mixed-with-iron . . . and that has changed the course of history. For Magic-mixed-with-iron is what the Witches have been waiting for, for so many, many years . . .'

Xar was still finding this hard to absorb. 'My father is always lecturing ME about not breaking rules, and

259

you're telling me HE broke the biggest rule ever?'

'Maybe this is what our quest has been all about!' said Wish excitedly. 'My father died years ago in a battle against the Grimogres. What about your mother, Xar?'

'She died when I was a baby,' said Xar**.

'So *your* father and *my* mother are free to fall in love all over again!' said Wish excitedly. 'We can help them by undoing the Spell of Love Denied!'

Both Xar and Bodkin looked at her as if she were crazy

'If my father made the mistake of falling in love with that dreadful polar ice cap that is your mother *once*, he's never going to do it TWICE,' said Xar in disgust.

'And oh dear, oh dear, oh dear,' said Caliburn, in great agitation. 'Undoing the Spell of Love Denied would be IMPOSSIBLE! What was Pentaglion thinking to cast such a spell?'

Eleanor Rose sniffed disapprovingly. 'Yes, sometimes it is the ones who think they are wisest who are in fact the most foolish. You're never too old to learn . . . Now, goodbye little humans, and other funny creatures,' she said.

** The narrator would like to gently point out that life was a whole load more uncertain in the Iron Age, which is why there are so many stepparents in fairy stories.

Oh dear... I hope this wasn't my fault....

'Oh, don't go!' cried Wish. 'We really, really need your help! And you never told me where the spoon was! Do you know?'

'I do know where it is,' agreed Eleanor Rose.

'OH!' cried Wish in delight. 'Please tell me where he is!'

'I can release it for you, but after that you should leave here *as quick as you can*,' warned Eleanor Rose. 'Us Frost-sprites are not really supposed to interfere with the affairs of the humans, you see, which is one of the reasons I can't kill THAT,' she said, gesturing upward. 'For that really would be interfering. And besides, I made THAT a promise . . .'

'What is THAT?' said Bodkin, looking up at the ceiling, where he thought he could see something, he wasn't sure what, but *something* lurking up there. They hadn't noticed before, but whatever it was was dripping, one small drop every minute or so, like a stalactite in a cave. Drip . . .! Drip . . .! Drip . . .!

Bodkin moved forward, peering upward, trying to

261

see what it was . . .

And just as Bodkin was staring upward . . .

Something rather LARGER than a drop of water melted from the dark thing it was attached to and landed on the floor with a bright clear ringing noise like a bell.

CLING!!! Cling! Cling! Cling! Cling!

Something that bounced around brightly on the floor before lying quite still.

Something about the size of . . .

an Enchanted Spoon.

Wish rushed forward, with a cry of joy. 'My spoon! *My spoon!*' and she caught the spoon up in her arms.

My Spoon!

'He's *fine!*' she exclaimed, in jubilant relief. The spoon was cold as ice, but she could feel it warming, and beginning to move, and the fork and the key and the pins curled round it gleefully, the key making purring noises,

Oh
bother.
I
hoped
we'd
lost
him
forever,
thought
the
fork.

and even the sprites and the hairy fairies were
pleased for Wish at this reunion. Xar and Bodkin
patted her on the back, and the snowcats and
wolves capered around in happy circles.

Wish turned to thank Eleanor Rose.

But Eleanor Rose had already left.

Off she flew, up and away, rocketing like
a tiny shooting star, pausing a moment at the
rim of the battlements, and then sending down
some sprite-writing as an afterthought, before
continuing on in the direction of the north.

The sprite-writing hovered in
front of them, for a few beautiful
flickering moments before
disappearing too, like
smoke into the sea.

'Remember . . .' said the sprite-writing.

'The universe often depends on

one . . .

unlikely . . .

chance.'

'Oh, I LIKED her!' said Wish, sighing and hugging the spoon very tight. 'She cared far more than she thought she did! And I felt somehow better when she was here to protect us . . .'

For as the spoon grew warm and wriggly in her arms, she could tell by its body language that it wasn't as joyful about this reunion as it ought to have been. It seemed agitated. It was jumping, sluggishly but anxiously, on her hand. It seemed to be trying to point to something . . . something up above their heads . . .

'What is the spoon trying to say?' asked Xar, as they looked around themselves, and realised that they were suddenly very alone in the castle, with the giant and Eleanor Rose gone. Some haunting spell had left it, and it felt . . . peaceful, and no longer sad, but also no longer alive.

But nonetheless . . . the silence was a little . . .

Ominous.

'Why do you think Eleanor Rose said we should get out of here as fast as we can?' asked Tiffinstorm uneasily.

Bodkin was slowly backing away as he looked upward, at where the Frost-sprite had pointed a few minutes earlier,

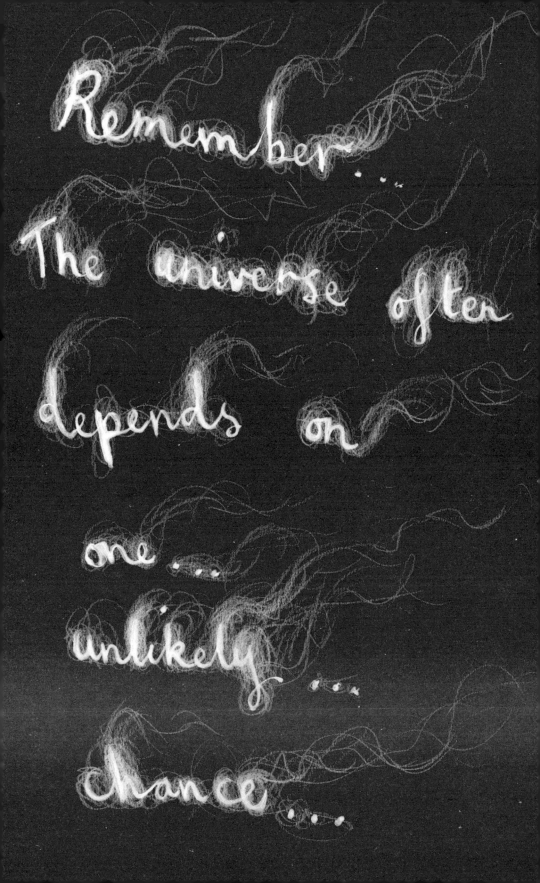

Remember...
The universe often
depends on
one...
unlikely
chance...

at the exact spot the spoon had dropped from.

There was *something else* hanging from the ceiling, like a gigantic vampire bat. A still thing, folded in on itself, quiet and malevolent and patiently waiting. It had witnessed the story. It had hung there for weeks. It had been there all along, and they had not noticed it.

A plotter.

A planner.

A thing with wings.

'What issss that?' hissed Tiffinstorm, drawing her wand, as sharp as any thorn.

Wish and Xar and the sprites and the snowcats and the wolves turned their own heads upwards to follow Tiffinstorm's pointing finger. The werewolf stiffened, sniffed the air as he smelt something wicked, and raised his shaggy head reluctantly.

Hissssssssss . . . hissed the sprites, bright as fire. How could they not have smelled that smell before? That stink, that reek, that corpse-like stench . . .

Because whatever-it-was had been frozen until that very moment.

Bodkin had been staring up at the thing for a while now, and he was so scared he could barely get the words out.

'*That,*' said Bodkin, 'is the Kingwitch. We need to get out of here NOW.'

We need to get
out of here
NOW

12. A Bad Moment for Your Escape to Get Held Up

s they all looked upward in horror, mouths open, at the great dark nightmare hanging above them like a sword about to drop, some more sprite-writing appeared, shooting down from above. It was a little wobblier and harder to read, for Eleanor Rose was now very far away, on the way back to the pole where she belonged.

'The giant and I promised the Kingwitch we wouldn't kill him, if he brought you all to this place together,' said Eleanor Rose's sprite-writing. 'I've frozen him for the moment, but the further I get away from the castle, the harder it is for me to keep him that way, so, I repeat, you will have a bit of a head start but you need to get out of there as soon as you can . . .'

'Oh brother, oh brother, oh brother,' moaned Xar, drawing the Enchanted Sword.

'Sorry about that,' finished the sprite-writing, getting fainter every second. 'But the ends justify the means . . . a fine outcome excuses a bad method . . . all in pursuit of a higher good, you know . . . You'll understand when you're older.'

Uh oh.

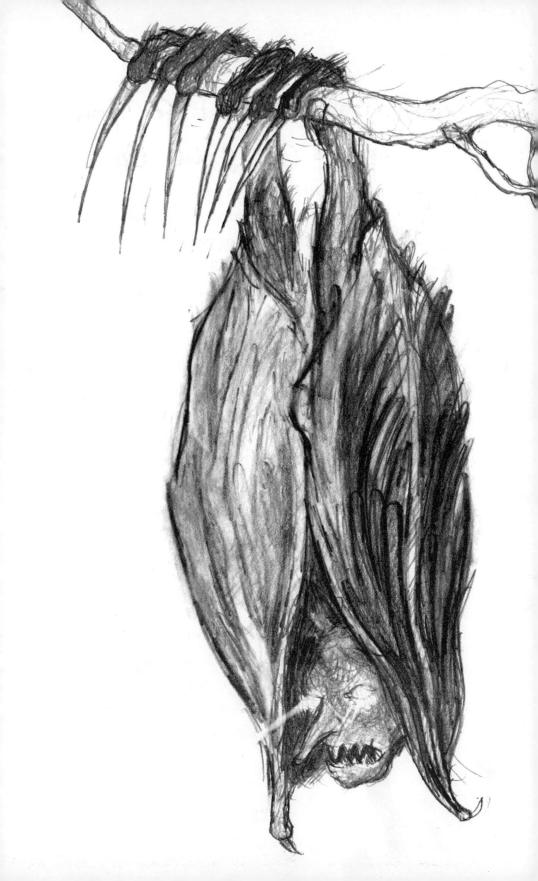

Uh oh uh oh uh oh uh oh . . .

They scrambled to get off the giant's table, and out of that hidden hall before the Thing moved. The sprites launched themselves into the air, the humans leapt on the backs of the snowcats, who ran down the table legs, scrambling to get across the hall, and escape from the castle before that THING woke up.

Up, out of the hall, and into the courtyard, the sprites zooming overhead.

However, as the sprites and the animals emerged shrieking and running as fast as their paws could take them into the daylight, an unwelcome sight met their eyes.

While they had been listening to the story, their pursuers had finally caught up with them.

Tiffinstorm gave a cry of distress, pointing her wand to the south, where up the southern ramparts were climbing Rogrebreaths, giants, Wizards, and the drifting ghostly shapes of Droods.

A golden eagle and a gyrfalcon flew in through two of the broken windows, and then swooped low over the heads of Wish and Xar and Bodkin, as they rode the snowcats through the ruined castle.

'Oh brother!' cried Xar, turning his head to look up. 'This is really going to hold us up!'

'What is it?' said Wish, riding Nighteye right beside him.

'My father,' said Xar. 'That's my father . . .'

'How can that be your father? It's a bird,' said Bodkin, but even as he said it, he knew it was a stupid statement.

The golden eagle and the gyrfalcon wheeled slowly around and hovered in front of the children. The long wings of the golden eagle turned into arms, and the body into the human form of Encanzo, and he landed lightly and coolly on the ground. The gyrfalcon's wings transformed into the long trailing sleeves of the Drood Commander, and he gave a grunt of satisfaction as he landed on the broken floor of the castle.

'SPLIT UP! DODGE!' yelled Xar, and the snowcats swerved – but it was already too late. They were surrounded.

The spelling staffs flew out of their pouch on Xar's back, and into the hands of Encanzo and the Drood Commander.

Birds flew in from all corners of the broken castle, peregrines and crows and seagulls, and transformed into hovering hooded Droods, landing with their long ominous sleeves trailing behind them. Wolves and bears and snowcats and mountain lions appeared, each with a Wizard on its back, armed for battle, and they took out their staffs, and the castle rang with Magic spells of overcoming, so that Wish and Xar and Bodkin could

271

barely move, and Bodkin struggled for breath.

'Going somewhere, Xar?' said Encanzo, coldly.

Xar cursed his father loud and long, as the spells from Encanzo's staff carried him up into the air, legs dangling furiously.

'LET ME GO!' shouted Xar. 'We need to get out of here right now! There's a Kingwitch about to unfreeze in the chamber below us!!!!'

'You will excuse me if I do not believe you, Xar,' said his father, in a voice of steel. 'For you have lied to me so many times in the past. We are here to take you back to Gormincrag. You were put in Gormincrag to try to HELP you but it seems you are determined to prove you are beyond help!'

'Why do you never listen to what I say?' raged Xar. 'That Drood there thinks I'm incurable! He just wants to keep me there forever! I am NEVER going back to Gormincrag, Father! Anyway this is all beside the point because as I just told you, there's this Kingwitch, about to attack!'

Wish stepped forward. 'Your son is right, sir . . . he's telling the truth . . . there really is this Kingwitch down there . . .'

Encanzo gave a start as he took in Wish and Bodkin for the first time.

'Who are you? And why are you with my son?'

There was no good answer to this question. 'Oh!' said Wish. 'I'm nobody . . . I'm nothing at all! I'm a friend of Xar's but nobody important . . . I'm just a . . . I'm a . . .'

What on earth could she be?

While Wish was desperately trying to think of a satisfactory answer to this question an ice-cold voice came floating out on the air from the right-hand side of the circle where all the Wizards, Droods and giants were gathered. A voice as cold as a frost drop and as sweetly pure as the point of a freshly sharpened knife.

'She is my daughter,' said Queen Sychorax, sweeping into the broken castle for all the world as if she were entering the emperor's imperial crown room far away in the Warrior capital. 'And *your son* has kidnapped her. In an act of war.'

13. Two Angry Parents

'Oh, great!' moaned Bodkin, in an agony of agitation. 'Now EVERYBODY'S here! We're never going to get Wish away at this rate!'

It appeared that Bodkin was right.

Down in the chamber below, the dark frozen shape of the Kingwitch was twitching, rocking, twitching, rocking, as if it were going to unfreeze any second.

But the humans up above were too concerned with their own problems to worry about *him*.

The words were hardly out of Queen Sychorax's mouth than one of the Magic-hunters threw a net woven entirely out of iron wires around Encanzo. Encanzo's Magic blazed out uselessly, as the net tightened around him, and the Witchsmeller stepped forward and placed iron manacles around his arms.

As soon as the iron touched Encanzo, Xar was released from the spell that held him, and he dropped heavily to the ground.

It all happened so quickly, no one had time to blink.

'Do not move! We have captured your leader, and one move, one attempt at a spell, and we will kill him!' cried the Witchsmeller.

'Ambushed!' swore the Drood Commander, cursing under his breath. 'I knew that boy would lead us all into a trap! He should be locked underground forever, and we should throw away the key!'

All around the circle the Magic things crouched low, growling, the sprites burnt bright with alarm and fear, the Rogrebreaths and giants grumbled deep in their great chests, but they dared not attack when their leader was immobilised and at the Warriors' mercy.

Queen Sychorax's Warriors trooped into the broken castle. The moonlight glistened off their iron helmets, their bristling weaponry, their Magic-catching equipment. Some were riding horses, others giant grey wolves.

'Forest destroyers!' hissed the Wizards.

'Wicked Magic-users! Followers of Witches!' shouted the Warriors.

'Well-poisoners!'

'Child-stealers!'

Encanzo was incandescent with annoyance to find himself overpowered and in chains so easily, and his expression became even more furious when he clapped eyes on Queen Sychorax. *She* was looking more beautiful and splendid than ever, in the manner of a particularly spectacular polar ice cap.

But her eyes were bleaker than midwinter frost.

275

And great
thunderclouds
steamed off
Encanzo's head, dark
with electric fury.

So the
atmosphere
was . . .
How can
I describe
it?

Tense.
Imagine
the foreboding
crackle in the
air and the spine-
jingling fizz in the
ground below
you if you just
so happened to
be standing on
the edge of a
volcano about
to erupt, and
then

multiply that feeling by about twenty, and you will have an impression of what it might have been like on that ill-starred moonlit night when Queen Sychorax met King Encanzo on the heights of Castle Death.

tap tap tap.

Not even Wish's hopeful gaze could make out
the slightest remains of past love in either of the two
monarchs' eyes. In fact, you could even say that they
were glaring at each other in what could be described as
most lively, and absolute, HATRED.

Queen Sychorax had her own reasons for being
particularly irritated at being dragged against her will
to this godforsaken blast of a doomed castle. She had
been here before, long ago when the castle had been
in considerably better condition, and she did not like
being forced to confront past deeds, and to be made to
discover the ruin that the castle had become – possibly
(who knows?) as a consequence of her own actions.

So Queen Sychorax was not in a good mood as
she stepped disdainfully across the broken rubble in her
golden slippers.

'Good evening, Queen Sychorax,' said Encanzo
with bitter, icy politeness. 'Ambushing a fellow royal
in neutral territory rather than meeting them in open
battle is treacherous and against your own Warrior rules,
but I gather your excuse this time is that in some way
unknown to ourselves *we* have declared War on *you*?'

(This seems like an unwise way to address a Warrior
queen who has you in handcuffs, but Encanzo was a
little too angry to be wise in that moment.)

Queen Sychorax might have been in a bad mood,

but it took quite a lot to get her properly angry. (People were so terrified of her, anger was rarely necessary.)

However, it turned out that *this* would do it.

'There is no question of excuses!' said Queen Sychorax, in a voice spitting like a nestful of infuriated hornets. '*YOUR repellently out-of-control and rude little son* has declared War on our nation by kidnapping *my* daughter, presumably on your orders!'

'I am NOT repellently out-of-control and rude!' snorted Xar, furious to see his father and his people overcome so humiliatingly easily by this dreadful queen. 'And if we're trading insults, *you* have the largest nose on a queen that I have ever seen!'

Queen Sychorax flinched.

The entire courtyard took in a breath.

For Queen Sychorax did have, as it happened, rather a large nose. It was a splendidly royally *beautifully* large nose, but a trifle on the enormous side of medium nonetheless and she was a little sensitive about that.

Queen Sychorax's eyes sharpened to splinters.

'*What* did you say?'

'BIG-NOSE!' shouted Xar. 'Cowardly, flat-footed, no-hearted, EVIL destroyer of forests! Skulking behind your Wall while we Wizards get destroyed by the Witches! You have a nose the size of a METEORITE! You have a nose the size of a TOWER! You're the wickedest woman in the whole forest but you also have a nose the size of a PLANET!'

'Be *polite*, Xar!' said Caliburn, in an agonised fashion. 'You're talking to the person who has the power to kill your father!'

'It is entirely unsurprising that the boy should be so rude!' raged Queen Sychorax. 'Like father, like son!'

'But in this case I disagree with Xar entirely,' said Encanzo. 'You, Queen Sychorax, have always had the most beautiful nose in the wildwoods. It is your *heart* that is the problem. The owner of the most beautiful nose in the wildwoods is also a queen who has no conscience.'

The most beautiful nose in the wildwoods flared in and out with temper.

'The cheek of it! You and your entire Magic people have only been allowed to exist because of MY mercy!' said Queen Sychorax. 'And I HAVEN'T left you to be destroyed by the Witches! I have personally hired this man here to get rid of them for me!'

She pointed to the Witchsmeller.

Encanzo sniffed. 'One look at this man tells me he is not the right person for the job.'

Sychorax's temper was not improved by the fact that she secretly agreed with Encanzo on that point.

'Enough of all this!' she snapped. 'I have been

patient with you for way too long. Encanzo, you must give me your solemn word as a king that you will stop using your Magic, right here, right now, and order your followers to do the same.'

The gathered Magic people gave furious murmurs.

'No, Mother, no!' cried Wish. 'For goodness' sake, everyone, please listen to me! This isn't the time for doing this! We're going to need all the Magic we can get, because there's this Kingwitch about to attack, just in the chamber below us . . .'

But Sychorax was too concerned with her fight with Encanzo to listen to Wish.

'You must stop using your Magic, Encanzo,' said Sychorax, 'or I will give the word for my Warriors to attack.'

Caliburn flew between them both. 'Sychorax, you know you do not mean that! The Wizards and the Droods do not have a hope of fighting your soldiers, for you are armed with iron!'

'Oh, but I do mean it,' said Queen Sychorax, with a glittering smile.

'How strange,' mused Encanzo, 'for you to ask me to stop using Magic, when I have heard rumours that you are not above dabbling in Magic yourself . . .'

Queen Sychorax blushed. 'Sometimes a queen can break the rules, in pursuit of a higher good. The ends justify the means . . . a fine outcome excuses a bad method . . .'

'Oh, is *that* what you believe?' said Encanzo, raising an eyebrow. 'How extremely convenient.'

'Fight them, Father!' shouted Xar.

'Your father is not the invincible person that you think he is, boy,' said Queen Sychorax contemptuously, quivering with temper. '*You* see him as a terrible, powerful Magician. But a little touch of my iron, and see how weak he is!'

'My father is not weak!' said Xar fiercely. 'He is the strongest person in the world!'

'No, Xar, the queen is right. Here, with my hands in iron manacles,' said the Enchanter with a smile, 'my Magic is useless. But however clever Sychorax may be, she still has much to learn. She can kill me, but I will still be here. And Magic cannot be destroyed, it can only be hidden.'

'I hate Magic!' cried the queen passionately. 'Magic is disorder! Magic is short cuts! Magic is chaos and anarchy!

'*Choose,*' she said.

'I choose that you should attack us,' said the Enchanter.

The queen looked at him in astonishment.

She stamped her foot. 'Choose *wisely*!' she cried.

'I *have* chosen wisely,' said the Enchanter. He laughed, and that infuriated Sychorax even more. 'Was it not the choice that you wanted?'

'I am trying to find a civilised way out of this mess!' said the queen in exasperation. 'I do not want violence, any more than you do. Giving up your Magic will still leave your people with a contented, happy way of life. Look at us Warriors . . .'

'It is very hard to be a leader, is it not?' said Encanzo sympathetically. 'Sometimes hard decisions have to be made. You gave me a choice, and I took it. Now you have to let your Warriors attack.'

The queen looked at him in baffled fury.

Queen Sychorax was a very, very tricky person.

But . . .

It is possible that the queen had been out-tricked.

'No!' she said sharply.

'Too late,' whispered the Witchsmeller, moving forward, purring. 'He chose death.'

The Witchsmeller stepped forward, sword drawn.

Encanzo braced himself for the final blow.

And Queen Sychorax leaned forward and knocked the sword out of the Witchsmeller's hand.

'What are you doing?' said the Witchsmeller in astonishment.

'Oh for goodness' sake, you stupid so-called

Witchsmeller!' snapped the queen. 'Don't you know anything? I can't possibly murder an unarmed enemy king in cold blood, however much he may thoroughly deserve it . . .'

Encanzo's expression was unreadable.

Surprise, satisfaction, relief, anger, despair warred for supremacy in his face.

But eventually despair won out.

'You may stop short of allowing your Warrior here to slay me, Sychorax,' said Encanzo, 'but you do not seem to understand that in taking away our Magic and destroying our habitats, you are killing us nonetheless . . . You leave me no choice. Xar, you are about to have your way. You wanted War, and you shall have it . . .'

'At last!' said Xar, his eyes brightening. In his Xar-like way, his excitement at finally being allowed to fight the Warriors in open battle, made him momentarily forget the impending doom of the Kingwitch.

At last they were going to stand up to these stupid Warriors and show them that Wizards could really *fight*!

'War it shall be,' said Encanzo sadly, 'and maybe, Xar, you will now see why I have gone to such trouble to avoid it.

'Magic people . . . *ATTACK!!*'

14. They Really Shouldn't Be Fighting Each Other

o! No! No!' cried Wish in distress. 'Why won't you *listen*? Both of you, this is all a waste of time! We shouldn't be fighting each OTHER! I keep telling you, there's this Kingwitch, just below us, and he's about to unfreeze, and he's the commander of a whole horde of Witches, so this really isn't the moment to do this . . .'

'WARRRIORS, *ATTACK*!' replied Sychorax, completely ignoring her. 'Be merciful, if you can be! If the Wizards surrender, take them prisoner!'

Wizard faced Warrior and they began to fight.

The Magic people were at a great disadvantage, for as you know Magic does not work on iron. But snowcats have teeth and talons, as do bears and wolves. Even sprites have fangs that sting like bees if they bite you. And Wizards and Droods carry bronze weapons with them as well as their Magic staffs if they are venturing into difficult or unknown territories.

So the sound of bronze sword on iron breastplate rang out with a bright terrible ring, and such was the volume of the roars of the wolves and the hissing of the sprites, the cursing of the Droods, and the bellows of

the giants that you could barely hear yourself think in the cacophony of the battle.

Wish looked on in horror.

'Why do they *do* this, Caliburn?' she asked despairingly. 'They're so stupid. I told them about the Kingwitch, but they're just not listening . . . I thought maybe, after the story, that we could make my mother and Xar's father see sense, but look at them now!'

Sychorax had made her guards remove Encanzo's manacles.

Both monarchs drew their swords, bowed to each other with exaggerated royal courtesy, and then lunged simultaneously, their sword-points meeting in dreadful song, as they began their battle.

'You might as well give up now,' spat Queen Sychorax, as she fenced

Squeezjoos biting a Warrior on the bottom (It's a classic)

superbly, 'for it is inevitable that you will lose. Your bronze sword is no match for my iron.'

'I cannot lose more than I have lost already,' said Encanzo.

Caliburn, on Wish's shoulder, sighed and shook his head. 'I don't know . . .' he said sadly. 'So many lifetimes I have lived and this is the way it always ends.'

'And look at Xar!' said Wish. 'Is *he* going to grow up to be as bad as the others?'

But even Xar found that *real* War was not the same as the *idea* of it.

What was he supposed to do now?

Fight Bodkin, who was running towards him? But he *liked* Bodkin.

The red mist of excitement faded from Xar's head and he paused, uncertain.

'Xar!' shouted Bodkin. 'We need to help Wish get out of here! In the confusion, we can get away . . .'

'Oh, yes!' said Xar, with a start. 'Of course we can . . .'

Too late.

As the Wizards and Warriors fought each other, some of the combatants lost their balance when the ground beneath them began to shake.

For in the chamber below, the sinister shape of the Kingwitch had finally unfrozen.

And with a noise louder than a thousand thunder

claps it burst up through the broken flagstones of the courtyard, creating such an outstanding noise that the people halted their fighting in their astonishment.

Up, up, it soared . . .

And then it dropped.

As it fell, it picked up speed, making a horrific explosive noise as the green sparks flew off it.

Someone pointed upwards in alarm, at what now seemed transformed into a huge boulder plummeting down towards them, and the small party running across the hall scattered, as . . .

BOOOOOOMMMMM!!!!!!!!!!!!

What-looked-like-a-boulder landed with an almighty explosion right bang-splat in the centre of the courtyard, shattering into a mass of tiny black shards and dust, and at the moment of impact, it burst into bright green flames.

'Look!' said Bodkin, pointing at the sky above them.

Above the castle, there was the sound of wings. Many, many wings. The crowd looked up. There they were, slowly turning visible in front of their eyes . . . the sky was thick with Witches.

'There are such a lot of them,' gasped Sychorax. 'How could there be so many Witches in the world, and we not know about them for so long? Where have they all been?'

Five of the Witches swooped down on the gigantic, leaping fire, and flew round and round it, turning the flames as they flew anticlockwise, as if they were winding some invisible clock, making a horrible keening sound.

With trembling fingers, Xar got a good hold of the Enchanted Sword.

The witches whirled faster, faster, shrieking in delight, as the fire burned and screamed and crackled.

And then great wings opened in the heart of the fire, wings that spread wide, slowly, unbearably.

Wings on fire . . .

Eyes like melting holes of hate . . .

A beak that screeched its loathing of the world and all the sweet good things that are in it . . .

The Kingwitch.

15. The King-witch

The queen shook the boulder dust off her white skirt, sniffing.

'We seem to have a slight problem,' said the Enchanter, betraying his agitation by a slightly raised eyebrow. If Queen Sychorax could play it cool, then, by mistletoe, so could the Enchanter.

The crowd stared in horror at the large crater in the centre of the courtyard, which now looked as if it had been blasted by the landing of a stray asteroid.

Power reeked from that feathered thing, as slowly, slowly it unfurled its wet black wings to their full extent. They dripped on the floor, black smoking drips, as it lifted its beak and looked around at the crowd until it could pick out Xar and Wish.

Sychorax was pale, very pale.

For she knew that this was all partly her fault. She had tried to be too clever. *This* was the horror that had been hiding in her Stone-That-Takes-Away-Magic all along. Wish had told her . . . but there is nothing like being confronted with the actual reality, to make you realise the extent to which you might have miscalculated.

She turned to Encanzo, white as ice. 'Algorquprqin,'

said Queen Sychorax uncertainly. 'I *think* . . . I may have made a mistake.'

Miracle of miracles! Stiff Queen Sychorax, proud Queen Sychorax, unbending Queen Sychorax who always thought she was right about absolutely everything, admitting that even *she* might not be perfect!

'We all make mistakes,' said Encanzo grimly. 'Even you and I, Queen Sychorax.'

'Oh, by hemlock and nightshade and all things mean and bad,' whispered the Witchsmeller. 'What is that?'

'*That* is a Witch,' said Sychorax. 'You see the difference, pest controller? Giants and fairies and Magical people, they're not really Witches at all, are they? A Witch is kind of unmistakeable.'

'And that isn't just a normal Witch, either,' said Encanzo grimly, '*that* is a Kingwitch'.

'What do you want, Witch?'

Now the Kingwitch began to speak, and it was a dreadful sound indeed, a harsh, grating, guttural noise that seemed to pain him to make, and every now and again, a word was reversed, as was the fashion with Witches.

'I want the children,' crooned the Kingwitch. 'Give me the children.'

There was a horrible silence.

'What children?' said Encanzo.

The Kingwitch pointed at Xar and at Wish.

'The boy iss mine already,' said the Kingwitch. 'And the girl is special . . .'

'There's absolutely nothing special about Wish, look at her!' said Sychorax, briskly, but there may have been a little anxiety in her voice. 'She's totally ordinary, and if anything, for a Warrior, just a little sub standard . . .'

They all looked at Wish, standing uncomfortably on one leg. She didn't look remotely special, a small, skinny little child with an eyepatch and hair sticking out in all directions.

'She has something I need,' continued the Kingwitch. 'I already have some of it, but only as much as was in the very tip of her very little finger . . . Now I want ALL of it . . . to share with my fellow Witches . . . Give her to me now.'

'And what,' said the queen, with considerable asperity, 'are you intending to do with her?'

'I will eat her,' said the Kingwitch.

Which was not very nice, but what did you *expect* a Witch to be like?

There was another horrified silence.

'That is ridiculous!' snapped Queen Sychorax, magnificently scornful and every inch a monarch. 'Of course you can't EAT my child, you disgusting creature,

I never heard of anything more barbaric!'

'Give me the child,' repeated the Kingwitch. 'I will swallow her whole . . . Give me the child . . .'

'I am the queen of these territories,' said Sychorax imperiously. 'We have a Warrior army, fully armed with iron. Take your Witches out of here, before we kill you all. Go!'

The Kingwitch gave a ghastly shriek and spread wide his great dark wings and leapt into the air, and as he flew up, up, up into the airy heights, it looked for one moment as if he was flying away, trying to escape.

Spare a thought for the poor Witchsmeller.

This was meant to be his moment.

He had been enjoying the battle with the Wizards, but this was even better!

As the Kingwitch soared upward, the Witchsmeller was rubbing his hands together.

OH, THIS WAS TOO GOOD.

All his wishes had come true at once.

A WITCH! At last he had found a real live Witch, after a lifetime of looking! And not just one Witch, a whole host of the creatures . . .

They weren't extinct after all!

'Get out the Witch-destroying weapon!' yelled the Witchsmeller joyfully. 'Prepare to face the full force of IRON, Thing of Evil!!!'

He put down his iron visor, almost chuckling to himself.

The Witchsmeller imagined, encased in iron as he was — iron breastplates, iron helmet — that he would be quite safe against the Witch. It might look scary, this creature, but no Magic could work against iron. He would first get rid of the big one and then turn the might of the weapon on all of the others. And then he would go back to the capital in triumph and in glory, with lots of Witch beaks to show the emperor.

The Witchsmeller was just enjoying this happy little thought . . .

When the Kingwitch turned on him.

High up in the air the Kingwitch turned, in a great beautiful glorious swoop, if you had been in the mood to admire the swooping of witches, which the Witchsmeller most certainly wasn't, and with a grand gesture of his feathered wing the Kingwitch pointed all five of his taloned fingers at the Witchsmeller and his two imperial giant-killers, who were struggling to launch the Witch-destroying weapon.

And the Magic came blinding out of the five fingers, with the fierceness with which it might blast out of five Wizards' staffs.

Fifty years the Witchsmeller had studied Witch-hunting, and the Pursuit of Magic, and now he was

looking up through his little iron visor
at the thunderous sky and realising, O my
goodness, that the Kingwitch was spelling at him, and
that was exactly the same moment that he had a tiny
flicker of concern as he realised, horror of horrors, how
small he was, how insignificant, how unprepared for the
spells coming down at him in brilliant stars of light.

The Witchsmeller didn't even have time to get the
imperial giant-killers to launch his Witch-destroying
weapon. It had taken years for the Witchsmeller's father
and for the Witchsmeller's father's father to design that
weapon, and they reckoned they had got it pretty much
perfect, but this is an excellent example of how things
that work magnificently in *theory* don't necessarily work
in practice.

The Witchsmeller got as far as shouting: 'LAUNCH
THE WEAP—!' before the spells hit him.

The stars of light hit the Witchsmeller full on the
chest, and bounced neatly off onto the other Magic-
hunters standing around him, one after the other.

One second the Witchsmeller was standing, in full
body armour, erect and splendid, if a little uneasy, with
his axe raised high above his head, shouting impressive
instructions.

"LAUNCH THE WEAP

The next second, the armour had stiffened around him and solidified, and he was caught within it, as if it were the trunk of a tree.

CLANG!

His visor came down.

'Hello?' said the Witchsmeller in a bewildered sort of way, and the echo of his own voice came back to him from within his metal prison. 'Hello?'

And all around him, his fellow Magic-hunters were similarly caught, stuck in their armour, frozen in various poses of attack, one of them bending down to light the fuse that might set off the Witch-destroying weapon (also frozen), another with arm above head about to launch a spear, others in the act of taking their swords from their scabbards.

IRON. Their armour was made of IRON. How could the Witch's Magic be working on iron? With a terrible sinking of the heart, Xar realised how . . .

Back in their last adventure, when they first met the Kingwitch in Queen Sychorax's dungeon, the Kingwitch had drunk up some of Wish's Magic, and NOW . . .

For the very first time . . .

He had a little Magic that could work on IRON.

The Kingwitch had not taken enough of Wish's Magic to do more than make the armour freeze. He couldn't make it move, or dance. But freezing was quite

enough to paralyse the Witchsmeller and his band of
Magic-hunters.

'Are you all right in there, pest controller?' snapped
Queen Sychorax, peering through the Witchsmeller's
visor. 'Enjoying your first encounter with a real *Witch*?'

'Help!' said the Witchsmeller in reply. And the
soldiers all around him echoed, 'Help!' 'Help!' 'Help!'
as they tried and failed to move the armour that had
solidified all around them.

Queen Sychorax sniffed. 'So much for your famous
Witch-destroying weapon.'

'The Kingwitch shouldn't have been able to do
that,' said Encanzo grimly.

But they didn't have time to absorb any of the
implications of this.

For the Kingwitch whirled round and screamed,
'Let me show you why you should do as I say.

'WITCHES! ATTACK!'

UH - OH ...

16. The Witches Attack

With a terrible smell of burning feathers the Witches swooped.

When Witches attack, they assault all your senses at the same time. Their stink is unbearable, the worst smell you can possibly imagine. Their scream is like the shriek of five hundred angry foxes, and it buries itself in your brain and reverberates around your head till you feel like you might go crazy.

'WARRIORS! WIZARDS! GIANTS! LYNXES!' cried Sychorax. 'Stop fighting each other! Fight THE WITCHES!'

And Encanzo held up his staff and yelled out the same orders.

Sychorax and Encanzo didn't really need to shout those instructions.

The noise and the smell were so horrid that the Wizards and the Warriors were instinctively banding together to fight these new, terrifying assailants.

Warriors and Wizards and giants were in one instant fighting back to back, on the same side. But there was an astonishing number of the Witches, a cloud of them, like a swarm of gigantic malevolent crows.

The Witches were happy to attack the Magic things. But they were still afraid of the Warriors, and they couldn't attack them like the Kingwitch could.

'HOLD FAST! DEFEND YOUR POSITIONS!' cried Sychorax, that great War leader. 'FIGHT THE WITCHES TOGETHER!'

The Kingwitch sharpened his talons against each other like a blacksmith sharpening a gigantic sword.

And then, quick as a weasel he stretched up his claw, and screamed an unintelligible gargle of command.

'We need to defend the children,' said Encanzo, jumping up aboard his lynx, and Sychorax glided up behind him, side-saddle, arms crossed, for she would have DIED rather than put her arms around Encanzo's waist. It was remarkable, the way that she did not lose her balance as the lynx leapt forward, but then Queen Sychorax was really rather a remarkable woman.

'Go away!' shouted Xar, as Encanzo pulled the lynx to a halt beside him. 'I don't need your help!'

'You have to let us defend you, Xar!' said Encanzo. 'I had no idea that creature was after you ...'

In the heat of the moment, and in his anxiety, Xar admitted something that he had not yet really wanted to admit, even to himself.

'The Kingwitch isn't after me, he's after *Wish*,' said Xar. '*Wish* is the girl of destiny ... We need to help Wish.'

Above Xar's head, the whirr of soft wings. Five witches soared, and they did not pause for Xar.

Xar was right, they were after Wish, while her Magic was still untrained, and uncontrolled.

Wish was in the centre of the courtyard.

She had been about to take off her eyepatch, but the Witches had attacked with such suddenness that she had only just nudged it up a smidgeon.

And as they attacked, Encanzo leapt from the back of his snowcat and pointed his fingers towards Wish, making a defensive Magical forcefield the size of a very large, round, invisible boulder spring up around Wish to protect her.

The forcefield burned bright, as the Witches struck again and again, like great black ravens attacking a tasty morsel. Such was the force of their onslaughts that Wish was rolled drunkenly round the courtyard, thrown about inside the forcefield with such violence that she was unable to take off her eyepatch. Every time she put up her arms to do it, she was thrown off her balance once more.

The Kingwitch landed in a blur of wings and crouched down, long black drips of saliva pouring from both sides of his jaws.

'It's weakening!' screeched the Kingwitch, three eyes glowing red as the great slugging force of the Witches' spell-attacks began to crush the forcefield protecting Wish, punching great dents in it as it rolled pathetically this way and that.

Xar ran towards them, the Enchanted Sword slippy in his trembling hand.

'GET OFF HER!' cried Xar, waving the sword at the Kingwitch.

The Kingwitch crouched lower.

'You fool,' he whispered. 'Do you not know, boy, that you are mine?'

'I am not yours!' screamed Xar.

'You have to be careful what you wish for,' crooned the Kingwitch, 'and *you* wished for Witchblood . . . willingly took it . . . put out your hand and made the cut yourself. X marks the spot . . .'

How could Xar deny it? His whole hand beneath the glove was burning a bright, terrible green of such vividness that it turned the glove itself transparent.

'And now I control you,' said the Kingwitch. 'It was I who urged you to escape from the prison of Gormincrag, and I who helped you to do it. You brought her to me.'

'No . . .' said Xar, very white, 'it's not true . . .'

But it is only sometimes when you reach the *end* of the quest that you realise what it has been about all along.

They had fallen into a trap set by a
Kingwitch. All along the way, they had thought
they were making free choices, but silent, frozen,
unmoving, the Kingwitch had been controlling them,
like the spider in the middle of a great grey web.

The Kingwitch turned his dead face to Xar.

'You can't fight *me*,' he said.

Xar's bright green hand burned hot with
such fire that it made poor Xar cry out, and
it was as if his arm had a mind of its own.

His own hand, holding onto the Enchanted
Sword, dragged him forward with his body
desperately trying to pull the other way.

But the hand was inexorable . . . it pulled him with
dreadful force . . .

305

He tried to resist, holding onto his
right elbow with his other hand, but like it
or not, for good or for evil, the rest of his body
was attached to that hand so what could he do?
Heels dragging, he was hauled toward Wish, who was
still being thrown about in Encanzo's forcefield.

'If the sword kills Witches, it can kill *her* too . . .
And I can eat her dead just as well as alive,' whispered
the Kingwitch. 'You can kill her for me, boy. Humans
are weak. She won't want to hurt *you* . . .'

'Remember who you are. You're a Wizard, and
she's a Warrior . . . Wizards hate Warriors . . .'

'I'm sorry, Wish! I can't stop it!' shouted Xar as his
bright green hand brought the sword down on the red
forcefield and broke through it,

BAM!

It shattered into thousands of pieces that exploded
round the courtyard like tiny splinters of bright red
glass, before melting into the air.

'Good, good,' crooned the Kingwitch. 'Now go for
the girl . . .'

Wish stood there, her fingers crooked now
underneath the eyepatch.

She couldn't lift it to fight *Xar* . . .

Poor Xar was still trying to control his own hand.
But the combination of his arm with the Witch-stain

and the Enchanted Sword was too strong for him and
he was being dragged nearer and nearer Wish, with the
sword raised above his head to attack her, even though
he was pulling in the other direction with all his might.

I can't fight this . . . it's too strong for me . . . thought Xar wretchedly.

'Don't think about your weaknesses, think about your strengths,' shouted Caliburn. 'Work with what you DO have, not with what you DON'T!'

'Use your disobedience, Xar!' ordered Queen Sychorax, shouting from behind him. 'You have PLENTY OF *THAT*!'

Xar turned, and raised the sword towards the Kingwitch. He couldn't fight the Kingwitch completely, he wasn't strong enough for that, but he could work with the Kingwitch's own desires.

(Xar had learnt that lesson from the Kingwitch, because that was exactly what the Kingwitch had been doing to *him*.)

'You want the sword, Witch?' shouted Xar. 'You can have it!'

With every single ounce of disobedience in his disobedient body, Xar shouted, 'NO! *Take that,* you stinking great feather-armed FREAK of a nightmare Witch!'

And he threw the sword with all of his might towards the Kingwitch.

There was a moment when it seemed as if the sword wasn't going to leave the green grip of Xar's hand.

But Xar had guessed rightly.

The Kingwitch DID want that sword, for it was a very powerful Magical object.

The Kingwitch's own wanting loosened Xar's grip . . . the sword sailed through the air, and landed a couple of feet in front of him with a loud clatter.

'I WILL NOT do it,' said Xar, chest heaving with the struggle of it. 'Because I LIKE Wish.'

The Kingwitch was astonished at this defiance. The boy should be his entirely! How was it possible that Xar would not do his bidding?

But it did not change the ending . . .

The Kingwitch would finish this himself.

He reached out his taloned hand and grasped the Enchanted Sword.

He said some very powerful words of a spell to bind the sword to his hand, so that the girl could not take it from him.

With one, two beats of his great wings he leapt in the air, wings spread wide, up up up.

And then he swooped, terrible mouth agape, to swallow the child whole.

17. Taking off the Eyepatch

nd Wish took off her eyepatch. Taking off the eyepatch was like opening the door into another world.

Looking through her left eye, it was as if she was standing on the top of a snowy mountain, where the snow was so glitteringly bluey-white that it dazed you. The colours were so forceful, the reds so red, the greens so purely green that it overwhelmed her, and she cried out now, as they hit her almost like a physical blow.

She'd forgotten just how sickening this feeling was, how terrifying.

Very few Wizards before or since have ever had the rare power of a Magic eye.

A power that misted up Wish's brain with such furious energy that her hair leapt up around her like an electrical ruff and the ground beneath her swayed like a sea, and the broken walls shook further, and all around lost their balance as the Magic came screaming out of her eye and met the blast of the swooping Kingwitch's Magic.

Closer . . . closer the Kingwitch dived, so close that Wish could see right down the ghastly maw of his open throat, the Enchanted Sword pointed right towards her.

Oh, by the gods of water . . . what can I do? I have all

this Magic but I don't know how to control it . . .

She tried to imagine removing the Enchanted Sword from the Kingwitch's hand. But it was stuck fast by the spell he had used.

What else can I do?

'Focus on what you DO know, not what you DON'T . . .'

Iron . . . thought Wish, *I know how to move iron . . .*

All that practising she had done in the Punishment Cupboard, and Caliburn's lessons back on the Sweet Track . . .

All around her were the figures of the Witchsmeller and his Magic-hunters, with their armour frozen around them, stiff as statues.

And then, almost the very second that the thought came into her head, the helmet of the nearest Magic-hunter began to untwist, as Wish's Magic made it move. She didn't even have to point her hand at it, all it took was a thought.

'Be careful what you wish for, Witch . . .' whispered Wish. 'You wanted Magic-that-works-on-IRON . . . and you . . . shall . . . have it!'

The Kingwitch was halted abruptly, mid-air, by a flying iron helmet that hurtled through the sky and, CLANG! attached itself to the Enchanted Sword, making the Witch's sword arm so heavy that his whole body lurched violently to the right.

The Kingwitch tried to shake off the helmet, but it was stuck fast, for the helmet had come into the orbit of the spell that the Kingwitch had cast to bind the sword into his hand, and it would . . . not . . . budge . . . however hard the Kingwitch shook it. CLANG! CLANG! Another helmet, and an iron glove soared through the air and stuck to the other side of the sword.

The Kingwitch said the words of the undoing, to take off the binding spell he had cast, and he had the first stirrings of unease.

'What is *that*?' the Kingwitch asked himself in a startled sort of way.

For as the Enchanted Sword sprang out of the Kingwitch's hand, and dropped point first into the ground, the Magic-hunters' frozen armour had exploded apart, leaving the bewildered Witchsmeller and his soldiers standing in their underclothes, staring upwards in astonishment while their armour rocketed towards the Kingwitch. Spears and helmets and chains and knives and swords and breastplates, not to mention an entire Witch-destroying weapon, the whole armoury of iron that the Magic-hunters carried with them on Magic-hunting expeditions, were sailing through the air towards the Kingwitch as if they were arrows fired at a bird.

MORE iron, thought Wish, *more and more and more . . .*

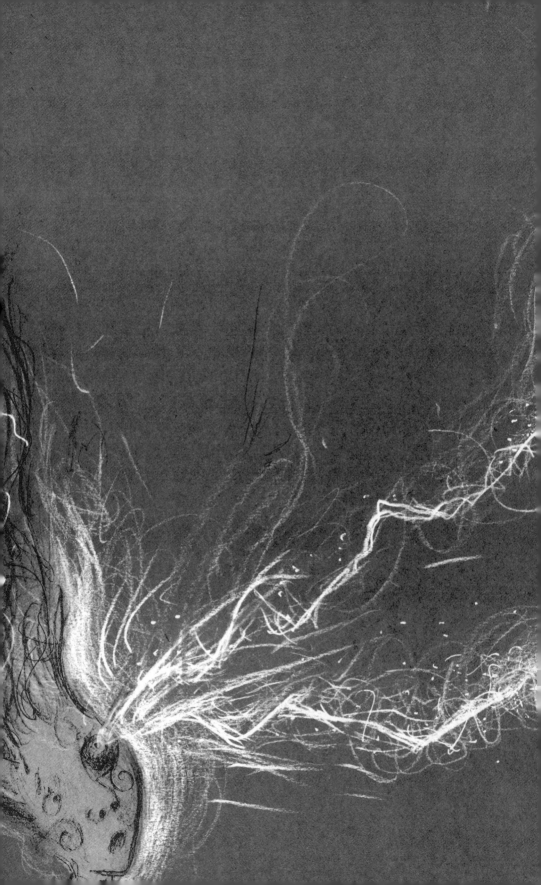

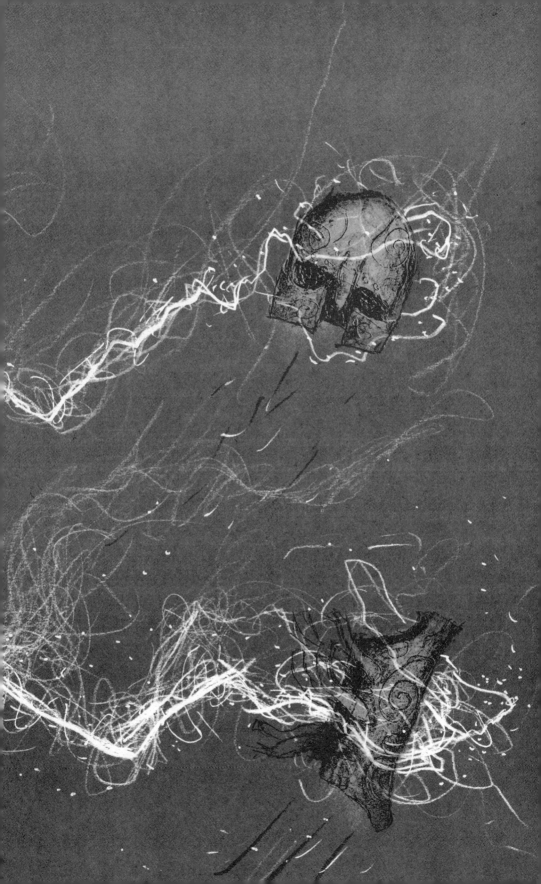

The army of iron attached itself to the Kingwitch as if he were a magnet.

The Kingwitch tried to beat all the iron things off, but they clogged up his wings, and the harder he tried to fight them off, the harder they stuck fast, until he became smothered in a thick ball of iron, iron that melted around him as it met the green heat of his Magic. It weighed the Kingwitch down, and he plunged deeper and deeper in the air, and Wish added more and more and more and more and more until he fell to the earth like a stone.

Xar and Wish scrambled out of the way over the heaving, tumbling earth as . . .

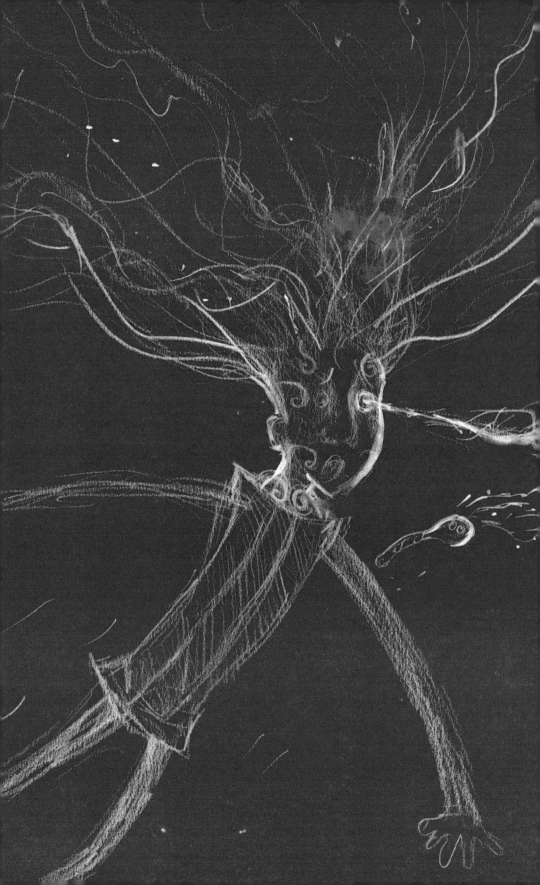

CRASSHHHHHHHHH!

The Witch encased in iron landed with such force that he created a great crater in the courtyard of the ruined castle of Pentaglion. Just as the iron solidified in a final, enclosing ball, the Kingwitch shot one last blast of Magic from his five taloned fingers and . . .

REOOW!!

The Magic came screaming out and hit Wish on the chest and there was a mind-blowingly loud noise, and a blinding white light, and something exploded with such energy that Xar was knocked over.

The earth came to a shuddering halt at last, and great clouds of dust billowed and wafted across the shattered remains of the courtyard.

The ball of iron that encased the Kingwitch was, strange to say, exactly the shape of the stone that used to be Queen Sychorax's Stone-That-Takes-Away-Magic, maybe because it was a shape that Wish had seen before.

The clouds of Witches who had been hovering, waiting, watching for the outcome of this battle, shrieked across the sky, howling and raging against the defeat of their leader, before dispersing, flying away, who knows where?

The ball of iron rocked once, twice, on its pointed axis . . . and then it rolled to the edge of the battlements . . . and fell over the edge . . . and down, down into the ocean below, before disappearing under the waves.

The Wizards and the Warriors, the Witchsmeller, the Droods and the Magical creatures staggered to their feet, coughing and choking, trying to work out exactly what had just gone on.

Queen Sychorax leapt up, and ran towards Xar, Encanzo and Bodkin running by her side. The dust fell all around them like blue rain.

Xar picked up the Enchanted Sword, which had landed right in front of him.

The writing on the blade had got so scratched and rubbed away on both sides by the helmet and the other iron things, that it now just read:

Once . . .

'We did it! AGAIN!' grinned Xar, as he put the sword into his scabbard. The two monarchs reached him where he stood, ragged and shaken, his quiff a little awry, but still Xar-like in his jubilation.

'I TOLD you we could do it, Father! 'And did you see, Bodkin? Did you see, Caliburn?' he cried, punching the air in triumph. 'I DID fight the Kingwitch! I TOLD you I could!'

'What on earth is the boy talking about?' snapped Queen Sychorax. *'Where is my daughter?'*

'There she is,' said Xar, pointing at the great cloud of gentle, shimmering, bright-blue dust falling around them.

Queen Sychorax was without words.

'She exploded,' explained Xar.

Queen Sychorax's chest heaved as she looked around at the clouds of blue dust before . . .

'EXPLODED?' she said in horror. 'My daughter *EXPLODED*???

What do you mean she *exploded*? And why are you celebrating? The child *saved* you, you horrible boy! You're as bad as that Witch!'

My daughter EXPLODED?

If she hadn't been such a very great queen you might have thought that Sychorax staggered a little. She certainly turned deathly pale, and then she knelt down on the floor where the Enchanted Spoon and thirty iron pins lay quiet and cold and lifeless.

She reached out a trembling hand to touch them.

Squeezjoos whispered, 'Don't you worrys ice queen, don't you worrys . . . she'll be back,' putting his little claw–like hands lovingly on the bewildered queen's cheek.

Queen Sychorax had given her heart away long ago.

But kneeling in the dust there, one, two, three tears dropped from her cold blue eyes.

'Outss of the way! Outsss of the way!' said the Once-sprite, swooping from nowhere, jumping from the back of the hovering falcon, and collecting the tears, one, two, three, as they dropped from the cheek of the mourning queen.

Encanzo stepped in hurriedly. 'For shame, Xar, you have to explain! Your daughter will regenerate, Sychorax. She has a Magic eye, which makes her a very great Enchanter, and very great Enchanters have more than one life.'

'Regenerate?' said Queen Sychorax, blinking blankly. 'Magic eye? More than one life?'

She had forgotten how horribly confusing Magical people were.

They couldn't even obey the normal rules about life and death.

'*When? When* will she regenerate?' gabbled Sychorax.

'In a moment or two,' said Encanzo soothingly. 'It can take a while . . . In the meantime, we have to be careful not to step on any of this blue dust . . .'

'This blue dust is MY DAUGHTER???' said Queen Sychorax, looking around in astonishment and horror.

'What issss that man doing?' hissed Squeezjoos, eyes narrowing.

That man was the Drood Commander.

The Drood Commander was behaving in rather a peculiar manner.

He was working frantically, and as they looked more closely they could see he was actually *spelling* the blue dust with his spelling staff, collecting bright clouds of it and putting it in a gourd.

'Yes,' said Encanzo, very puzzled, 'what on earth are you doing, Drood Commander?'

'Didn't you see? The girl, the Enchanter, has Magic-mixed-with-iron, which makes her very very dangerous!' said the Drood Commander. 'Quick! We don't have much time! We must trap her in here and then she won't be able to regenerate!'

'Be careful there, Commander!' said Encanzo sharply.

'We're talking about the pieces of a human being here.'

'An extremely hazardous human being!' said the Drood Commander.

'How dare you take advantage of my daughter's dust-like state to attempt to imprison her?' snapped Queen Sychorax.

'Don't you move any closer, Queen!' warned the Drood, pointing his staff at her. 'Or I will put the lid on this gourd and throw it into the sea! And that will be far worse for your daughter than you can imagine, for she shall be half here, and half there . . .'

Encanzo and Sychorax froze, for a state of limbo was a dreadful fate.

But the werewolf stepped forward, growling, low, ominously, deep in his throat.

'Get back!' ordered Encanzo. 'That Drood is dangerous . . .'

The werewolf ignored him.

'What are you doing, werewolf?' screamed the Drood Commander, madly sweeping the blue dust into the gourd in great drifts. 'Step back, you evil-bound beast! Halt, you loveless furball! I'm doing historically important work here!'

And then Xar had a brilliant idea . . .

And he did a Good Thing.

A really, *really* Good Thing.

Xar needed to get rid of those Witches. He knew that it was unlikely that the Kingwitch would have been defeated forever. His hand was still burning bright green. He needed all of the ingredients in the spell to get rid of Witches, and they had just gone to considerable lengths to get hold of this one.

Xar NEEDED what was inside this bottle...

BUT...

But for the first time in Xar's life, he cared about somebody else more than he did about himself.

So Xar undid the stopper on the collecting bottle he was carrying.

In a great glorious roar the Giant's

Last Breath blasted out of the collecting bottle into which it had been shrunk only an hour or so earlier.

'FORGIVE THEM!' roared the Giant's Last Breath.

'FORGIVE THEM!!!' at a decibel so loud that Sychorax and Encanzo and Xar and Bodkin had to put their hands over their ears.

'FORGIVE THEM.'

18. Forgive Them

The released giant's breath was a roar so loud, and it made a wind so strong, that the bright pieces of blue dust that the Drood was trying to collect whirled up into the air in a flurry of excitement, and out of the Drood's reach.

The Drood gave a howl of frustration as up and into the wind they went, round and round, impossible to catch, and the Drood, arms flailing, dropped the gourd which rolled on the floor, all the dust spilling out of it in great glorious swoops . . .

And the Drood himself lost his balance in the tremendous roar of the blast, and fell out and over the edge of the battlement that had been broken by the ball of iron that encased the Kingwitch only moments before, with a furious shriek.

Down the Drood fell, becoming smaller and smaller, and when he had nearly reached the ocean, his pin-prick of a body transformed into a gyrfalcon, before spreading wide his wings and flying out, out across the waves in the distant direction of the islands known as the Giant's Footsteps.

Just in time, for all around them the freed blue dust was singing . . .

Singing a beautiful sweet
song of life returning, as all the
whirling innumerable little pieces of
Wish came joyfully back to life again, and they
rushed around, those tiny fragments, in a confusing
blur of reshuffling Magic, whizzing back together
in the memory of where they were, the impossibly
complicated reality of a human body, forming the
perfect sculpture of what-once-was-Wish, until: Oh!

Bodkin would never tire of the heart-stopping
moment when up above, the small brown heart of Wish
re-formed in the air, and then down it plunged through
the chest, and Wish sat up and
took in that breath that was life
itself, in sweet, thirsty gulps.

Caliburn had found
Wish's eyepatch in the
rubble, and he hurriedly
handed it to her, before
the earth started trembling
again.

'Wish!' cried Queen Sychorax, extremely shaken, for it is not every day that you see your daughter blown into pieces, her heart flying through the air and her entire body reconstituting herself in front of your very eyes. 'Are you all right? Is everything in the correct place?'

She held her daughter's hand and patted her down to check that she was real, and alive, and breathing, and that all of her was there.

'I'm sorry, Mother!' said Wish, gasping for breath. 'I know it's a bit unusual . . . but it seems that I have more than one life . . . I do hope you don't mind?'

'I do not mind,' said the queen, in a definite tone of relief, 'as long as you promise never to do all this . . .

all this *flying about in little pieces* in an untidy fashion . . .
all this . . . *making your heart go jumping through the air* . . .
ever EVER again . . .'

'You were *worried* about me, weren't you?' said
Wish shyly.

'Perhaps I was,' admitted Queen Sychorax.

And then . . .

'The way you defeated the Kingwitch, was, I have
to admit, *clever*. Queens have to think on their feet,' said
Queen Sychorax.

The queen did not smile at her daughter very often,
but when she did, Wish's whole world lit up with
sunshine.

Wish smiled back delightedly.

And as Queen Sychorax smiled at Wish,
Encanzo embraced his son.

'You said you'd make me proud of you,
Xar,' said Encanzo. 'And I AM proud of you.
You resisted the power of the Kingwitch. I never
thought you could. I said "be good" and you were.
You really are growing up.'

Xar stuck out his chest in delight.

'It's all going to be fine!' said Wish, joyously, holding out her arms. 'Thank you, Lonesome, thank you, Squeezjoos!' she said, hugging the hairy fairy.

The werewolf was so surprised he actually let her hug him too.

'*URRRRR URRR URRRRR! URRR URRR URRRRRR! URR URR URRRRR!*' roared the werewolf.

'*URR URR URRRRR!*' shouted Xar. 'Join in, everyone! She's alive!' Completely forgetting themselves in the excitement of the moment, the Wizards and the

Warriors responded to Xar's demand, and they also looked up to the sky above and echoed this wild cry:

'URRRRR URRR URRRRR! URRR URRR URRRRRR! URR URR URRRRR!'

Miracle on miracle.

What a sight it was, Wizards and Warriors howling at the sky alongside the most reviled, the most feared, the most despised beast in the wildwoods.

And then . . .

'WORRA WOORA REARRGH! WORRA WORRA CREAGGGGGLE!' screamed the werewolf, abruptly tilting his head downward, and fixing his savage gaze on the crowd with alarming intensity, foaming at the mouth, and making tearing-limb-from-limb motions with his arms, while gnashing his teeth. 'GOORAGGOOGLE!'

And the crowd's happy supportive howling halted rather abruptly as they scrambled fearfully out of the way, pushing each other over, and screaming a little, in case the teeth-gnashing and limb-tearing was intended for *them*.

This is the problem with werewolves, you see.

They're hard to love, even when you're on their side, because they're so . . . well . . . *scary.*

'Now it really IS all right!' said Wish, with a sigh of contentment.

It had been a terrible adventure, but it had all been worth it, thought Wish. She had been dreading the moment that her mother found out her secret, but now that she had, it was sort of a relief. Now could be the start of the Wizards and the Warriors finally working together to fight the Witches. Her mother would fall back in love with Encanzo, they would stop this silly war between them, it was all going to be fine . . .

But now that she was over her initial relief, Queen Sychorax was no longer smiling.

She was standing, her immaculate hair covered in bits of brick dust and dripping wet. Her once-white dress dragged behind her in the dirt, streaked with mud and mess, torn by Witch's talons, and dripping in green Witchblood. She had made the unwelcome discovery (Sychorax may have suspected this already, but actual *proof* is always a bad moment) that she had an exploding daughter, with a Magical eye and a historically unfortunate Magic-mixed-with-iron component . . . it was all very irregular indeed.

'All right?' snapped Queen Sychorax. '*All right*? It most definitely is NOT all right! This is a disaster, and I am now going to take my daughter home, and I do not want to hear ONE WORD about this ever again.'

She adjusted her dishevelled hair, and brushed down her white dress briskly.

All Wish's wonderful fantasies about this being a new start collapsed in an instant.

'But this adventure has been a lesson to all of us that things are going to have to change round here!' said Wish. '*People* are going to have to change, people like US. The Witches have returned to the wildwoods, and Wizards and Warriors have to join together, to fight them off, just like we did this evening.'

'Never!' cried Encanzo.

'Not on your life!' spat Queen Sychorax. 'Wizards are incapable of change!'

'As are Warriors!' said Encanzo, if anything, even crosser.

'No, no, don't say that!' said Caliburn. '*Everyone* is capable of change! What the children need is *education* . . . For the Witches are still out there, and when they come back, then this girl Wish is going to be tested, and she may be all that stands between us and oblivion . . .'

'Yes, and Caliburn's been giving us lessons while we were on the run!' said Wish. 'He's a brilliant teacher, not just of Magic, but all the Warrior spelling-and-words-and-maths stuff, and when *Caliburn* is teaching me it seems to all make sense!'

'I am not going to have my child taught by a talking *bird*!' said Queen Sychorax. 'I know perfectly well how to educate my own child, thank you very much.

'You have both been saved from the Kingwitch,' she went on, 'and now we must put things back to the way they were.'

'But, Mother! You and Encanzo were in *love*!' said Wish, very distressed. 'Remember the wolves? Every second Thursday!!! *It's the reason I am who I am*! The true love's kiss of a Wizard remained in your blood and it made me Magic even though I am a Warrior!'

Encanzo and Sychorax went very still.

Wish quailed before the look of utter horror in her mother's cold blue eyes.

'WOLVES? *THURSDAYS?*' said Queen Sychorax in arctic outrage. 'Wizards and Warriors in *love*? Impossible!'

'Inconceivable,' echoed Encanzo bitterly, in a voice hard as a diamond. 'A queen like Sychorax was always going to marry some idiot Warrior with a thick neck and a big sword, so she could enjoy all these knick-knacks, these golden plates, this Warrior jewellery trash around her neck . . . A queen like Sychorax would never be in love . . .'

'I had duties!' retorted Queen Sychorax. 'Responsibilities! And *you* married one of your own kind, just as I did, Encanzo, for your disobedient son here must have had a mother once!'

'But the giant Proponderus told us the whole story . . .' said Wish, now miserably muddled. They were talking as if it had actually happened, while at the same time denying it.

Grown-ups were so confusing.

Was it true or was it made up?

'The giant must have been listening to the fairies,' said Queen Sychorax firmly. 'Fairies are terrible liars. This is *real life*, Wish, not a fairy story. Therefore, I repeat, for the final time, Wish will return home with me, to the safety of Warrior Castle, and as far as I am concerned, this JUST . . . NEVER . . . HAPPENED.'

At that moment the Witchsmeller stepped forward.

It was difficult for the Witchsmeller to be quite as scary as he had been only a couple of weeks before when he'd left Queen Sychorax's iron fort in the full screaming cry and splendour of the Magic-hunt.

He had his sniffing nose, of course, but even *that* wasn't quite so alarming now that he and his Magic-hunters had no armour, weapons, shields, spears, sprite-catching equipment, anything. All of it had been used by Wish's Magic to create the great grim iron prison that now enclosed the Kingwitch. They were standing there in that cold draughty castle, wearing mostly their underclothes. Some of them had even had to cover themselves with hastily arranged brambles (which make rather prickly trousers).

A person always feels at a disadvantage when they

are trying to address a queen while dressed in little more than their knickers, so the Witchsmeller spoke with less than his usual authority.

'Your Majesty!' he objected. 'You can't possibly take this child Wish back to Warrior territories! This child here is, as I suspected, an extremely dangerous *Fule.*'

A person feels at a disadvantage when they are only dressed in their underclothes and a few hastily-arranged brambles.

He lowered his tone in horror. 'And the Fule is MAGIC, there's no two ways about it . . . and when I say Magic, I mean . . . really, really *Magic*.'

It was not wise to disagree with Queen Sychorax once she had decided something had JUST . . . NEVER . . . HAPPENED.

So now she turned on the Witchsmeller and fixed him with a stare that a Frost giant would have been proud of and her voice dropped to about fifty degrees or so below freezing. 'I hope you are not suggesting, pest controller, that *my* daughter, MY daughter, who is the product of nineteen lines of Warrior good breeding and is a direct descendant of Brutal the Giant-Killer himself on *both* sides of her family tree, is some kind of common CHANGELING?'

'Well . . . er . . . I don't know about that, but you have to admit something very odd has gone on . . .' spluttered the Witchsmeller, quailing under her stern gaze.

'Or perhaps,' continued Queen Sychorax, in a voice so grim it could have shrivelled a snail at fifty paces, 'you are putting forward the notion that I, Queen Sychorax, exchanged a true love's kiss with a rascal of a Wizard and that that has in some way turned my impeccably pedigreed Warrior of a daughter treasonably and untidily *Magical*?'

'But she was exploding all over the place! Into an enormous cloud of dust! Shooting spells out of her eye! Making all the iron fly about like this!' babbled the Witchsmeller, waving his arms around energetically to recreate the moment. 'We ALL saw her do it, right in front of us!'

Queen Sychorax's eyes narrowed to splinters. 'So you *all* saw her do it, did you?'

She turned to the crowd and her voice was as brisk and as meaningful as a freshly sharpened knife. 'Step forward, if you have seen *my* daughter explode like some sort of badly raised Wizardly firework! Put up your hand if you witnessed *my* daughter making spells with iron like some sort of ghastly Magical blacksmith!'

There was a dreadful silence.

Nobody put up their hand.

And then such was the force of Queen Sychorax's personality that everyone took a step *backward*, Wizards and Warriors alike, muttering things like: 'Oh no, we saw nothing . . . nothing at all . . . it's difficult to see in this kind of light.'

Queen Sychorax raised one splendid eyebrow and turned to the Witchsmeller. 'It appears,' she said, in a tone like a cat bite, 'that *you* were the only one who witnessed this spectacle, pest controller . . . You and your Magic-hunters are dismissed, and don't expect me to offer you any references to the emperor.'

The Witchsmeller trembled with indignation. 'This

is an *outrage!*' he said. 'I shall report this whole story to the Warrior emperor *myself*, and he shall remove your crown, and bring the might of the Anti-Magic Commission down upon you and upon that Fule!'

'You're going to tell the emperor that *you* failed, and that the Kingwitch was defeated by a couple of thirteen-year-olds?' said the queen, in a tone of gentle surprise. 'But you're supposed to be his crack Magic-hunting troops! The emperor doesn't like *losers*, pest controller, and what *I* would do if I were you, is to take some of these Witch feathers lying about around here back with you to the capital, and make up some story about how it was YOU who destroyed the Kingwitch. And then maybe he will forgive you for losing all that expensive Magic-hunting equipment.'

'*You* are the most appalling woman I have ever met in my entire life!' said the Witchsmeller bitterly.

Queen Sychorax gave a small smile.

I *think* she took that as a compliment.

The Witchsmeller drew himself up to his full height, and adjusted his underclothes. He and his Magic-hunters gathered up as many Witch feathers as they could find. And then they stalked out of the courtyard with as much dignity as they could manage considering they were half-dressed and unarmed.

I'm afraid that the watching Wizards and Warriors

did not entirely hide their laughter, and the sprites certainly didn't.

'Very good. In which case, order can be restored,' sniffed Queen Sychorax with satisfaction, for there was nothing that Queen Sychorax liked better than order being restored. 'I will take Wish back to iron Warrior territory behind the Wall, so she will be safe if the Witches return.'

'And as for *Xar . . .*' continued Encanzo, sorrowfully, 'don't take this badly, Xar, but I do still have to take you back to Gormincrag.'

'*Why?*' asked Xar, in shock.

He had never heard anything more unfair in his life.

'Let me explain,' said Encanzo. 'Gormincrag is not supposed to be a prison so much as a rehabilitation centre . . .'

'They always say that!' yelled Xar in outrage. 'But "rehabilitation centre" is just a fancy way of saying jail! *You* said you were proud of me! *You* said I was growing up! *You* said I did a great job at controlling the Witch-stain and being good! And now you're going to PUNISH me for it?'

'Look, I am impressed, Xar, with how you've been trying to be good, I really am,' said Encanzo. 'But here in real life you cannot wish away that Witch-stain, and it is only going to get worse. The Drood Commander was a bad lot, but I will go back to Gormincrag with you, and make sure a new and kinder regime is installed, for that is where you will be safest until we can get rid of the Witch-stain entirely.'

'That *isn't* what we need to do!' howled Xar. 'We need to find the ingredients of this spell to get rid of Witches, that we found in my Spelling Book. Show him, Wish!'

Bodkin took out the Spelling Book, and gave it to Wish, and she showed Encanzo and Sychorax the right page.

'Who wrote this spell?' asked Encanzo after a while.

'I did,' said Wish. 'With Caliburn's feather.'

Encanzo sighed and gave the book back to Wish.

'This isn't a *real* spell. Wish just made it up,' said Encanzo gently.

'What do you mean it isn't a real spell?' said Xar, very crestfallen indeed, for he had been pinning all his hopes on that spell.

'Look!' said Encanzo, 'it's in the Write Your Own Story section, right next to a whole load of stories about Xar being the biggest hero the world has ever known. No one single spell could defeat the Witches on its own.'

'Encanzo is right, and it is just as I said,' said Queen Sychorax. 'This is *real life*, Xar, not a fairy story. You have to be reasonable and do as you are told.'

Wish stepped forward hurriedly.

They were all going to be there *forever* if they had to wait for Xar to be reasonable and do as he was told.

But at least she could finally say the words she had been intending to say all along, a couple of weeks back, on the Royal Stage in the iron Warrior fort.

'You are wrong, Mother, wrong!' said Wish defiantly holding up her fist.

Sychorax started in shock.

And then she gave Wish *That Look*, a Look of Deepest and most Furious Disappointment, the look that generally meant that all the words that Wish had been *intending* to say went completely out of her head.

But standing by her friends' sides, with Xar, Bodkin, the spoon and all her Enchanted Objects, and the werewolf, the snowcats, and with weeks of terrifying and challenging adventures behind her, Wish opened her mouth . . .

And carried on speaking despite That Look.

'You are wrong, Mother, wrong!' repeated Wish fiercely. 'And so is King Encanzo! You HAVE to believe that the world can change, that the spells can work, that you can write your own story whatever the odds that are facing you! For it is surprising how often the universe depends on one . . . unlikely . . . chance!'

Queen Sychorax looked at her daughter.

A girl who ROARED . . .

That Look unfroze.

She remembered, once more, that she should not underestimate her peculiar little daughter.

Sychorax touched Wish on the shoulder.

'I'm sorry, Wish,' said Queen Sychorax. 'You'll understand when you're older.'

Oh, for goodness sake! Why do they keep saying that? thought Wish crossly. The adults clearly weren't going to see sense *whatever* their children said.

You are WRONG, mother, wrong!

The grown-ups had some growing up to do *themselves*.

So Wish turned with a sigh to Encanzo.

'All right then. I don't agree with you, but if I can persuade Xar to go back with you to Gormincrag without a fight, will you and my mother at least grant us one wish?' asked Wish.

'If you can persuade Xar to go back with me without a fight, that would be a miracle,' said Encanzo. 'I make you no promises about the wish, however.'

Wish took Xar aside, and whispered something in his ear.

Xar looked thoughtful.

'All right,' he said grumpily. 'I'll go back.'

'A miracle!' said Encanzo in amazement. 'I must come to you, daughter of Sychorax, for Xar-training tips . . .'

'What is your one wish?' asked Sychorax suspiciously.

'I wish you would both grant us *just one night* of ceasefire,' begged Wish. 'One evening banquet, here, Wizards and Warriors sitting and eating together, one night to celebrate the ONE time that Wizards and Warriors fought together side by side and defeated the Witches, and when a werewolf and a Wizard saved a Warrior princess's life. One night, stolen out of time.'

'Just this one night?' said Encanzo thoughtfully.

'And then we go back to real life' said Wish.

'It's a beautiful evening,' she added persuasively. 'And look! One of the giants is starting to dance!'

It was true. One of the larger giants was gently moving his long limbs in a slow dignified country dance, humming to himself and the moon above.

'And then in the morning I PROMISE I will go back to Gormincrag and even tell you how to turn my brother back from that creature into being Looter again,' said Xar, gesturing at the furious form of the Creature-that-was-Looter, being held, rather gingerly at that moment, by one of the Droods.

Queen Sychorax gave a start.

'Have you no control over your repellently disobedient son?' she said to Encanzo. 'He turned his brother into *that*?'

'Your own offspring is not exactly a perfect example of obedience herself,' snapped Encanzo. 'Do Warriors normally jaunt about the countryside in the company of Enchanted Spoons?'

This was unanswerable, and the two monarchs bonded silently for a moment over the problems of parenting.

And they were at least *considering* Wish's request.

'I will not dance myself,' said Sychorax thoughtfully, 'I never dance . . . but I would normally give my troops a little celebration after a battle like that one . . .'

'We in the Wizarding world would feast into the small hours,' said Encanzo.

Everyone was tired.

Everyone was hungry.

If they went their different ways right now, they would have to climb down that mountain again, and nobody particularly wanted to do that after a long, exhausting fight against the Witches. It would be irregular . . . *most* irregular . . . but it would mark an irregular event. And it was, by chance, Midwinter's End Eve, the day before spring finally turned to summer.

Midwinter's End Eve was also known as 'Fool's Day', and things that happened on that day did not really count.

'As long as you absolutely understand, Wish,' said Sychorax sternly, 'that it will be *just one night*, out of time. It will change nothing. We go back to War with the Wizards tomorrow morning. Both of you have to give your Wizard and Warrior words that you will come back with us tomorrow.'

Wish blinked at her innocently.

'Oh, yes, mother, what you are saying makes total sense. It would just be one night, out of time. We give our word, don't we Xar?'

'Absolutely,' said Xar.

'Hmmmmmm . . .' said Encanzo.

'Hmmmmmm . . .' said Sychorax.

Quite by chance they were both thinking the exact same thing, which was that they would give in to their offspring's request but they would not let them out of their sight for one single second.

We give our word...

but they both had their fingers crossed behind their backs...

19. Midwinter's End Eve, Also Known as 'Fool's Day'. One Night Out of Time

So Sychorax and Encanzo turned to their subjects, and ordered one night out of time.

'WARRIORS!' cried Queen Sychorax. 'For this one night, I decree a ceasefire between the Warriors and the Wizards, to celebrate a historic defeat of an ancient enemy, the Witches! Tomorrow we return to our battles . . . tomorrow we carry on our War . . . but tonight, we FEAST!'

'ONE NIGHT OUT OF TIME!' cried King Encanzo.

The Warriors and Wizards gave wondering murmurs, for this was all most unusual. But the fight had been won, and the word 'feast' acted on them all like a Magical elixir.

'ONE NIGHT OUT OF TIME!' the Wizards and the Warriors cried back to their monarchs.

And so began one of the most extraordinary evenings in the history of the wildwoods.

A great bonfire was built in the centre of the courtyard, and the flames burnt red, yellow, and also eerie blues and purples, as the Droods and the sprites added Magical fire to encourage the real flames to burn higher, and hotter.

Warriors danced with giants, whooping around the fire. The hairy fairies whizzed around in a state of high excitement, as everyone made music, Queen Sychorax's Warriors blasting out joyful horn noises, Encanzo's fiddles hanging in the air magically playing themselves, the giants humming happily, linking arms with each other, the sprites singing their high bright songs, of things too high for the human eye to see, sounds too low for the human ear to hear.

The giants sang their giant songs, which rolled out across the landscape:

I need the space to run my fill
I need to jump from hill to hill

And if you take my woods from me
I'll wander out into the sea
And try to find another world

So I can live a GIANT life!

The Warriors sang their own songs:
'*NO FEAR!* That's the Warrior's marching song!
NO FEAR! We sing it as we march along! *NO FEAR!*
Cos the Warriors' hearts are strong! Is a Warrior heart

a-wailing, is a Warrior heart a-failing, is a Warrior heart a-railing? *NO FEAR!*'

And the songs of the Warriors mingled with the melancholy song of werewolf:

I'm running for the moon
Up to the moon where I can be good
When all the world gives up on me
When everyone thinks bad about me
I still have the moon
It's me and the moon
Mostly its me and the moon

Every now and then the werewolf would break off to howl, *'Ooooooww ooow OOOOOOOOWW!'*

The sprites rushed around, wildly overexcited, playing tricks on every one with naughty games like:

Hinkypunk cast a Spell on one of the Warrior's bowls of stew, making it rise up into the air and land on his head in a sticky stewy mess. Tiffinstorm lobbed a Softening Spell onto some of the Warriors' knives and forks so they went all floppy in their hands and they couldn't lift their food up to their mouths . . . Bumbleboozle cast little 'Stopping Time' Spells so that he could nip in and steal everyone's food while time stopped for a blink of a second . . .

And Caliburn flew around, very harassed, trying to stop all these things from happening.

Xar and Wish and Bodkin watched them all dancing. 'You see?' said Wish. 'They *can* get on if they try.'

'It won't last,' said Bodkin gloomily. 'Your mother said "one night" and when your mother says something she means it . . . Tomorrow they're going to be quarrelling and fighting all over again.'

'Grown-ups are so annoying! They always think they know best. Why won't they listen?' said Wish.

Bodkin sighed. 'Yes, but it probably IS for the best. You will be safer back in Warrior territories, Wish, and Xar, I know it's uncomfortable at Gormincrag, but now the Chief Drood has gone, maybe they can find an antidote for the Witch-stain.'

Both Xar and Wish looked at him as if were crazy.

'Oh, Bodkin, we're not going

back to Warrior territories, or to Gormincrag,' said
Wish casually.

'Wha-a-a-a-at? But you promised! You gave your
Warrior and your Wizard words!' said Bodkin.

'A promise can be broken,' said Xar, piously, 'in
pursuit of a higher good. Anyway they lied to us, and so
that promise doesn't count.'

'What are you going to do?' squeaked Bodkin in alarm.

One of the many reasons Bodkin wanted to go
home was that back in the Warrior fort, he had Wish
all to himself, he and the spoon were her only friends.
But out here, in the wildwoods with the wayward but
undeniably charismatic Xar, Bodkin had to share her.

Bodkin told himself it was for Wish's own good,
that all he was concerned about in his official capacity
as a bodyguard, was Wish's health and safety – but he
knew really in his heart of hearts that he was ever so
slightly jealous. Even though (and this made Bodkin
very sad), out here in *real life*, an Assistant Bodyguard
would *never* end up with a Warrior princess, not even a
slightly odd one.

That was just in fairy stories.

'We're going to run away, while they're all busy
celebrating,' said Wish. 'We have work to do. We have
to find the rest of these ingredients for the spell to get
rid of Witches.'

'But Encanzo said that spell wouldn't work!' cried Bodkin. 'Caliburn! Are you going to let them do this?'

The old bird flew hither and thither. 'Yes, the bodyguard is right!' said the bird in extreme agitation. 'It's probably a really bad idea . . .'

However, Caliburn said this without total conviction because frankly he had not been looking forward to going back to Gormincrag. It was all very well for the bodyguard to speak. *He* hadn't been there, in those dripping gloomy depths.

'But then,' said Caliburn, 'the adults are making such an almighty mess of things maybe we have to put our faith in the children, crazy and unrealistic and reckless though they are . . . What did I say earlier?'

'You said, and actually I wrote it down because I thought it was rather good: "I suppose this is all such a disaster that it doesn't really matter WHAT we do, as long as we're with our friends and we do it together . . ."' said Wish, checking back in the Spelling Book.

There was a small scuttling sound from behind them, and the werewolf pounced, and when he straightened up, he was carrying in his mouth the Creature-That-Once-Was-Looter, who had broken away from the Drood holding him earlier, and had been spying on them. The Creature-That-Once-Was-Looter was now on his way to sound the alarm, and warn

The SPELLing BooK
Write Your Own Story

So Xar Boy of Destiny triumphs yEt
aGain aGainsT the eViL Graxerturglebur
kin!

ThE EViL GRaxertuRgleburkin

3 ears

lots of eyes

gripping claws

armouR PLATing

SPECial powers:
Can drown you in RiVers of sNot
Bigger than a RoGreßBREath

pagE 3,284,631

everyone that Xar and Wish were planning to run away, for the Creature-That-Once-Was-Looter was absolutely determined that Xar should go back to Gormincrag, preferably indefinitely.

The bulging-eyed Unknown-Creature-That-Once-Was-Looter, swinging upside down by his four hind legs, looked so absolutely petrified to find himself actually in the JAWS of a werewolf, that he passed out for a second.

'Don't worry, Whatever-You-Are!' said Wish. 'This is a very NICE werewolf, and he wouldn't bite you, would you, Lonesome?'

Lonesome shook his head, a little too vigorously, but stopped when the creature woke up with the shaking, and squeaked fearfully.

'*Greeaggle Barg,*' apologised Lonesome.

And then he added, '*Greaggle Barg Rurgle*' – this time apologising because Caliburn had told him that he shouldn't speak with his mouth full.

'Xar, you promised you would tell Encanzo what that creature is, so he can turn him back into Looter,' urged Caliburn. 'And remember what the giant said, you're supposed to be forgiving your enemies . . .'

Xar sighed. 'He's going to be hopping mad when he gets back to being Looter. Trust me, he's never going to forgive me back.'

But Wish passed him the Spelling Book, and Xar tore out the page where it said what Looter was. It was in a section of the book where Xar had been making up mythical beasts, just beside that section where Xar had made up a whole load of stories about 'The Exploits and Superdeeds of Xar, Boy of Destiny', and what Looter was, apparently, was a Graxerturgleburkin.

No wonder they'd never guessed what he was, for Xar had made that up. Xar had drawn a rather marvellous picture of the Graxerturgleburkin, and they all admired it, for it really was very like the Graxerturgleburkin itself, slowly turning a deep purple as it hung upside down, dripping from the werewolf's mouth.

With a flourish, Xar showed the picture of the Graxerturgleburkin to Looter. 'You actually got away pretty lightly, Looter,' said Xar. 'You've only been a Graxerturgleburkin for one month. I was stuck in Gormincrag for over *two months!*'

The Graxerturgleburkin didn't look like it was looking on the bright side of things.

Wish wrote a message to her mother on the bottom of the piece of paper, and the message read:

'I'm sorry we lied to you, Mother. But the ends justify the means . . . a fine outcome excuses a bad method . . . You'll understand when you're older.'

Xar wrote beside it, a message to his father: 'I'll be good, Father, I promise.'

And then, carefully, Xar put the torn piece of paper on the ground, and got the werewolf to put the Graxerturgleburkin on top of it.

'Now he can't move,' said Xar with satisfaction. 'Because it's a windy night, and if he moves that piece of paper will fly away, and then Father won't know what to change him back from again . . .'

The Graxerturgleburkin's eyes bulged with fury, but also alarm. His many little talons gripped that piece of paper for dear life. He squeaked, as loud as he could, curses and insults in the Graxerturgleburkin language, but no one understood that language or would hear that squeaking above the sound of merry-making and dancing.

He was stuck there now, to that piece of paper, and he did not dare scuttle or sludge away to sound the alarm.

But Xar was right.

There was a look in that Graxerturgleburkin's eye that said Looter wasn't going to be forgiving Xar anytime in the immediate future.

'We'll never get away,' said Bodkin, in a last-ditch

attempt to change their minds. 'Encanzo and Sychorax are watching you both like hawks . . .'

Encanzo and Sychorax were indeed clever enough to know not to trust the children's words, so they had been keeping a sharp eye on those little rebels.

Sychorax was sitting on a rock, ramrod straight, her face a lofty regal mask, to show she was above such common things as dancing or celebrating. But every minute or so her eyes snapped across to check that her daughter was there, and that she wasn't escaping with any bad influences. (And maybe the very TIP of her toe was tapping in time to the music. She *was* human, after all.)

And Encanzo was prowling in the shadows, his face bleak as a midwinter cliff, great stormclouds billowing from his head, muttering under his breath: 'I can't go back to that dark place . . . I can never go back . . .' while gripping tight to his Wizard's staff. 'Never again . . . never more . . . ' (And what he meant by that I have no idea.) But every now and then he cast a Magical glance over to check that his rascal of a son wasn't running away with Queen Sychorax's dangerous little daughter.

Xar told Crusher that he could join them later, at an agreed meeting place, because a Longstepper High-Walker giant was a little visible for a stealthy escape. But in the meantime he said the Once-sprite, perched like a little nightingale on Crusher's shoulder, should start up a song.

Wish suggested the song choice, and it was an unusual one.

It was a song that had not been heard in the wildwoods for many a long year, a song that began like this:

I am young, I am poor, I can offer you nothing
All that I have is this bright pair of wings . . .
This air that I eat, these winds that I sleep on
This star path I dance in, where the moon sings . . .

As soon as Sychorax heard the opening words, she turned white as a spirit, and Encanzo stopped still, and lifted his head.

Sychorax marched right up to the giant and shouted up to the Once-sprite. 'Stop singing that song!'

But Encanzo heaved a great sigh as if he could no longer bear it, stepped forward out of the shadows and said, 'Wait a moment, Sychorax!'

And then Encanzo gave her a look that was a question, and he said:

'Just one night ... one night out of time ... for old time's sake ...'

And he held out his hand towards her, and Sychorax paused as the sweet haunting words floated on the midnight air, for the Once-sprite had not listened to her, and he was singing on regardless.

It was Sychorax's own fault really, for it was *she* who had created that voice, in her dungeons at Warrior Castle, when she removed the Once-sprite's Magic. Beautiful things can be created out of loss and out of pain, and the Once-sprite's voice, which had always been sweet, now conveyed such a yearning sense of longing for the Magic that had been lost, the love-that-might-have-been, that it seemed like he was no longer a mere mortal, but a supernatural ghost of a sprite, blown in like a white winter leaf from the underworld, singing the past into the present with such pure intensity that it could even pierce the iron breastplate of the frozen queen herself.

See the swifts soar, they live well on nothing,
You are young, you are strong, if you'll give me your hand ...
We'll leave earth entirely and never go back there
We'll sleep on the breezes and never touch land ...

366

'It IS true, the giant's story about Encanzo and my mother, whatever she may say!' whispered Wish triumphantly, looking at her mother's white face, which was unfreezing just a tiny, tiny fraction as she listened to the music. 'I knew it! Otherwise it would not affect her like this . . .'

I promise you gales and a merry adventure
We'll fly on forever and never will part . . .
I am young, I am poor, I can offer you nothing
Nothing but love and the beat of my heart . . .

. . . sang the voice of the Once-sprite. He sang with a little less melancholy than he had before, in Queen Sychorax's dungeons, because the Once-sprite had found a new life as a spell-raider, but there was still an overpowering bittersweetness to his song that was hauntingly seductive.

Sychorax, diamond-hard Sychorax, could not resist.

It *was* Midwinter's End Eve, after all.

And what happened on Midwinter's End Eve did not really count. Even a *queen* can be a fool on Midwinter's End Eve.

Queen Sychorax reached out her own hand, touched Encanzo's.

For old time's sake.

They both bowed, very regal, very courtly, very stiff.

367

And they began to dance.

They danced a little more stiffly than they might have done, once. Time had tempered them, just as bendy little saplings harden into immoveable tree trunks. Fine lines had traced their way across their faces.

But their eyes were the same eyes that had gazed out on the world a couple of decades before. One pair a fierce blue. The other a wild grey.

The two of them danced, and they were lost in the music for one fatal moment.

The song took them up into the air like the swifts, out of time, where there were no rules . . .

And in that fatal moment the children left, tiptoeing out of the courtyard. Crusher gave them the broken door, which he had kept in his pocket. So engrossed were the adults in their dancing and their merrymaking and eating and singing, that nobody noticed the broken door soaring off quietly into the night.

It was Midwinter's End Eve, ages long ago.

In a British Isles so old it did not know it was the British Isles yet.

A broken door, soaring through the quietness of the midnight sky, like a small flying carpet. Three children, all thirteen years old, poised in that moment between childhood and adulthood, lying on their backs, looking up at the stars. A talking raven, perched on

Wish's foot. A spoon, lying fast asleep on her heart. The sprites, joyously swooping and diving, and buzzing around them. Down below them three snowcats, a werewolf, a bear and a pack of wolves running, softly, quietly, their footsteps disappearing Magically as they ran, in a spell cast by Ariel.

After a while of peaceful contemplation, Wish sat up and peered over the edge of the door.

'All right, we couldn't persuade our parents to join us, but let's not forget that we're doing really *well*!' said Wish. 'The werewolf has learnt some manners . . . The Once-sprite is happier now he's a spell-raider . . . and Xar is making definite progress in being good . . .'

'He still has some way to go,' said Caliburn, a trifle gloomily, for only Encanzo had the power to set Caliburn and Ariel free***.

'And we do have ABSOLUTELY NO IDEA where we are going NOW,' Bodkin pointed out.

Xar's arm was burning, and it gave him an idea. He sat up and opened the Spelling Book onto the page with the spell to get rid of Witches. And then he gave Wish Caliburn's feather. 'Write!' urged Xar. 'Write down the next ingredient! Think as hard as you can, and write!'

'Oh, that won't work,' said Wish, dipping the

*** When Xar grew into a wise and thoughtful adult, and helping Xar run away from his own parent may have put Caliburn's moment of freedom back a bit.

feather in the ink. 'I've tried that so many times before and it just won't – *oh!*'

To her astonishment the feather, warm in her hands, began to write, almost as if by itself.

'Four scales of the Nuckalavee from the Western Whirlpools . . .' read Bodkin, in growing horror, 'and five tears of the Drood from the Labyrinth of the Lake of the Lost . . .'

'Is there any more?' asked Xar.

'No, that seems to be it,' said Wish, for whatever had animated the feather had run out, and all she was making now were a series of unintelligible blotches.

'I knew it! I knew it! We have the last ingredients in our quest!' said Xar, punching the air in his excitement. 'Key!' he said to the key, who was steering them from the lock of the Punishment Cupboard. 'Turn due southeast! Next stop . . . *THE LAKE OF THE LOST!*'

'Wha-a-a-a-a-a-t?' cried Bodkin, waving his arms around in horror. 'But the Lake of the Lost is the DROOD STRONGHOLD! We can't go there! It's a suicide mission! Didn't you learn anything AT ALL from the Giant's Last Breath Story? Pentaglion just took TWO tears of the Drood and those scary Droods came and destroyed his whole castle and his giant, and we're thinking of taking *FIVE* . . .? They're not listening to me are they, Caliburn?'

'No,' sighed Caliburn, 'they're not listening.' Trying to control the uncontrollable little princess was bad enough, but trying to control both her and Xar together ... well ...

'It's impossible,' moaned Bodkin, lying back on the door and putting his helmet over his head.

But Xar and Wish were not paying attention to such gloomy thinking. They were excitedly surveying the spell to get rid of Witches.

'We'll get rid of those Witches in *no time* at this rate!' said Wish, with great enthusiasm. 'Let's put a tick against the ingredients we've already *got* to make us feel like we're progressing. We've got the tears of the queen, and the Witch feathers ...'

'Yes, but I'm annoyed that we've lost our first and most important ingredient in the spell to get rid of Witches by using it on the Drood,' said Xar.

'The *moral* of that is worrying me,' said Caliburn. 'The giant's last words were about forgiveness, but it was the breath of forgiveness that actually *got rid of* the Drood in the end. So how does that work?'

This is the problem with stories.

Stories always mean something. The question is ...

What exactly *do* they mean?

'It means we're going to have to start all over again finding ANOTHER Giant's Last Breath before we can find anything else!' said Xar. 'It's very annoying.'

Squeezjoos hovered joyfully above them.

'Yous don't have to start again!' said Squeezjoos. '*I* hass a secret that I's hassn't told anybody! I's saved the day without anybody realising!'

'Nonsssense . . .' hissed Tiffinstorm. 'An insignificant little hairy fairy like you could never save the day.'

'But I has!' said Squeezjoos, triumphantly. He paused for effect.

'*There'sss a tiny little bit of the breath left in the collecting bottle!* I sssaved it! I's put the sstopper back in just in time!'

Xar got out the collecting bottle, and there was the very, very faint whisper of green smoke in the centre of it.

The last remains of the Giant's Last Breath.

'You see! I may's be sssmall but I is mighty! I is NOT too tiny to be a spell-raider after all!' crowed Squeezjoos.

'You most certainly are not,' said Xar heartily. 'That was extremely quick thinking of you. For this, Squeezjoos, I make you not only an official spell-raider, but the *Chief* Spell-Raider of our entire team!' said Xar, and the little hairy fairy was so overcome with excitement that he blew up like a puffer fish and turned three cartwheels in a row, and collapsed panting on Wish's shoulder. The spoon, who had woken up, gave him a celebratory bow.

'And look!' said Wish. 'I can now tick off THREE of the ingredients! And there are only two more to collect!'

Wish lay back down on the door with a sigh of satisfaction, and went back to dreamily surveying the stars.

'The universe is sending us a sign,' she said. 'Look! I'm sure that star up there is winking at us!'

And indeed, one of the stars did seem to be blinking on and off at them.

'Is it winking in a friendly way, though, or in a laughing-at-us way?' worried Caliburn. 'Is it a good sign or bad sign? Are we really only being led by Xar's Witch-stain in escaping from your parents for the second time? Look! The Witch-stain is worse than ever! How can we know if Xar is EVER going to be able to control or get rid of it?'

Xar's hand was indeed still burning green in the moonlight.

'We just have to believe and hope that he can,' said Wish simply. 'If we believe in Xar hard enough, then we'll find our way to a happy ending.'

'But you only think that because you're young and don't know any better!' agonised Caliburn. 'When you're young you think that love conquers everything . . . you don't know the problems it can cause . . . you haven't seen the times where the Witches triumph, there is no second life, and the werewolf dies!'

'Well, I never want to grow up, then,' said Wish. 'I want to stay young forever. You know I'm right anyway,

Caliburn. It's why you came with us, and didn't betray us to our parents . . .'

'And if you want to *stay* with us, Caliburn, you have to stop being so negative!' said Xar. 'Wish is right, it's a good sign. It's a sign that everything will be all right in the end.'

Caliburn sighed.

Some of his thoughts he kept to himself.

About LOVE, for example.

For as they lay on the door, the key, swivelling happily in the lock, was looking longingly at the spoon, and the fork was lookingly longingly at the key, and it was not so very different from the longing way Bodkin looked at Wish sometimes, and the longing way Wish looked at Xar.

There may be trouble ahead . . . thought Caliburn.

Who knows if Wish and Xar were right, on that midnight long ago?

For there would be storms tomorrow, there is no doubt.

But if we worry too much about tomorrow, how can we enjoy today?

So let us leave our heroes there, in the happiness of NOW, soaring gloriously through the sky, in the triumph and satisfaction of a quest completed, and in that blink of a moment before another quest begins.

And let us leave the grown-ups dancing.

In a while they will discover their children gone, the birds have flown, and then there will be tears, and rending of clothes, and wringing of hands, and Warriors blaming Wizards, and Wizards cursing Warriors, and their War and their worrying will begin again anew.

But for now they are *dancing*, in a moment out of time.

So let us enjoy that moment, lost in the music, a small sweet bittersweet smile on Queen Sychorax's face, for she knows this is a stolen time.

In that moment Sychorax and Encanzo are young again, free from all parental and regal responsibilities of being mothers, fathers, monarchs. In that moment they have no tribes to run, worlds to conquer, countries to rule, traditions to uphold.

They have earned those moments, the poor parents, just a few minutes to go back into the past, and unbend, relax, for an eyeblink or two, to be once more a young Warrior princess, who has just met a Wizard in the wood.

The Once-sprite is singing a different song now, another forbidden one.

Once we were Wizards,
Wandering free
In roads of sky
And paths of sea . . .

And in that timeless long-gone hour,
Words of nonsense still had power.

Doors still flew and birds still talked,
Witches grinned and giants walked . . .

We had Magical wands and Magical wings
And we lost our hearts to impossible things
Unbelievable thoughts! Unsensible ends!
For Wizards and Warriors might be friends.

In a world where impossible things are true
I don't know why we forgot the spell
When we lost the way, how the forest fell.
But now we are old, we can vanish too.

And I see once more the invisible track
That will lead us home and take us back . . .
So find your wands and spread your wings
I'll sing our love of impossible things
And when you take my vanished hand
We'll both go back to that Magic land
Where we lost our hearts . . .
Several lifetimes ago . . .
When we were Wizards
Once.

Dance on, Sychorax.

Fly on, door, through the quiet night.

With the three young heroes, lying on their backs, looking up at the stars.

And a very pleased-with-himself little hairy fairy, buzzing on Xar's chest, with his ear to the collecting bottle in Xar's breast pocket, whispering to himself.

'*I's* saved the day! ME, Squeezjoos! The smallest of them all has saved the day!'

For it was definitely the final fragments of the Giant's Last Breath in there.

There was no doubt about it.

If you held the bottle up to your ear, extremely close, you could still hear it, very, very faintly like an echo.

'Forgive them,' the echo whispered.

'Forgive them.'

Epilogue 1

wo weeks later . . .

Many fathoms down, far further than five, for the ocean was terribly deep at the bottom of the Cliffs of Eternity, lay the Ball-of-Iron-That-Enclosed-the-Kingwitch, on a bed of coral.

The ball of iron was silent, still.

But then from within it, there came a faint, muffled scraping, as of talons against something metal.

And the ball of iron began to move . . .

Softly, at first, and then a little faster.

The Kingwitch hadn't died.

He was in there.

He would keep scratching.

He had a little Magic-that-works-on-iron and he would keep using that Magic to break out of his iron prison.

The Kingwitch was nothing if not patient.

In the meantime he rolled over the watery landscape of the bottom of the ocean steadily, gradually, like a dark malignant glacier, or a slow but certain fate.

Epilogue 2

S o that was the story of . . .
A word that froze, a heart that soared,
A boy who flew, a girl who ROARED.
Have you guessed which of the characters in the story I am yet?

I could be any of them, Wish or Xar, or Caliburn-the-raven-who-has-lived-many-lifetimes, or Bodkin the Assistant-Bodyguard-who-wished-he-was-a-hero, or Crusher-the-dreamy-Longstepper-High-Walker-giant, or one of the sprites, or the hairy fairies, ANY of the characters at all. (Not Eleanor Rose or the werewolf – I couldn't be either of THEM, because they weren't in the first book, so that would be cheating, and the narrator can be tricky, but they should not actually cheat, otherwise it's extremely annoying for the reader.)

I still cannot tell you who I am, I'm afraid, for as you can see, the story has not yet ended.

I can only tell you at the end . . .

but the end is getting closer.

Wish and Xar's stars have crossed for the SECOND unlikely time, and for good, or for evil, their stars are now joined together and they are travelling in the same, very dangerous, direction.

I left them, peacefully enjoying the present.

One of the reasons that looking into the future, or dwelling too much on the past, are such dangerous practices, is that what we see there might stop us enjoying the excitement and pleasures of the 'now'.

But pity me, for I have the curse of being able to see into the future, and although they do not know it yet ... that door our heroes are lying on so peacefully is headed towards the Lake of the Lost, which, as Bodkin pointed out, is the Drood stronghold, and Droods are unrelenting, unforgiving, and the greatest Wizards in the wildwoods, and they will want to obliterate anyone who has Magic-mixed-with-iron.

The emperor of Warriors will be told by the Witchsmeller about Sychorax's daughter, and he too will want to eliminate the threat posed to the Warrior world by Magic-mixed-with-iron ...

Encanzo and Sychorax will be chasing Xar and Wish, but Encanzo is in trouble with the Droods himself. And Sychorax is in trouble with the emperor of Warriors ... and everyone will be chasing everyone else.

The forces of darkness will be closing in on our young heroes.

But WORST OF ALL ...

The Kingwitch will be after them both. And he will not rest until he gets them. And he has a single piece of tiny blue dust that he thinks he may find helpful.

Can Wish and Xar break out of the sad circles of the history of the wildwoods?

They are young, they are hopeful.

Can they really write their own story?

Is that even possible?

Keep hoping . . .
Keep guessing . . .
Keep dreaming . . .

The Unknown Narrator

Never and Forever (Tor's Song)

Don't blame the wolves, for winter is bitter,
Don't blame the wolves, for wolves need to eat,
The winter has chased all the game from the forest,
The wolf cubs are hungry, and I would taste sweet . . .

I don't want to die before I have children,
I don't want to die when the world is so young,
I don't want to die on this glorious midnight
With words not-yet-said and songs not-yet-sung . . .

I am young, I am poor, I can offer you nothing,
All that I have is this bright pair of wings,
This air that I eat, these winds that I sleep on,
This star path I dance in, where the moon sings . . .

See the swifts soar, they live well on nothing,
You are young, you are strong, if you'll give me your hand,
We'll leave earth entirely and never go back there,
We'll sleep on the breezes and never touch land . . .

I promise you gales and a merry adventure,
We'll fly on forever and never will part . . .
I am young, I am poor, I can offer you nothing,
Nothing but love and the beat of my heart.

See the swifts soar,
They live well on nothing,
You are young, you are strong
if you'll give me your hand.

We'll leave earth entirely
and never go back there,
We'll sleep on the breezes
and never touch land..

ACKNOWLEDGEMENTS
(THANKYOU)

A whole team of people have
helped me write this book.

Thank you to my wonderful editor,
Anne McNeil, and my magnificent agent,
Caroline Walsh.

A special big thanks to Samuel Perrett,
Polly Lyall Grant and Rebecca Logan.

And to everyone else at Hachette Children's Group,
Hilary Murray Hill, Andrew Sharp,
Valentina Fazio, Lucy Upton, Louise Grieve,
Kelly Llewellyn, Nicola Goode, Katherine Fox,
Alison Padley, Rebecca Livingstone.

Thanks to all at Little Brown,
Megan Tingley, Jackie Engel, Lisa Yoskowitz,
Kristina Pisciotta, Jessica Shoffel.

Thank you to Eleanor Rose and her Mum for
donating money to the National Literacy Trust
for her name to appear in this book.
Find out more about the vital work the
NLT does here: literacytrust.org.uk

And most important of all,
Maisie, Clemmie, Xanny.

And SIMON for his
excellent advice
on absolutely everything.

I couldn't do it
without you.

Discover the Magic of Cressida Cowell

visit

www.cressidacowell.com

to find out all about her books, events, and lots more!

Read all about Hiccup and
Toothless and their HILARIOUS
adventures in the EPIC series:

HOW TO TRAIN YOUR
DRAGON

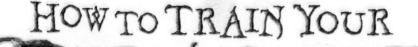